I0556255

WHERE IS MY MIND?

SHIRLEY BENTON

POOLBEG

Copyright © Shirley Benton 2020

This book is a work of fiction. The names, characters, places, businesses, organisations and incidents portrayed in it are either the product of the author's imagination or are used fictitiously. Any resemblance to actual persons, living or dead, events or locales is entirely coincidental.

Published 2020
by Poolbeg Press Ltd
123 Grange Hill, Baldoyle
Dublin 13, Ireland
E-mail: poolbeg@poolbeg.com
www.poolbeg.com

© Poolbeg Press Ltd. 2020, copyright for editing, typesetting, layout, design, ebook

A catalogue record for this book is available from the British Library.

ISBN 978-1-78199-342-2

All rights reserved. No part of this publication may be reproduced or transmitted in any form or by any means, electronic or mechanical, including photography, recording, or any information storage or retrieval system, without permission in writing from the publisher. The book is sold subject to the condition that it shall not, by way of trade or otherwise, be lent, resold or otherwise circulated without the publisher's prior consent in any form of binding or cover other than that in which it is published and without a similar condition, including this condition, being imposed on the subsequent purchaser.

Typeset by Poolbeg Press Ltd

www.poolbeg.com

ABOUT THE AUTHOR

Shirley Benton is an Irish author. Two of her books, *Looking for Leon* and *Can We Start Again?*, were also published by Poolbeg Press Ltd. She lives in County Meath, Ireland.

ACKNOWLEDGEMENTS

Thanks to Poolbeg Press Ltd for the opportunity to get up to mischief together again! Thanks are also due to my family and friends for lending me their ears while I bounced ideas around as I was writing this book.

To all readers out there – thank you.

PART ONE

NOW

PANIC SETS IN THE SECOND I WAKE. I know immediately that everything is horribly wrong and I wait for recognition of what's happened to come flooding into my consciousness.

It doesn't.

My brain is foggy. The pain in my head is unfathomable. My hands are tied behind my back and there's a rope around my arms and stomach, tying me to the chair on which I'm sitting. I try to move my feet but they, too, are tied, only to the legs of the chair. My entire body aches. Why am I tied to a chair? Why does everything hurt? Where the hell am I?

I look around, willing understanding to come. To my right is a curtain-less, glassless, partially boarded window, through which light is seeping. It's either the light of dawn or dusk, I can't tell. There's a range in front of me and to my left is an old threadbare couch. The room I'm in is falling down around me. As the seconds tick by, I still have absolutely no idea where I am or why I'm here. Am I inside a derelict house? Why would I be inside a derelict house with my body tied to a chair? Who would do this to me?

Before I realise it's about to happen, I'm screaming. I try to flail my legs and arms to free them, but it's no use. I cry for help, but nobody comes. I scream and struggle against the ropes binding my hands and feet until I have absolutely no energy left. It's then that I start to wonder why I'm not gagged.

Thoughts come slowly. What's the last thing I can remember before waking in this place? An assortment of scenes from my life come flooding into my head, but the details are blurry. I close my eyes and see myself with my boyfriend, Jake Ryan. I'm breaking up with him. When did that happen? Did I do that shortly before all this? Then a memory of meeting some of my friends for lunch and talking about Jake's abject disappointment at me ending our relationship fights its way into my mind. After that, there's nothing. What came after that? What came before *this*?

My head throbs incessantly. I'm not sure if it's a physical external injury or something internal. My mouth is dry. Dust dances before my eyes.

Focus. I listen for any sounds coming from outside. The rustle of the wind through trees is about all I can hear. I listen for a very long time. I can't hear the sound of any cars in the distance. Other than nature, I hear no signs of life other than my own.

Wherever I am, it's off the beaten track. Hardly a shocking revelation, given the circumstances. Whoever left me here doesn't want me to be found.

The last thought I have before I black out is that I've been left here to die.

When I wake an indeterminate amount of time later, everything in my body aching even worse than before, the light that's streaming through the gaping hole that was once a window is brighter. I try to remember what day it is. Nothing. What month is it? I think it's November. My mother's birthday is at the end of October, and I remember it was her seventieth a while ago, for which my sisters and I organised a big party. The memory feels recent. I try to

4

remember the details of the party, but they're hard to grasp. Was Jake there? I think so, but I can't be sure. Everything is fuzzy and that fact scares me as much as being tied up in an unknown place.

I'm horribly thirsty but so nauseous that the thought of drinking anything makes me want to vomit. It doesn't look like drinking is an option, anyway. Even if I managed to free myself, I very much doubt there would be running water in a building like this one. It looks like it's been uninhabited for decades.

The thought flits into my head that it's also surprising I'm not blindfolded. Isn't that what's usually done in these situations, along with gagging? Then again, when it comes to the latter, whoever brought me here probably didn't need to have me gagged once we'd arrived at this place. I haven't heard a human sound outside since I woke and it's clearly later in the day now. People may not be up and about at dawn, but they surely would be at this time. There's nobody here to hear me scream. Was I gagged before though, when I was taken and brought here?

How can it be that I can remember nothing about it? Did I get a blow to the skull? I consider the thumping pain in my head. It's several leagues worse than a pounding hangover yet not dissimilar. Whatever the reason, I can feel that I'm dehydrated and that surely isn't helping the problem. Surely a serious head injury wouldn't even allow me to think or reason. But if I haven't sustained a head injury, what's caused my memory loss and current confusion?

I try to work out what I am sure of in this situation. I'm Katie Turner. I'm thirty-six years old. I have two sisters and I'm the youngest in the family. I'm a journalist. I work for the *Irish Bulletin*, a broadsheet daily national newspaper. I enjoy my job – most of the time, anyway. I live in Carrickmines, a suburb in South Dublin. I have – *had* – been going out with Jake for six months. Again, I can't remember why I ended our relationship. Things had been very good from the minute we'd first met. When did it start to go so wrong that I wanted to end things? And why is the memory so hard to grasp properly?

I squeeze my eyes shut against the light and force myself to think. Was I out on a night out when this happened? Did a stranger take me and bring me here? I look down at what I'm wearing – a blouse and jeans. I recognise them both. I remember buying them. The jeans are designer and were very expensive, and I bought the blouse in a boutique. I wouldn't be wearing them unless I'd been out at the time this happened. Was I wearing them at the lunch that flashed into my head earlier? I can't remember. They're both in a bad state now. It looks like I've been sick on the blouse and the jeans, and that I've wet the jeans as well. What took place that made me sick?

All the horrible reports I've read in newspapers and online of young women going missing flash into my head. Is that what happened? Was I walking home late at night and somebody grabbed me and brought me here? Why would they even do that? Did I challenge them and this is my punishment? I realise with great relief that it certainly doesn't feel as if I've been sexually violated in any way. But maybe something worse than being left here to die will happen. Maybe my abductor will return and do unthinkable things to me. Is this all part of some sick, twisted game, culminating in the unimaginable?

I need to get out. Wherever I am, whatever has happened, I need to undo the ropes that bind me and get as far away as possible. *Now.*

THEN

THE GROUP OF WOMEN ENTER THE RESTAURANT. Prosecco is ordered, accompanied by food. The prosecco disappears fast while the group lingers over their lunch. One woman in particular is drinking faster than the others, the food an afterthought.

When the group leaves the restaurant several hours later, they immediately make their way to a bar – the first bar on a verbal list that's been compiled over their meal. The woman who's been drinking the fastest is the first one to reach the counter. She's downed half of her drink before the others have even taken their first sip.

"Here's to the rest of a long overdue catch-up," she says, clicking her glass against those of her friends before draining her drink.

NOW

I LOOK AROUND THE ROOM, BREATHING THROUGH my mouth to try to avoid inhaling the stench of vomit and urine or the horrible damp smell in the place. There's very little here that can be used as a tool to help me, even if I could reach anything. The old couch on my left is small and filthy, and looks like it'd be infested with rats if you lifted up what's left of the cushions. To the right of the couch and in front of the left-hand side of the wall I'm facing, with the range in front of me, lies an ancient-looking wooden table and three wide-legged chairs. From the limited amount I can see of the legs of the chair I'm on, I think it's safe to assume that I'm sitting on the fourth in the set. I try to turn my head further to the left, but I can't see anything else that might be of use to me in the restricted amount that's visible to me.

I turn round again and look at the basin on a small table to the right of the range. Behind the basin and the tables are a few ground-level cupboards, presumably where the kitchenware and tableware were once kept. It looks like this room is the kitchen and sitting room all in one, but the doors are missing and it's immediately obvious that there's nothing in the cupboards. To my right is the window and nothing else. The bit that's boarded up is at the bottom. It looks like the strips that would have been across the top half of the window have fallen off. With such a restricted view, all I can see outside the window is bushes, a field and trees in the distance.

Again, I try to turn my head sideways to see what's behind me to the right. In my peripheral vision, I can just about make out that there's a door on the extreme left-hand side of the wall behind me, presumably leading out into the hall of the house. Anything else that may be there is directly behind me and out of my line of vision. I try to throw my head back, but I can't. The top of the chair won't allow me to do that.

I consider the chair I'm sitting on. It doesn't feel too sturdy. Would it move? There may be something else behind me that would help me if I could get to it. And if I can move the chair, maybe getting to it is a possibility. At five foot ten, I'm of a strong build and while I'm not overweight, my body isn't light, either. I think of the kettlebell classes I've been doing recently and how they've increased my muscle density. Although I've visibly slimmed down, my body is heavier than it used to be. That thought makes me realise something: it can't have been easy for my attacker to take me. I'm fit now. He must have been strong – I know I wouldn't have let him take me without a fight. At least, I presume it's a he, as why would a woman want to do this to me? I rock myself forwards on the chair. It moves slightly. I jerk myself sideways, trying to move the chair. It moves again.

It'll take a while, but I'm going to turn this chair right round.

My toes are touching the ground. I'm not wearing shoes or socks. My abductor has raised my heels and tied the rope under the middle of my foot and around the leg of the chair an indeterminate amount of times. It strikes me that it's a rather amateurish way to tie someone up. Was my abductor in a rush? And where is he now? Then again, what would I know about the right or wrong way to tie someone's feet to a chair? And I can't fault its efficiency. After all, I'm securely tied up here.

I flex my feet and try to pull my feet upwards to slip them out of the rope, then push my heel down into the ground while wriggling my feet to try to loosen the rope in the hope that I can slither my feet out. Neither approach works. It's not long before my ankles start to ache. Whoever tied this rope tied it tight, amateur or not. There's no give in it at all.

After a few minutes, I stop trying to free my feet and return to my plan of turning the chair round. I push my toes into the ground and push myself up as much as I can, as if I'm trying to stand up, then throw my weight down on the chair again insofar as I can while tied up, simultaneously leaning to the left. I jiggle and wriggle and flail around on the chair for so long that rivulets of sweat begin to drip down my forehead. This is dangerous work

– I know I'm not far from becoming completely dehydrated as it is and the exertion of this task is already starting to take it out of me. Not to mention the fact that my head is thumping so hard that it feels like it's about to explode and I'm still terribly nauseous. But staying here, doing nothing but waiting, could be far more dangerous. I have to try.

Slowly – ever so slowly – I start to make progress. I still can't see behind me, but something more important is happening. The chair is loosening. Its legs are starting to wobble now under my weight. If I can break it, it could be the first step towards getting out of here . . .

Feverishly now, I thrash my body against the chair as much as my limited mobility will allow, despite the fact that I'm feeling horribly groggy. I know that regardless of how awful I'm feeling, I mustn't stop. The legs of the chair feel like they're moving even more now, which spurs me on further. And eventually, just when my energy is starting to sap, it happens. As I'm throwing myself sideways to the left, the leg on the back of that side breaks. As the chair crashes down, I feel the other leg on the left crushing under my weight too, but the bottom of that one is tied to my ankle. I plop unmercifully on the floor, my left shoulder crashing onto the rough uncarpeted ground and my left leg getting crushed. I ignore the pain. I need to work out my next move.

I'm now lying on the ground, the left-hand side of my body against the floor with the seat of the chair still under my bottom and the back of the chair still tied to my back. A small portion of my back is supporting my weight along with my left arm, my right leg tied to the front right leg of the chair. Grateful that I can at least move my left leg now, I slowly slide it forwards and then move my lower left leg upwards insofar as I can, my toes pointing towards the

10

ceiling. Then I try to shake off the leg of the chair that's tied to my left leg by jiggling furiously. After several minutes of shaking my left leg and foot left and right, front and back, trying to dislodge the chair leg with very limited capability to move with everything else that's still tied to me, I accept that it's not going to happen. Instead, I decide to focus on moving myself round again.

With great exertion, I try to dig my left foot into the ground while shifting myself to the left. I use my left shoulder, the rump of my left leg and my scuttling foot to edge myself to the left again and again. It takes almost every drop of energy remaining in me, not to mention how long it takes, but eventually I'm finally in a position to see what's right behind me.

I almost cry when I see virtually *nothing*. To the left of the door I spotted in my peripheral vision, there's absolutely nothing but a high sideboard with zero items on it and a blank wall behind me. The sideboard is a capacious effort. It must be about six foot high and evidently had lots of useful storage and display space when it was in use. There are two storage areas to the bottom left and right of it, containing three wonky-looking empty shelves each. The doors to these areas have either fallen off or have been removed for some unknown reason. An area in the middle of the sideboard once housed drawers, by the looks of it, but these areas are empty now. There's a wide open storage area on top. None of this helps me at all when there's absolutely nothing in this huge sideboard at present. There's nothing there to help me.

The earlier adrenaline surge I'd experienced when I was thrashing in the chair has left my body and a horrible lull of energy has descended in its wake. I suddenly feel shattered and so, so thirsty. This is crazy. I'm fooling myself to think I'm going to get out of this situation. How can I? I don't even know what my next move is. My shoulder is starting to ache badly now. But my options are to lie here and let pain and fear overwhelm me, an option I am dangerously close to, or to do something.

I need a next move.

I can't think of any way that I can free my hands. If I could release my other leg though, I might be able to manoeuvre myself into a standing position . . .

I'm not sure if that will help me when I can see nothing in the room that will help me to release the ropes that bind me. And surely the door to this room is locked, because it really wouldn't make sense in this crazy situation for it not to be locked. But I can't think about any of that. I've found my next move and that's all I need to think about now.

I look down and consider where the knot is in the rope, grateful that the legs of the chair are wide enough for me to have visibility of this. It's at the back, slightly inwards. Did my abductor move behind me to tie my feet to the chair? Did he tie my hands behind me first, then tie the rope around my chest, then secure my feet? I prise my thoughts away from that and slide my left foot towards the rope binding my right leg to the remains of the chair. Could I wriggle a toe into the knot to loosen it?

I try to stick my big toe into the knot, but there's absolutely no leeway in the rope at all. I try again, burrowing inwards as energetically as I can. It's no good. The weight of the leg of the chair on my left leg isn't helping, and my energy is depleting and plummeting by the second.

I let my left foot crash to the ground and wait for the ache in my leg to diminish before I restart. I look at the position of the knot again. If I rubbed it against the ground repeatedly, would it loosen?

Only one way to find out.

THEN

SOME OF THE GROUP ARE STARTING TO slow down. Some have had enough, both of alcohol and of being out. Thoughts are drifting to the rest of the weekend and the tasks that lie ahead when they go home. Conversation is starting to involve children and work that needs to be finished before Monday morning. An uneasiness has set in with some – they're silently planning their exit strategy. Others are determined to make the most of the opportunity to be out.

One of the latter category orders another round of drinks. Some of the former shake their heads – they've had enough and are leaving soon. The drinks are bought anyway. The round is quickly consumed by some and lingered over by others, and it's decided, amid hesitation from some, that they'll leave where they are and visit just one more pub to round off the evening.

It turns out to be a very, very bad decision.

NOW

I SHIFT ALL OF MY WEIGHT ONTO my left shoulder and throw myself forwards as much as possible to try to connect my right foot with the ground. It proves to be exceptionally hard and the angle isn't in my favour – the position of the rope means that it only partially connects with the ground at any point of my endeavour. Nevertheless, I push my foot forwards and backwards repeatedly insofar as my limited mobility will allow me to, the rope scraping against the ground. When I haven't the energy left to do it for another second, I throw myself back onto my left-hand side and stop to try to regroup, mentally as much as physically.

I eventually summon the energy to examine my right foot and assess what good, if any, my actions have done. The rope looks exactly the same, but when I lift my left foot towards my right and try to wriggle my big toe into the knot again, I'm sure it's looser now. It can't be my imagination, can it? I try again – yes, it's definitely looser. Not loose enough for my toe to get through, but looser. That's enough for now to get me through.

With renewed verve, I repeat the process of burrowing my toe into the knot for as long as I can. No, it's not my imagination. My toe is getting in further now.

I'm going to do this.

And I do. It takes forever and I feel like I've run a marathon by the time it happens, but after a long process of scraping the rope against the ground and working my toe against the rope, it finally starts to give way. When it does, my left foot is like lead and I have to take a break before I can use it to unwind the rope. I see glaring red friction marks round my right ankle, some of which are weeping blood, but they don't matter. I've completed my next move and it feels damn good.

As I'm congratulating myself, the reality of my situation comes crashing in on me anew. My abductor could come back at any moment to do horrifying things to me, or else I've been left here to die. I'm getting dangerously thirsty and I have no means of drinking anything. I know I'll soon be dehydrated. I still have a chair both on my back like a mutated turtle shell and under my bottom – not to mention the fact that part of it is tied to my leg. I have very little to be congratulating myself about or celebrating.

I flex my newly freed right leg forwards for a moment before moving it towards the leg of the chair that's still stuck in the rope attached to my left ankle. I bring the weight of my right leg down on the middle of the chair leg and sweep upwards, hoping that this action will pull the leg of the chair upwards against the bindings of the rope and that the movement will eventually loosen it. When that doesn't work, I move the big toe from my right foot up against the bottom of the chair leg and try to push it upwards. When I've pushed it as far as I can, I slide my right leg against the leg of the chair in an upwards movement again. It takes a lot of attempts, but eventually, it falls out and plops on the ground between my legs.

I give my right leg a minute to relax before I draw both knees upwards as high as I can, then roll onto my left knee with the intention of subsequently rolling forwards onto both of them. Once I've done that, I should be able to lift my torso and then make an attempt to stand up, even with the seat of the chair still under me.

My shoulder doesn't want to play ball – it's had enough. I wince as I shift the weight of my body and the chair onto my left shoulder and the side of my left leg. I throw myself over, aiming to land face down. It sounds like an attainable aspiration, but I soon find that I have so little room to manoeuvre that it feels virtually impossible for the first few attempts.

It isn't long before I realise that I'm trying to do this without hurting myself. I know the uneven ground underneath me will tear the skin from my cheeks if I do this too fast. I'm worried that the weight of the chair, in conjunction with a sudden jerky movement, will injure my body. But if I stay here, who knows what worse things will befall me?

That thought spurs me on to fling myself forwards once more, heaving my weight and the bulk of the chair inwards until I land face down with my weight on my knees, my nose pressed into the ground. As predicted, pain swells down my face and I'm sure my skin will be in tatters after this, yet I'm elated.

I foolishly tell myself that the next step should be easy – I just need to lift my head and then heave my torso upwards. However, I hadn't factored in that I'm totally dehydrated. I lift my head, but I try to move my body upwards too quickly. A wave of dizziness overtakes me as soon as I'm in a semi-upright position and I lose my balance. I topple to the left and crash to the ground.

My first thought relates to the pain this movement has resulted in. My head has hit the ground and although the side of the chair has taken a lot of the impact that my head would otherwise have taken, the pain is still significant. My second is *Was that noise what I think it was?*

It is. The impact of the fall has caused the seat of the chair to break off, bringing the remaining two legs of the chair with it.

"Yes!" I yell into the emptiness of the house, trying to put the pain aside and immediately scooting myself away from the broken seat by scuttling my legs like a crab away to my left while shifting the weight of my upper body with them. Now, all I have to contend with is the back of the chair tied to my back – something that would be a major obstacle in my ordinary, everyday world, but I'm very far from there now.

I focus on my breathing, waiting a few moments until my head recovers a little, then I try to carry out my attempt to get upright again. It's easier this time – once I've summoned my energy, I raise my knees as high as I can and then roll onto them, pressing my face into the ground once more but allowing my knees to take the impact of the manoeuvre this time. I take about ten seconds to breathe deeply before using every ounce of dwindling resources that remain in me to lift my head slowly, then my torso. I hold my breath as I complete the task, hoping and praying that I won't lose my balance again.

I don't. It worked. There's sweat dripping down my brow and I feel dizzy from my exertions, but I'm now essentially kneeling and all I need to do is stand up.

In theory, it should be simple to do after what I've already done, yet it seems like a mammoth task. I breathe deeply for a few moments.

The dehydration is getting worse. I close my eyes and visualise a jug of ice-cold water . . . then a glass sitting on a table with condensation dripping down the side . . .

Stop it! No good can come of this, unless perhaps I can use it as a spur to get myself moving and out of this place. It's that or drive myself mad.

Slowly, I bend my right knee then gingerly use the momentum to push myself up to standing. My legs feel like jelly and an image of a newborn giraffe with weak legs comes to mind. A wave of dizziness overcomes me and almost has me back on the floor again, but I fight it with everything I have and somehow manage to stay upright.

Although what I've just achieved has been a huge step forwards, there's no time for feeling triumph of any kind. My exhaustion is getting serious. I know I'm starting to fade. I wonder again how long it's been since I last ate or drank anything. I have to get out of here straight away, or . . .

With that thought, I immediately make my way to the door, any elation I might have felt about getting into a standing position being eclipsed by how weak and groggy I feel. I put my back to it – or rather, the chair's back – and feel around until my hands connect with the old doorknob I saw as I walked towards the door. Even though my hands are tied together at the wrists, I can still twist them somewhat.

Feeling hopeful, I twist the doorknob with my left hand. It doesn't open. I twist it again and try to pull it forwards at the same time, wondering if the problem is that it's an old lock and the door needs a sufficient amount of pulling to open it at all, but that does no good, either. When my left hand feels like it's going to fall off, I start to use my right. Still no joy. My hope wanes as fast as it had arisen. Either the door is locked, or it's going to need a gigantic full-force, two-handed yank to get it open – one that I can't give without my hands being free.

If I do manage to free my hands and the door is locked anyway, that only leaves one option. The window, although high, is my gateway out of here. No glass remains to cut me if I made my exit through it, although I'd have to deal with the boards that cover half of it. I walk towards the three chairs at the dining room table and bring the one that's closest to the window right over to it using a combination of pulling one leg of the chair along with my left leg and kicking the chair forwards.

I carefully stand up on it and peer out. There's a thicket of brambles and thorns outside the window. If I could kick the boards down, in theory I could just step onto the windowsill and jump straight out – but I know I'm going to need my hands to break my fall and possibly protect my eyes from the neglected, angry-looking bushes. The thorny thicket looks so dense that I'd imagine even standing up in it after I fall into it would be a challenge without having the use of my hands. I'd probably lose my balance trying to kick the boards down anyway while standing on this chair with the back of another tied to me. I have no option but to get these ropes off before I leave the house. I'm so close to freedom and yet so far.

I get down from the chair and walk around, considering every object in the room to free my hands with – a short process. The edge of the top of the sideboard looks jagged and damaged, with one piece of wood sticking out almost as if it had been hacked away. If I rubbed the rope against it repeatedly, would that action wear it down? But the sideboard is too high.

I stand in front of it, turn round and lean forwards, lifting my hands as high as I can, but they don't even nearly connect with the edge. Besides, the ache it generates in my shoulders is almost too much to bear. I need a chair again.

I walk towards one of the two remaining at the table that's closest to me, feeling now like I'm only fuelled by adrenaline. My steps are heavy, but I keep moving. As I did with the other chair, I pull this one out from under the table with my foot and use my legs to push it forwards. I keep pushing until the chair is in front of the sideboard. I consider the damage to the sideboard again. A small piece of wood is jutting out at the top right, as if the sideboard was once sliced by something. What could have caused that? It doesn't matter. All that matters is making this work.

I push the chair with my foot again until it's exactly where I need it to be. Then, carefully, I put one knee on the chair, then the other. Pressing my elbow and lower arm against the back of the chair, I carefully pull one leg up and

19

press my foot into the chair base, then the other. Now, it's down to balance again.

I slowly move myself upwards until I'm standing on the chair. I turn to face the window, lean forwards and push my hands back until they connect with the sideboard. I try to spike the small protruding piece of wood through the knot.

At first, it's impossible. At that moment, I see myself as a little girl trying to catch a helium balloon that had been tied to my wrist and somehow came loose. The more I tried to catch it, the further it floated out of my reach. I'm putting everything I have into focusing on connecting that spike of wood with the centre of the knot that stands between me and freedom, but it's not happening. I take a break and try to rally my fading strength, gearing myself up for another effort. If this fails, I don't know what I'll do. I'll probably die here, or be killed. I'll die not knowing what happened to me, or how I came to be in this situation.

I lift my hands again, but too fast and to the wrong place. I've misjudged where I should have lifted them to. I'm really slowing down now, the effort of the last few hours – has it been hours, or has it just felt that long? – starting to take its toll. I move my hands back again to where I think the protruding wood should be, then realise I've cut the skin on my wrist.

Suddenly, I feel significantly more alert. That wood is *sharp*. It's as sharp as I need it to be. It's just a matter of making it work for what I need it to do. I need to try harder.

I lean forwards and move my hands back towards the same area again, more gingerly this time, and locate the damaged wood. It's so sharp that my fingers instantly recoil, but the sharper the better. I try to judge the position of the wood as accurately as possible, then move my hands and arms down while pushing the rope against the wood, moving back and forth. I work slowly at first as I try to maintain my balance on the chair, then faster as I get into a rhythm.

The angle isn't as good as it could be, so I go through a painstaking process of climbing off the chair, moving it, climbing back up on it and going through the procedure of rubbing the rope against the wood again from my new vantage point. After an indeterminate period of time, I flex my wrists to see if there's any give in the rope. There's none at all. With a sigh that comes from somewhere so deep within me I didn't know it existed, I start again. I wonder if I'm mad to think this will work. But then, I got this far. I should still be tied to that chair in the position I woke in, but I'm not. I have to give this everything I have left in me.

I get into a groove and work methodically. My thoughts start to wander as I repeat the same action over and over. Will anyone even realise I'm missing? As I've broken up with Jake, does that mean I'm living on my own now? I can't remember. Why can't I even remember that much?

I try to imagine what I'd do in those circumstances. I wouldn't go to stay with a friend, I know that. I like to sort these kinds of situations out myself in my own head. A lot of my friends either have children or are pregnant right now, so I know I wouldn't impose on them with my problems when they're all so busy. The house is mine. If we broke up, Jake would probably have left. Unless he was taking it badly and being obstinate, but surely he wouldn't stay on in the house? Surely that would have been unbearable for both of us. He has his own house and he'd only been renting it out on a very short-term basis to a friend who needed a place for a few months. His friend had moved out a few weeks ago – I remember that much – so he's probably moved back there. So, on the assumption he's left, I'm now living by myself and unless I'd arranged to meet someone, nobody knows I'm missing.

I try to refocus my thoughts on the lunch and drinks I had with the girls. That must have happened on a Saturday or a Sunday. I'd have been working otherwise, and my friends would have been tied up with work and the routines of the school run during the week. My limited memories of being with them are the ones that are coming through the strongest, so I think I might have met them just before all this. If only I could remember how I'd got here. Did I leave them and walk out of the pub by myself? Will they all assume that I got a taxi, arriving home safe and sound? If they've just seen me, they probably won't be contacting me for a chat today. They might send a text, but that's all. And they probably won't get too freaked out if I don't reply immediately, instead assuming I'm just busy.

My family! My sister Claire usually rings me twice a week, but that isn't set in stone and if she has a busy week it mightn't happen. My other sister, Sandra, is usually too busy between work and her own family to ring much. As for Mam, she used to ring me every day until we came to an agreement that we'd stop that as it had started to feel too Big Brothery. Mam's the best in the world, but she finds it hard to accept sometimes that her children have grown up and need some space. Now, she rings twice a week for long chats. It could be another few days before she rings, though.

And it's doubtful that anyone will call round at my house looking for me without putting a plan in place first. I'm usually either in the office, at work dos or at the gym.

What about my friends? I think of Penny, Jake's sister. Although we hang out a lot, long-term, our friendship will probably be blown apart now that I've ended things with Jake. However, in among the memories of the lunch that are coming back to me, she's there and there's no weird vibe between us. But still, who knows? Penny's very good at putting on her public face.

Realistically, work is my best chance of my presence being missed. If today is a weekday, I'll be missed instantly. I never, ever miss a day at work. Even when I'm sick, I'll show up or work from home if things are super bad, but I'd never fail to contact work even in this instance. *Please let it be a weekday!* I try to remember the facts about missing people. Don't you have to be missing for twenty-four hours in Ireland before any action will be taken?

Everything I've done up to this point since I woke has been a huge strain on my body, but this is the worst. The ache in my arms makes them feel like lead and soon every move is torture. I can almost visualise elephants sitting on my shoulders, such is the feeling of heaviness that's started to seep into my bones and muscles. I can't give up – I know I can't. But, God, it's torture now. The weariness in my body has started to seep into my mind. Is this ultimately impossible? Am I putting myself through a task that's doomed to fail? I thought the protrusion of wood was sharp enough to file the rope away, but how would I really know? It's not as if I've ever attempted to do anything like this before.

Just when I'm at the point where I feel I can't go on a second longer, I hear the rope tear. I push my hands in opposite directions from each other. Yes, there's a discernible difference in the rope's tightness now! My heart soars and adrenaline floods my body. I resume my work, with more than a touch of frenzy to my efforts this time.

I don't know how long it takes, but eventually I wear the rope away. I want to scream with delight as I hear the rope tear some more and I'm suddenly able to wriggle my wrists freely, but I don't. I stay focused. I quickly shake off the rope around my wrists and get down off the chair. Now, I need to work on the rope around my body. My arms are still tied behind my back. I know the knot where the rope was bound isn't at the front as I can't see it when I look down, so it's tied somewhere behind my back.

I move my newly freed hands up my back and soon connect with the knot under my left shoulder. It's actually reasonably loose, probably from all the thrashing around on the ground I've been doing over the last while. It doesn't take me long to slip a finger into the heart of the knot and work it loose. I wriggle my hands to my sides and push them outwards until the rope loosens and I'm able to pull it off my body. The back of the chair crashes to the ground, the sound reverberating throughout the empty house.

Or at least, I hope it's empty.

Do I dare to yank the door open and see what lies behind?

THEN

"KNOW THE ONE THAT'S ONE TOO MANY." That's what a radio ad for alcohol consumption awareness that I heard years ago recommended. The final drink is the straw that breaks the camel's back, although it's fair to say that more than one too many has been consumed by now. For one person, the final drink ends it all.

Not long after the final drink has been purchased, the much-planned, much-talked-about day is over for everyone. And nobody thought it would have ended this way.

NOW

I VISUALISE MYSELF OPENING THE DOOR and finding my abductor standing there, sneering at how futile my bid to freedom has been. I can't bring myself to think about what might come after that.

There's always the window, of course. I can get out of here without seeing the rest of this house! What if he's in another room? But then, why would he be? This isn't exactly the type of place that would have a lovely bedroom for a leisurely lie-down after the exertion of abducting someone. And even if he is in another room in this house, he's lying in wait. Me getting out of the window isn't going to stop him. I've made lots of noise up to now. If he's here, he's heard it. He's not going to do all this and then let me escape out of the window. I wonder where he is. It makes no sense to take someone to a place like this, tie them up and then leave them. What could I possibly have done to this unknown person to deserve this treatment?

I close my eyes and try again to remember where I was before this happened. Perhaps it's procrastination while I decide what to do. I don't know. Procrastination isn't something I usually indulge in, but maybe this situation merits it. Or maybe I should make a decision and run for my life. But what if it's the wrong decision? Will it make any difference either way?

Nothing comes back to me. I try to visualise myself standing in a nightclub, or walking around the city after leaving a nightclub, trying to get a taxi. Surely that's when this happened to me. It's not as if someone would drive up to my door, ring my doorbell and drag me into a waiting car when I answered the door. Is it?

I have no answers. I open my eyes and rub my throbbing head. There's a huge lump on my forehead, so I must have sustained an injury while I was being taken – although the throb is probably a combination of this injury and my dehydration levels. I walk to the door and place my hand on the doorknob again. There might just be something else in this house that will help to protect me if I meet my abductor after I leave this house.

He's not here – he *can't* be. Other than the sounds of nature outside and those generated by my struggle to free myself, I haven't heard a single sound. He'd surely have come in if he'd heard the sound of the chair breaking. He's either away for some reason and is on his way back, or he's left me here to die. Those are the only plausible options.

I turn the doorknob with conviction. I push it outwards. Nothing happens.

I turn it again and pull it in with all my might – and again, nothing happens. And then something does. The door handle comes off in my hand and I stumble backwards.

Okay, the window it is.

As I walk over to it, another wave of dizziness floods me. I really, really, badly need water now. I can feel myself moving on to some other plain I've never been to before. Everything feels muddy. I'm swimming through it in my head as I wade to the window. When I get there, the prospect of either removing the rest of the boards or somehow climbing over them feels more daunting than escaping from the ropes had done earlier. Even standing on the chair seems like the biggest task in the world at this moment, even though my hands are now free.

I take a deep breath and put one foot up, then the other, then I kick the boards with all my might. I do it quickly, because I know the minute the adrenaline stops pumping, there will be nothing left to sustain me. Thankfully, like a loose tooth, the remaining board is ready to fall out. God only knows how long it's been there, but it comes away easily and falls outwards with a soft thud on the green area below.

I look out. The landscape doesn't look any more inviting than it did the last time, but at least the board is covering some of it now. I cover my eyes with my hands to protect them and jump down without thinking any further about it. As I land on the board, I somehow end up rolling off it and into the assortment of greenery. My skin on my legs and arms instantly rips from the brambles. My legs have also hit concrete. I remove my hands from my eyes and see that there's a concrete border round the green area, boxing it off from the gravel driveway before me. It looks like this was once a huge flower bed in front of the window, housing rose bushes and other plants. Now, all that remains is weeds.

I don't even survey the damage to my skin. Instead, I look back at the window. I almost expect my abductor's face to appear. I crawl out of the greenery onto the small driveway and look higher. I'm looking at the front of the remains of a very old cottage with a roof that's badly in need of repair. It seems to be missing more slates than it has left. The house looks tiny overall, with a narrow door in the middle and a small window to the left of the door, matching the window I've just come through. In front of the window is another selection of brambles, another former flower bed.

I consider the gravel driveway. It's overrun by weeds and moss, but it's certainly possible for a car to drive up to the front door. To the right of the driveway is an old shed and the path leading away from the house snakes to the right behind the shed, so I can't see from here where it leads to, or how far it is to get out of here and presumably – hopefully – to a road.

I listen again for the sounds of traffic. Even now that I'm outside, I can hear absolutely nothing. My mouth suddenly goes even drier than it was before. Just how far inland am I? I consider the land around me. It looks rich and fertile, the kind of ground I'd imagine would be good for farming, but having grown up on an estate in a town I don't have enough knowledge of land to say that for sure. If it's good farming soil, why are there no animals around? Or at least, I can't hear any. Surely I'd have heard some by now! Does anything at all exist here other than myself?

If I don't get out of here, *I* soon won't exist, either. It's sunny and I'm already sweating from my exertions, but the sun is making it worse. If only it was raining and I could catch rainwater in something. Maybe there's a barrel around the grounds that would contain rainwater from the previous day, if it was raining.

I creep towards the front of the house, a part of me expecting my attacker to appear from somewhere. While there's no car in the driveway, who's to say it isn't parked further down the road, behind the shed? But then, why would he even do that? I run past the front door towards the other side of the house, desperate now to find something containing water. There must be something. Except there isn't. There's absolutely nothing here except grass, grass and more grass – and the wreck of a house from which I've just escaped.

I start to make my way to the back of the house, trying to dodge nettles but finding it impossible to do so. A thicket of brambles impedes my progress and I have to push it back and down with my arms and legs before I can move forwards. Each footstep rustles in the long grass. I look back to see I'm leaving a trail of flattened greenery behind me. As I battle through it, I trip and land face down in brambles. I instinctively squeeze my eyes shut as I fall and miraculously, they're okay. But my face has been torn by the brambles, and when I lift my hand to my cheeks and forehead, they come away covered in blood.

I get up, wipe my hands on the side of my filthy jeans and continue through the vast expanse in front of me, my blouse repeatedly getting caught on thorns. I hear the sound of material tearing as I fight my way through the greenery, getting caught on something or other every few seconds. Eventually, I get through it and find precisely nothing behind the house except more grass and a dry ditch running parallel to the house around five feet behind it. For the first time since this nightmare started, I'm tempted to sit down and cry. I need water. It's like a form of hell not to have some. Everything about this experience is hell on earth. I've never felt so groggy in my life. After everything I've done to get to this point, I don't know if I can do any more. Maybe it all ends here.

No. I shake that thought from my head. I can feel my body slipping out of my control. I can't let my mind go the same way. I go back the way I came and walk towards the front door. Is there anything to be gained from trying to get inside and see the rest of the house? Surely my attacker isn't in there. Maybe he might have left some form of liquid behind from when he brought me here – for himself, not for me, of course. Surely abducting a woman is thirsty work. I might even find a clue as to who has done this to me.

Without further thought – I'm running out of time to

mull over decisions now – I push my body against the door. It doesn't budge. I move forwards then throw my weight against the door again. Still nothing. For an old door, it looks pretty sturdy. Whoever brought me here had a key.

I consider the other front window. It's also partially boarded up and as with the window I jumped out of, the thicket of weeds and brambles in front of it is so high that I'm risking tearing what's left of my skin to shreds if I even attempt to go through it, not to mention my eyes. I'd need goggles even to attempt to go through that thing. No. It's time to move on.

Once I've made my decision, I find myself running. I know it's unwise given that I hardly have any fluids – or energy – left in my body and yet I find myself unable to stop once I've started. I want to get as far away from that house as possible and never see it again.

I round the corner of the shed, hoping that I'll now see how long the path is leading away from the house, but all I see is a ditch a few feet ahead as the path snakes to the left. When I reach that point and turn left, the path suddenly becomes straight and I can see it extending ahead of me. My brain can't process how far it is in a measurement, but it's far. It'll take me at least two minutes to run it. What's at that point, though, I don't know.

I don't see a gate, just more greenery. From here, I can't work out if it's snaking to the left again or if it's the exit point of the house. But to where? To my left and right, there are nothing but trees and bushes. I can't see if the areas to the left and right of the end of the lane look like they're bordering a road because my visibility is hindered by the trees. And if there is a road up ahead, does nobody use it at all?

I run and run and when I'm halfway down the lane, I still can't hear anything other than the sound of my own panting. I thought I was fit, but when you're running for your life it seems you run faster than you do in the gym. I'm finding it harder by the second to keep running, but I force myself to keep doing so.

I consider the path to keep my mind focused. You can clearly see that the grass on the lane has been driven on recently but that it hasn't been used frequently of late. It's so overgrown with grass and weeds that it's almost become part of the landscape, like one big green blanket. I run on the parts that the wheels have flattened somewhat, still finding it hard to run fast through it.

As I approach the end of the part of the lane that I can see, I know this isn't the end. It becomes more and more obvious that the path is going to snake to the left again. I slow down, unwilling to face the imminent disappointment. For the first time since I started running, I look around. I've come a long way already. How much further will I have to go?

I round the corner to the left then instantly stop running and sink to my knees. Ahead of me is another long expanse of path, approximately twice the length of the stretch I've just battled my way through.

It's only when I've stopped running that I realise how hard and fast my pace was. I'm suddenly gasping for breath on all fours. Starbursts of light appear before my eyes and a wave of dizziness hits me, accompanied by a swell of nausea.

Things start to go black. I can feel myself going and I try to rail against it, but it's too late.

And then there's nothing.

PART TWO

Chapter 1

When I open my eyes, I see Jake.

I feel immense fear, followed by a strange sense of crushing disappointment. I really didn't think Jake was capable of doing something like this to me. I realise that a part of me had been hoping some random, opportunistic abductor had taken me, not the man I'd shared the last six months of my life with.

And then I realise I'm no longer outdoors. I'm in a bedroom – a luxurious one. I look around and quickly take in white lace curtains on the window, a chaise longue, a silver chandelier and linen bedding. I don't know where I am, but I'm certainly not back in the derelict cottage.

That knowledge isn't enough to stop me from screaming, though. I try to scramble out of bed, away from where Jake is perched at the side of it staring at me, but my body is heavy and I find myself unable to move very far. This makes me scream even more.

"Katie, it's okay," Jake says. "Calm down."

"What have you done to me?" I say. My voice sounds groggy. Getting the words out was a huge effort.

"Me? Nothing!" Jake sighs. "You've done this to yourself, Katie."

"What?" My fury at his words forces mine out. My fear is completely displaced by my anger now. "I tied myself up and left myself somewhere to die, did I?"

Jake frowns then shakes his head. "You need water." He nods towards the bedside table beside me. "There's plenty there."

I look at the jug of water. "No. You've probably poisoned it. I need a bottle of water with the seal unbroken."

Jake looks at me as if I'm mad. Is that part of his act? Is he trying to pretend he's not behind all this?

"Katie—"

"Where am I?"

Jake pauses before speaking. "You don't remember anything, then?"

"Where the *hell* am I, Jake?"

"Penny's house."

"Penny's house?" Yes, this room does look familiar. I couldn't place it at first. "Why?"

"She brought you here last night after you passed out."

"Last night? What day is it today?"

"Sunday."

"Where was I last night before Penny brought me here?"

"Out in town with her and your other friends. You went for lunch and stayed out afterwards. Don't you remember?"

So that memory in the cottage of being out with the girls for lunch was yesterday. How did Jake do this to me, then, without any of my friends seeing it, especially Penny?

Jake shakes his head. "How did it come to this, Katie?

36

I've always been concerned about how much you can drink and you know we've had conversations about whether you drink too much when you're out, but this – this is at a whole new level. I've never seen you like this."

I'm completely perplexed. Words spill from my mouth again, even though I know it's not wise to antagonise the man who tried to kill me, and yet I can't help it. I'm too incensed to keep my counsel.

"You took me to a derelict cottage, left me there for dead and you're telling me I have a drink problem? Don't you think you might be the one with the problem?"

"*What?*"

"And why are we back here? Did you get cold feet? *How* could you have done that to me? I was hoping it was someone else. Some stranger. Anyone but *you*."

I would say more, but speaking hurts. Everything hurts. I look down at my arms. I'm now wearing a short-sleeved pyjama top and three-quarter length pyjama bottoms. I can see the tears in my skin from battling through the brambles and falling into them. My head is still throbbing – what did Jake do to me to cause that injury on my forehead? – and I feel even weaker than I did at the cottage. I know I should be terrified at what's to come now, but I'm too angry to let even more fear in. It'll probably follow shortly, but there's no room for it at this moment. My anger is suffocating everything else.

Jake exhales sharply then walks to the door and leaves the room. I sit up in bed, intending to throw my legs over the side and stand up. Dizziness hits me instantly and I sink back into the soft downy pillows behind me. I close my eyes and breathe deeply, trying to regain control of my body. I'm in a sorry state, one that will hardly allow me to escape. Fear finally starts to creep in now. What exactly is Jake planning to do with me next?

And yet, none of it makes sense. Jake never had a threatening bone in his body. How could he go from being the person I knew to someone who'd do this?

I hear Jake's footsteps returning. My heart starts racing and the fear starts to come back. I've no idea what's going to happen next.

"Here." Jake walks over to me and hands me a bottle of water. "Check the seal. It hasn't been opened."

I check it. He's right. I tear the bottle open, which proves to be harder than I'd imagined in my present state, and gulp the water furiously.

"You should eat. What do you think you can stomach?"

I hesitate before answering.

"I won't poison it, Katie, for heaven's sake. I can give you a sealed bag of crisps, or I can cook you something substantial. Surely you must be hungry by now."

"What time is it?"

"Just after seven in the evening. Penny says you haven't eaten all day. You guys had lunch at two yesterday and you didn't eat anything after that, so it's well past twenty-four hours since you last ate."

Seven p.m.?

"I thought you'd never wake."

"How long have you been here?"

"About four hours." Jake shakes his head. "I just can't believe what you've done to yourself. No wonder you think I'm trying to poison you. The drink is destroying your mind."

38

All fear leaves me as anger takes over again. I can't just lie here and let him speak to me like that after what I've just been through.

"Jake, the last thing I remember is being out for lunch with Penny and the girls, then I wake up in a derelict cottage in the middle of God knows where, tied up and left for dead. I escape but then pass out. And when I wake again, I see your face." I struggle to speak, but I know I must continue. "Do you honestly think you're going to be able to convince me that it was all some drunken dream?"

Jake gives me a strange look. "Katie, did you take something?"

"What?"

"Drugs. Did you take drugs? This isn't like you at all. Something isn't right here."

"Of course I didn't! And don't try to change the subject! Why did you come back for me? What changed your mind?" I start to cough, but I'm determined to continue. "No, actually, let's take a step back," I say when my breath returns. "What possessed you to do something like that to me in the first place? Just because I broke up with you. What you did is the behaviour of a psychopath, Jake!" I'm crying now. *"You left me for dead!"*

Jake's eyes widen. The expression on his face that follows is full of something I can't quite read. Is it . . . pity?

"I'm going to send Penny up to you," he says, standing up. "You can let her know if you want something to eat."

"No!" I wipe my eyes furiously. "You can't just walk out after what you've just done to me!"

He does just that but turns round before he walks

39

down the stairs and looks at me through the open door. He gives me that look again. I want to kill him just then, in exactly the same way that he wanted to kill me. Perhaps he still does. Perhaps he's going to get Penny to help him finish the job.

Penny. We get on well, don't we? At least, we always got along well enough for us to go on nights out together – both with and without Jake – but we wouldn't be ringing each other constantly during the week for chats, either. Her career is a lot more high-flying than mine. She's the CEO of operations for Europe, the Middle East and Africa in a huge multinational corporation that employs 2,000 people in Ireland alone. At thirty-eight, she's considered in professional circles to be very young to hold this position and she's garnered plenty of attention in media columns as a result. How do I react to her now? She'll help me, surely. She'll see sense. Maybe she's protecting me from Jake. Maybe she found out what he did and was the one to stop it from happening.

I consider what Jake said about my drinking. Okay, I like my alcohol. Yes, I can probably drink more than the average person, given my height and slightly broad build. I can put away a bottle of wine no problem without feeling more than a little tipsy and without many adverse effects the following day. I've been known to drink two bottles over the course of a long day, such as a lunch date that goes on until the late evening, and still function reasonably normally the next day. Although I'm always careful not to drive the next morning when I do that and I'd never drink that much other than at the weekend – even then, it rarely happens.

The speed at which I drink usually determines the outcome, though. If I drink slowly, I'm fine. Too fast and I'm hammered like everyone else, which is why I usually drink reasonably slowly. At home, anyway. Sometimes when I'm out, I do get a bit carried away and knock back my drinks. I usually have a glass of red wine with my dinner, sometimes two, but generally one.

I'd never considered my level of drinking to be problematic, but Jake, who doesn't drink in large volumes owing to being health conscious, thought my drinking was unnecessary at best, excessive at worst. "It's empty calories," he'd say, to which I'd counter that I don't eat chocolate, crisps, biscuits or most other forms of junk food, and I deserved to have something as a treat. Besides, red wine was the one form of alcohol that could boast a certain amount of health benefits, such as lowering the risk of heart disease. "It'll dehydrate your body," he'd say, to which I'd say I'd have a large glass of water directly after finishing my wine. "It's an addictive substance," he'd offer, to which I'd say some classed love as an addiction, too. And coffee. He loved coffee. That usually stopped the conversation.

But whenever we went out, I knew he was always silently monitoring my alcohol consumption. It annoyed me and it sometimes made me drink even more. I'm a work-hard, party-hard type of person now. I wasn't always that way, but that's certainly how I've been recently. I definitely never considered myself to be a nuisance when drunk and was never aggressive while I was under the influence of alcohol, either – on the contrary, it softened me. And I could hold it, I know I could.

I may have consumed a considerable amount of wine

on the day I met Penny and the girls for lunch, but I find it hard to believe that I drank myself unconscious. I've had times when I've forgotten certain things that have happened and yet people have said to me that I seemed normal. That's the kind of drinker that I seem to be. I look fine even when things are caving in inside me.

Of course, to everyone else's eyes, it's plausible that the amount I apparently drank would have knocked me out – it certainly might have done so to other people. But I know my body and I know how it reacts to certain substances.

Lunch is coming back to me in more detail now. I remember sitting at the table with Penny, Barbara, Rose and Gabrielle. Some of us had prosecco, I think. We were all talking a lot at that point, some people favouring catching up to drinking. I think I had two glasses of it before switching to red wine. I also vaguely remember what I ate for lunch. I'm quite sure I had fish cakes as a starter and a sirloin steak with vegetables and potatoes for my main course – that's what's coming to mind, anyway. I may even have had a dessert, accompanied by Irish coffee. I can visualise Irish coffees being brought out to us – I *think*. That part of the memory is hazy. Nonetheless, it was a substantial lunch overall – not lettuce leaves.

I'm pretty certain we went on a pub crawl then, but I've been on many of those without ending up in a deserted cottage afterwards. Something isn't adding up.

Penny's appearance at the door puts an end to my recollections.

"Penny, I'm trusting you to tell me what the hell is going on here," I say, calmer now, as she walks into the room. "Jake hasn't told me anything."

I'm expecting reassurance, but her expression is colder than I've ever seen.

"From what he just told me, you didn't give him a chance. You were too busy accusing him of trying to poison you. Oh, and of leaving you in a cottage to die. Seriously, Katie? Have you lost your mind?"

"Penny, just tell me what happened."

"Okay. I'll tell you." Penny folds her arms across her chest. "You got drunk – messy, disgracefully drunk. I could see that you were too far gone and I wanted you to go home, but some guy was chatting you up and it was obvious that you had no intention of budging. Not long afterwards, you collapsed in the pub.

"I carried you outside with the help of the girls and the bar staff and brought you back here because you had nobody else to look after you, and you certainly weren't in any condition to look after yourself. You vomited all over my house, wailed and cried. You called me all sorts of names, called Jake worse ones, and told me how much you hated yourself."

"What?"

That doesn't sound like something I'd say at all. I'm rarely dramatic when drunk and I certainly don't feel like I hate myself on a day-to-day basis. Sure, I've had a hard time in the past, but it was a long time ago and I'm over it now.

"Yes. You were hard work, Katie. You went to sleep sometime around three o'clock, when there was nothing left in you to throw up. When I came in to check on you this morning, I saw that you'd gone wandering downstairs and had brought a packet of my sleeping tablets upstairs with you from the cupboard downstairs. You'd taken two of them. Maybe you thought they were paracetamol, I don't know. Richard was keeping an eye on you on and off during the night, but you must have gone downstairs when he was asleep."

Richard Stapleton is Penny's current other half and someone I don't gel with very much, to put it mildly.

"You've only just woken. I thought I was going to have to call a doctor, you've been out so long."

I can't believe what I'm hearing. "Penny, that can't be right. I—"

"No!" Penny puts a hand up. "Don't you dare deny it just because you can't remember. The last twenty-four hours around you have been *hell*. I flew in from the States on Friday, as you know, and the last thing I needed was to spend all day yesterday and today wiping your butt for you – literally, Katie. You have *no* idea of the state you were in."

Oh yes, I vaguely remember something about Penny being in the States last week. It seems like a very long time ago now, though. Something that I heard about in a different life. I shake my head, suddenly shivering. I fold my arms and rub my hands up the opposite arms.

"Cold? The reason why you're in such skimpy pyjamas instead of a warm woolly one is because you got sick on everything else I gave you! You even got sick on your socks and refused to put on another pair. That's how petulant and hard to deal with you were. And now you're accusing Jake of complete nonsense! Why? Just because you two broke up? That's crazy. *You* ended things with *him*. You really and truly need to take a good long look at

44

yourself and where you're at in your life before you push everyone away."

Penny turns round and marches out of the room, closing my door as she leaves. I'm too shell-shocked to say anything at first, but as soon as she's left the room, I'm yelling after her, pleading with her to come back. I know she can hear me through the closed door even though my voice is weak, but she doesn't return.

I'm petrified now. I *know* what happened to me. It wasn't a drunken dream. I only need to look down at my bruised wrists, my torn arms, my swollen ankles to know that what happened to me was real. I touch the lump on my forehead. I still don't know what caused that, but that injury was there in the house and it's still there. I run my fingers over my face. It's torn to shreds from the brambles and it's sore on the side that crashed to the floor – as is my nose. Is Penny covering for Jake? What other possibility is there but that?

I won't let them get away with it. I *can't*. I throw myself out of bed and onto the ground, fuelled by the same adrenaline that got me out of the cottage, and I start to crawl. I escaped once. I can do it again. I'm getting out of here and going straight to the gardai.

I crawl to the door. Damn Penny for having closed it!

Slowly, I get to my feet and open the door. The dizziness takes over again. I walk into the hall but immediately lose my balance and crash against the wall opposite the door. I feel the oblivion overtaking me as I slide down the wall.

This time, there will be no escape.

Chapter 2

I wake up. Jake and Penny are sitting on chairs, staring at me.

"What's going on? Where am I?" I say, looking around the room. My surroundings are unfamiliar. "Is this a hospital room?"

Jake nods. Before I can ask any more questions, I start to remember what happened in Penny's house – and before that. The last thing I remember from being in Penny's is trying to escape. Clearly, I didn't get too far. When I try to sit up, I see that there's a drip in my arm.

I notice that both Jake and Penny are looking a lot more sympathetic now.

"You collapsed and we brought you to the hospital," Jake says, "but everything's going to be okay now."

"How can everything be okay?" I say, but Jake shushes me.

"Katie, you were drugged," Jake says. "A test was done on your urine after you were admitted. There were traces of Rohypnol in it."

"Rohypnol?" Is he lying? "I don't remember giving a urine sample."

"They took it from a catheter, Katie." Penny looks almost pitying. "Don't worry, I'm sure it's normal to feel confused after everything you've been through. And for my part, I'm sorry about how I spoke to you earlier. I assumed it was the drink. I had no idea you'd been drugged."

"How could something like this have happened? I don't remember . . . "

I trail off. I was going to say I didn't remember leaving my drink down anywhere for long in the bars we'd been to, but of course I don't. I don't remember anything much beyond lunch with the girls and little snippets of memories of the bars we went to.

Penny glances at Jake. "You might remember me saying that a man was chatting you up when we were out. You were talking to him at the bar in the Kildare Lounge for about fifteen minutes. Do you remember that?"

I shake my head. *We were in the Kildare Lounge?* Yes, now that she's specifically said it, I do hazily remember walking there with the group, but the memory is misty. I can just about remember us leaving the pub we'd been in before that and walking towards the Kildare Lounge. And I have a fuzzy memory of walking in through the door, but that's all.

"You and the man started talking at the back of the bar. The pub was jammed, so the rest of us decided to move upstairs to find a quieter place to stand and I said to you to follow us, but you said you'd join us in a minute and turned away from me. We were worried about you. You'd had a lot to drink, much more than the rest of us, so we all went downstairs not long after to tell you we were leaving. By the time we got to you, you'd collapsed.

"We got you outside and I brought you back to my place in a taxi around 10 p.m. But, Katie, I have to reiterate that I had absolutely no idea that your drink had been spiked. You drank so much that your behaviour seemed to be alcohol-related, although you seemed pretty okay before we went into the Kildare Lounge. I wouldn't have let you have another drink if I'd thought otherwise.

"I thought that last drink was the straw that broke the camel's back and tipped you over the edge, but it seems that's not the case. As soon as I leave here, I'm ringing the gardai to report that this took place and to get them to check the CCTV in the pub for footage of this man. There's no way I'm going to let someone get off scot-free after drugging you without trying to identify them and bringing them to justice!"

"But . . . " This doesn't make sense. "What about what happened to me?"

"Nothing else happened, Katie," Jake said. "It was a hallucination. We told the doctor what you've been saying and he said hallucinations are a possible side effect from Rohypnol."

"But look at me! Look at my arms and wrists!" I hold out my arms. "And my face! Brambles caused these scrapes. A rope caused these bruises on my wrists. This is physical proof of what happened to me! And look at my ankles, too! And the bump on my forehead."

Jake and Penny look at each other. They both give me that sympathetic look again.

"You scraped your arms and face with your nails yourself, Katie," Penny says slowly. "I saw you doing it. You were agitated after I brought you home. You also kept grabbing your wrists and squeezing them. I didn't know why, but you were so upset at that time that I assumed it was some form of self-harm."

"Self-harm? I've never self-harmed! Ever! Why would I do that?"

Penny shrugs. "You were so drunk and upset, Katie. You weren't yourself at all. And now we know why, but at the time I thought it might have been a reaction to . . . " She glances at Jake again, who looks uncomfortable. "Well, the break-up. As for your ankles, I don't know what happened there. But with regard to your forehead, I'd take an educated guess that you sustained that injury when you collapsed in the pub. I didn't see it occur, so I can't say for sure, but I'd imagine that's what happened."

I shake my head. "It was so real. Are you absolutely sure I came home with you?"

Penny looks cross now. "Of course I'm sure. Ask the girls if you don't believe me."

"I do believe you," I say. "It's just . . . honestly, I'd swear this happened to me, Penny."

"Do you feel like you've been sexually assaulted?" Penny says.

"No."

"Well, there you go. Do you really think if there was any chance at all that a man in a bar had drugged you and taken you somewhere that it wouldn't have been for the purposes of having sex with you?"

I glance at Jake. He looks uncomfortable.

"Katie, you have my every sympathy for being drugged. It's wrong and it shouldn't have happened. But I can assure you that I took you home and looked after you. And nobody had the chance to take you to a cottage and tie you up in the meantime.

"Richard can verify that if you need further proof. He called over after I got home and he helped me to look after you. He was there all day Sunday with me, too. We stayed in to keep an eye on you. I know you can't stand him and *he* knows you can't stand him, but he was willing to help you when you needed it all the same. It was a hallucination, as the doctor said."

There's nothing else I can say. I want to scream at Penny that she's wrong, but how can she be? And yet, how can a hallucination feel that real? Also, the thought of Penny's boyfriend – or *partner*, as she always insists on calling him – helping me in any way makes me want to scream, too. I find him creepy and hard to be around.

"They won't keep you here long," Penny says. "They've checked you out and other than the Rohypnol finding, they said you're okay. You were just dehydrated and hadn't eaten in too long. I'd imagine they'll let you out in the next few hours – they'll need the bed."

I feel worse than ever now, like I'm taking a bed from someone who genuinely needs it while I'm apparently just a drunken, drugged-up mess.

"I've called in sick for you at work, by the way," Penny says. "I didn't give your manager any details. He asked, but I just said I didn't know exactly what had happened. Just that I wasn't sure when you'd be back but you'd keep him posted."

"I'm sure he questioned you further on that," I say.

"He didn't get a chance. I politely said goodbye and hung up before he could ask anything else."

I try not to think about how busy things must be at work this week. I remember working late on Friday and I know we have a lot on this week, too. I'll have to ring my manager, Henry, later and sort something out. But what? Right now, I'm not sure if I have the strength to walk to the bathroom.

"Katie, I'm sorry for judging you so harshly about your drinking," Penny says while Jake continues to hold his tongue. "But while this new information does change my perspective on the issue, I still think your drinking is something you need to look at. You drank at least eight quarter bottles of wine on Saturday. That's the equivalent of two bottles of wine, you know. That's way too much in one day. *Plus*, we had prosecco and Irish coffee with lunch."

"But we were out since lunchtime, so the drinks were spread out over a long period and we'd had lunch."

Penny shakes her head. "If this was a one-off, I wouldn't be questioning it, but I've been out with you often enough to know this is normal for you. I never drink the same volume as you do when we're out. I simply wouldn't be able."

"My system is well able for wine, Penny. I never get hangovers from it."

"But it's not right that it's able to process that volume of wine, Katie! It must be well used to it, which is extremely worrying. You're going to have to learn to drink in moderation. If you can't do that, you'll have to accept that you have a problem and then do something about it."

"Stop making me out to be an alcoholic! You're just as fond of a few drinks as I am!"

"Yes, a few. I only drank half of my drinks in most of the pubs. I drink a lot less volume than you do."

"Only because you can't handle it," I say immediately. I can't stop the words from coming out, but I know as soon as I've said it that I've dug a hole for myself.

"And you can?" Penny inevitably says. "You're in a hospital bed right now and I'm not."

"I'm in a hospital bed because I was drugged!"

"Which you didn't notice happening because you were *drunk*."

"Penny, leave it," Jake says. "Katie's not strong enough

to have this conversation right now." He stands up. "I have to go to work. Penny will stay on with you for a while, Katie."

"So it's Monday now, right?"

"Yes, it's Monday morning," Penny says. "You've been here overnight. Do you remember anything after you arrived here?"

I think about this. Yes, vague memories of waking up in the middle of the night last night and wondering where I was but feeling too tired to do anything other than go back to sleep straight away are coming back to me. I can't remember arriving at the hospital, though.

"Only fragments," I say. "Don't you have to work too, Penny?" Penny *always* has to work.

"I'm going in later. I'll leave here in a while and then ring the gardai before I go in."

"I hope it's not causing trouble for you to be here."

"I don't answer to anybody in work, Katie. *They* answer to *me*. Barbara's coming in to see you in an hour's time. I've filled her in on everything. Your handbag is in your bedside table, by the way. I brought it in, along with some spare clothes and some toiletries."

Barbara was out with us on Saturday, too. I'm torn between wanting to see her and question her as much as possible, and being ashamed at the thought of her inevitable disapproval of what my drunken behaviour has led to.

"Penny, I'll ring you later. Take care of yourself, Katie," Jake says as he leaves.

I say goodbye, attempting a smile. I'm not afraid of him now, I realise. Did the drug cause paranoia? I'm suddenly mortified in his presence. I accused this man of wanting to kill me. But I thought *someone* did. Logically, he seemed like the most likely option. Who else would have had a motive to do it?

And now they're telling me it didn't happen at all. That it was all in my mind. I don't know whether to be thankful to be told that such a horrific experience didn't actually occur, or to scream with frustration at how nobody believes me, because I'm still not convinced that it didn't. I can't fathom how any hallucination could possibly be so authentic. And there are still unexplained marks on my ankles . . .

Chapter 3

A few minutes after Penny leaves, I ring the buzzer beside my bed and ask the nurse if I can see the doctor as soon as possible. I'm told he's busy right now and will be with me in a while. I start to argue, but then I see Barbara standing at the doorway. Despite the fact that Barbara and I have been friends for years, I start to feel nervous when I see her.

Barbara looks tentative as she walks in. I wonder how visibly I wear the same emotion on my face. What did she see me doing that night?

I attempt a smile. "Hi, Barbara. Still alive."

She frowns.

"Me, that is. Not you."

Her frown intensifies. This isn't going well.

"Sit down," I say quickly. "These hospital beds are surprisingly comfortable if you'd like to sit at the edge there. Jake and Penny didn't look too comfortable on those chairs earlier."

"I'd imagine that might be more to do with this situation than the chairs, Katie." Barbara perches herself on one of the seats. "They seem fine to me. How are you feeling?"

"Sore," I say.

"That's to be expected, I'd imagine. God, Katie, *Rohypnol* . . . You were so lucky we were there. I can't believe this happened to you. It could have taken a much more sinister turn."

"What happened?" I say. "I know the general details, but what did you see happening to me?"

Barbara's frown, which had just about left her face, returns again.

"I don't know what you mean. I saw you drinking a lot over the course of the day, then reaching a point where you collapsed and had to be brought home, or do you mean what did I see of the man you were talking to at the bar?"

"Well, yes. And . . . did you actually see me getting into that taxi with Penny?"

Again, I've said the wrong thing. I know it instantly.

"Of course I did, Katie. I helped to *carry* you into that taxi. Hasn't Penny told you all this?"

"Yes."

"Well, you hardly think she's lying about it, do you? Because if you're in any doubt, I can confirm that she isn't."

I say nothing. It's not that I think she's lying, but how can a hallucination feel so *real*?

"She told me about the side effects of the drug," Barbara says, her voice gentler now. "Look, don't worry about it, Katie. I'm sure hallucinations feel real at the time, but they probably fade after a few days. Don't let it mess with your head. The important thing is that you got out of this situation in one piece. Some people aren't so lucky."

I nod. What else can I do? But I don't feel lucky. I don't feel like I got out of this situation in one piece. My head is destroyed with thoughts of that cottage and yet everyone's telling me it couldn't possibly have happened. So what does

55

that mean? Am I mad? Has the drug altered the chemicals in my brain? Maybe Barbara's right. Maybe if this is a hallucination, it'll fade soon. But every time I look at my swollen wrists, I'm back there. I'm in the cottage, in that never-ending moment. I can *smell* the place.

"It could have happened to any of us," Barbara continues.

I know there's a but on the way.

"But, Katie, you can't put yourself in this situation again. If you'd been sober, you'd have seen that man putting something in your drink. I *know* you would have. He couldn't have done it without it being in some way obvious, I bet. And I know how much pressure you're under at work and how much you like your social drinks at the weekend – we all do, or at least I certainly did before I had the kids. But imagine if this had gone wrong. He could have murdered you, for all we know!"

I think about how it felt to be tied up, thinking I could well have been about to be murdered. Or how I *thought* I was tied up, apparently. Tears fill my eyes and start to spill over. It was so *real*.

Barbara moves to the bed and takes my hand. "I know, Katie. It's such a scary thought, isn't it? And we all have to learn from it. We all need to be more vigilant. There are bad people out there."

"There sure are," I say.

"How has Jake been about it all?" Barbara says.

I think about this. "He's been . . . non-judgmental," I eventually say.

I hadn't really known what I was going to say until it came out of my mouth. Penny, although she's trying very hard to hide it, is more than likely disgusted at me for ending up in this situation. A part of me thinks I'm probably a huge inconvenience to her and her high-flying lifestyle, but I bury that thought instantly. If I'm wrong about all this actually happening to me – if it actually *was* a hallucination – I have a lot to thank Penny for. If she hadn't taken me home and kept me safe, it could have happened for real, or something even worse.

Jake, though, has said very little and has almost been quietly supportive. I'm not sure I deserve that after breaking up with him and accusing him of trying to kill me, but it is what it is nonetheless.

Things that happened before all *this* happened have come back to me. I've been so busy dealing with this horrible mess that I haven't even acknowledged that realisation to myself. I remember now why I broke up with him. I remember that Jake has indeed moved out. I remember every horrible messy detail. I almost wish I didn't.

"I still can't believe you ended things with him," Barbara says. "I really think you're making a mistake."

"I did it for him," I say. "It's better this way."

"He doesn't seem to think so."

"What do you mean? Have you been talking to him about it?"

"Only briefly. He thinks it's a huge mistake. So do I, Katie," Barbara says. "And look at what's happened to you since you broke up with him! No good has come of it."

"I don't need Jake to protect me," I say. "I drank too much. It was a mistake – one I won't be repeating."

The doctor comes to the door.

"Barbara, could you give us a second, please?" I say.

Barbara nods and leaves the room. I thank God it's her here and not Penny. Penny would probably insist on staying, too. She means well, but she can be overbearing.

Right now, I need time alone with this doctor. I need to know how a hallucination can feel so real. If I can't get an understanding of that, I know I'm going to struggle in moving forwards from this.

He starts by telling me what I've already been told – that I collapsed, was brought into hospital and a urine test showed traces of Rohypnol.

"Did my friends tell you about my hallucination?" I say.

"It was mentioned briefly," he replies.

"It was so real," I say, vocalising my earlier thought.

I start to tell him about it. I can see he wants to end this conversation as soon as I start talking – he probably has an endless list of patients to see – but he stays and listens. I spill out as many details as I can. As I talk about it, it feels more real than ever.

"As I told your friends, hallucinations can be a side effect of Rohypnol," he says when I eventually finish speaking. "It should start to fade soon. You were lucky your friend Jake asked us to test you for drugs," the doctor says. "At least you know the reason for your hallucination now."

I frown. "You didn't run the test as standard? Jake asked for it?"

"Yes. He said he had a suspicion that something untoward had happened to you – that he's seen you drinking quite a bit, but nothing like this has ever happened to you before."

If I was right and everyone else was wrong, and this whole thing wasn't a hallucination, it mustn't have had anything to do with Jake like I first thought when I woke up and saw him there. Why would Jake ask for a drugs test if he was the one who'd drugged me, or had arranged to drug me? He personally wouldn't have had the opportunity to drug me. He wasn't there. The only way he could have done it was if he was in cahoots with this guy I was talking to, but why would he be? That's not Jake. He's not that person. I'm pretty sure of that. And yet earlier I thought he was capable of drugging me himself.

The doctor talks on about how my head injury seems relatively innocuous and consistent with a fall. And how they're happy to release me but I need to look after my diet and fluids – and watch my alcohol intake to make sure I never fall prey to something like this again. I'm listening, but I don't quite feel present in the moment, either. I've never felt so confused in my life. At least physically I'm feeling much better today, though. I certainly feel well enough to go home, although I'm still a lot weaker than I usually am.

"Do you have someone to collect you from the hospital?" the doctor asks.

"I'll get a taxi," I say.

"Try to arrange for a friend or family member to be with you when you get home," he says.

I assure him that there will be someone, even though there won't. I'm anxious to get out of here now.

When he leaves, Barbara returns. She asks me for an update, and I tell her I'm fine and will get out later today. I'm vague with the details because I'm hoping she'll leave. Much as I appreciate her visit, I want to be on my own now. I still can't process the trauma of my supposed hallucination. I don't know what I'm supposed to do now. The doctor said the hallucination will fade, but when? What do I do until it does?

"I'd better go," Barbara says. "I have to pick Ivan up from preschool."

I try to mask my delight. Finally, time on my own to try to think straight.

"Thanks so much for visiting, Barbara. I appreciate it."

"How will you get home?"

"I'll ring Jake for a lift," I say, telling her what I know she wants to hear. "He's finishing work early today." A lie but a necessary one. "I'm sure, despite everything that's happened, that he'll help me out."

"That's a good idea." She gives me a hug. "You mind yourself, okay?"

I assure her I will. As soon as she's gone, I reach for my handbag. I need my phone to call a taxi.

I rifle through my handbag quickly. It contains plenty of things – my wallet, make-up, a hairbrush, among an assortment of other items – but not a phone.

I resist the urge to throw my handbag across the room. When did I lose my phone? I try to remember when I last had it. I know I took pictures of the girls at lunch on Saturday. I think I may have taken some in the pubs afterwards, but I'm not sure. I have a vague recollection of Jake texting me at one stage and of me being annoyed about it because I felt he was crossing the line by continuing to text me after things had ended. He knew I was out with the girls that day and wasn't ringing me, but there were plenty of texts, if my memory serves me right. I suppose I lost the phone in one of the last few pubs we went to, if not *the* last. I'm sure I won't get it back now, anyway.

I sit back and close my eyes, suddenly exhausted again. When I open them, I can't quite believe what I'm seeing. Is this another hallucination?

"Mam? What are you doing here?"

Just when I thought things couldn't get any worse . . .

Chapter 4

Mam's not alone. She's with my sisters, Sandra and Claire. All three of them are looking very solemn.

"Hi," I say tentatively.

Mam instantly bursts into tears.

Shit.

"Mam, I'm fine," I say.

"Fine?" Mam says in a wobbly voice. "You were drugged! Your face is torn to bits! You're as far from fine as you've ever been, Katie!"

I can't think of anything to say to that. She's 100 per cent right. I'm not fine at all.

"Did Jake ring you?"

"No, it was Penny." Mam's voice is stronger now. Harder. "She told me you finished with Jake last week."

I nod.

"How's that working out for you?" Sandra asks.

I know it's a rhetorical question. Sandra has a sharp tongue at the best of times.

"I hoped you'd get engaged!" Mam says. "You seemed happy together at my seventieth birthday party. Why on earth would you end things with a man like him?"

"It's . . . complicated, Mam."

"No, it's not. You're throwing a good man away. It's that simple. Just when I was finally starting to think I needn't be as worried about you any more, that you were getting yourself together. Then you go and break things off with a decent soul like Jake, the nicest man you could ever meet and a far cry nicer than your ex-husband, I might add. And now you're having these hallucinations!" Mam's face starts to crumple.

God, I wish Penny hadn't told Mam about the hallucination! If that's what it was. But then, Penny doesn't know what happened years ago.

"It was only one and it's nothing to worry about," I lie.

I've never been so worried about anything. But if Mam gets too involved in my life, I'm in serious trouble.

"That's what you said the last time," Mam instantly retorts.

"I was eighteen years younger then," I say. "Am I ever going to be allowed to forget about all that? I've moved on. I thought we all had."

Mam starts to cry again. "You don't remember," she says. "You've blocked it out. You have no idea how bad you were."

"Bad in the sense of sick," Claire chips in, speaking for the first time since she's entered the room.

She likes to interpret Mam-speak for everyone else when Mam's having a politically incorrect moment. That's Claire – always the peacemaker. She can't bear conflict. I know right now she's wishing this entire situation would just go away.

"But you got better, Katie," Claire continues. "And you will again now. We all have ups and downs in life."

Mam's wringing her hands. I feel a flash of pity for her

and disgust at myself. She's seventy. She's not able for this.

"Mam, I made a mistake. I drank too much. I know I like a drink, but I never take it that far usually and unfortunately, someone saw that I had this time and took advantage of me. It was just a case of wrong place, wrong time. Believe me, I've learned my lesson. I'll never drink that much again – ever."

"You should give up drinking, full stop," Mam says fiercely.

"I know, I know. You're probably right."

"And the hallucination, that's what worries me most of all. This is exactly what happened before—"

"This isn't the same thing at all," I say quickly.

And it isn't. It's far, far worse this time. But I can't tell Mam that.

The doctor walks in. "We're happy to discharge you now, Katie," he says.

"Okay. Thanks for your help, Doctor."

"Are you in full-time employment?"

"Yes, I'm supposed to work tomorrow. I'm supposed to be working today, really."

"My advice to you would be to take a few days off, possibly a week."

"A *week*?"

"That would be the optimal recovery time, yes. While the drug passes through the system quickly, I'd recommend taking some time to recover from a mental and emotional perspective. And obviously, you also have some physical injuries that need to heal, too."

I can just imagine Henry's reaction when he hears that I need to be off for a week. Usually, the thought of his disdain at me calling in sick for a week would make me quiver. You don't *do* sick in our office. There was a time when I broke my arm a few years ago on a skiing holiday and I still went into the office and typed my articles with one hand when I came back.

Henry takes his position as the newspaper's editor very seriously and he expects everyone else to take their jobs seriously, too. We've been busier than ever in the past few months owing to a few staff members leaving and the budget for hiring their replacements being pulled as a result of reduced income revenue. Everyone's had to take on more work and everyone's way more stressed than they used to be. The fact that Henry's possible ire is little more than a passing concern for me right now is a measure of how mentally messed up I am at this moment. However, I don't want him finding out about this. Anything that's logged about me in a doctor's report could be dangerous to my future career prospects, depending on the extent of the information.

"I'll go to the doctor during the week for a check-up and get a certificate from him," I say. "I'll tell him to liaise with the hospital's administration department for information if needs be. Would that be all right?"

"Sure." The doctor seems anxious to get away now. "Will one of your friends be collecting you, or . . . ?" He looks at Mam, Sandra and Claire.

"I'm Katie's mother – Jackie's my name – and these are her sisters, Sandra and Claire. We'll take her home," Mam says.

"Oh no, that's not necessary," I say. "You probably need to get going soon."

Mam flaps a hand in my direction. "Not at all. You're coming with us. That's that decided."

The doctor tells me to make sure to eat and drink plenty

of healthy foods over the coming days and to abstain from alcohol until my body has had a chance to recover, to which Mam says that she's certain that I'll be giving up alcohol completely from this point onwards.

I nod and smile, trying not to let my internal panic show. When Mam said they'd bring me home, she'd better have meant *my* home. I try to avoid Mam's house as much as possible. It was never the same to me after Dad died and even seeing it now reminds me of the hellish aftermath of his death. If she even tries to get Sandra or Claire to drive back there, I'll jump out at some traffic lights and run for my life.

Mind you, if it's Sandra driving, she'll lock the car internally the second she gets inside. Someone opened her passenger door once at traffic lights and whipped out her handbag. Luckily for her, it was the day before pay day and all she really had in it were snotty tissues and Halls Soothers because both she and her children had bad colds that day. She even laughed afterwards at the thought of the thief plunging his hand into her bag and getting nothing more than a handful of snot. Still though, she never forgot it, so God help anyone who wanted to do a runner from her car. I hope Claire drove to the hospital.

We leave. They lead me to Sandra's car.

"Shit," I say.

Shit. I can't believe I said that out loud.

"What's wrong?" Mam says.

"I . . . I think I left the immersion on before I went out on Saturday," I say. It's all I can think of.

"You don't have an immersion, Katie. Or at least you didn't the last time I visited you."

She's right. I don't.

"Electric showers are overrated," I say just to say something while I think of an excuse for what I've just said.

I've got nothing.

Eventually, Mam says, "They said they checked out that bump on your head, didn't they?"

"They did. I'm just tired, Mam. I need to get home to my own bed. Sandra, you know the way to my house from here, don't you?"

"I'll set the satnav," she says.

Mam doesn't contradict her. *Phew.*

We pull up outside my house. I fervently hope I have a key for the house in my handbag. I hadn't checked for that in the hospital. I rummage through the bag and find it, offering up a silent prayer of thanks. I can't wait to get into my own house. I'm hoping the refuge of my home will make me feel safe again.

We go inside. Mam's already talking about tea. I welcome the thought of the familiar ritual and instantly offer to make it, but Mam's already halfway to the kitchen. I hang up the coat Claire gave me before we left the hospital and breathe in the familiar scent of my home. It feels like a long time since I was last here.

It feels like Jake should be here, too.

I bury that thought. I go into the sitting room and sit down. Sandra and Claire are already inside and sitting down, at Mam's instruction. They're talking about Sandra's children. I sit down and try to listen, but my mind soon wanders. It must be obvious, because Sandra stops talking and stares at me intently.

"Are you okay?"

I nod. "Just trying to work out how to get back to normal, I guess. Things feel pretty weird right now."

I don't say that that's mostly because of the hallucination. I can deal with Jake and I no longer being together. I can take accountability for the fact that I drank too much and didn't notice someone drugging me, ending up in hospital because of it. But that cottage, the cottage they're telling me never happened, well, it's haunting me. I know if I say another word about it, though, that Mam's going to think I need to be locked up.

"Take a few days off work to recover like the doctor advised and then when you go back to work, things will settle down," Claire says.

Mam appears. "There's no bread left for sandwiches, Katie. Will I put on something from the freezer for you?"

Mam lists the things I have in my freezer and asks which one I want her to cook. I can see she disapproves when I say chips, but that's all I can stomach the thought of right now, even though they must have been there months because I don't really eat stuff like that any more. They were emergency hangover chips and are probably covered in ice.

Mam puts on the chips. "Your phone is blinking, by the way," she says, looking into the hall to where the landline lives on a small table. "It must be your answering machine. Will I press Play?"

I nod, although I have no interest in listening to phone messages right now. I suppose I'll have to do it sooner or later. Mam goes out to the hall and I plod along behind her.

"Hello, Katie," an unfamiliar voice rings out in a message that was left an hour previously. "It's Garda Brian Houlihan here and I'm ringing in connection to a report your friend Penny Ryan-Thornton made about an incident that occurred in the Kildare Lounge last Saturday. Can you ring me back on this number, please?"

67

Mam grabs a pen and writes down the number on her hand as the guard calls it out in the message.

"Penny must have given him my landline number as well as my mobile," I say aloud when the message finishes. I assume my lost mobile is going straight to voicemail.

"Here." Mam hands me the landline. "Ring him back straight away. You might not have the energy to do it later and you seem all right now. You may as well get it over and done with."

Mam inputs the number of the garda station from her hand and passes the phone to me. I'm in no form for a chat, but she's right. I need to speak to the gardai about the drugging.

I get through to Garda Brian. He greets me in a friendly tone. It calms me somewhat – he sounds personable.

"Katie, could you meet me today? It'd be best if we could talk in person."

"I'm just out of hospital. Give me a minute and I'll check if someone here can give me a lift to the garda station."

"I can call round at your house, if that's easier?"

"Yes, that'd be great," I say straight away. I know this needs to be done and I'm definitely feeling too weak to leave the house. The journey home has taken it out of me. "I'll be here for the rest of the day."

"I can leave the station now and be over to you in ten minutes. Would that suit?"

"Sure. Thanks, Brian."

True to his word, Brian lands at the door ten minutes later.

We go inside and head for the sitting room. Brian tells me what Penny reported and asks me if that's my recollection of events.

"I actually have no recollection of events in that particular pub, I'm afraid," I say, mortified. "Well, very little. I vaguely remember walking in, but that's all. I must have been more drunk than my friends realised. The last thing I properly remember was leaving the pub we'd been to before that."

The dining room door is open. I see Mam setting the table for the chips she'll give me when Brian has left, having postponed her cooking when she heard he was calling over. I'm sure she heard what I said. Even though she's only in my peripheral vision, I know she's frowning. I can *feel* her frown. I should have closed the dining room door, but if I do it now, it'll look like I have something to hide.

"I've no memory at all of the man Penny says I was talking to," I continue. "There's no way I could possibly identify him. Penny could, though. She said she was going to ask if there was CCTV in that pub."

"I rang the pub earlier and they do have CCTV, so I'll check that out with them as soon as I get a chance."

"Penny said the pub was really busy. I hope it's not hard to make me out on the CCTV. Also, I'm sure I looked quite different that night than I do now," I add as an afterthought. I haven't a scrap of make-up on me and I threw on an old, cosy tracksuit before Brian arrived. "I hope you'll be able to identify me on it. At least I'm tall, I suppose."

"Penny's told me as precisely as she could where you were standing and approximately what time you entered the bar, but did anyone take any pictures of you earlier that day?"

"Actually, yes. Barbara took quite a few of all of us over lunch." I can remember the lunch clearer now that the fog of the drug has lifted. "She asked one of the waiting staff to take a group picture of us. Barbara also took pictures of us in twos and threes. They should clearly show what I'm wearing from the waist up. Would they help?"

"Yes. Could you ask her to email them to me ASAP? I'll give you my email address if you have a pen handy there."

"I'll get one."

I get up and dash out to the kitchen. Sandra and Claire are sitting at my small breakfast bar, magazines open in front of them. They clearly hadn't been expecting me to dart out so fast in my weakened state, because they stop whatever they were saying mid-whisper when I come out. Their eyes drop to the magazines they'd been browsing through when they see I've caught them whispering. My kitchen opens on to the dining area and the entire surface area is quite small. It's clear that they've been trying to listen to my entire conversation with Brian too, but they're pretending they're not. I go to a drawer where I keep spare pens, pick up a notepad and pen, and return to the sitting room. I notice Mam walking towards the table again with a salt shaker.

Brian calls out his email address. "Is there anything else you need to tell me about that night?"

"Well . . . " I want to tell him about the cottage, but what would he say if I did?

Mam's still fussing around the table.

I know if I say a word about the cottage to the garda, Mam will be ringing the nearest mental health institution and booking me in. No matter how real it felt to me, everything is pointing towards it being a hallucination. If I say a word, I know she'll think it's back to the bad old days again.

"No," I say eventually. "That's all."

"Okay, Katie. I'll be in touch if there are any updates. Is this the best number to get you on, or is your mobile better?"

"I don't know where my mobile is," I say. "It's not in my handbag, so I assume I lost it on the night out. Good job Penny gave you my landline number."

70

"I rang her back and asked her if you had a landline when I couldn't get through to your mobile. I rang it several times earlier."

"Oh, I see. Unfortunately, I don't think I'll be seeing it again."

Brian repeats that he'll be in touch and leaves. I get the landline and ring my mobile to see if anyone will answer it. When Brian said he didn't get through to my mobile, I'm not sure if that meant the call didn't connect or if someone just didn't answer. But I'm not surprised when it goes straight to voicemail. The battery is probably dead by now if it's just lying somewhere. Or if it was taken by someone, they probably have their own SIM card in it at this stage. Another thing to sort out, although buying a new phone is the least of my concerns. I also look up Barbara's mobile number in my address book and ring it from the landline. I ask her to email the pictures to Brian and she says she'll do it straight away.

I must look worried when I get off the phone and come into the kitchen, because Claire smiles kindly at me.

"It'll all be fine, Katie. You'll feel better in a few days."

"But God Almighty, lay off the booze," Sandra says. "You dodged a bullet this time, but you might not be so lucky the next time."

"Yes, Katie," Mam says as she hands me a cup of tea. "God, when I think of what could have happened . . . "

"I'll never drink that much again, I promise. Things have been a little strange recently because of the Jake situation. I just lost control."

"Sounds to me like you need Jake in your life to look after you," Mam says.

I try not to get mad. I knew this was coming and I'm surprised it hasn't come sooner, really.

"No, Mam. It's over. I'll take care of myself and I'll do a better job of it from now on."

"Well, Claire and I are staying tonight to keep an eye on you."

"No, no, that's not necessary."

"Necessary or not, it's happening. Isn't that right, Claire?"

Claire nods. "It'll be handy for you to have someone around tonight, Katie. I'll get some shopping in for you later and I'll order a takeaway as well."

"And I'll stay tomorrow as well if I think it's needed," Mam says. "Sandra has to go home tonight to look after the kids and give her husband a break – poor Liam must be exhausted – but she'll pop in and out over the next few days when she can. And don't forget work. You'll need to ring to tell them you'll be off for a week, as the doctor recommended."

The thought of talking to Henry now and answering his inevitable questions is just unbearable. As for "poor Liam", that's nonsense. Aren't they his kids as well?

"Claire, if I give you Henry's number, could you ring him for me? Tell him I'm really sorry but me being off is unavoidable owing to . . . a medical emergency. I'll give him a ring later in the week when I'm feeling stronger. Oh, and tell him that I'll have the documentation to verify my sick leave when I come back. I'll organise that later this week."

"Okay, but I'm sure he'll ask what the nature of the medical emergency is, unless Penny said anything to him?"

"She didn't. She kept it vague."

"So what will I tell him?"

Henry's someone I have to tread carefully around. I can't have him knowing too much about what's going on, in case it compromises my position at work.

"Tell him some of the truth – that I was drugged by Rohypnol when I was out and that I've suffered a range of injuries as a result. Just leave it at that. Say I'll tell him the rest of the story when I get back." Hopefully, by then, I'll know who's done this to me.

I give Henry's mobile number to Claire and she goes into the kitchen to ring him. A few minutes later, she comes back in and says Henry sounded concerned and that he said to let him know if there's anything he can do. I'm sure he's probably going mad at the thought of me being off for a whole week and although I hate putting pressure on my colleagues, the doctor was right. Me going into work is out of the question at the moment.

I drink my tea as fast as I can. "I'm going to go and lie down, guys. Do you mind?"

"It's your house," Sandra says somewhat sulkily.

I leave before Mam can say anything. I know she's only trying to help, but I feel suffocated. I run upstairs and close the door firmly behind me.

Chapter 5

I wander around my bedroom, wondering what to do now. I pick up a CD. It's a 2007 release called *Puzzle* from one of my favourite bands, Biffy Clyro. The cover, created by renowned graphic designer Storm Thorgerson, depicts a man sitting on a stool with his head resting on one hand, the other hand touching his chin. His body is covered in jigsaw pieces with one piece missing from his body, having fallen to the floor beside him. It's a perfect depiction of how I feel right now. There's definitely a piece of my jigsaw missing since that fateful lunch date, and I don't know if I'll ever be able to find it and put it back in.

I take the CD out of its case and put it on to play. *Puzzle* is a glorious album, each song full of surprises on first listen that become more nuanced the more you play them, and I know exactly what song I'm going for. It's a short track called "9/15ths", an ominous, eerie tune that perfectly encapsulates what I'm feeling right now. I select the song, sit on the bed and close my eyes, letting the music wash over me as I sit there listening to the band's singer, Simon Neil, singing about being on a hell slide and asking for help.

Nothing has ever sounded so relevant to me and for a

few minutes I feel less alone in the world. Other people have problems, too. It's easy to forget that when you're in the depths of it yourself. Other people find a way out of their problems eventually. Don't they? Surely we can't all slide into hell. Surely someone can save us if we can't save ourselves. I don't usually have these thoughts. Most of the time, I don't have a reason to question things the way I am right now. But between breaking up with Jake and now this, I feel as if my security rug in life has been pulled from under me and I'm currently floundering in uncertainty.

At least I've avoided talking to Henry. Things have been frosty between us since an incident a few months ago when I took it upon myself to do something that he didn't agree with. At the time, a garda whistle-blower had just given interviews to the media, reporting incidents of alleged harassment and bullying within the force. When I was out one night not long after the controversy broke, I saw the former Irish garda commissioner in a quiet bar and decided to approach him to ask his opinion.

Henry is someone who's always encouraged staff members just to go for the story and not to be afraid of the consequences. Obviously, there were caveats to this mindset in that if we could avoid the kind of legal action that could shut down the paper while we were busy being fearless investigative journalists, so much the better. But he always encouraged us not to stick to the limits of what we were "supposed" to do. As journalists, his view was that we had an obligation to the public to expose the truth. If he was particularly busy, which he pretty much always was, he told us to use our own judgment when it came to deciding whether or not to run with something if we couldn't get hold of him. Because of that mindset, all of us in the paper had become accustomed to using our own initiative. If we saw an opportunity, it was part of our culture to go for it.

I saw an opportunity as I walked past the former Irish garda commissioner in that restaurant. When I asked him for his thoughts on the controversy, he initially ignored me. But as I persisted, he became apoplectic, to the point that the bar manager came over and led me out of the pub. His reaction made me convinced that there was something to hide and I was sure Henry would agree with me when I relayed the story to him the next day.

Instead, he told me that I'd made an error of judgment in encroaching on the commissioner's personal time and space, stating that I shouldn't try to contact him again, or any other member of the garda force. I argued furiously with him that day, trying to fight the cause of truth and justice, but Henry stonewalled me and ended the conversation by pulling rank, saying he was the boss and he made the ultimate calls on what we'd cover. Things haven't been 100 per cent between us since that and although we've gone back to some sort of normality, it's still there in the background.

And it doesn't help, either, that my work email was hacked last month, even though it obviously wasn't my fault. Emails of a sensitive nature – downright insulting emails, to be very honest – were sent from my work email to key figures in the media. It caused an awful furore. Although the IT crowd who we outsource to were able to ascertain that my account had indeed been hacked and the emails had been sent from a different IP address, all at a time when I was sitting at my desk in the office, Henry hadn't been impressed at the fall-out. We reported it to the gardai, but nothing ever came of it. They said the hacker had covered their tracks well and they didn't seem bothered about taking it any further.

I was seething with resentment at the time that I somehow seemed to get the blame when I hadn't done anything to compromise the security of my account to begin with, but I'd been forced to get over it. Nonetheless, I'm just not feeling strong enough right now to deal with Henry on top of everything else.

I let the CD play to the end. It doesn't take long – there's only one song on the CD after "9/15s". When it ends, I sit in silence until I hear footsteps approaching my room.

"Katie?" Claire knocks at the door.

"Yes?"

Claire opens the door and comes in. "I thought I'd come in for a chat. Do you mind?"

Claire knows very well that "going for a lie-down" means getting away for a while when Mam's either giving out or in mother hen mode.

"Erm, no, of course not."

"Here." She hands me a hot-water bottle. Her excuse to Mam for coming up to me.

"Thanks. Sit down."

I gesture to the end of the bed. Claire sits. I pull the pillow away from the headboard, toss it to the other side of the bed and sit with my back to the headboard. I wrap my arms around my legs and rest my chin on my knees, wondering what Claire wants to talk about. I'm presuming she wants to assess my mental state, too.

"What happened between you and Jake? You never told me the full story. I was surprised to hear you'd split up, I must say."

I shrug. "He wanted things I wasn't ready for."

"I'm presuming you're not talking about the BDSM type of things. You mean commitment."

I smile, despite myself. "Children. I was happy with the thought of marriage, but children . . . "

"Well, not everyone wants to have them. It's an individual choice."

I didn't expect that. I thought I'd have to justify my words. That's usually the way it works when I tell someone that I'm not sure about trying for children. The only other person who seems to understand my ambivalence is Penny, albeit for different reasons than mine. She feels she's too involved in her career to do justice to the role of motherhood. She can't see herself ever not wanting to work the way she does now and she thinks it'd be unfair to put a child through a lifetime of having an absentee mother.

"Yes. But Jake's certain that he does want them. And therein lies the problem. I can't promise him I'm going to change my mind on this, so how can I marry him knowing this is something he wants?"

"But you'd marry him otherwise? The problem is purely this?"

"Yes. I had to let him go. It's the only fair thing to do."

"And did he *want* to be let go? Was the children issue bigger for him than what you had between you?"

"He said he didn't want it to end. Then again, he didn't not want to have children, either. I knew he wasn't going to walk away, but I also knew he'd be unhappy in the long run if he stayed. I had to do something, for his sake. And for my own. He'd only end up resenting me in a few years and we'd have split then anyway. But he certainly wasn't happy about it."

78

"That's to be expected."

"I suppose, but it's better this way. As you know from my previous experience, marriage doesn't always work out. Declan and I don't even speak to each other since we divorced."

"Well, that's probably for the best – too many bad memories there. But just because it didn't work out with Declan doesn't mean it wouldn't have worked out with Jake."

"No. Jake wants all the same things that Declan did. All the things I can't give him."

"Although I understand your decision, I have to play devil's advocate here and point out that you don't know that for sure. Aren't you willing to take the chance and find out?"

"And waste Jake's life? Years could go by like that. It's not fair on him and it'll destroy me."

She grimaces. "It's such a shame. Jake's a good man. Do you still love him?"

"Claire, please!" I hadn't expected such directness. "This is hard enough as it is."

She smiles sadly. "That's a yes, then. Feck."

"He's probably thinking he's had a lucky escape after the last few days," I say, proceeding to tell her what I accused him of.

"Wow," she says when I finish. "You *really* thought Jake would be capable of doing something like that to you?"

"No, not really. You don't understand, Claire. I've had hallucinations before. You know . . . "

"Yes. I remember."

"I thought you would. But this one – well, it felt more real to me than sitting here right now does."

I tell her about my cottage experience in great detail. By the time I've finished speaking, I'm shaking.

"I'd swear on my life that it happened, that someone

had done that to me. And Jake seemed to be the only person with a motive to do it, but then he was the one who asked for the drugs test in the hospital, so that makes no sense, either. I honestly feel that it happened, though. I just don't know how."

"But you were with people all the time until you woke up, right?"

"Apparently so. Penny said she took me home in the taxi on Saturday night and she and Richard minded me. Barbara said she helped to put me in the taxi with Penny. After a night of me being sick, Penny said I took two sleeping tablets at some stage towards Sunday morning and I was out for the count until Sunday evening. Penny and Richard stayed at home all day. Jake was there when I woke up at 7 p.m. and he said he'd been at Penny's house for about four hours. All of my time seems to be accounted for, with people present."

"I guess Rohypnol must have affected you in a different way than the drugs you took in the past, then. That's the only plausible explanation."

Claire's voice goes down an octave as she makes reference to my torrid drug-taking period years ago. It wouldn't do for Mam to hear it mentioned. Any mention of that time sends her into a total tizzy.

I shake my head.

"What is it, Katie?"

"Claire, like I said, I could honestly swear it happened. I know it'll sound crazy, but do you think Penny could be wrong about me being there all night?"

Claire frowns. "Do you really think someone took you from Penny's house in the middle of the night, brought you to a cottage and tied you up, and then brought you back to Penny's again without her noticing?"

"I don't know! All I know is that everyone's telling me this didn't happen – that it *couldn't* have happened – and yet I really feel that it did. No hallucination could be that vivid, surely." I bury my head in my hands. "I feel like I'm going mad, Claire. I can't fathom how real it all was."

Claire moves closer to me. "When you told me the story about the cottage, you said it was bright when you escaped and it had been light for quite a while. If that's the case, surely Penny would have been up and she'd have noticed you were missing? Is she an early riser?"

I nod. She sure is. Penny gets up every day at six o'clock to work out in her home gym for an hour before she starts work. No matter what day of the week it is, she always has work to do. But if she'd been up really late, with me being sick, I'm sure she must have had a lie-in. Even a superwoman like Penny must need some sleep.

"She probably checked in on you, then," Claire says before I get a chance to voice this thought. She rubs my arm. "You can ask her if it puts your mind at rest. It might help you to let this go."

I try not to shake her hand off my arm. I'm irritated by her words. She sounds like she's speaking to a child or, at best, a troubled teenager.

You're being unfair, Katie. At least she's trying to be kind to you. And if you heard a story like this, would you believe it?

"I'm sure in a few days' time it'll fade away naturally anyway," Claire continues. "You can put this whole thing behind you and . . . you know, focus on not letting something like this happen again."

"Oh please, Claire, not you as well! I know I drank too much and I definitely won't be doing that again."

"Good, good. All you can do then is learn from this and move on. You have so much going for you, Katie. You don't need alcohol to be a part of your life."

"I won't be binge drinking any more," I say vehemently.

Claire looks pleased. What I don't tell her is that I won't be binge drinking because I just can't shake the feeling that I have to watch my back. I'll need my wits about me from now on.

No matter what anyone says, something about this situation still isn't sitting right with me.

Chapter 6

I took it badly when my father died. It was so unexpected. At fifty years of age, he dropped dead of a heart attack and that was that. I was eighteen and had just done my Leaving Cert. I was so full of hope for the future. His death changed everything. I'd applied to be a primary school teacher and I felt my exams had gone well, so I was hopeful of getting the points for the course. Suddenly, I couldn't care less whether I did or not. Nothing mattered any more.

In the hen house that was our family home, my dad was the only one who looked out for me. My two older sisters were both in college and thought they were great because of it. They had no time for little inexperienced me, bothering them with questions about this, that and the other. Over the years, Mam had always been too busy making dinner, cleaning or doing something practical for someone ever to sit down and talk. The only one who had any time for me was my dad.

For the first few weeks, I could do nothing. I barely ate. I barely moved. I lay in bed all day and stared at the ceiling or, when Mam or a sister literally dragged me out of bed, I sat on the couch and stared at a wall. I had nothing to say to anyone. Everything my mother or my siblings said to me had me piqued. Everything felt pointless.

My mother dragged me to the doctor and told him that although everyone in the family was suffering, I didn't seem to be able to cope with what had happened at all. The doctor was reluctant to prescribe any medication and said to give it time. He suggested counselling. My mother thought it was a good idea. I downright refused to entertain the thought. Mam and the doctor tried to talk me into it, but I wouldn't agree.

When the college offer of my first choice of a place on a primary school teaching course came through, Mam was thrilled. I could see she thought it would be the panacea to lift me out the hole I'd fallen into. I knew instantly that I wasn't going to take the place. I wasn't *able*. I couldn't muster the energy to take a shower some days. How was I meant to do a college course?

When I finally got it through to Mam that I wouldn't be accepting the course, she freaked. After days and days of non-stop arguments, she begged me to at least accept the course and defer it for a year. Eventually I acceded to that, just to keep the peace and calm the situation. I still couldn't imagine myself being able for college in a year's time, but at least it brought an end to the bickering.

I spent the next few months trying to get myself together. Mam lobbied for a job for me in a local pub and I took it. I found it depressing though, to see the same people coming into the pub every night, talking about the same old things and drinking their families' money away. There was a sense of hopelessness about it all.

Even though I felt this way, it wasn't long before I was buying alcohol with my wages and drinking every night after work until all hours of the morning. It passed the time, or killed it, more accurately. I got fired after calling in sick too many times after numerous benders that rendered me lifeless. Mam went crazy, which was to be expected, but I didn't care. I'd gone beyond caring about anything.

When things reached the point where I couldn't take the fighting at home a minute longer, I talked my way into a waitressing job in a restaurant in town. The pay was awful, so I was only able to afford a bedsit in a really horrible building in a very bad part of the city centre, but at least it wasn't home. I didn't tell anyone in my family where I was living and I made sure they didn't find out, either.

I got friendly with a guy called Frank who lived in another bedsit in the building and that was when my next problem started. Frank was a regular drug user. I hated my job – I was a useless waitress who could only carry two plates, no matter how hard I tried to balance a dozen up my arm – and I had no other friends in my sad, lonely eighteen-year-old world.

It wasn't long before I wanted in on the oblivion Frank seemed to get when he was high. It started innocently enough with us sharing joints during the week. Frank kept his harder drug usage to the weekend when he went out partying. I started accompanying him to these parties, but I stuck to heavy drinking at first.

My contact with home was sporadic. I'd ring the landline once a week, tell Mam I was alive and well, and put down the phone. I rang from a different public phone box every time in case she tried to trace the number.

As time went on, I got more disheartened. Things didn't get any better in my job and I was always tired and hungover, yet I couldn't seem to stop myself from going round to Frank's every night and having a few drinks and a joint. I didn't even want the alcohol most of the time – just the company – and as for the joints, they were a camaraderie thing more than anything.

Frank and I struck up a casual sexual relationship and it wasn't long before he was encouraging me to take ketamine with him at the weekends. Special K, he called it. The first night I took it, I didn't think what I was doing was too serious. I'd never even heard of ketamine. It's not as if we were taking heroin or cocaine. Frank said it was just a relaxant to help me to disassociate from the worries of the world. As disassociation was exactly what I was looking for at that time in my life, I decided to try it. We smoked it, which again seemed relatively harmless to me. It wasn't as if we were injecting and sharing needles with strangers.

At first, I wasn't sure if I liked the effects of ketamine or not. The first time I took it I definitely felt detached from myself, which I saw as a positive, but I also felt confused and nauseous. Frank said the next time I took it I had to make sure to take it on an empty stomach. The next day I felt sick and disorientated and I wasn't sure if there would be a next time. Then the following weekend rolled around and by then I was bored out of my brains from my working week, so I decided to take another trip on ketamine.

And so it continued every weekend for the next two months, with Frank and I moving on to taking ketamine orally. The phone calls home started to slip to once a fortnight. And then one night, in a pub in Temple Bar, it all came to a head. I was out with Frank and a group of his friends when I bumped into Sandra. She was out celebrating a friend's birthday. I couldn't believe I'd been unlucky enough to run into her. Sandra rarely went out in town.

She ranted and raved about how thin I was and how unhealthy I looked, and how I was going to worry Mam into an early grave with my antics. We had a huge row and Frank had to drag me out of the pub to settle things down. Frank and I went to the pub next door, leaving our group behind, and to calm myself I took more ketamine.

My memory of what happened after that isn't very detailed. According to Sandra, she covertly followed me into the busy pub I'd gone to with Frank and watched from a distance as my behaviour became increasingly erratic. Then Frank had taken me outside, where I lay down on the pavement. Sandra followed me outside and said I was hallucinating wildly about elephants dancing on my stomach, sharks eating me alive and being cremated while still alive. And that was only the ones she could make out from my slurred speech. She instantly rang Mam, who drove to town to collect me. Sandra and Frank carried me to where Mam had parked, and Mam brought me back to her house.

When I woke the next morning, clueless to a large extent as to what had happened, Mam bundled me into the car and took me straight to the doctor. She told him that I'd been experiencing mental health issues ever since the death of my dad, leading to excessive drinking and a drug addiction. She asked for a referral to a psychiatric hospital and she got it. She was so persuasive that even I believed I was mental by the time she'd finished talking about me. She'd expected resistance from me about attending the psychiatric hospital, but I was feeling so low and so desperate not to feel that way any more that I went without hesitation.

It was only when I was there that I realised it wasn't the right place for me. The team working with me realised that quickly, too. I was depressed, they told Mam, and experiencing post-traumatic stress syndrome, but I certainly didn't have psychiatric issues, in their opinion. They also felt I didn't have a serious addiction issue and was reacting to the circumstances more than anything, so the chances of me pulling things back were high.

I moved back to Mam's and resolved to try to pull myself out of the hole I'd fallen into. I never saw Frank again. When I went back to my bedsit after I got out – accompanied by Mam – to collect my things, all my stuff had been thrown out and someone else had moved in, and Frank had moved out of his. In those pre-mobile phone days, I had no contact details for him. It was probably a blessing. I often wondered where he'd ended up, though, and if he'd made it out of the drugs trap or got lost in the k-hole.

The following year, having decided not to accept the deferred place on the primary school teaching course – refusing it because I felt it would always remind me of my dad's death – I took up a place on a journalism college course. I'd applied for it after spending months and months of doing nothing but hanging around the house. If my time working in the pub and waitressing had taught me anything, it was that I was no good in the services industry and I really needed to try to find my niche.

I resolved to sort myself out both mentally and physically, having become very interested in health, fitness and nutrition after my foray into the dark side of life with drugs. I was determined to turn my life round and I did. I was warned by Mam over and over never to tell anyone about the time I took ketamine, aka "the time Katie got herself in trouble". In Mam's eyes, I was right up there with the hardened city centre street addicts she feared so badly. She said that if it ever got out that a trainee journalist had taken drugs, I'd never get a job. There was a very definite sense of "if the neighbours found out . . . " about her reaction too, but they never did. As a family, we closed ranks on my "episode".

In the years that followed, while I recognised that Mam was just trying to help me, I resented the labels I felt she'd put on me within the family. I took drugs for two months in my life, but I never saw myself as an addict. I hadn't been using every day and I often felt that it was a stopgap phase I'd have got out of either way. "A problem with alcohol" had often been bandied around too, but everyone else my age had been drinking as much as I had at eighteen. Were they all addicts as well? Most of them were married with children now and rarely drank at all. Why was I labelled when they weren't? And as for my mental health, well, Mam might as well have just tattooed "mental" across my forehead. I knew it would never be fully forgotten.

And sure enough, eighteen years later, it was being brought up again.

After Claire leaves, I decide to take a shower. Not only is it time to, but my thoughts are still racing. I hope the ritual of shampooing and conditioning my long, thick hair will stop my mind from spinning.

I go to the main bathroom. When I look in the mirror, I'm shocked. Although I saw myself in the hospital, this is the first time I've taken a good look at myself. My face is in tatters. I lean in closer to the mirror. The wounds aren't deep and I doubt they'll scar, but they're nasty nonetheless. I can't see how I'd have done this with my nails and I feel it's something I wouldn't do, drugged or otherwise. It's not something I ever did while on ketamine. Whenever I've had plenty of alcohol and been upset about something, I've never felt the urge to claw at my face. It looks exactly the way scrapes from brambles look. *Exactly.* And the side of my face that crashed on the floor in my apparent hallucination has more scrapes than the other side.

I look away and begin to undress. As I move my arms behind me to undo my bra, I feel a sharp twinge in my shoulder blades. Back pain has been bothering me on and off all day, but there's been too much going on for me to acknowledge it fully either to myself or anyone else. I rub my shoulders and instantly squeal. The muscles are so sore to the touch. I walk towards the full-length bathroom mirror and tip the top of it slightly backwards, then turn round.

What I see shocks me so badly that I have to kneel on the ground to stop myself from falling to the floor.

There's a raw purple bruise around two inches wide extending from my left shoulder blade to my right, slightly less intense in the middle. It's in exactly the position where the chair I was tied to in the cottage met the top of my back. At the base of my spine is another long bruise from left to right, thicker at the sides where I thrashed furiously against the chair to try to free it from my body.

It happened. I know it did. It *happened*.

Chapter 7

I'm suddenly frantic with the need to take action. I dress myself, run downstairs into the hall and grab the phone.

"Katie . . . " Mam says.

I run back out before she can finish. I know there will be questions asked afterwards, but right now I need to report what happened straight away.

Once I'm upstairs, I ring the garda station and ask for Brian.

"He's finished his shift," says the lady who answers. "Can I help?"

No, no, no. I wanted Brian. He sounded like he'd give me a fair chance. This woman's tone is polite but abrupt. She doesn't sound like she wants to help at all. But I can't wait until tomorrow to report this.

"What's your name?" I ask, hoping that knowing her name will make it easier to talk to her.

"Grace," she replies.

I fill Grace in on what I'd already reported – and what I hadn't. When I eventually finish speaking, there's silence.

"So, you think you were abducted and subsequently freed, is that right?"

"I can't remember what happened after I blacked out on the lane."

"I see. And you didn't report any of this to Brian?"

"No. I only realised for sure a few minutes ago."

"Why is that?"

I explain to her about the bruises.

"I see," she says again. It sounds very much like she doesn't. "I'll pass on all this information to Brian and I'll make sure he calls you back first thing when he gets into work tomorrow, okay?"

"But isn't there anything we can do now?"

"As Brian's dealing with your case, he'll be the one to do a full investigation with you," she says.

She's speaking in a tone that I feel could either be interpreted as soothing or patronising, as if she's talking to somebody very young. Or crazy.

"But what if I'm in danger in the meantime?"

"Do you think you're in immediate danger?" Grace asks.

"I . . . I honestly don't know," I say.

"Are you alone?"

"No. My mother and my sisters are with me, and my mother's staying here tonight."

"That's good. If an incident occurs, call us immediately and we'll send a car out, okay?"

She's being nice, but again I detect something in that tone. The word that comes to mind is disbelief. I resist saying that I think it might be too late for a car if I'm kidnapped again and instead thank Grace for her help – or lack of it.

I sit down on the bed, feeling completely deflated now. The adrenaline that came with my need to take action is seeping out of my body now and I can't think of anything else to do. Brian was my only plan of action.

I curl up in a foetal position and close my eyes, trying to block out where I am now and desperately trying to put myself back in the moment when I was taken in the hope that I'll remember something to report to the gardai, but nothing comes to me. The effort of it drains me.

When Mam walks in and asks me if I want a cup of tea, I have to bite my lip to stop myself from crying at the normalcy of her words. I nod and follow her downstairs, formulating my excuse in my head for running upstairs with the phone. No good will come of me showing her what's on my back or telling her that I was in contact with the gardai again. I know she'll find another way of rationalising my bruises, because the fact is, she just doesn't believe me.

I plaster a weak smile on my face as I walk into the kitchen, horribly nostalgic for a time when everything was okay – a time that was only a few days ago. Now, it feels like my circumstances will never be normal again.

Chapter 8

I'm being pulled up. From where, I'm not sure. All I'm aware of is the sensation of hands under my armpits, tugging me sideways. I try to open my eyes, but I can't. I thud onto something lower. Was I on a bed? Was I pulled off and thrown to the ground? The hands are under my armpits again, dragging me backwards this time. I can't see the face of the person dragging me. I can't gauge if they're finding it easy or hard to pull my weight. All I know is that I'm leaving wherever I was and going elsewhere. And I'm scared. I know that much. I can sense the bad feeling coming from the person who's pulling me. This person is out to do me harm.

I wake up screaming.

It takes me a few seconds to realise where I am and what's going on. I'm on the couch in my sitting room and I must have fallen asleep. Mam said she was going out to the corner shop for ingredients for a fry-up in the morning. I said I didn't want one, but she insisted on going anyway. I look at my watch. She left about twenty minutes ago, if I remember correctly, and I must have dozed off after she went out. It's not unusual that it's taking her a while – she's probably buying up half the shop, as is her wont – but I hope she finishes soon and comes back. Claire and Sandra have gone home to their kids.

The doorbell rings. I frown. I'm sure Mam said she was taking the front door key. Maybe she forgot it. I get up and peer out of the window.

Jake. What's he doing here? If I let him in, nobody knows he's here with me. What if he's here to hurt me?

As I stand there hesitating, Jake looks over. I dart away from the window.

"Katie, please, let me in!" I hear Jake's voice at the window.

I move into the hall. Putting the chain on the door, I open it only as far as the chain will allow.

Jake hears the door opening and comes back. When he sees the chain, he shakes his head.

"Jesus, Katie. It's as if the last six months never happened. Surely you can't think I'm a threat to you."

"Why are you here?" I say.

"Your mother rang me to talk about you. She asked me to call over."

I weigh up his words. He could be lying. He could be using my mother as a way to get into the house and then who knows what he'll do to me? He's probably seen her leaving.

"She told me about your drug-taking experiences after your dad died," Jake says. "Why did you never tell me? You always said you were anti drugs."

I sigh. It sounds like he's at least telling the truth about my mother ringing him. Where else could he have gleaned that information?

My neighbour passes, out walking her dog.

"Hi, Emer!" I practically scream, making sure she looks over and notices both me and Jake.

I want there to be no doubt about the fact that he was here. I want him to know that he's been seen standing at my doorstep.

Emer says hi and waves. Jake looks from her to me and frowns.

"That wasn't necessary," he says.

He looks so hurt that I feel thrown. Then an image of the marks on my back flash into my mind. I can trust no one, I remind myself. Somebody tried to harm me and was possibly going to kill me or leave me to die alone, slowly. Maybe it wasn't Jake, but I owe it to myself to question everyone who has a motive to hurt me now.

I close the door, take the chain off and open the door. He's been seen. He's not going to do anything to me.

"You'd better come in, Jake."

We go into the sitting room. I sit in an armchair, leaving Jake no choice but to sit on the couch, away from me.

"Your mother's very worried about you," Jake says.

I can't play the game of pretending that nothing happened around Jake. I just can't.

"I'm very worried about me too, Jake. Someone abducted me. Mam probably *should* be worried."

Even if Jake reports my words to Mam, I feel better for having said them. I *had* to say them. I study his face, trying to weigh up his reaction to my words. He looks at the ground, breaking eye contact.

"Katie, your mother said you had a history of hallucinating after taking drugs. It obviously happened to you again after you'd consumed the Rohypnol. It's clear that this is the effect drugs has on your body." He looks up at me again. "Do you honestly, for one moment, think that I'd hurt you?"

96

I stare at him. He doesn't flinch. He doesn't look like he's bluffing. He looks sincere. My heart breaks all over again.

"I don't know what to think any more," I say finally. It's all I have.

Jake shakes his head. "I can't believe you'd think that of me. When you accused me at Penny's, I was shocked. Then when I heard you had Rohypnol in your system, I told myself that it was the drug talking and not you. I assumed you were still confused and disorientated. But now, you clearly still believe it's possible that I'd do such a thing. That's really messed up, Katie. I wanted to *marry* you. I want a future with you! Why would I hurt you?"

Because I can't give you what you want, I think, but I say nothing. I'm dying inside. Seeing Jake here, listening to his words, makes me think he couldn't possibly be the person behind all this. But I need to keep a very pivotal fact in mind: I've only known Jake six months. There could be a lot about him I don't know. He could be playing me and it's all too soon, too fresh, for me to see it. I think about showing him my back, but I decide not to.

"Okay," Jake says after a long pause. "There isn't much else to say then, really, is there?" He stands up.

I put my head in my hands. I feel so alone. Nobody believes me.

Jake walks over and puts his hand on my back.

"I hate to see you like this, Katie."

I don't shrug him off. For a second, I want him to stay. I want to forget all this ever happened.

But I can't. It did happen. And I need to work out who did it to me and what I'm going to do to stop them from coming for me again.

I stand up. I cross my arms and stare at Jake.

"I'm sorry if I caused you any offence, Jake. I'm going to have to ask you to leave now, I'm afraid. I need to rest."

Jake gives me that look of utter disbelief again. If he's acting, he's doing a good job. If he's not . . . God, I can't bear to think of how I'm treating him if he's innocent. Jake, to give him his due, was never anything but decent and respectful to me.

"You're right. It's time for me to go."

He turns and walks away, violently slamming the front door behind him as he leaves. I'm almost relieved he's exhibited some sign of anger rather than maintaining a dignified front. I feel bad enough as it is.

Chapter 9

I had to be like that, I tell myself after Jake leaves. I wasn't being cruel. It was self-preservation. How well do I *really* know Jake, anyway? And yet, all I want to do now is curl myself into a ball on the couch and howl at how stupid I've been for pushing him away after he extended an olive branch.

Slowly, I walk to my computer and log on. When I'm in, I open the Photos folder on my hard drive and push the cursor towards the subfolder entitled Jake. I know I shouldn't. I've been trying not to open this folder since we broke up in case the memories plunge me into a horrible strain of despair over us no longer being together. But I need to see his face again now that he's gone and probably won't come back, thanks to my actions. I need to work out if the person behind it is capable of doing something terrible to me, or if I'm crazy for suspecting him.

Within the Jake subfolder is a sequence of other folders, ordered by date and spanning a period of six months. I go through them one by one. The first folder contains tentative, almost stolen selfies of the pair of us that I took on nights out when I wasn't sure if doing so was too keen and would scare him off. It turned out that Jake welcomed the selfies. The second folder is far bigger. There are pictures of a weekend break to Berlin in there – a surprise trip Jake organised – numerous nights out, even a random trip to the zoo. As I go through them, it gets harder to look at how happy we were, particularly when he moved in with me on month three.

The first four months were absolute bliss. Although I'd never wanted to fall in love again after my marriage to Declan ended badly, that was exactly what had happened when I met Jake and there was nothing I could do to stop it. We still look very happy in the last two months of pictures, but I can see the strain on my face of what was going on behind the scenes.

Six months. It's not a very long time to really get to know someone . . .

It happened at the top of Croagh Patrick. I was euphoric at having made it to the zenith of the mountain, never having done much in the line of hillwalking or mountain climbing before. I was taking in the sights of Mayo's Clew Bay from my vantage point, visibility on the day being excellent owing to perfect weather conditions. For a few seconds everything felt just right, there at the top of the Holy Mountain with the love of my life.

And then he got down on one knee and proposed – and ruined everything.

I really hadn't seen it coming. Yes, things at that time had been as close to perfect as I'd ever experienced with anyone, but proposing? I was shell-shocked. For several minutes I couldn't even speak. It didn't take Jake long to realise that he wasn't going to get the reaction that he'd been hoping for – or the answer, either.

The descent from Croagh Patrick was far more punishing than the ascent. Those few moments on top of Croagh Patrick changed everything. And although I tried to assure Jake that things were ideal as they were and I loved him beyond belief, things were never quite the same afterwards. My refusal to accept his proposal was the beginning of the end.

It wasn't the thought of marriage that scared me. It was what I knew Jake hoped would come with it. That being said, the way my last marriage ended wasn't exactly the biggest incentive ever to get married again, either.

Chapter 10

The mark of what happened in the last few years of my marriage has never fully faded. Looking back now, it's easy to see where it all went wrong. To begin with, I was still too wild and immature to get married, but we also got married far too quickly. I met Declan when I was working in a junior position in a newspaper. It was my first journalism job after I graduated from college, one that I'd been in for a few years when I met Declan. I was getting on well in the position and was putting my time in with it, determined to work my way up within the paper.

He joined the paper as a crime correspondent. He was ten years my senior and very *together*. I was so impressed by him, but I never let on. I had a feeling he was interested in me from the way he interacted with me, but I didn't show any signs of reciprocating. I wanted him to chase me and he did.

When he first asked me out I said no. He left it a few weeks before asking again, a few weeks during which plenty of flirty exchanges took place, but again I told him it wasn't the right time for me. I wanted to test him to see if he really wanted to be with me, but if I'm honest, I also wanted to strengthen whatever longing he had for me. I wanted to be the ultimate girl he couldn't obtain, because I could see how easily women were attracted to him. He could have had his pick of the girls in the office and always had women after him whenever we went out as a team. But I knew he was the type of man who wanted a challenge and I was adamant that the way to get him for good was to give him just that.

He refused to give up, just as I'd suspected. Declan was the type of man who was used to getting what he wanted. I gave him the runaround for six months before finally agreeing to go out with him. After that, it was a whirlwind of weekend breaks to European cities, days at the races, fine dining in the best restaurants – all very respectable and a far cry from the life I'd been leading a few years previously. When he proposed a year later, there was no giving him the runaround then. I said yes instantly. Our wedding was big and extravagant, just like our relationship.

It wasn't long before Declan started talking about babies. I was initially resistant to the idea – at twenty-six, I wasn't sure if I was ready – but the more he talked about it, the more it seemed like the right thing to do. I was in the peak of my physical health and Declan wanted to have children while he was still young. Although I'd been determined to rise through the ranks at work, I'd still be young enough to get places in my career when the children were older.

Declan had it all worked out. After my maternity leave, I could either give up work instantly and focus on the baby – Declan earned enough to support the whole family – or go back to work until we had our second child. Then I could give up work for a few years and go back when both children had started school. Neither of us saw ourselves having more than two. I came round to thinking that having a baby was what I wanted, after all, and we started trying.

Meanwhile, we bought a cottage with a 100-foot garden in a south-side suburb and applied for planning permission to extend it into a four-bedroom house with a large open-plan kitchen and dining area. If permission was granted, it was going to be a dream home in a hugely sought-after location, close to the sea and two minutes' walk from a LUAS tram station.

The months went on and planning permission was granted, but there was no sign of me getting pregnant. Neither of us thought too much of it at the start. We were busy and I wasn't buying ovulation predictor kits or being too scientific about it. We were just hoping that nature would take its course. But the next few months after that initial disappointment involved plenty of ovulation kits, no alcohol, lots of food containing zinc, folic acid and calcium, and vitamins C and D for Declan to help create healthy sperm. Plus arctic conditions in the cottage, because I'd read that heat kills sperm. Another four months passed and I still didn't get pregnant.

I knew Declan was perplexed. This wasn't supposed to happen to someone like him. From everything he'd told me about his life before we met, it sounded like a charmed one. The lovely upbringing in a nice quiet suburb, the private school education, the degree, postgrad and masters from a top university, the great career and now the perfect marriage. I think he'd assumed that life would continue giving him what he wanted when he wanted. I was more aware than him that things didn't always go to plan.

After a year, the extension was built and yet there were

still only two of us in the family. Declan wanted us to get help, so we got ourselves checked out and no problems were found. This seemed to rile Declan more than the possibility of either of us being diagnosed with something. Problems were, to his mind, things that were fixable. How did you fix something that didn't seem to be broken, yet didn't work? And that was how I was starting to feel about our relationship, too, at that time.

After the initial whirlwind of our romance started to mutate into ordinary, everyday life, I frequently found myself questioning how compatible we really were when it came down to it. I also found myself a lot less concerned about the fact that I wasn't getting pregnant than Declan was, which forced me to ask myself how much I really wanted this anyway. I even wondered if a part of me was relieved that it wasn't happening – although I'd never in a million years have articulated this to Declan.

When he inevitably suggested IVF, I agreed to do a round of it, with great trepidation. If it didn't work, I truly didn't know what Declan was going to do with himself. "Getting me pregnant", as he called it, had almost become an obsession for him. I'd anticipated some possible mild side effects of the IVF, as per the discussions I'd had with hospital staff, but I'd never dreamed that it would all go so badly wrong.

Although I'd read that ovarian hyperstimulation syndrome (OHSS) was a possibility, it was something I glossed over as being too rare to be something to worry about. And God knows, I was worried about too many things already to have the headspace for the unlikely scenarios as well. I soon learned that the unlikely scenario can also happen. My body overreacted to the fertility drugs used to stimulate egg production during my IVF procedure, causing my stomach to swell and me to contort with stomach pains. Vomiting soon followed and, more worryingly, shortness of breath.

Declan rushed me to hospital, where I was diagnosed with OHSS and treated, but it was a terrifying experience and at the end of it all I discovered I wasn't pregnant. I told Declan in no uncertain terms that I wasn't trying IVF again after having such a frightening side effect first time round and at first, Declan said he understood.

But as time went on, Declan couldn't accept it. As far as he was concerned, that was the end of his hopes and dreams of getting everything he'd ever wanted. He was more than a little dramatic in conveying his feelings on the subject too, which annoyed me beyond belief. At that point, everything about Declan annoyed me. It felt as if the blame for us not having a baby lay entirely on my shoulders and there was never a word of comfort from him for me. It was all about him and his life plan lying in complete disarray.

I discovered four months later that he was having an affair. It wasn't a total surprise given that we seemed to have very little to say to each other any more, but I was stunned nonetheless that my marriage had come to this point. Although things were difficult, I never expected the marriage to fail and despite what we'd been through, I was still in love with Declan. The trouble, I realised, was that Declan was in love with Declan, too. Nothing in his life could be less than perfect and the only way he could redress the balance of the things that were going wrong was to find perfection elsewhere.

When he told me he was leaving me for a girl called Pippa who was five years my junior, something about it all made sense. He'd been stopped in his tracks by her beauty the second he laid eyes on her and there was nothing he could do to stop himself. I felt as if I was seeing Declan from the outside for the very first time. If things weren't perfect, Declan didn't want to know. I was damaged goods and therefore dispensable. Self-preservation and common sense stopped me from begging him to stay, even though it broke my heart to watch him walk out on me. I deserved better than someone who'd left me behind at the first hurdle to jump.

Declan moved in with his new Barbie doll and asked if I'd enter into a separation agreement. I initially resisted to agreeing – I saw no reason to make Declan's life easier in any way after what he'd done. But after seeking legal advice, and as time helped me to come to terms with what had happened, I decided that the agreement would be in my own best interests. Our solicitors drew up the agreement and I resolved to move on with my life, just as Declan was doing. I was still young.

We sold the house. I threw myself into my career, changed jobs and eventually bought my own house. It was a much smaller three-bedroom semi-detached and it wasn't in one of the most salubrious areas of town like the cottage was, but it was mine. Not having to see Declan's face every day in the corridors at work helped me to move on. Mind you, it was around then that I decided to lift my "no alcohol" embargo and recommence social drinking, something I'd never really been bothered about after I first went on my health, fitness and nutrition buzz. But everything came at a price. Unfortunately, it looks like I'm now paying the price for that, too.

For the first time, I consider Declan's possible culpability in my situation. Could he be behind all this? Surely not. Granted, he hadn't taken it very well when I'd filed for divorce. His reaction had surprised me – *he'd* left *me*, after all. Once four years had passed since we'd separated, it seemed to me like a logical thing to do. There were no feelings left on my side by that stage and awful as it sounds, getting the divorce done was, in my mind, another piece of admin to tick off the list like paying the car tax or renewing my insurance.

I thought he'd be delighted that I was putting the wheels in motion to put the marriage he couldn't wait to get out of completely behind us both. But one night shortly after the divorce papers had been issued to Declan, he turned up at my house blind drunk. He said he was sorry for how things had ended four years previously and that he'd always regretted it. I ascertained that things with Barbie had ended badly and Declan was now alone, in his early forties and again wondering where it all went wrong. And feeling very, very sorry for himself.

I tried to send him packing, but he quickly turned nasty and blamed me for how everything had gone wrong. I threatened to call the gardai and he eventually left. The next day, he rang me on the same number I'd had years ago and apologised profusely. He was mortified and swore that nothing like that would ever happen again. I told him it had better not. His outburst had not only upset me, but scared me, too. I was a single woman living on my own. What if things had escalated into physical violence? But he'd been true to his word and had never come near me or contacted me again. When the divorce finally came through a few years ago, that also passed without incident. I rarely even thought about Declan any more.

It's highly improbable that he had anything to do with all this, but I make a mental note to mention him to Brian, just in case.

Chapter 11

The following morning, Claire calls round after she's dropped the kids off at school. Although she's not in full-time employment right now, I know she has lots of jobs to do during the day between running her house and ferrying the children to school and after-school activities, so I feel bad about her morning being taken up on me. When I voice this concern, she says she was just passing, which is a total lie, because she lives on the other side of town.

Mam, however, looks delighted to see her. I can feel Mam's discomfort around me at the moment. I can't help but feel resentful, even though I know she's trying to help. But much as I appreciate her help, I didn't ask for it and the feeling of being watched is starting to stifle me. It's not as if I'm going to shoot up in the kitchen when her back is turned. She doesn't need a partner in crime to keep an eye on me. More than anything else, I want to show Claire the marks on my back and find out what she thinks about them, but I know I can't do that with Mam around. And Claire probably won't believe that they were made by a chair anyway. She'll come up with some other reason for them and leave me even angrier and more frustrated than

I am now, no doubt. I suppress a sigh, reminding myself that family dynamics can be complicated and the best thing I can do right now is say nothing. They're only trying to be of help.

"Are you all right, pet?" Mam says as Claire fills the kettle for tea.

"Yeah, I'm fine, Mam, thanks," I say.

"You look very pale. I suppose you're still getting over that horrible Rohypnol experience." Mam tuts. "I still can't believe something like that was done to you."

"I'll be okay. Honestly."

"You need to eat bigger portions at mealtimes, love. Your clothes are falling off you."

"I wish," I say. "I've plenty of meat on my bones, Mam. Don't worry."

"But I do worry, Katie," Mam says. "I always worry about you and I always will. And right now, you don't seem to be getting back to yourself at all."

"I suppose being drugged really took it out of me, as you mentioned," I say, unwilling to tell her the truth about what I'm really worried about and alarm her further. "And I guess I almost poisoned myself with drink too, which wasn't very smart of me. My appetite still isn't back properly. It's no wonder I'm looking pale, really."

"You have to start eating better," Mam says. "Are you sure nothing else is bothering you?"

"I'm sure. I'll be just fine," I say, hoping that's the truth.

As soon as I find out who's out to get me and I put a stop to it, things should be okay again. I'm not sure how soon that day will come, though, and what I'll need to go through in the meantime to get to that point.

All three of us are sitting in the kitchen with cups of tea

when the phone rings. Mam says, "I'll get it," and walks out to the hall to answer it before I can think of a reason to stop her. If it's Brian, I need to talk to him without her listening to what I'm saying. If she knows he's ringing me, I just know she'll find an excuse to earwig outside my bedroom door.

She answers with a rather curt "Hello?" but her tone soon changes.

"Ah, Jake! How are you?"

Out of the corner of my eye, I see Claire looking at me. Gauging my reaction. It's a mixture of shock that he's bothered to contact me again, relief that he's contacted me at all when there's a possibility that I might have blamed him wrongly and apprehension that he's about to give me an earful for what I've accused him of, but I try not to show any of this.

"She is, yes," Mam says. "I'll get her for you now."

"So much for 'checking you're there'," Claire says.

Mam walks into the room with the phone in her hand. "Katie, it's Jake on the phone," she practically shouts. "Here you go now."

She pushes the phone into my hand, leaving me no option but to talk to Jake. This must be about the gardai this time. I'm going to get an earful.

I shake my head at her and go out into the hall.

"Hi, Jake," I say somewhat tentatively.

"Hi, Katie. How are you feeling?"

"I'm okay."

"Good. That's good."

I wait for Jake to say why he's rung, but instead, silence reigns.

Eventually, I can't take it any more and ask him what's up.

"We left things badly," he says. "I shouldn't have stormed out like that."

"It's okay. Forget about it."

"I'm trying to understand how you could have thought me capable of doing bad things to you," Jake says after another silence. "It makes me wonder if you really knew me at all."

I don't know what to say. It's not as if I haven't asked myself the same thing.

"I know you've been through a hard time recently, though, so I'm trying to be sympathetic," Jake continues. "I'm trying to *understand*."

I run upstairs with the phone. I've a feeling Mam's listening to every word and I don't want her to hear what I'm about to say.

"Jake, you don't owe me your understanding. It's over between us," I say as kindly as I can.

"I think it shouldn't be," Jake says. "I feel it was a knee-jerk reaction on your part. Just because you're not ready for the things I'm ready for doesn't mean we have to break up."

"But I might never be ready for the things you want," I say. "We've discussed all this already."

"I know. I don't want to put any pressure on you, Katie. I just want you to know that as far as I'm concerned, this isn't over. Not for me."

I sigh. "My head is all over the place right now, Jake. I need to sort myself out before I can even think about there being an 'us' again. I'm sorry, I really am. I just can't give you any more right now."

"All right. I expected you to say that. But I just want you to know that I'm here, okay? I'm not going anywhere."

A part of my heart is leaping for joy. Another part of it

is breaking. I can never be who Jake wants me to be, I know that. Sadly, he doesn't.

"I have to go now, Jake. Thanks for calling," I say.

I hang up and throw the phone on the bed before throwing myself on it, too. I've never felt so perplexed.

In a bid to delay the process of going downstairs and facing the inevitable Jake-related interrogation, I rifle through a drawer looking for an old pay-as-you-go phone I had several years ago. I soon find it, with its charger. It's old-fashioned, but it'll do until I get a chance to buy a new one. It's even partially charged. I put it in my pocket.

When I eventually go back downstairs, the questioning begins. And to add to it, Sandra has also "popped by" since I went downstairs. Mam's clearly assembling her entourage again today. I want to scream at how unnecessary it all is, but instead I exchange greetings with Sandra.

"So, how's Jake?" Mam asks innocuously.

"He's fine."

She cuts to the chase. "What did he want?"

"Just to see if I'm okay."

"Ah. That's nice of him, considering you accused him of abducting you. He's such a lovely man."

Claire frowns. "Yes, that *is* nice of him. Not many men would be so understanding."

Oh no! not Claire as well. I thought she wasn't judging me as harshly as Mam and Sandra are.

I need a bit of breathing space.

"I have to do some food shopping," I say, even though the house is full of food from Mam's groceries foray.

I walk to the hall, grab my car and house keys and handbag, and leave as fast as I can before someone tries to stop me, hoping Brian won't ring while I'm gone.

113

Chapter 12

I drive to a shop and buy credit for the phone. I need to ring Penny. She knows more about the facts of Saturday night than anyone else. I put the credit into the phone and ring Penny's mobile. She doesn't answer. I'm not surprised – she's probably in a meeting – but I'm disappointed nonetheless. The only other person I could ring and grill for information is Richard, but I'm not going there. Richard is non-communicative with me at the best of times. If I rang him out of the blue and he answered, he'd probably hang up straight away when he found out it was me ringing. In any case, I don't even have his number. And it's not just that I can't remember it. I didn't have it on my old phone, either.

Penny could do so much better than Richard, although in some way they're well suited. Jake and I used to call them the power couple, both doing very well in their careers, both very well respected professionally. However, there was a catch. Richard was married. It was something that Penny never mentioned to me initially – Jake had told me. Penny was firmly of the belief that Richard would leave his wife for her one day, Jake had told me.

"I can't believe she really thinks that," Jake said. "That's the oldest trick in the book and Penny's no fool. Love really is a great leveller."

As someone in a prominent position at work, Richard was often interviewed by the media and a quick Google search showed that he was married with four children, all in their teens. But as far as Penny was concerned, it was as if they didn't exist when she spoke to me about him after Jake and I first started going out. If Penny was aware that I knew Richard was married, she never mentioned it. Nor did she ask me to keep their relationship quiet. It was just never addressed.

The day came when I had to bring it up. While I didn't judge Penny for seeing a married man, I didn't condone it, either. We were becoming friends and as her friend, I didn't like to see her so caught up with someone who could never fully be hers. But I also had to work out what made her think that what she was doing was right if I was to understand her as a friend at all. It seemed to me that there wasn't much to our burgeoning friendship if we couldn't talk about the hard, real issues going on behind our public faces.

I was dreading bringing it up, yet I couldn't sit in front of Penny any more over dinners and drinks listening to how amazing Richard was and how their relationship was everything she'd ever wanted. I couldn't live a lie any more, nodding and smiling while really thinking that she was making a big mistake. I expected a huge level of defensiveness, but what actually happened shocked me.

"I saw this in the paper," I said to her on the day I knew I finally had to bring it up. I produced a picture of Richard and his wife at an awards ceremony, as shown in a Sunday newspaper. "Why did you never tell me Richard's married, Penny?"

I braced myself for her to tell me it was none of my business, and that I should focus on my own relationship and my own problems instead of worrying about hers. Penny could be very sharp when she wanted to be.

Instead, she burst out crying. Loud, body-engulfing sobs that I'd never expected to hear from her.

"This isn't a surprise to you, surely?" I said.

According to Jake, Penny had known Richard was married from the very beginning.

"No, of course not. It's just so hard to see them together!"

She tore the newspaper cutting from my hands and ripped it up violently, throwing the pieces on the ground when she'd finished before stomping out of the room.

I was utterly thrown by Penny's reaction. I'd never seen "not in complete and utter control" Penny before. If she were to lose control, I didn't anticipate that it would be in such a spectacular, almost childish fashion. I also didn't realise she felt that strongly about him. Although they're a good match on paper, they're a strange pairing in reality. There's very little affection between them, but Jake says that's normal for Penny.

"Penny doesn't do affection," he said when I remarked on it once.

"They're probably different in private, though," I said. "Maybe she wouldn't like to be seen to be affectionate in case it makes her look needy."

Jake shrugged. "I don't really want to think about what those two get up to in private," he said and that was the end of that subject.

A few minutes later, Penny came back into the room. She apologised and was completely herself again, as if it had never happened. It was disconcerting. I haven't brought up Richard's marriage since, but there's always an underlying note of tension between us whenever she mentions him. And I don't know if she told Richard that I'd brought up his marriage, but even if she did, that's not the cause of his coldness towards me.

He's been like that with me from our very first meeting. I don't know if that's how he treats people in general – when you take into consideration the lack of affection between him and Penny, it could well be – or if it's just me. Either way, I find Richard strange to be around. I find Penny and Richard's entire *relationship* strange. I'm in no position to judge there, though. Relationships are complex. I know that as well as anyone.

I go home and after a bit of small talk with my family I go straight upstairs, feeling like a moody teenager who's gone to hide in her room. I ring the gardai and ask to talk to Brian, but I'm told he's in a meeting. I leave a message and my new mobile number, asking if he can call me as soon as possible. Then I try to ring Penny again, but there's no answer. I ring twice in case she just missed the call the first time, but I don't get through to her.

A wave of exhaustion hits me, so I lie down while I'm waiting for Brian and Penny to call me back, hopefully. The incident at the weekend has taken it out of me physically as well as mentally.

I sleep for several hours and when I wake, I try to ring Penny once more. While I can only imagine how little free time the CEO of operations of a multinational company has and I'd never usually ring Penny at work, I desperately need to speak to her now. It's late afternoon and I'm getting nowhere with my enquiries. My call rings out again. I leave a voicemail.

A few minutes later, Penny rings me back.

"You were trying to reach me, Katie?" she says quickly. Penny doesn't really do preamble.

"Yes, I was."

I relay the day's events to Penny.

"I had countless missed calls from the same number, but didn't realise it was you until I listened to your voicemail. Did you get a new phone?"

"It's an old pay-as-you-go one I had before."

"Oh, right. I have a fairly new smartphone here that I don't use if you need it."

"Thanks for the offer, but this one's fine for now. Penny, listen. I need you to go through everything that happened with me again that night, step by step."

Penny sighs. "Oh, Katie, we've been through all this already."

"No, we haven't. Not in *detail*. I've heard snippets of what happened from you and other bits from Barbara, but I was too shocked and messed up when I woke in hospital to ask a lot of questions. I need a more detailed discussion about it all."

"There's nothing else to say."

I'm having none of that. I know she wants to get off the phone and attend to the million important things she has to do, but this is important, too.

"I'm sure there is. There might be something we've missed. There are things that I'm not clear about. For example, did the man initiate the conversation, or did I?"

"He did, from what I saw."

"From what you saw? So, there's a chance I might have?"

"I wasn't monitoring you that closely, Katie. I'd been talking to Barbara about how we should try upstairs to see

118

if it was quieter there and I had my back turned to you. When I turned round, you and the man were talking. From the way he was leaning in towards you, it looked to me like he initiated the conversation."

"But you didn't see him actually coming up to me and starting to talk to me?"

"No. Why, does it matter?"

"I'm just wondering if this man targeted me for some reason. And you think I was talking to him for about fifteen minutes before I collapsed?"

"About that. I came downstairs. You told me you'd follow us up, but you never did. And I tried to drag you away from him after about that length of time, which is when I got a good look at him, but you wouldn't budge. Then I had to go back upstairs and get the girls."

"Did you talk to him at all at that point? Did I introduce you?"

"No. I grabbed your arm and pulled you aside to try to warn you that you should stay with us, but you got very aggressive with me. I could see you were on the edge of losing it, so I thought it best to walk away at that moment and not antagonise you further. I know what you're like when you're drunk, Katie, and I assumed you were enjoying the attention after the break-up.

"I went back up to the girls then and told them that we as a group should tell you we're leaving and get you to come with us. I know you've had issues in the past thinking I'm too bossy and I thought you'd react better if it came from all of us."

I decide to let that go without remarking. I only said that to Penny once, a few months ago, but it was never forgotten and she's made several references to it since.

"What did I say when you guys came up to me?"

"By the time I'd explained the situation to the girls and we'd got our coats and bags together to leave, it was too late. It took a while as there was no sign of Gabrielle and we didn't know where she'd gone. Turns out she was on her phone in the bathroom, but we couldn't leave until she came back. After I'd gone upstairs to get the girls, we came back down, which took another five minutes at least. But in the time since I'd last seen you, something had changed.

"As we were walking over towards you, we saw you falling forwards and down. Then you just went out cold. A barman saw what was happening and he came over. We carried you outside between us to get some air."

"And what about the guy I was talking to? Where was he?"

"He was there when you collapsed, but I took very little notice of him at that point, Katie. I didn't think for one second that you'd been drugged. I assumed you'd blacked out because of the alcohol."

"And after I was brought outside?"

"We all went out with you. I hailed a passing taxi and told him I'd pay him double if he'd take you. He said no. Most taxis won't take very drunk people because of the risk of soilage. I had to ask five different taxi drivers before I managed to sweet-talk one into letting you get in – for treble the price. Barbara physically had to help me get you into it."

My cheeks burn. It's hard to hear this, but I have to get all the facts.

"Sorry, Penny. It sounds like I was really hard work. I'll pay you back for the taxi, by the way. So, nobody saw that guy leaving after we did?"

"No, but we weren't looking for him, either. As I said,

we didn't think there was anything to suspect him of at the time."

"I wonder if he followed us out and got a taxi home after us. You didn't notice anything strange after we got home, did you?"

"No, Katie. I was too busy with you to notice anything, truth be told."

"Sorry. Sounds like you had a hard night with me. That reminds me, what time did you check on me the following morning?"

"It was late enough. I slept in after being up so late with you. I'd say around ten thirty."

"And I was asleep then?"

"Out for the count."

"You actually saw me, though? I wasn't just a shape in the bed – you actually *saw* me?"

Penny sighs. "Yes, Katie. I actually saw you. So did Richard. He checked you several times throughout the day." Penny sounds distinctly impatient.

"I just had to ask."

"You don't seriously think this man followed you back to my place, do you?" Penny's voice is softer now.

"I don't know what to think, Penny. I'm just trying to work it all out. So presumably, he put that stuff in my drink between the time you came over and the time I collapsed. You said something about me had changed, so that must have been when he did it."

"Maybe. If only you'd come with me when I asked you to, Katie. I'm your friend. I was just looking out for you."

"I know. And sorry if I was a wagon to you that night."

"You were a bit, particularly when I was trying to change your clothes."

121

That's another thing that's bothering me. In the cottage, I was wearing the clothes I was wearing on our day out, but Penny said I'd been sick on my clothes and she'd cleaned me up and changed me into pyjamas. If I was taken from her house in the middle of the night, why wasn't I wearing pyjamas in the cottage?

I can't ask that, though. I have to keep the focus on trying to find out who drugged me, for the purpose of tracking him down and bringing him to justice – and to stop him from doing this to someone else. If I bring up the cottage, Penny will just think I'm losing it again. The last thing I need is for her to contact Mam and tell her stuff I don't want Mam to hear. It's bad enough that I've said stuff to Jake that could get back to Mam.

"How many changes of clothes did I go through?" I say, trying to bring the clothes issue into the conversation somehow.

"So many that I lost count. We used up most of my spare pyjamas and I own quite a few. But look, it doesn't matter now. They're all washed and sorted."

"Are the jeans and blouse I was wearing the day of the lunch at your house, too?"

"Oh yes. I've been meaning to talk to you about them. I didn't realise that blouse was dry-clean only, so I put it in a hot wash in the machine to get rid of the vomit and then it went into the dryer. I'm really sorry, Katie, but it shrank like you wouldn't believe.

"You told me where you bought it though, when we were out at lunch, so I bought you a new one from the boutique online to make up for it. It was my mistake, after all. I got your size from the label on the shrunken one. The jeans are in the house, all clean and ironed."

"Oh, okay, thanks. There was no need to buy a new blouse."

"There was every need. I should have realised the material would shrink, but I just had so much washing to do that night that I threw everything into the machine without thinking. I was annoyed at myself afterwards. Anyway, I gave your address for delivery, so the new blouse should be with you soon. And call round to collect the jeans whenever you want."

"Okay. Thanks, Penny."

"Sure. Anything else I can clarify? It's just that I have two conference calls with the States in the next few hours and I need to prep for them."

"Only two?" I say, trying to inject a bit of levity into my voice. "Sounds like a half-day for you."

"Yeah, I'll have more demanding days this week," Penny replies without so much as a hint of humour. "I'm travelling to London at seven tomorrow morning and it's going to be a busy day over there. I'm really looking forward to it."

And she is. Penny lives for the kind of thing that would put other people six feet under from exhaustion.

"Just one other thing. Is there anything else about the man's physical appearance that's worth mentioning? Anything at all that could be considered a distinguishing feature?"

"No, he was very nondescript. Other than the way I've described him already to the gardaí – medium height, medium build, balding dark hair, regular features – there's very little to say about him. He was wearing dark jeans and a black blazer, so his dress sense wasn't particularly different, either. There was just nothing untoward to report about him."

"One thing I can't rationalise is why he'd bother giving it to me at all right then, Penny. Surely he knew the effect it would have on me. And that he'd never get me out of the pub and home with him before I blacked out. And after he saw you coming over to me, he must have known I was with a group of friends who were keeping an eye on me. How did he think he'd get away with it?"

"Well, he has, hasn't he? He did this to you and we have no idea who he is. He might not have got what he wanted from you, whatever that was, but he still walked away from it with no repercussions. Plus, Katie, you have to remember that there are weirdos out there who'll do things like this just for kicks. Just because they can. Maybe it made him feel powerful to see you collapsing and knowing he did that to you."

"Do you think?"

"There are all sorts out there. We can never make sense of the motivation of some people."

Penny's voice sounds like she's trying to be comforting, but the thought of never making sense of any of this makes me feel even worse. It's time to get off the phone.

"Well, safe travelling, Penny. Thanks for taking my call."

"It'll all be fine, Katie. Take care," Penny says before hanging up.

I wish I could believe that. Nothing that I've heard today gives me anything to go on at all and I have absolutely no idea what to do next.

Chapter 13

I'm passing through the hall on my way to the kitchen, when the call comes through on the landline.

"Hello?"

"Katie?"

"Yes."

"Brian Houlihan here, Katie. I got your messages. Sorry about the delay in getting back to you – busy day here."

At last. I was getting scared Brian wasn't going to ring me back at all.

"Hi, Brian. I'm sorry I didn't tell you the full story last time round."

"Could you relay it to me again first-hand? Grace gave me an overview, but I'll need to hear the details."

I tell Brian everything. When I finish speaking, he doesn't offer anything on the other end of the phone. I wonder, have I stunned him into silence?

"I know it sounds unbelievable, but it happened," I eventually say. "If you're in any doubt at all, the marks on my back make it very clear. They couldn't have been made by anything other than a chair. It happened, and now I need to work out how. And I'll need you guys to help make that happen. I could be in big danger here, Brian. Someone changed their mind once about possibly killing me. What if there's a next time and they don't change their mind then?"

"Is there any reason I should know of why someone would want to do something like this to you?"

"No, I don't think so."

"Have you fallen out with anyone recently?"

"I broke up with my boyfriend. I haven't fallen out with anyone else."

"What's his full name?"

I give Brian Jake's full name, along with a few other details he asks for.

"What about your professional life? Any significant recent changes there?"

"I'm a journalist. Significant *recent* changes – no, there hasn't been any big change in my role recently, and I don't think I've upset anyone through my job. Journalists can sometimes be a target for ire owing to articles they've written, but I haven't worked on anything contentious lately."

One of my former colleagues, a crime writer, has received several threats from criminals he's written about over the years – even a death threat – and now he has 24-hour armed garda protection. But as for me, although I occasionally do write-ups about court cases, crime isn't my area. Most of my work to date has been in Lifestyle – articles about the home, family, travel, health, beauty and wellbeing, and food and drink reviews. In the last year or so, though, I've been covering Irish and international news related to politics, education, social affairs, banking and so on, but I don't think I've written anything too controversial. I haven't had a run-in with anyone. My pieces are factual, not opinion based.

"You've never received threats from anyone?"

"No. I don't understand any of this, Brian. I don't know why it happened. All I know is that it did."

"Okay, Katie. Let's work through this. Is it your opinion that the man in the bar who you told me about did this?"

"I have no idea. It might have been. It seems most likely and obvious that it *would* be him, although I don't know how feasible it is that this man would have somehow managed to follow me home to Penny's house and spirit me out without anyone noticing. Then again, it might have been someone closer to home. I honestly don't know."

"Someone closer to home? Anyone in particular?"

I'm afraid to say the words. And yet, if I don't say it now, I might not get another opportunity. I could be completely wrong and if I am, I'll antagonise everyone. And yet, how can I let this go without investigating it thoroughly?

"Katie? Is there someone you have in mind?"

"I need you to check where Jake was on the night this happened to me."

Guilt floods me as soon as I utter the words. But I need to take action and rule out the most obvious people. I can't just sit here and do nothing.

"Do you have a reason to believe that your ex-boyfriend would want to cause you harm?"

"No. I don't know. I just think it's possible that whoever did this might have been in my circle. And if you look at this situation clinically, the most likely person would be the man I broke up with recently, even though it wasn't particularly acrimonious."

"Particularly? So, is it fair to say that it was *somewhat* acrimonious?"

"It was more distressing than acrimonious, really. Break-ups are never easy, but I didn't think there was any bad blood between us at the end of it, either. Surely it couldn't have been a stranger if Penny's saying that I was in her house all the time – if that's even true."

Can I believe Penny, either? Can I trust anyone? I'll need to ask Brian to check Penny and Richard out, too. I think of the call I had with Penny and how friendly we were, and I feel dreadful.

"From my interaction with Penny in relation to your drink being spiked, I have no reason to believe that she's lying about you being in her house that night. She mentioned that her partner, Richard, was in the house that night, too."

I try not to scream with frustration.

"Someone along the way is either not telling the truth, or they're getting their facts wrong, Brian! I know I'm right about this. I was *not* in Penny's house for all that night. I might have been put to bed there, I might have woken up there, but there was a period of time in which I wasn't there."

"I wasn't finished, Katie. I was about to say that although we have no reason to believe Penny and her boyfriend aren't correct in what they're saying, let's work through this from all angles. First of all, let's assume that what Penny is saying might *not* be true. Do you have a reason to think Penny's covering for her brother?"

I feel a flicker of hope. Finally, he's giving me a chance.

"I have no concrete reason to believe that, Brian, but they're siblings, so surely it's a possibility."

"Okay. Let's also consider the people in the circles you move in. First, what about Penny herself? Do you have any reason to believe she might want to cause you harm?"

"No, none at all."

"And Richard? What kind of relationship do you have with him?"

"A 'hi' and 'bye' one. He's rarely around and when he is, he's usually stuck to his mobile or on his laptop."

"So, there's been no discord with either of those two?"

"Not discord as such. I get the impression that Richard doesn't want to get to know me. It may be something to do with my profession. I don't know. Maybe he's just like that with everyone."

"And the connection with your profession is?"

"As a banker, he doesn't seem too keen to interact too much with a journalist. I suppose there's been quite a few articles written by journalists about bankers in recent years – me being one of them."

"I see. What about your friends? Let's start with the ladies you were out with on the day you've told us you were taken."

"Well, there's Barbara Flood. We're on good terms. She wouldn't have had anything to do with this, no way. She's lovely and a very supportive long-term friend. Plus, even if she wanted to organise for someone to tie me up and leave me for dead in a derelict cottage, she wouldn't have had the time. She's run off her feet between work and the kids and by her own admission, she barely has time to wipe her bum."

"Okay."

I can tell from Brian's voice that he's smiling. It puts me at ease somewhat.

"Who else was there?"

"Rose Doyle. She's a friend of mine since college."

"How is your relationship?"

"It was always close . . . "

"*Was*?"

"We did have a bit of a falling-out recently, but Rose would never be behind something like this. We go way, way back. We made up anyway before that day when we all went out together."

"Why did you fall out?"

"We had a row about Jake. It got a bit personal. We sorted it out afterwards."

"You're sure it's sorted and there's no lingering ill feeling?"

"Yes."

"And there's no historical issues between you from all the years you've been friends?"

"No. I wouldn't still be friends with her if there were."

"Okay. Anyone else?"

"Yes, Gabrielle Quinn. She's a friend from a previous job."

"What's the situation with her? Any fallings-out in the past?"

"No. Gabrielle's pregnant. I don't think her thoughts are anywhere but on her impending arrival and her three-year-old daughter. I've no reason at all to believe she'd want to do me any harm."

I feel awful even having this discussion. Of course Gabrielle wouldn't do me any harm, any more than my other friends would. Yet, a part of me is willing to investigate the possibility that Jake would. Jake, who's always been so lovely to me. Am I mad?

It's self-preservation, a voice inside my head says. Someone's done this to you and until you find out who it was, you can't trust anyone.

"Anyone else?"

"There's Declan Campion, my ex-husband."

"Tell me about him."

"We're divorced. We don't communicate now. Things aren't hostile as such, but at the same time we're better off staying away from each other."

I give Brian a brief background into my relationship with Declan and tell him about the incident when Declan showed up at my house drunk.

"Right," Brian says when I've told everything there is to tell about Declan and that there's nobody else in the frame I can think of who we need to be thinking about. "I'm going to need to speak to all of these people and gather as much information as I can from them about the day you were out, okay? They're not under any suspicion. I just need to talk to them in order to investigate this as thoroughly as possible."

"All right."

"Maybe your friends remember other things about the man who we believe spiked your drink. Things that Penny might not have observed. Everyone sees the world differently. The more information we have, the better."

Brian asks me for the contact details and other relevant information for those I've named, and I call them out to him.

"Now, let's talk through the timeframe here. You left the bar with your friends at around 10 p.m. Penny says she took you home with her. You said that when you came to in the cottage, it was morning, right?"

"Yes. Early morning. I'd say it was around eight o'clock when I woke, but that's just a guess from the light at the time."

"So, you believe you were abducted between when Penny took you home and sometime before eight o'clock the following morning?"

"I would imagine so, yes."

"And Penny says you were in her house all that time?"

"Yes, but you need to question her more deeply on that. I mean, I'm sure she wasn't watching me throughout the night. She said after a certain point when I stopped being sick, she put me to bed and left me to sleep it off. I must have been taken then."

I don't mention that I've had a conversation with Penny in the meantime. I want Brian to try to get as much information out of Penny as possible and cross-reference what he tells me. I know that makes me a horrible friend, but I can't fully trust any of my friends until I get to the bottom of this. Anyway, it's more the men in Penny's life I'm doubting than her. If Penny pulls me up on being questioned by Brian after she's given me the details, I'll have to pass it off as a misunderstanding.

"So, this person took you and brought you back without Penny noticing?"

"I know it sounds absurd, but it's the only thing that makes sense."

"Is it possible that you somehow brought yourself back to Penny's house?"

"I don't see how that's possible. I seemed to be in a very rural, faraway place. How would I know the way back to Penny's from there? Why wouldn't I remember something?"

"But you don't remember anything about someone else bringing you back, either?"

"No, but I presume I was still out cold when that happened. I certainly wasn't in a fit state to bring myself anywhere. That's not to say that someone else couldn't have transported me in the meantime. All they'd have had to do is lift me up and put me into a vehicle."

"Did you have anything with you when you woke in this place, such as your phone?"

I know Brian's probably thinking that the mobile phone might have used phone masts in particular location but unfortunately, that line of thought probably isn't a goer.

"No. I had absolutely nothing with me and my phone is missing. I noticed it was gone from my handbag when Penny brought my stuff to the hospital after I collapsed at her house."

"Do you know when you lost it?"

"The last time I remember using it is in one of the previous pubs we'd been to that day. I presume I lost it in one of the last pubs we visited. It might be worth you checking the masts to see if it picked up any signals after 10 p.m., though. Who knows? Maybe it came with me to wherever I was brought to and was lost there. I honestly have no idea."

"Okay, Katie. We'll leave it at that for now. First, I'll need to talk to everyone. I should also have the CCTV footage later today. I'll get back to you after I've made contact with everyone and I've watched the footage."

That doesn't sound like much action to me.

"And then what?"

"I'll need to speak to everyone first before I can determine that," Brian says.

In other words, he doesn't know. Or else he *does* know and he just doesn't want to verbalise it at this point. He'll talk to Penny – she'll confirm that I was at the house all night and he'll come back to me saying that's that. Nothing happened. There'll be no checking of phone masts because it's all in my head. Nothing to see here, folks.

But I don't say that. I need to keep Brian onside as much as possible. If I start ranting at him that he's doing nothing, it won't do me any favours.

"Brian, can you take the angle that you're mainly trying to find out who drugged me when you're doing your information gathering? I don't want this to turn into an item of gossip among my friends, you know.

"I also don't want them turning against me for having them investigated. I know I can't have it every way, but I want to minimise the amount of harm I'll do to my relationships as much as possible while also getting things thoroughly investigated."

"I'll need to be completely transparent with the people I contact about my reasons for doing so, Katie," Brian says. "However, I assure you that I'll be as discreet as possible."

"Thanks, Brian," I say instead. "I'd appreciate it if you could get back to me as soon as possible with your thoughts. I really don't feel safe right now. The other thing is, I want you guys to see the marks on my back before they fade. You need pictures of them. Can I come in to meet a female guard – perhaps Grace – and she can take photos of them?"

"Yes. We should do that. You can come in now, if you wish. Grace is here. I have to leave here soon, but Grace will be here for another three hours."

"I'll come straight in."

Before we end the call, Brian promises he'll get back to me as soon as he's spoken to everyone. I feel slightly better and yet horribly guilty.

But I have to get this sorted. After all, if the person who did this gets away with it, how do I know they won't come after me again?

Chapter 14

I wake up and instantly check my mobile. I'm on high alert since last night.

After my landline call with Brian, I picked up my mobile to text those whose numbers I'd passed on to Brian from my address book. I noticed that there was a message waiting. From Jake. I decided to read it after I sent my message. I typed out the following and sent it to the relevant people:

Hi, just a heads-up that I had to pass your number on to Garda Brian Houlihan in relation to me getting drugged. He wants to talk to everyone in my group in the hope that gathering information will help to find the person who drugged me. I hope that's okay.

Once that was done, I opened Jake's message.

Hi, Penny said this is your new/old mobile number. Hope you're feeling okay now. As I said before, you know I'm always here.

I didn't know whether to reply or not, or what to say if I did. Eventually, I typed: *I'm fine. Thanks for texting.* I couldn't believe he was being so nice to me after what I'd accused him of. It almost made me more suspicious of him, which is probably horrible of me.

Jake's a very forgiving type in general. I've seen it in how he interacts with his friends and family, and I've always thought he lets people get away with far too much. But that's who he is and I always found it endearing before. This behaviour is actually consistent with his character. Although, I know I certainly wouldn't be reacting this way if someone had accused me of the things I've thrown at him. Most people wouldn't. But most people aren't Jake.

A few hours later, I received five missed calls from a blocked number. Thinking they were from Declan, who'd no doubt be livid at getting dragged into all this, I let them go to voicemail. Nobody left a message. What if the calls were from Jake, though? Declan had always been a great man for leaving voicemails, particularly if he was angry about something. I suppose he'd probably approach it differently having been asked his whereabouts on the night something happened to his ex-wife, though. Declan is no fool – he'd probably be far too smart to leave a ranting voicemail.

I probably should have had the courtesy to answer the calls after getting people involved, but I just wasn't feeling strong enough at that point to deal with Declan, if it was him, and I could hardly have hung up if I'd answered and it was him. Nobody else reacted adversely, although there were a few cold *okays* among the replies. And some of the recipients didn't reply at all – like Jake.

I could have sworn that Grace was looking at me like I was totally crackers, too, when I went in to get the photos taken of my back yesterday. She passed no comment other than to say that Brian had told her to expect me in to get the photos taken, but she didn't need to say anything else. I could tell from her face that she was dubious about me. When I asked her what her thoughts were about the marks, all she would say was that Brian was investigating the matter and it was best if she didn't comment. I left the station trying not to cry from sheer frustration.

There are no new messages on my phone from overnight. It's eight o'clock and Mam's pottering around downstairs already. I put the phone down and go downstairs to help her. Well, I'll offer, but I know she'll refuse, even though it's my house. That's Mam – she has to do everything herself.

"Ah, you're up, love. Sit down and I'll make you a cup of tea and toast."

"It's fine, Mam. I'll make them myself."

"Not at all, would you stop! Sit down there now and I'll bring them over to you in a minute."

I sit at the breakfast table, knowing I won't win this particular argument.

An hour or so later, Claire calls over. Sandra can't make it this morning and I have to admit, I'm glad about that. I already feel like I have more breathing space now. While Sandra's a good person, we habitually clash too much for us to feel fully comfortable around each other.

We were never all that close when we were younger anyway, but she was never right with me again after the Temple Bar incident. I always feel like a nuisance at best around her. I also feel she enjoys what she sees as her right to act in a superior manner towards me because she's older and I messed up eighteen years ago. Sadly, this new material will probably give her ammunition against me for years. All the same, I know she'll do whatever she can to help me if it's possible. That's just how we roll as sisters.

Mam and Claire go through the rigmarole about who'll make the tea and toast, and Claire sits down as Mam serves. We chat about this and that, me firmly steering the conversation away from anything related to the last few days. Claire has nothing on today and none of us are in a hurry to be anywhere. It feels good just to relax and have regular, everyday conversations. I'm starting to feel normal again, for however long it lasts.

We're just starting on our third cup of tea of the morning, when the doorbell rings.

"I'll get it," Mam says, and she's up from her chair and out of the door before she's even finished speaking.

I frown at Claire. "I'm not expecting a delivery or anything," I say.

I get up and follow Mam, just in case it's anyone dodgy at the door. I walk into the hall to see Mam being swamped by a gigantic bouquet of flowers.

"They're for you, love!" she says, bringing them in. "God, they're heavy. Aren't they lovely? I wonder, are they from your workplace?"

"Hmm, probably," I say.

I bring the bouquet into the kitchen and take the card out:

I hope you feel better soon. Whenever you're ready, I'll be here waiting for you.
All my love,
Jake

"They're from Jake!" Mam squeals. She couldn't be any happier if she'd received a bunch of flowers herself from

George Clooney. "Oh, my! Didn't I tell you he's a lovely man? They must have cost a solid fortune. Look at all the roses."

I leave the card on the table. Again, I don't know what to think or feel, other than the fact that Jake would be sorry he'd spent money on those flowers when the gardai are investigating his whereabouts last Saturday on my insistence. He would have ordered the flowers before I'd texted him about that.

Claire picks up the card and reads it.

"He texted me this last night as well," I say. I don't even know why I'm saying it.

Claire puts the card down on the table. "What exactly did he say?"

"Pretty much the same as what he wrote on the card."

Claire just looks at me. I've no idea what she's thinking. I've no idea what *I'm* thinking.

"Let's get these in water," Mam says, swooping on the bouquet and taking it to the sink.

"Guys, would you mind if I left you on your own for a while? I feel like I need to lie down. I didn't sleep very well last night."

Mam turns round and frowns. "Katie, love, are you okay?"

"I'm fine, Mam. Honestly. I think maybe that Rohypnol incident took more out of me than I thought. I'll be fine after a while, particularly now that I have a bellyful of tea and toast. I just need a little rest, that's all."

"Go on up so, and I'll bring you up another cup of tea and a hot-water bottle."

I smile. Any time is a good time for a hot-water bottle, according to Mam.

"That'd be great. Thanks, Mam."

I get straight into bed when I go upstairs. I'm anything but tired, but I need to think about why I'm so conflicted by all this attention Jake's giving me.

Not long afterwards, there's a knock on my bedroom door. I know it must be Claire, because Mam would just walk straight in.

"Come in, Claire," I say.

She comes in with the promised tea and hot-water bottle.

"Mam's canonising Jake downstairs," Claire says. "I swear she'd marry him herself if she could."

I take a sip of the tea rather than saying something, even though I can barely fit another drop into my belly.

"What do you make of the flowers?" Claire says.

"I'm assuming you're not asking me if I like the variety and choice of colour."

"No."

I put the tea down. "I don't know, Claire. Look, Jake's a very decent person. When I think about it, him sending me flowers even after I accused him of doing something awful is probably very consistent with the type of person he is."

"But?"

"I know it was hasty of me to accuse him, and deep down I don't think he's capable of doing something like leaving me for dead in the middle of nowhere, but he seemed like the most obvious person. And let's face it, I haven't actually known him for a long time, so I had to investigate it as a possibility.

"As for the flowers, I just don't think I'd be sending flowers to someone who'd accused me of trying to kill them, so they've made me feel a little unsettled. But as I said, that's Jake. He's very different from most other people.

"He might feel differently now, though, because I asked Brian at the garda station to investigate where everyone I was out with was on the night I went missing. I don't think Jake's going to take that well. Although, who knows? Based on how he's reacting so far . . . "

"Oh, it's being investigated? Wow."

"Yes. But I know none of you believe I was actually abducted anyway, so us having this conversation is probably pointless."

Claire sighs. "I'm not saying I don't believe you, Katie."

I sit up. "So, what *are* you saying? That you do?"

Claire shrugs. "Oh, Katie, I really don't know what to make of it all, but I'm starting to think that maybe we should all be listening to you a bit more. The whole situation sounds hugely improbable. However, I can't stop asking myself what if you're right? We're your family. We should be supporting you.

"As for Jake, I feel like he's being a bit over the top with you at the moment. You broke up with him, you accused him of locking you up in a cottage, and he's sending you supportive text messages and flowers. And this thing of 'I'll be here waiting whenever you're ready' doesn't sit right with me either, Katie. If you want to break up with him, you can. He doesn't get to tell you he's not going anywhere if you don't want him to be around! I find it a bit creepy that he'd say something like that."

"I really can't work out if that's his way of being sympathetic, or . . . "

"Yes. *Or.* Look, he could be completely innocent and I could be barking up the wrong tree. He most likely *is* completely innocent, to be fair. But we've all heard stories of people who lived with someone for years, only to find out their partners lived double lives with another partner and children elsewhere.

"You weren't with him all that long, Katie. I'm just putting it out there that we should be suspicious of him – and everyone else who was around you that day. So where are things at exactly with the gardai?"

I decide to confide in Claire, but before I do, I get her to promise that she won't relay any of the information I'm about to tell her to Mam. She promises and I fill her in fully on my conversation with Brian the previous day. Then, I take my top off and show her the marks on my back. She doesn't say much about them, but when I turn round to gauge her reaction, she looks shocked.

"As I said, everything's being investigated at the moment. I'm going to ring Brian later to see what he's uncovered since our conversation yesterday."

"Okay, well, make an appointment to go in and see him. Don't have the conversation over the phone and don't accept no for an answer when it comes to seeing him in person. If you have any difficulty, let me know and I'll sort it out. And let me know what time you're going in, because I'm going in with you."

My eyes fill with tears. Finally, someone's listening to me.

I'm being dragged out of Penny's house by my legs. I can't move or react in any way, but I can see it as clearly as if I'm outside my body, looking down on myself from some vantage point. The man who's taking me out of the house is of medium height, medium build and balding. It's the man I spoke to in the pub. I recognise him now. He hasn't even made any attempt to disguise himself. He knows he's going to get away with this.

Once we're outside the house, he drags me down the street as brazenly as you like. He's not concerned about anyone seeing him. My head is hopping off the pavement as he pulls me along like a sack of coal he's trying to drag into a garden shed. From outside my unconscious body, I can still feel the friction of the rough ground tearing away the hair at the back of my head and wearing into the skin underneath. Soon that, too, will be gone and the bone underneath will be exposed. This man won't be happy until my brains are spilling out all over the street.

I pray for a car to come along, but none does. It's late – everyone's tucked up, fast asleep. Surely I'm leaving a trail of blood behind me on the pavement from my head injuries. Just as I think that, it starts to rain heavily. Even the elements are against this man being held accountable for what he's doing to me. Why? What have I done that's so bad that I deserve to be treated like this and have someone get away with it? Why didn't Penny or Richard wake up? Has he drugged them? Has he killed them?

We get to the end of the street, where he stops near a car. He drops my legs on the ground. They crash against the pavement. He opens the boot of the car. He doesn't even look round before he picks me up and throws me in, shoving my knees up against my chest. My mid-air form of being is screaming at my unconscious self to wake the hell up and fight before he closes the boot, but it's too late. The door is closed.

He's getting into the driver's seat now, to bring me to the cottage. It's as he's pulling away that I finally come to and start to scream . . .

"Katie, you're okay! Katie, love, it was just a bad dream."

I wake on the couch to find Mam staring at me. The look of fear on her face soon dissolves the terror of my nightmare and my panic mutates into anger. This isn't right. This shouldn't have happened to me. My mother shouldn't be going through all this.

If it kills me, I'm going to find out who did this to me.

Chapter 15

The following afternoon, Claire and I are sitting at a desk in the garda station across from Brian. He's a busy man and not an easy one to pin down, but Claire has managed to do it. After I told her I'd been ringing Brian's office all morning only to be told he was busy, she rang up herself and tore strips off everyone in the place until she got the answer she wanted. Once she decides she wants something, she's very good about putting a plan in action.

"Brian, I need you to fill me in on exactly what your enquiries in relation to Katie's incident have come up with. I'm very concerned about my sister's welfare. She believes she was abducted and I need to know what you guys are doing about that."

I almost cry with relief at having someone on my side. Being honest with myself, though, I don't think Claire truly believes me. She's taking care of the what-if scenario – what if Katie isn't actually mad and there's a smidgen of truth in what she's saying. But right now, it's enough.

"Investigations of this nature do take time. The list of people alone who needed to be spoken to since Katie and I spoke yesterday was extensive and a few people were hard to get hold of, although I've now spoken to everyone."

For a few seconds, I feel sorry for Brian. It's impressive that he's managed to talk to everyone in such a short timeframe. He's clearly taking this seriously, yet we're in here demanding answers from him as if he's done no work at all. I would apologise, only I know Claire would kill me if I did.

Penny dropped me a text a few hours ago to say she'd heard from Brian last night and had told him everything she could about the evening. She said Richard had also been contacted. I didn't hear from anyone else about what Brian had to say to them.

"Katie, in the initial report you made to me, you expressed concerns about the man who Penny said was chatting you up on the night in question. I told you I'd liaise with the pub you were in to get the CCTV and I've done that. Unfortunately, the quality of the CCTV wasn't great. The pub was extremely busy on the night in question, and although both you and the man of concern can be seen on the footage, you're quite far away from the camera.

"You both appear to be holding your drinks constantly and the man's back is to the camera, with you – and your drink – directly in front of him. I can't see him putting anything in your drink from the footage I have, but it would appear that he'd have explicitly had to drop the drug into your drink right in front of you. You're surrounded by people and nobody seems to react adversely at any time. Nobody seems to have seen anything strange happening."

"That doesn't necessarily mean he didn't do it, though, does it?" Claire asks. "Maybe he did it slyly. Maybe he's experienced at this."

"As I say, I didn't see anything to indicate that this man

146

put something in your drink. The quality of the footage isn't the best I've ever worked with, admittedly, but there's nothing in it to pin the incident on this man.

"In terms of even identifying him, I've spoken to staff in the pub and shown them excerpts of the footage, and they've all agreed that the man isn't a regular. They've never seen him before."

"What did he look like?" Claire asks.

"White, average height, mid forties, balding dark hair."

"That's pretty . . . generic," I say. "That could be anyone."

"God, no wonder you can't remember him," Claire says.

Appropriate or not, I find myself smiling. But the smile dies quickly.

"Could I see the footage?" I say.

Brian hesitates. "I'm not sure that will serve any purpose."

"No, really, I'd like to see this man."

Brian shakes his head. "I think you'd be better off not seeing it, Katie. You might find it upsetting."

I presume he's talking about me seeing myself collapsing, but if I even saw the part before that, it'd be enough. I'm about to argue, when Brian starts talking again.

"I did, however, print off some still images of the man to show you."

Brian opens a folder. His *Katie* folder. It just doesn't seem right that there's a folder in the garda station about me. He hands several sheets of A4 paper to me.

My heart races as I start to look at them. He's right – the quality isn't good at all. Grainy is a euphemism. The woman in the picture is obviously me – there I am in the blouse I loved so much – but my features are undefined. As for the man, I could be talking to anybody. He's not tall, he's not small. And while he's not fully bald, he also doesn't have much hair. We're surrounded by other people. I can imagine how shitty the video quality would be. It's not worth fighting Brian to see it.

"We've investigated the whereabouts of the people who were around Katie on the day she believes she was abducted," Brian says. "Katie, you were particularly concerned about the movements of your former partner, Jake. When we interviewed him, he told us that he met friends the night that you believe you were abducted. He gave us the name of the bar he was in and he said that he stayed with a friend afterwards. He'd driven to his friend's house before going out and had left his car there, so that's why he stayed the night—"

I can't help but interject. "Do you mind me asking, what friend did he stay with?"

"Ronan Phillips," Brian says. "Do you know him?"

"Yes." Ronan is a colleague of Jake's and I'd met him several times.

"We have CCTV footage of Jake entering and leaving the bar he said he'd gone to: The Duke. He told us that he went to a nightclub with Ronan and a few others from work after leaving the pub, and again, we found footage of him entering and leaving the club. He went to a fast-food outlet on Grafton Street after the club with his friends – we have that footage, too. We've spoken to Ronan, and he confirmed that Jake came back to his house and stayed that night."

"He might be lying about it," Claire said. "If Jake was responsible, maybe Ronan was in on it, too."

"Ronan's wife was in the house when they came home. Apparently, they were quite loud, so she had to get out of bed to tell them to pipe down. She's confirmed to us that she saw Jake in her kitchen at three thirty in the morning."

"What about the rest of the night?" Claire says. "Katie has no idea what time she was taken, but it could feasibly have been any time during the night."

"The Phillips have a home CCTV system because they were burgled about six months ago. I called round to view it this morning. Jake didn't leave the house that night. He left the following day, around midday."

"Is that footage covering all parts of the house? It's not possible that he left via a back door and accessed his car on the street, out of view of the CCTV system?" Claire asks.

"It does cover all parts of the house, yes, and Jake's car was visible from the outdoor view. It wasn't moved."

I swallow hard to stop myself from crying. It sounds as if it's not possible that Jake had any hand, act or part in my abduction. I'm so relieved, but also mortified at having accused him of such a heinous thing in the first place.

"What about the women Katie was out with that day? Have you checked up on all of them?" Claire says.

"I've spoken to all of them, yes. Let's start with Penny. Penny says she brought Katie home. The other women who Katie was out with that day confirmed that they helped Penny to put Katie into a taxi. Penny's boyfriend, Richard, has confirmed that he saw Katie in Penny's house later when he called over. He also confirmed that he saw Penny putting Katie to bed late that night, when she'd stopped being sick.

"He stayed the night at the house and says that Penny definitely didn't leave the house that night. He's told us that he woke several times that night and Penny was there on every occasion. He has no reason to believe that Katie wasn't in her room."

"Did he check?" Claire says.

"Not that I'm aware of," Brian says.

"Claire, I'd be worried if I heard that he had checked," I say. "I'm not a baby."

I don't say aloud that the thought of Richard checking on me creeps me out beyond belief. Maybe I should be more open to the idea, though. If he had checked on me, he'd have seen that I wasn't there. I *couldn't* have been there.

"What about CCTV?" Claire says. "Surely someone who earns as much as I hear this Penny woman does has CCTV!"

"It was broken," I hear myself say before Brian can answer. "I remember her telling me about that a few days before we went out. Wasn't it? Did she tell you that?"

Brian nods.

"How trustworthy is Richard?" Claire says.

She seems to be directing the question to me.

"How trustworthy is anyone?" is all I can say. "I don't know Richard very well. I can't see why he'd have any motive to hurt me, though."

Then again, I can't see why anyone would. But somebody did.

"We also spoke to Barbara and Rose," Brian says. "Barbara went back home to her husband and children after Katie was brought back to Penny's in the taxi. Gabrielle also went home. As for Rose, she went back out. She met her sister in the city centre. She stayed with her that night."

"What about Declan?"

"Declan was on a stag do in Frankfurt last weekend. Many of his friends have verified he was there."

"That's very Declan all right," Claire says. "Stags in Frankfurt. He hasn't changed." She rolls her eyes.

"Everyone has alibis," I say aloud.

I'm not sure if I'm saying it to myself or to Brian and Claire.

He closes my file. Gently but firmly. I know what's coming.

"Katie . . . " he says almost kindly.

No.

"We need something else if we're to progress with this investigation. Everyone who was around you that day was with someone else the night you claim you were abducted. This, coupled with the fact that the hospital confirmed that Rohypnol can have hallucinogenic side effects, makes it very hard for us to move things on any further."

"You think it didn't happen," I say.

Brian says nothing for a few seconds. That in itself says it all.

"If anything else comes to light, I'm happy to investigate it. For now, though, there's nowhere else I can take this."

"This is ridiculous!" Claire says. "We're all aware of the statistics regarding unsolved crimes in this country. We have a history of young women having gone missing and decades later nobody has the faintest idea what's happened to them. Their families wake up every day and wonder if today will be the day that they find out what happened to their loved one. Sometimes, the parents of missing people go to their graves never having found out what happened. Katie could have been another one of those statistics!

"For all we know, the guy in the bar who you can't seem to identify could have followed her back to Penny's in his own car or a taxi. He could have taken her out of that house during the night without Penny or Richard hearing. There's no CCTV to say he didn't, is there? Anything is

151

possible. You only need to turn on the news any day of the week to realise that. My sister could still be in danger and if anything happens to her, it'll be your fault for not taking this seriously!"

"Claire, I understand your concerns, but I've explained the situation. Without something else to go on, there's nothing we can do. If anything else does come up in relation to Katie's case, I'll be more than happy to investigate it—"

"Katie is *not* a case. She's a *person*. A person who could have been killed! And you're sitting there saying there's nothing you can do."

Claire stares Brian down. If I were him, I'd be intimidated, but Brian seems unfazed. I'm guessing that in his line of work, he's heard and seen it all before from people who are a lot more threatening than Claire.

"It happened, Brian," I say. "I know it sounds improbable, but Claire's right. Think of all the strange cases we read about every day in the papers. The improbable happens, too. The improbable happened to *me*."

"Maybe so, Katie, but without proof . . . " Brian trails off.

"It's as if it didn't," Claire says. "Well, that's just great."

"What about checking the phone mast for my missing phone?" I say. "I can give you the number for it and you can run a check."

"That's out of the scope of this investigation at this point in time, I'm afraid."

"Roughly translated as you're not bothering," Claire pipes in.

Brian remains composed and doesn't react to Claire's statement.

"I'm here any time if you remember anything else, Katie," he says.

The note of finality in his voice is unmistakable. He's being perfectly pleasant and professional, but I know he thinks this is all in my head.

I stand up, unable to think of a way to move this conversation forwards in a meaningful way. Claire reluctantly gets up too, glaring at Brian as if he were the one who abducted me. I feel a rush of affection for her. It feels good to have someone on my side, fighting for me, even if she isn't fully convinced of the veracity of the situation.

"We'll be in touch," Claire says. "Everything comes out in the wash, Brian. And if you're not going to load the machine, we will."

She flounces out, throwing one last dagger at Brian before she goes. For someone who doesn't like conflict, she's trying very hard to defend me. I'm quite impressed.

"I'll be back, Brian," I say a lot more confidently than I feel. "I'm not giving up until I find out the truth behind all this."

I say goodbye to Brian and follow Claire.

"Load the machine? Nice analogy," I can't help but say with a smile in the corridor.

"I'm afraid you have nothing to smile about, Katie."

"It's laugh or cry, Claire," I say. "Well, smile, at least. God, this is a mess."

Claire puts an arm around my shoulders. "Come on. Let's get out of here."

Chapter 16

Claire's quiet in the car. After how vocal she was with Brian, her silence is somewhat discomfiting. I can barely focus on driving with the weight of it.

"What's up?" I eventually say. "You're much quieter than usual."

"I'm just thinking about what Brian said."

"Claire, I don't want to cast aspersions on Brian's integrity, but do you think it's possible that he knows who I am from the paper and is consciously trying to get me to drop this investigation for his own reasons?"

"What do you mean? What motivation would he have to do that?"

"Do you remember me telling you about the time I approached the former Irish garda commissioner in the restaurant to ask him his opinion on the alleged bullying and harassment accusations within the gardai? And how Henry went mad with me and made me drop the whole thing."

"Oh, yes."

"Well, what if Brian's aware of that incident? What if he's been advised not to investigate this any further because it suits the gardai to believe I'm going mad?"

"Ah, hang on a second now! You can't accuse the gardai of corruption."

"I'm not accusing them of anything. I'm doing a what-if scenario here. Anything's possible, Claire. Anything. I'm long enough in journalism to know that for a fact."

"I find the scenario you've described to be highly unlikely. First of all, there wasn't even a huge amount of attention given to the incident when you approached the former Irish garda commissioner. It never got out in the media. If what you're saying has any validity, that would mean that the former Irish garda commissioner himself must have told senior staff within the force about it, and to keep an eye out for you. Brian himself would have to have been aware of the incident. It just doesn't make sense, Katie."

"He just seemed so quick to want to drop this – to *dismiss* it."

"He probably just didn't see anywhere else he could take the investigation," Claire says in a gentle voice. "He'd exhausted all of his avenues."

"But had he? I don't believe that. I just don't think he thought it was worth his while investigating any more. That kind of thinking is all well and good until a woman disappears and her body is found in the Dublin mountains a year later by someone out walking their dog."

"I know I said something similar to Brian when I went to the station, but I was just trying to shock him into making sure he'd done everything. There's a difference between looking at all the angles of a situation, though, and being completely paranoid. I'm aware that you've trained yourself to consider all possibilities because of your job, but you need to rein it in now or you'll drive yourself mad."

"No. Someone tried to harm me, Claire, and nobody's

taking it seriously. Nobody believes me."

Claire sighs deeply. "I think now, honey, that you're going to have to focus on how you'll move on from all this."

"I can't move on until I find out what happened," I say.

"But what if you don't? You heard what Brian said. The gardai aren't going to help you any further. You don't have any ideas on what to do next, unless you're keeping them to yourself. You might need to write this off and put it behind you, Katie. Just watch your back and keep your eyes open. In the meantime, you have to try to live a normal life. This will swallow you whole if you let it."

I hadn't expected this. The speed of my driving slows with the effect of her words. I wish I could pull over, but I don't want to be dramatic or cause a fuss.

She doesn't believe me. If she did, she'd never be saying this. She was just covering the "What if she's right?" factor in the garda station. She was so vehemently on my side, though, that I really thought she believed me.

I should have known. I'm not mad at her – after all, she's listened to me and given me more of a chance than anyone else has. She wants to believe me, I can tell. The problem is, she just doesn't *fully* believe that it happened, no matter how much she wants to.

"I think the best thing you can do now is to stop drinking and maybe take a bit of time out from the social scene," Claire continues.

It sounds like something that she's said before, not something that just came into her head. Possibly something that was discussed with Mam.

"Maybe even take a bit of time off work and just relax, you know? Everyone needs downtime."

"Maybe you're right," I say eventually, almost choking on the words.

If Claire, Mam and Sandra start talking too much and getting too concerned about me, I'll be suffocated. If Claire doesn't truly believe me, I'm better off on my own. Clearly, I *am* on my own in this.

Claire has a few jobs to do, so I drop her in the city centre. While I'm there, I decide to drop the car in a multistorey and wander around town myself. I don't need to buy anything, but I do need to distract myself before my situation overwhelms me completely. I think about going to the promenade in a suburb called Clontarf to sit on a bench and stare at the sea – something I love to do when I need to gain perspective on life – but the rain is pounding down today and it would probably be a miserable experience. Winter has well and truly set in.

I go to the nearest coffee shop I can find. I look at all of the people around me in the coffee shop, eating and drinking like they haven't a care in the world. Or maybe they do and they're just masking it well. Do I look normal? Do I look like I might be a happy person, even if I'm not smiling right now? Or can they see my problems written all over my face?

I stop people watching and stare at the table before someone asks me what I'm looking at. Instead, I relay in my head everything that Brian said. Essentially, I'll get no answers unless I can produce new evidence that this actually happened to me. How can I do that? I'm not sure I can accept Brian giving neat and tidy explanations for where everyone I know was that night. Perhaps he just wanted to finish this case up and get it off his desk. If so, it seems that he's achieved that. I don't know how thoroughly he's investigated things, or if I can trust him and his professional capabilities . . . what if he's missed something?

I try to grab the attention of a passing waitress.

"Sorry, do you have a pen I could borrow, and some paper, please?"

The waitress looks at me as if I'm the biggest nuisance in the world. To be fair, I'm sure she has more than enough to do without providing stationery for customers. But she goes into the kitchen and returns with a pen and a page from a food order duplicate docket book, saying that's all she has in the line of paper. I thank her.

When she walks away, I write "Possible Suspects" on the top of the page. As soon as I've written it, I can't help but grin, despite everything. I can just imagine Sandra's reaction if she saw this. "Who needs Jessica Fletcher from *Murder, She Wrote*?" she'd say with an accompanying eye-roll. Not to mention the fact that she'd see it as further proof that I've lost my marbles. But no more of that. I must continue. If I stop, I'll fall into an abyss of helplessness and I don't know if I'll be able to get out of it again.

Maybe this is mad. Maybe I should just accept that the gardai have investigated things as thoroughly as anyone can. And yet, I can't help but suspect that they might have missed something. They don't have the same motivation I do to look into every nook and cranny of this situation. While Brian seems like a genuine man, I'm sure he has countless other cases going on right now. They probably include burglary, domestic violence, rape and other heinous crimes – possibly even murder. I'm sure if he's assessing the urgency of them, there are many cases that rank higher than mine.

Surely there's no harm in me going over everything – and every*one* – one more time? Even if I'm driving myself mad, I can't help but feel like that's the route I'll be going down anyway if I can't get to the bottom of this. There is no moving on, as Claire suggested, when I feel like I have to look over my shoulder constantly now.

Under the heading, I write a subheading "Unknown Perpetrator". My first entry under this subheading is "guy in bar". What can I do about him? I've seen the CCTV. The guy's looks weren't particularly distinctive. If he was behind this, surely he'd never be stupid enough to go back to that bar, so me planning a trip there next Saturday night with Penny to see if he comes in again would be a waste of time. Besides, Penny wouldn't agree to it. I wouldn't recognise him if I went there by myself. The gardai had no idea who he was.

I put the words "cul-de sac" beside his name, reluctant to write "dead end". Not only does it sound too negative, but "dead" is just too close to the bone for me right now.

Under that I write "another person". This one is wide open. Could someone random have come into Penny's house and taken me? Why would anyone even want to do that? Why would anyone care enough about me to take the risk, and why then? A house like Penny's is one that anyone with a bit of sense would assume has CCTV. But then, I can't account for how someone else would act in that situation. Maybe the person who did this was on drugs and didn't even think about the CCTV. Or maybe, as Penny says, it just didn't happen. It seems unlikely even to me that someone came in.

I put a note beside this entry saying "possible, but how to prove it?" It bothers me that I don't know what I can do to move that line of thought forwards, but at least it does seem like the most unlikely option. Sadly, far more likely is the possibility that someone closer to home is responsible for what happened to me. Even if a stranger took me from Penny's home and knew where to bring me back to, would someone who didn't know me risk returning to the scene of their crime even if they'd had a huge attack of the guilts? It just doesn't make any sense at all that they would. But someone who knew me and who reconsidered would have more of a chance of making it all go away by pretending it never happened. Particularly if it was Jake, Penny or Richard, all of whom could easily get back into Penny's house.

I write another heading: "Known Perpetrator". With a shaking hand, I then write the first name of the people I need to consider: "Jake".

An avalanche of guilt causes me to drop the pen as soon as I've written Jake's name, particularly after Brian has said that he has an alibi and Brian believes he's not in any way responsible for this. I close my eyes and remind myself of a few things. How many articles have I read where murder victims were found to have been killed by their partners or spouses? How many of those killers were rejected by the object of their affection?

Although I know Jake to be one of the nicest, most decent souls on the planet, I try to look at the situation objectively. Jake is my spurned former partner. I am the person who destroyed his dreams of the future. And while I've never seen him exhibit anything that would indicate the potential to abduct a woman and leave her for dead, I've only known Jake for a very short period of time. The gardai are sure they've investigated him fully and they're confident he didn't leave Ronan's house, but what if Jake has somehow doctored the CCTV when he came back from Ronan's house?

He used to work as a video editor for a TV station before he took up his current role as the manager of the Irish arts council. It wouldn't surprise me if he had the technical know-how to do something like that. But the real question is – would he be capable of hurting me?

Perhaps it comes down to which emotion is stronger in people – love or hate – and which one holds the most power over our actions. Which one drives Jake?

I thought I knew the answer to that. Now, all I know is that I know nothing any more.

I write "strong possibility" beside Jake's name, wondering how it's all come to this as I do so. Under Jake's name, I write "Penny".

Even though Penny's my newest friend in terms of how long I've known her compared to the other people I hold as friends, she's the one I spend the most time with now. Despite her busy life, she's child-free and therefore seems to have more time to meet up than my other friends with children, who seem to be tied to their routines of school runs and work, with children's classes in the evenings and at weekends.

I can't think of any possible reason Penny would have to want to hurt me or give me a scare. We haven't had a serious disagreement about anything. It's certainly not down to jealousy. I don't have anything that Penny doesn't have. Penny has *everything*. She's someone whom everyone wants to know in the hope that her success and self-confidence will rub off them, but she's very selective about who she lets into her life.

She guards her time preciously because time means money. I've often thought that she wouldn't have let an ordinary, mid-level career person like me into her life at all if it wasn't for the connection to Jake. I wouldn't be at all surprised if she phased me out now that Jake and I are no longer together. If I remove myself from the friendship and look at it objectively, I'd have to say that much as we get on well, our friendship isn't old enough or deep enough for her to see it as a lifelong thing, either – or so I'd imagine.

She wouldn't cut me out straight away, though. Like Declan, she's too smart for moves like that. She might need me again for something work related. Penny always keeps in with her contacts, which would be why she hasn't cut me off yet, even though it's over with Jake, if cutting me off was something she wanted to do.

The ending of our friendship is something I've never even thought about before and I realise that it's a highly unpleasant one. I enjoy my time with Penny. While she can be overbearing, she's always the first one in line to try to help out when there's a problem. And in her own unique way she's been supportive since my abduction, even if she doesn't believe that that's what it was. However, the fact is undeniable that I disappeared from *her* house. I was returned to *her* house. *Her* CCTV was conveniently broken. If someone close to me has done this, she'd be the one with the means to do it and get away with it.

But the big question is, *why?* What would her motivation possibly be to do such a messed-up thing? She doesn't even seem all that annoyed with me for breaking up with Jake. She was stoical about it, knowing the reason why I did it and understanding to some extent.

Now that I'm actually going through this process of analysing everyone around me, I'm starting to wonder if I'm actually going mad, after all.

I write Richard's name down next. Although he barely speaks to me, there's something about Richard I don't like. My nose for a story instinctively tells me that Richard is a man with something to hide. The fact that he's always avoided talking to me or getting to know me in any way when we're in mutual company also indicates to me that he doesn't want to get to know a journalist. In my experience, if someone doesn't want to get to know me, they're trying to keep something under wraps. And yes, I've written quite a few articles about the banking sector over the last year, but nothing related to the bank he works for. Maybe I've touched on something relating to something he doesn't want to get out there.

Again, this is a lot of ifs and buts and maybes, but I need to look at all angles. Richard was there that night. He has no affection for me or friendship with me. He's in a very high-up position in his career and surely he didn't get there without a degree of ruthlessness in the competitive industry he's in. However, the same could be said of Penny.

If Penny was responsible, she'd need help. She'd never be able to drag me in and out of the house on her own. If it was her, Richard must have helped her. If it was Richard, he'd have easily managed it. Richard is a behemoth of a man, around six foot five and of a very broad build. I put the words "strong possibility" beside both of their names, hating myself for suspecting Penny but telling myself that this needs to be done.

Barbara, Rose and Gabrielle seem to be unlikely candidates. Barbara has three children, one of whom is only three months old. It took a miracle to get her out the day all this happened. Her new son is still waking up through the night and her husband works night shifts, so unless she walked out of the house in the middle of the night and left her three children to fend for themselves, it's highly unlikely that she had anything to do with what happened. Neither her family nor her husband's live close by. She can't find people to mind her children at the drop of a hat.

Rose went out after she left us that night. Not only does she have alibis, but I know Rose and her drinking patterns. She hits a point where, after a long day, she'll literally just fall asleep on a table and then she's out cold until the morning. There's no way Rose would have been capable of even staying awake beyond a certain point in the night. The fact that she even managed to go out again that night after our meet-up was good going for her.

As Gabrielle is heavily pregnant, she was probably fast asleep when all this happened to me. She'd spent the entire day yawning on our day out. She said she'd been feeling the strain recently of working full-time and minding her three-year-old daughter while in the third trimester of pregnancy. Gabrielle's probably the last person one could possibly imagine who'd have the wherewithal to do something like what happened to me.

Plus, they're all tiny women, none of them taller than five foot four. Unless the three of them worked together, they wouldn't have had a hope of carrying me. And again, why in the world would they want to hurt me? Not only have I known them a long time and clearly nothing has happened to me in the course of our friendship up to this point, but what possible reason in the world would they have to carry out such an act of hatred?

I close my eyes for a second as the realisation of what I'm doing hits me again. I hate myself for doing this, for questioning every single person I hold dear in my life. I try not to question what kind of a person I am for thinking all this. I could be fighting for my life again in the future. I know the person who did this to me has the potential to hurt me again. It might not happen today, or tomorrow, or next week, but what if one day I'm going about my business, my guard down again when all this unpleasantness has settled down, and I'm targeted all over again? And what else am I meant to do when nobody else believes me or supports me in finding out the truth?

I write "highly unlikely" beside the names of Barbara, Rose and Gabrielle, and then write Declan's name.

When it comes to my ex-husband, I really don't know what to think any more. By the time we separated, I felt like I'd never known him. His over-the-top reaction to me asking for a divorce reinforced that feeling of him being a total stranger. He is, however, no stranger. He's my former husband, a man I spent a portion of my life with and a man who could see a twisted justification in being angry at me because his life hasn't worked out the way he wanted.

At the time of our last face-to-face contact, when he'd turned up at my house drunk, he certainly didn't seem, or sound, stable. He was highly strung and seemed to be in a very bad place in his life. Brian said that the gardaí are satisfied that Declan had nothing to do with this incident because Declan was in Frankfurt, but out of everyone I know, Declan would be the most resourceful in both setting this thing up and hiding it. He could easily have organised for someone to follow me and hurt me. Just because he wasn't in the country doesn't mean he's not behind this.

Declan's the type of man who gets an idea in his head and then just does it. Nothing stands in his way. Of course, this very aspect of his character was the root of the problems in our marriage. Although on paper what happened to me sounds bizarre and impossible to implement in a real-life situation, Declan could do it. But would he *want* to? Surely if he had any residual anger towards me or if I was on his mind in any way, there'd have been more frequent contact from him before this happened? This possibility doesn't add up, either. Nothing is adding up, no matter how I look at it or what angle I take. I just write one word beside Declan's name: "possible".

Who else is in my life? Mam, Claire and Sandra don't count. Surely, no matter what, my own flesh and blood wouldn't do this to me. Sandra and I might not get on great, but she's my sister. I won't even consider my family. And although I understand that for some people in life the biggest enemies are sadly within their own family group, we've never been that bad. I can't even go there.

I look back at the list. My key takeaways from it are that if it's a stranger, I'm very limited in what I can do, but I must think of something. If it's someone closer to home, it's most likely to be either Jake, Penny or Richard, with Declan also in the frame as a possibility. Out of those four, on paper, wouldn't anyone suggest that crime of passion is the most obvious one? And as Declan has had years away from our relationship, that means Jake is the most likely suspect.

If only I could remember what happened after I walked into the pub. *Fuck* that pub. If only we'd never gone there.

I can't get the pub out of my head as I sit there sipping my coffee. I grasp at memories from when we went in there, but they're slippery. While I can vaguely remember walking in, the drink must have hit me at that point. Sometimes in the past when I've been on nights out where too much alcohol has been consumed, I'll be told a story about something that happened and I'll initially have no recollection of it at all. And then, like a flash of lightning, I remember it. Is there any chance at all that this will happen this time?

I don't expect to remember anything after I took the Rohypnol, but if I could even remember talking to the man who supposedly did this to me, that would help. There must have been a good few minutes of talking done before he somehow managed to slip it into my drink. If I could just picture his face, at least I'd have something to bring back to the gardai.

I need to go there. Maybe if I sit down at the bar in the pub, something might come back to me. It's a long shot, but it's all I've got right now. After throwing my list into my handbag, I take money for the coffee out, leave it on the table and dart out of the coffee shop.

It takes me ten minutes to get from the cafe to the Kildare Lounge. I'm surprised, really, that we ended up there that night. It's a real old man's pub rather than the trendy hipster types we usually go to on nights out. Barbara and Gabrielle always say that because they never get to go out, they want to try the new pubs when we do. I have a feeling that I was the one to suggest this place, being a fan of old-man pubs, but I honestly can't remember. As a traditional Irish pub built towards the end of the nineteenth century, some would argue that it looks ancient and feels draughty unless you're lucky enough to get a plum seat in front of the open fire, but others find the snugs and partitions throughout the pub cosy and intimate. The upstairs section looks and feels just like sitting in a 1980s sitting room, complimented by peeling wallpaper and a sticky carpet.

I walk in through the grocery and snug bar. It's my favourite part of the pub, having once been a grocery and still containing not only a low grocery counter, but also a cosy snug. I've often sat here, enjoying leisurely drinks. However, this time I make my way to the back of the bar, where Penny said I was when I met the guy I was talking to.

I hope to be instantly flooded with memories – that perhaps even the smell of the place will bring something back to me – but I'm not. I walk in and nothing happens. I go to the bar and sit down. When a barmaid appears, I order a sparkling water. I notice that my voice sounds shaky and wonder if the barmaid has noticed it, too.

"Em . . . sorry, but were you working here last Saturday night?" I say to the barmaid when she returns with my drink.

"I was, yeah," she says.

"Do you by any chance remember me? I was here with a group of friends. Someone spiked my drink and I collapsed."

I can tell straight away by the expression on her face that I've said the wrong thing.

"I don't know anything about that," she says.

"I'm not looking for someone to blame," I say quickly. "At least, I'm not apportioning any blame to the pub at all. I was just wondering if you might remember seeing me here talking to a man, that's all. He's the one I'm interested in finding out about. We were in this section of the pub."

"I'm sorry. I don't remember you," she says. "I was working upstairs on Saturday night."

"Okay, no problem. Is there a manager here that I can speak to? I believe the gardai were in touch with the management here about the possibility of getting CCTV of that night."

"The manager here is Greg, but he just popped out a while ago to meet a supplier," she says.

"When will he be back?"

"Hard to say. He'll be gone at least an hour," she says. "Could be longer."

Tears of frustration spring to my eyes. Every single little step to try to move this situation forwards seems to be such hard work.

I blink them away, but the barmaid must have seen them, because she says, "I can ring him and see if he'll speak to you, if you like? He has a hands-free kit in his car to use while driving."

"That would be great," I instantly say. "Thank you."

She takes out her phone and rings the manager. After explaining the situation to him, she hands me the phone and says he's happy to talk to me.

"Hi, Greg. Thanks for speaking to me," I say.

I explain my situation as succinctly as possible and ask him if he remembers seeing me speaking to a guy.

"I do remember seeing your friends helping you outside all right," he says. "I just happened to be in that section at the time checking something with one of the lads working there and I saw them bringing you out, so I followed them to see if they needed any help. As I told the gardai, though, I have no memory of the man you were speaking to. I didn't notice him at all. The pub is always absolutely packed to the rafters on Saturday night, so someone really has to give us a reason to notice them before we'll remember them," he says.

"I guess I'm one of those types, so," I can't help but say.

"Ah, you weren't the first and you won't be the last. Besides, from what I heard, it wasn't your fault. This man you're talking about is believed to have slipped something into your drink, the gardai told me. From our point of view, I asked the two barmen who were working in the section you were in that night and they don't remember serving you. They'd never serve anyone who seems to be strongly under the influence already, you see, so you must have been okay when you came in."

I'm torn between doing a fist pump – I knew I hadn't been that drunk! – and tempering my relief at his words with the knowledge that of course the manager of the pub where I was carried out of would say that. He's never going to say that his staff sold me drink regardless of whether or not I looked legless. I probably didn't, though. I always seem to wear my level of intoxication well and Penny said I looked okay going in, as far as she was concerned. Clearly, my other friends must have thought the same.

Also, Brian has seen the CCTV. If he thought I looked very drunk when I went to the bar, if that was in the coverage of the CCTV, surely the pub would be in trouble and he'd have mentioned that to me. However, I might have been okay going in there – or at the very least, I might have *looked* okay – but clearly I wasn't okay for long when I can't remember anything beyond walking through the front door of the pub!

"Did anything else strange happen that night, Greg? Did any other women seem to be out of control, or did anyone else collapse?" That's something that never occurred to me to ask the gardai. "I'm wondering if perhaps he might have found another victim after I was taken home."

"Not that I observed," Greg says, "and none of the staff reported anything like that happening, either."

"I was just wondering if maybe another woman might

have been able to identify him," I say. "I'm very surprised the quality of your CCTV is so bad and that's not a problem for you guys," I can't help adding.

"We've never really had reason to question the quality of it before. Nothing that bad has happened here."

"Take it from me, Greg, bad things happen. Thanks a lot for your help," I say before hanging up and handing the phone back to the barmaid.

"Did you by any chance find a lost phone in here recently?" There's no harm in asking, surely.

"I'll take a look in the office. We often get phones handed in."

I name the model of the phone I had and describe the pattern on its cover.

The barmaid disappears but returns soon after holding a phone that looks distinctly like mine.

"This looks like the phone you described."

"Yes, that's it! Thank you so much! You've saved me the price of eventually buying another smartphone."

"You're welcome. We usually ring someone in the person's phone list if the phone isn't password protected, but your phone is dead and we don't have a charger for that model here. We figured someone would come in looking for it anyway and we'd match it up with the owner easily – that phone cover is distinctive."

"You don't know where exactly it was found, or who handed it in, by any chance?"

"I've no idea. One of the other people working here just told me it was there if anyone was looking for it. I'd imagine they won't remember, either. Saturday nights are always crazy busy here."

"I understand. Thanks so much for your help."

Delighted as I am to have my phone back, a part of me was hoping that the phone would be found somewhere that would help me to identify where I was brought to when I was taken to the cottage. Now, it's clear that the phone never left this building.

I give the barmaid the price of a drink for herself for her help and leave, glad to be leaving with my phone. Perhaps there's some information on it from the day I went missing that might help me. But I can't help feeling disappointed that visiting the pub hasn't brought back any memories. I make my way home, wondering what to do next and feeling hopeless when I come up with nothing.

Chapter 17

I spend the rest of the day in a state of heightened anxiousness. I try to mask it from Mam when we return home, though, as she's watching me too closely for me to feel comfortable. I can see the worry on her face every time she looks at me.

When I got home from the pub, I charged my phone and checked the messages I both received and sent before everything happened. There had been quite a few interchanges between Jake and me earlier that day. It had started with him saying he hoped I would enjoy my day out with the ladies. I had sent back a curt *Thanks.* When I read the texts, I realised that I remembered receiving his message and sending my reply. That much, at least, was not a blur, but it had been early in the day and I remember everything from then.

I presumed that Penny had mentioned what was going on that day – I certainly hadn't told Jake about it. I was annoyed that Jake had even acknowledged it, because I was trying to make a clean break from our relationship. It was easier that way and I felt he was muddying the waters by texting as if nothing had changed.

A few hours later, he'd sent a text saying that if we were going to a particular bar in Temple Bar that serves craft beer, I should make sure to try one that he named in the text and highly recommended. I probably should have ignored the text, but I replied saying that I was uncomfortable with him texting me in the aftermath of our break-up and I needed a bit of space. That I'd be grateful if he didn't text again and how I hoped he understood.

I remember thinking that this day out was the first time I'd managed to put the break-up to the back of my mind at all and I was angry that he was dragging it back into my mind by texting me. I felt I'd made it clear when we broke up that I needed a total break, yet he kept contacting me. And I couldn't help feeling that he was disrespecting my wishes by texting like we were buddies and all was fine.

He replied saying that he was only trying to keep things civil and that he hoped we'd somehow get to the point where we could at least be friends. I didn't reply to that. I didn't want to give him false hope. I knew us being friends just wasn't a viable option.

Other than that, there was nothing significant to note on my phone. I didn't see any new contacts added to my list. I wonder when I lost my phone. Was it before or after I met the guy in the bar? Presumably after. Maybe it fell out of my pocket or handbag when I collapsed. I don't remember where I had it.

I pace around the kitchen, trying to find something to do to take my mind off my worries. Something has been preying on my mind all day and I can't shake it, something I voiced to Penny when I asked her on the phone for all the details of what happened that night. I'm trying to work out why the guy in the pub would drop Rohypnol in my drink just then if he wanted to do certain things to me, which I presume he did. Why else would he be carrying Rohypnol with him?

As I now know from googling the drug, it can take effect quickly. Surely that man didn't think I'd leave the pub with him a few minutes after we started speaking. What was there to gain from him drugging a woman's drink and having her going unconscious straight away? Shouldn't he have tried to lure me back to his house or something and then have drugged me there? Although from his perspective, if a woman was happy to go back to his house, maybe there was an assumption that consensual sex could be on the cards and therefore there'd be no need to drug her. Surely he'd wait and see, anyway.

Is that even the point, or was something more sinister at play with the Rohypnol? How am I supposed to second-guess the intentions of a person who'd want to give someone Rohypnol? When I said all this to Penny, she said some people do things like this just for kicks. Maybe she's right. It just all seems so pointless though, for someone to do this to another person when they wouldn't even get anything from it. It's so hard to make sense of any of it.

I decide to clean out the fridge and rearrange all my food in the presses, jobs I hate doing. If anything will keep my mind off my woes for a while, that will.

I'm taking the food out of the fridge five minutes later, when the doorbell rings. I answer the door to see Penny standing there with two hampers: one of chocolate and one of fruit.

"Gifts from work," she says immediately. "I think you deserve them right now more than I do. Ah, Jackie, hello!" Penny says as Mam comes up behind me.

"Hello, Penny! My, my, you're very good to be calling round with such lovely gifts. Aren't they lovely, Katie?"

"Lovely. Very lavish. But honestly, there's no need."

"There's every need. You've had a hard time and you need your friends to spoil you."

"Come in, Penny, come in! I was just about to put the kettle on."

"I can't stay long, Jackie, but thanks. A quick cuppa would be great."

Penny comes in and it's not long before she's holding court with Mam. It's nice, but I almost feel extraneous to events. Mam's definitely feeling the Penny effect without Penny even trying to make her feel so. I smile ruefully to myself as I unpack the hampers. Somehow, I can't see Penny ever getting herself into the situation I'm in.

True to her word, Penny doesn't stay long. She has the promised cuppa, we retire to the sitting room, she gets us another round of tea to give Mam a break and off she goes. While it was nice of her to call with such lovely gifts, I can't help but feel relieved when she's gone. I feel like a hopeless case who everyone has to keep an eye on, even though I feel terrible for thinking like that after Penny was so generous.

After dinner, Mam insists that Claire, Sandra and I watch *Coronation Street* with her before Sandra goes home. Sandra's anxious to leave straight after dinner as her husband is looking after the kids tonight and she wants to get a few jobs done when she gets home. But Mam points out that the kids will be in bed by the time she gets home anyway and there's no household job that can't wait if push comes to shove. And while Sandra agrees to stay, I know it's more for Mam's sake than mine.

It's obvious that this whole episode has rattled Sandra, too, and has brought back bad memories. We've just had yet another argument. I let slip that I went to the pub and asked a few questions, although I tried to make it sound like I was just passing and decided to go in. And when I mentioned that the manager said the barmen wouldn't have served me if I was falling around the place drunk, Sandra went into a rant about how they'd say that to cover their asses either way. Which in fairness is something I'd thought myself at the time – and that my drinking is undoubtedly the main thing behind me being in so much trouble right now.

I should have said nothing, yet I couldn't help myself and ended up squabbling with her. I wanted to prove that I don't have a drink problem to the extent that Sandra seems to think I have. It feels as if she actually *wants* me to have a drink problem and I'm getting tired of it. Still, though, I should have had the sense to keep my mouth shut. I'm thankful that the TV will prevent too much further talking for now.

As the *Coronation Street* theme tune plays at the end, I realise that I've watched the entire thing and yet couldn't name a single character or relay any of the scenes I've just watched. My mind won't stop racing, trying to work out what I can or should do next, and yet all that racing is getting me nowhere. I have no idea what to do next.

Just as Mam picks up the remote to flick the channel, no doubt hoping to lure Sandra into watching *Fair City* as well before she goes, a voiceover says that after the break there will be a show about missing people in Ireland.

"Oh, leave it on, Mam," I say. "*Fair City* isn't actually on tonight – there's a football match on. I'd like to watch that show about the missing people."

"Oh no, don't go upsetting yourself watching that," Mam says.

"Why would it upset me?" I can't help saying. "It was all in my head, remember? I'm not missing!"

"Missing people is an upsetting topic in general," Sandra chimes in.

"Well, it's a reality," I say. "We should be aware of it and have enough respect for those people not to change the channel just because it makes for uncomfortable viewing."

I know I sound a bit snotty, but I don't care. This could have been *my* reality, even though nobody believes me.

Mam puts down the remote, albeit somewhat reluctantly. "It's your house."

What I see over the course of the next hour chills me to the bone. I watch as one woman after another is introduced to us as a person – her age, where she's from, what she looks like, what was going on in her life around the time she disappeared. Each woman – six in total in the documentary – disappeared suddenly and unaccountably. Although the gardai launched large-scale searches to find them, no trace of them was ever found again. Not even significant clues were found as to what happened to them.

I watch in horror as a picture of a beautiful German student flashes up on the screen at the start of the documentary. She was twenty-one at the time of her disappearance in 1995 and was living in North Dublin. She'd left the house early on the day she'd vanished and had left a note for her housemates to say that she was going hillwalking in the Dublin mountains. She was never seen again.

The documentary moves on to Charlotte, a 35-year-old woman who told her husband she was going out for a walk one night around the local estates in Portlaoise. She left the house with her Sony Walkman cassette player and earphones in 1994 and never came home. Neither did forty-year-old Catherine, who went walking her dog one summer's evening in Kildare in 1998. The dog was found wandering the streets near Catherine's home, but Catherine had disappeared.

My sense of horror increases further when we're told about twenty-year-old Anna, who disappeared after walking to her local village in Carlow in 1999 to buy the Sunday papers for her family. She was seen by a neighbour that morning walking back towards her country home with the Sunday papers in her arms, a half-mile from her house. She never returned, nor were the papers found.

A picture flashes up on the screen of fifteen-year-old Louise, who went missing after walking home from basketball practice close to her home in County Kerry in 2002. It's heartbreaking to see. She looks about ten in the picture. Only a child.

Finally, we hear about a student who was home from college for the weekend in Thurles, County Tipperary and went to her local nightclub one Saturday night in 2003. She left the nightclub early without telling any of her friends. She was seen on CCTV leaving and going to a nearby fish and chip shop. After that, there were no further sightings of her.

How did nobody see anything? How could these women have disappeared without any trace at all? And yet, after what happened to me, it's not that unthinkable in my eyes.

The narrator of the show states that it's believed by the gardai that the disappearances were the work of a serial killer. That killer has never been caught.

When the show ends, there's complete silence in the room. Sandra eventually breaks it.

"I should really go now," she says, standing up. "I've stayed longer than I meant to and Liam will be expecting me home."

Mam seems relieved that something has been said to break the tension. She stands up, too.

"Drive safely now, love, won't you? The roads are very wet tonight."

Claire and I say goodbye to Sandra, and Mam walks her to the door.

"Are you okay after watching that?" Claire asks. "You look as white as a sheet."

"Any of those women could have been me," I say. "I know you don't believe me, Claire, but I know what happened. Maybe the circumstances weren't exactly the same, but the essence of it was. I could be a missing person, just like those women. If my abductor hadn't decided to come back for me, I'd probably be dead by now."

Claire says nothing.

"I know you don't know what to think about all this any more, Claire," I say, "but *I* know what happened. What I need to do now is work out what I'm going to do about it."

Mam comes back into the room. I excuse myself, saying that I need to sort out my laundry. I leave the room quickly before Mam can offer to do it for me.

Mam and Claire eventually leave, although it took a lot to persuade Mam to let Claire drive her home and leave me on my own for the night. I badly needed the space from everyone in my family and I'm relieved to see them go. As I lie on the bed staring into space after their departure, I can't get away from the theory I put to Penny before: that maybe the man in the pub followed Penny and me in a taxi back to Penny's house. Even if he didn't hang around, he knew where I was. Isn't it possible that he came back during the night and took me without Penny or Richard hearing?

Penny had had quite a bit to drink as well, after all. Even if she's saying she only drank half of her drinks in some of the pubs, that would still amount to quite a bit with the wine at dinner. And Penny mentioned before that Richard always has a few whiskies on a Saturday night. Perhaps he'd been drinking before we got back. They'd both have been tired from looking after me earlier that night, too. Maybe they were out for the count and didn't hear him get in. But Penny didn't mention any indications of a break-in.

Something hits me. I sit up.

I got drunk in Galway once, a few years ago. I was on a hen night and we all drank far too much. When we all got back to the hotel, I felt very sick and thought I needed some air. I left the hotel without telling anyone and went wandering around the town. I must have walked around for a full hour and then, in my drunken wisdom, I decided to walk down to the prom to watch the sea at night.

I fell asleep against a wall on the beach and woke up when it was bright, feeling nauseous. I hobbled back to the hotel and went straight to bed. The next morning – or afternoon, really – I was too embarrassed about my night-time ramble to tell anyone. Why I decided to do it in the first place was beyond me. I could easily have been taken advantage of in the state I was in.

I ask myself over and over what I potentially might have done in Penny's house after she and Richard went to sleep. If I went walking once while drunk, isn't it possible that I might have done it again while drunk and drugged? While the Rohypnol caused me to black out, that doesn't necessarily mean I remained that way for the entire night, does it? I realise I can't say for sure. I don't know enough about the effects of the drug to be able to say with certainty what I could or couldn't do.

But I could find out.

I run to my laptop and research everything I can about Rohypnol online. Of course, I shouldn't be relying on a search engine for my information. I should go to a healthcare professional. But who's going to entertain my questioning? I'm sure as far as the doctor who treated me on the day I was admitted is concerned, that's old news. Hospitals are always insanely busy anyway, so the likelihood of getting that doctor to speak to me about this several days later when he and all the other staff are dealing with life-and-death situations every hour of the day is slim. I, like everyone else in the country, know how much pressure the hospitals are under. I had my window with him when I was there and I've a feeling that's as much as I'll get.

Half an hour later, I can only conclude that it's entirely possible that I returned to consciousness after Penny put me to bed. According to the information I've read, the sedative effects of the drug would have begun around fifteen minutes after I ingested it in my drink. The peak effect is supposed to occur two hours after ingestion, but I assume from what I've read that I blanked out immediately because the drug was taken in combination with a large quantity of alcohol.

Then as the night wore on and the alcohol in my system would have started to wear off somewhat, there's every chance that I could have woken and not remembered. But would I have been able to walk? The articles I read said the drug can cause impaired motor skills and difficulty standing or walking. It also said that Rohypnol can completely wipe the memory for a period of time. Is it actually possible that I made it outside somehow and just can't remember a thing about it?

Maybe all this had nothing to do with the man who drugged me. Perhaps someone else took advantage of my state and took me somewhere with the intention of doing me harm then had second thoughts. How did he get me back into the house without anyone noticing? It sounds unlikely, but not impossible, surely.

It's all a lot of ifs, buts and maybes. Taken in its entirety, it all sounds unlikely. But, as I remind myself for what feels like the millionth time, something happened. Every possibility needs to be considered if I'm to get to the bottom of this.

The days are ticking on. If I did go outside in the middle of the night and anyone saw anything, their memories are soon going to fade. I can hardly go door to door in Penny's neighbourhood and ask if anyone saw me wandering around at a time I can't even precisely pinpoint.

After midnight, the phone rings while I'm still sitting in front of my laptop, googling things related to Rohypnol and making notes in a Word document about possible scenarios that could have happened. It's a withheld number. I let it ring, dubious about answering it when I don't know who's ringing.

In the next two minutes, I receive three more calls from the withheld number. I'm starting to get worried now. Who would be calling me at this hour unless something is wrong? My mind starts to run away with itself thinking of the possibilities and when the withheld number rings my phone for a fifth time, I answer.

"Yes?"

"Katie?"

"Who is this?" I ask, although I'm pretty sure I recognise the voice.

"You've hardly forgotten me already, I'm sure. In fact, I *know* you haven't."

As I thought. Declan. And he's pissed.

"Why are you ringing me at this hour of the night, Declan?" I can't keep the annoyance out of my voice.

"*I* should be the one asking *you* questions. Like, why did the gardai contact me today to find out where I was last Saturday night?"

I hold the phone out as Declan launches into a drunken diatribe about how he doesn't want to be dragged into whatever trouble I'm after getting myself in, after all the trouble I've caused him. His rage meanders into tales of woe about all the things that have gone wrong for him since we broke up. By the time he's graduated on to how he wishes he'd never met me in the first place, I've had enough.

"Declan, shut the hell up. *You* are the one who left *me*. I've accepted that with grace over the years, I feel, and I've never given you too much of a hard time over it. I've moved on. The gardai contacted you as a matter of course, just like they contacted everyone else in my life to check on their whereabouts. It wasn't anything personal.

"I'm sure you were probably too drunk last Saturday night after a full day of drinking even to consider kidnapping someone, quite aside from the fact that you were abroad, from what I hear. You'd probably have done well to get your zip down in time to piss at the time I was taken. Now, kindly fuck off and leave me alone. I have enough to worry about."

I hang up, shaking. Declan could be very intimidating when he was angry. I'm just glad the conversation was over the phone and not face to face.

It takes a while before I eventually fall asleep, wondering what tomorrow will bring.

Chapter 18

Tomorrow brings trouble all round.

I wake to the sound of the doorbell being pressed over and over. I instantly look at my phone on my bedside table to see what time it is, having taken my watch off before going to bed: 7 a.m. I have eight missed calls from Sandra.

I run downstairs and peep out of the door. Sandra's standing there, looking harassed.

"I've been ringing this doorbell for ten minutes!" she says before I get a chance to ask her what's wrong.

"Oh, sorry . . . You know I'm a sound sleeper."

"Why the fuck didn't you answer your phone? You message me at 3 a.m. telling me to call round and you won't even answer your phone when I call you? What's going on?"

"What do you mean?"

"What do you mean, what do I mean? What's going on, Katie? What is it now?"

I can only stare at Sandra while I try to make sense of what's going on here.

"Oh, let me in, for fuck's sake." Sandra pushes past me and storms into the hall. "So?"

186

"Sandra, I didn't ask you to call round. I don't know what's going on here—"

"So what's this, then?"

Sandra unlocks her phone and hands it to me. There's a text on it from me, sent at three in the morning, saying that she needs to call round straight away.

"I didn't write that," I say. "I've been fast asleep all night."

"So it just sent itself, did it?"

"I . . . I don't know."

"So, can we just ascertain here that nothing is actually wrong? Nothing bad has happened."

"No. I've literally just woken."

"Christ, Katie, you gave me such a fright! I've had to drop everything to rush over here. Liam will be late for work now because we couldn't leave the kids on their own in the house. Such messing about! You must have sent that text in your sleep. Were you having nightmares or something?"

"Sandra, I did *not* send that text!"

"I don't see anyone else here."

"I must have been hacked again," I say.

"Again?"

I tell Sandra the story of my email account being hacked.

"But who would do that? And you never hear of anyone's phone getting hacked, Katie."

"I know, but I didn't send that message."

"Christ Almighty. I don't even know what to say. Okay, look, if everything's fine here, I need to get home."

"Okay. Sorry. I can't explain what's just happened, but it wasn't me."

"Sure, sure. I really have to go. Talk to you later."

Sandra leaves as quickly as she entered. I stand at the

door until she drives away, wondering what in the name of God just happened.

I'm still thinking about it all when Rose touches base.

"There are things about Jake you don't know," Rose says immediately when I answer the phone.

She'd texted at 11.30 a.m. and said she needed to speak to me as soon as possible. I was instantly worried – her tone sounded off – but not enough to panic. I thought the issue might not be directly related to me, anyway. That maybe Rose needed a sounding board to talk about her problems. She didn't have a partner, a lot of her friends were married with children now and she didn't get on very well with her family. She didn't have many people in her network to talk to at the drop of a hat.

Rose and I have been friends a long time and whenever she needed a friendly ear, I tried to be there for her. I told her to feel free to call whenever suited and she suggested ringing at 1 p.m. when she was on lunch. I just hoped that whatever was bothering her wasn't anything too serious and she wasn't in any kind of difficulty.

But now it sounds like it's me who has reason to worry.

"Have you just seen a preview of the new series of *The Secret Millionaire*?" I say, trying to diffuse the tension by keeping my tone light.

Rose worked for the national television broadcaster and always had the inside scoop on new shows.

"No, I'm afraid Jake isn't in the line-up for our latest set of secret millionaires. It's nothing as good as that, I'm afraid – or anything good at all."

"Jesus, Rose, get me scared, why don't you! What is it?"

"I met Anna this morning. She was in the studio

188

working on a new show. We went for a coffee at break time to catch up. She told me a few things about her time with Jake – and afterwards."

Anna is Jake's former girlfriend. She used to work with Rose in another TV station. In fact, I met Jake through Rose. I was out with Rose one night when she bumped into Jake, whom she'd occasionally met at work dos with Anna when Jake and Anna were still going out. He was with a group of friends the night we bumped into him. Jake and I hit it off instantly. At the end of the night, he asked for my number – and that was that. We were inseparable from that time until recently.

"How did Jake come up in conversation?"

"She asked how things were between you. I didn't know why at the time. A few minutes later, it was clear that she was looking for a chance to warn you about a few things so that you wouldn't go through what she did. I didn't know if you wanted her to know things were over between you, so I just said things were going fine as far as I knew. And then she just started talking . . . "

My stomach churns. "What did she say?"

"That Jake was intense. Super, super intense. She said they were only together a few months when he asked her to marry him."

Tears instantly spring to my eyes. Just like he'd done with me! When we'd spoken about former partners, he'd dismissed his relationship with Anna as being nothing serious.

"What else?"

"When she ended it with him, she said he became obsessed with her. Ringing her morning, noon and night, waiting outside her workplace at close of business and trying to force her to talk to him. The word she used to describe him was stalker, Katie. She had to threaten to call the gardai to get him to back off. I'm really sorry. I hate having to tell you this, but I felt you should know."

"Why? Do you think he's the one who put me in the cottage?"

"Oh, no, that's not it. I just thought you should know in case you ever consider taking him back. I would strongly advise against it, bearing Anna's story in mind."

"But Jake didn't behave like that with me when we broke up," I say. "He was upset, but when I told him to give me space, he respected that. He contacted me, yes, but he wasn't over the top about it. It was mostly just texts."

"Well, maybe he wasn't as obsessed with you as he was with Anna. I don't know. All I'm saying is if you're ever tempted to go back with him, do it at your peril."

"If you feel that way, don't you think it's feasible that he's behind my disappearance?" I say, testing the waters.

Rose says nothing.

I knew it. "You don't believe me, either."

"It's not that, Katie. I understand that you fully *believe* it happened, but it *had* to have been the drugs. It's just not possible that all of what you said happened could possibly have taken place in such a short timeframe, especially when both Penny and Richard were in the house all the time."

"In light of what you've just said, who's to say they weren't covering for Jake?"

The thought, and the words, come unbidden. I instantly regret saying the thought out loud, but it's too late now.

"They wouldn't do that!"

"I didn't think my former boyfriend was someone who'd become obsessed with a woman and stalked her, but that's what you've just told me happened. Things aren't always what they seem, Rose. Isn't there even a part of you that believes me?"

"I . . . I really don't know what to think."

"Rose, some part of you must be worried that Jake might be a threat to me when you've told me this as a matter of urgency!"

"No, Katie. I just wanted to tell you as soon as possible because I'm so busy that things fall off the radar if I don't do them straight away. I just thought as well that it might help you to move on from the break-up if you heard that he isn't as great as you thought he was. That's all."

But that's not all now! What she's said gives me reason to believe my theory about Jake being behind all this, that it might have legs after all, despite evidence to the contrary.

"Maybe I've said too much. I know you're still in a bad place after everything that's happened recently. I don't want to make it any worse for you. I just thought you should know what I heard."

"Look, I appreciate your honesty, Rose. I just don't know what to think any more."

"You'll work it out," Rose says. "Keep your chin up. I'll be in touch, okay?"

"Yeah. Thanks, Rose. Bye."

I hang up. I'm trying not to choke on the golf ball that's erupted in my throat. Did I really know Jake at all? Or was I just another woman in a series to him, falling for all the same lines he'd spouted many times before?

I sit on the couch for a while after Rose's call, feeling completely numb. Then I do the only thing I can think of – I go to my computer and google Anna. This isn't the first time I've done this. I looked her up before when Jake and I had our first chat about former partners. Rightly or wrongly, I wanted to see what she looked like. Now, I just

191

want contact details for her. I have no idea yet what I'm going to say to her if I get them. I just need to do something.

First, I google Anna's full name and the word Facebook. It returns several women of the same name, but I know from googling her image before which one is the correct profile to click on. Her page is private and I currently only have a very limited view of the content of her page. That doesn't bother me – all I want is the ability to message her. I can see the "Message" button is enabled on her page. I'm not sure if she'll definitely be able to see a message from someone she's not connected with on Facebook though, so I google that, too. It seems that she'll receive a connection request when I send her a message and she can then choose to read it or not. I'm sure Rose has probably mentioned me by full name to Anna before, so I'm not sure if she'll be keen to accept a connection request from someone whom she'll recognise as being her ex-boyfriend's girlfriend – well, ex-girlfriend now.

However, I decide to go for it.

Hi Anna,

My name is Katie Turner and I'm Jake Ryan's former girlfriend. You and I have a mutual friend in common: Rose Doyle. I believe you went out with Jake, too. I hope this doesn't sound too strange, but there's something I'd really like to talk to you about if you'd be happy to talk to me. Don't worry, it's nothing for you to be alarmed about. I'd just like to have a chat with you about Jake if you'd be up for it, that's all. I'd love to hear back from you.

Thanks,

Katie

I press the Send icon. Surely it won't do any harm to talk to her, if she's willing to engage with me.

I could ring Jake and ask him about what Rose said, but what if he fills me with lies? Maybe it's better to play my cards close to my chest and try to get to Anna first.

It's not long before my thoughts return to Jake. I haven't heard from him since I texted him to tell him the gardai would be in contact with him – although his flowers arrived, they'd have been ordered before he got my text. The gardai seem to think he's innocent, but what if they're not taking this seriously and it suits them to close the case based on the fact that he was confirmed as being at his friend's house? What if he's fooled them somehow?

If the gardai aren't going to investigate further, that only leaves me. *I* am the only one who can save myself. If someone around me did it, I need to find evidence of that to ensure my future safety. But how do I do that?

Do I know any of Jake's passwords to email and Facebook accounts? Even as I'm thinking this, my face burns in shame. Normally, I'd never do something as intrusive as look at someone's private correspondence. But right now, nothing is normal. Normal was my old reality and it'll never return if I don't get to the bottom of what happened to me. And I need to start with Jake. I need access to everything that he uses.

It'll kill me to do it. The last thing I want to believe is that Jake would do me any harm. I *adored* him. I still do, although I try not to acknowledge that fact to myself too often now. It's easier that way. But I must do it, not just to Jake but to everyone in my life. If I don't, there's a chance that I might not be alive for much longer. If I have any doubts about what I'm doing, I need to remind myself that it really is as simple as that.

Then it hits me. I have a key to Jake's house. He'll be at work right now. And he always, but always, leaves himself logged into his various accounts on his home computer.

I immediately stand up and run to the kitchen to get my car keys. I almost shock myself at my reluctance even to think about what I'm doing. But the will to survive has brought out something primal in me that I didn't know was there. Right now, I'll do anything to protect myself.

Chapter 19

I park my car near a playground at the back of Jake's estate and walk the short distance from there to his house. He often referenced that playground when we were out for walks around the estate and the surrounding areas, saying we might be hanging around there ourselves someday as we walked past the families pushing children on swings and guiding little people up the steps of the slide. That was when I'd always walk faster and change the subject.

I turn into Jake's empty driveway and walk to the front door, the key in my hand. I ring the doorbell first, just in case. If he answers, I'm not sure what I'll even say – but I'm confident that he's not there. And I'm right – he doesn't come to the door. I put the key into the lock, turn it and push the door. I instantly hear the beep of his alarm. For the first time since I left my house, I have a moment of panic. What if he's changed his code? I run to the alarm and press in the code that I know. I close my eyes with relief when I hear the words "System unset", then open them again quickly. I bang the front door shut behind me. I have work to do.

I run upstairs to Jake's office. The house smells exactly

as it always does. It feels strange to be back. The smell is familiar, comforting and yet very bittersweet now. The office is exactly as it always is – untidy. Jake always seems to be too busy working to tidy his house, other than doing the bare minimum to keep things ticking over.

I sit down at the computer and press the On button. I know that Jake's password to his computer is just "Password", because he mentioned it once and we had a debate about it. I argued that it was crazy for someone not to change their password from the default when they got their home PC, but Jake didn't see the point of having yet another password that he might forget. He'd only have to write it down and leave it in front of the computer anyway, which defeated the purpose. Besides, he said it was highly unlikely that someone was going to come into his house and go up to his office to use his computer without him knowing about it, and even if they did, he had nothing to hide anyway.

You were wrong, Jake. And I'm going to find out if you were telling the truth when you said you had nothing to hide.

A wave of guilt crashes into my consciousness, but I try to ignore it. I'm protecting myself. Nobody else can or will.

I enter the password and the computer starts up. I go straight to an Internet browsing window and type in the address for Facebook. I don't know Jake's Facebook password, but he mentioned before that he has "remember me" set up on his PC so that his passwords are autofilled. He doesn't log out of things a lot of the time when he's at home either, to save himself the hassle of having to log in again when he sits back down at his PC. As I was hoping, Jake's left himself logged in. His page comes straight up when the Facebook website opens.

I sit back for a second. Jake told me all this about his

logins because he trusted me. I know I'm crossing a line. What I'm doing is so wrong and a part of me is growing hugely ashamed of myself. Another part, though – a stronger part – is urging me to continue. To fight, not sit back passively and wait for more danger to come.

The words of a Manic Street Preachers song, "Motorcycle Emptiness", come to my head – a lyric about how survival is as natural as sorrow.

Despite myself, I smile wryly. *Katie, if you wanted to make yourself feel better, that quote probably isn't the most cheerful way to do it.* But the will to survive *is* natural. I'm discovering that more and more every day.

I lean forwards and put my hand on the mouse. I direct it to Jake's messages.

The first message thread in the list is to Penny. I click on it. My shame grows, but I continue. The most recent messages are just general chat between them and some talk about me. The last thing that Jake said to Penny, sent last night, was that he was worried about me. In response, Penny told him he'd have to accept that he no longer has a place in my life and that she'd keep an eye on me to make sure I was all right.

I scroll down the list of messages and realise that Jake and Penny have had various formats of essentially this same conversation ever since the cottage incident, always initiated by Jake. But it's the messages on the day I went missing that I'm really interested in.

They begin shortly after midnight:

00.03 Hi, P. How did your lunch go?
00.34 Hey, just saw this now. You really don't want to know.

197

00.35 ??

00.35 Ask your ex-girlfriend. Actually, you can't. She's out cold. For now. She's coming and going.

00.36 What?? Is she okay?

00.36 She's ridiculously intoxicated. I haven't seen anyone that bad since I was a teenager. She's been sick all over my house.

00.37 What was she drinking?

00.37 What wasn't she drinking? Prosecco . . . red wine . . . Irish coffee . . . But particularly red wine. My house has the stains to prove it.

00.38 Shit. That's not good. I'm just out with the lads. Do you want me to get a taxi over?

00.39 No, don't come out. Richard's here. We can handle this. She's out for the count now anyway. But even if she wakes, I don't know if seeing you right now is a good thing for her. Not while she's in this state anyway.

00.42 Jesus! She'll be dying in the morning.

00.42 Yes. Look, I have to go. As I said, the house is in a real mess and I'm trying to do damage control here.

00.43 Okay. I'll check in later to see how things are going, in case you're still up. I'll be out a while.

00.43 Okay. Bye.

She'll be dying in the morning . . . No. I can't read into that. Jake always uses that expression in relation to hangovers. It means nothing. Surely.

I continue reading through the messages and see that there's another string of conversation from just after 2 a.m. onwards:

02.11 How is she now?

198

02.12 She's been sick again – several times. She's disgracefully drunk. I've never seen anyone this bad.

02.12 Jesus. Do you think she should go to a doctor?

02.13 What good would that do? She needs to sober up, not be pumped out. Besides, she's done the pumping herself. I've got a mountain of washing to prove it.

02.14 I really think I should come over.

02.15 Don't you dare! She's mellowed into a manageable state now. If she sees you, God knows what way she'll react. I can't take much more of her after the week I've had at work.

02.18 Okay. Look, I'll check in again later.

02.18 Jake, do you know what time it is? I'm planning on not being awake later. I'm hoping she'll sleep now for the night and hopefully that means I will, too.

02.19 Okay.

02.20 I don't mean to sound cross. I'm just exhausted. Richard said he'll keep an eye on her if I go to sleep.

02.20 Let me know in the morning how things went, if you can.

02.21 I will. Bye.

02.21 Bye.

The next communication is at nine fifty-six the following morning:

9.56 How is she today?

10.34 Just saw this now. She's sleeping it off. I haven't gone in to her since around three last night. She was sick again after you messaged me, but eventually it stopped. I left water by her bed and I'm leaving her to it to recover now.

10.37 Shall I call round today?

10.40 Jake, stop it. She ended it with you. She won't want to see you. Just leave it and stop making a fool of yourself over her. I'm going back to sleep now. Your message woke me and I really need more sleep. I was up so late with her and I had such a hectic week at work.

10.41 Are you sure she's okay?

10.44 What would be wrong with her other than a hangover? She's a grown woman, Jake. She wouldn't have choked on her vomit in the middle of the night, if that's what you're worried about. Trust me, there's NO vomit left in her.

10.45 Can you just check her quickly anyway?

10.45 Okay. Wait while I check her.

Penny's next message is two minutes later:

10.47 She's fine. Fast asleep.

10.47 Thanks for checking. I'm just worried about her.

10.51 I know you are, but there's no need to be. She just needs to sleep it off and never repeat this experience. As for me, I need to get myself some rest for another busy week tomorrow. I don't mean to sound cruel, but she's made her own bed and I've done all I can for her. All that will help her now is staying in bed for the day. I'm going to sleep again now, Jake.

10.52 okay. I might call over later. Let me know if you need me.

That ends that conversation. Penny doesn't reply and Jake doesn't say any more.

I rifle through the rest of Jake's messages to see if I can find anything suspicious, particularly any more messages from that night and where they were sent from. There's nothing else from Saturday night. In fact, there aren't many messages in his message bank at all. They're either messages to me or Penny, for the most part. There are a few messages to male friends of his, but they're very brief ones setting up various arrangements to meet up and none took place last Saturday. Since Saturday, the only messages he sent were to Penny.

I type the website address for Gmail into a browser and get the login page. I begin to type Jake's email address into the email section, speculating as I do so as to what his password could be. But as I type the first few letters, his email address appears in a drop-down menu. I select it and his password is automatically entered via autofill. I feel another flash of guilt, but I remind myself that I have to do this. I have to do a variation of it to everyone I know until I discover the truth.

But what if it costs me my friendships? And what sort of a friend am I anyway, suspecting everyone around me and investigating them?

I push that thought aside and skim through the list of Jake's emails before me. His account is full of emails about deals and coupons for local services, shopping and travel. Then there's Twitter notifications and updates, with alerts from a property website about houses for sale, which he set up before he bought this house and never bothered to unsubscribe to afterwards. There are very few personal emails in there.

I move to his sent items. There's nothing of note in there either, unless he's deleted them. Jake told me before that he never bothers deleting anything from his Gmail account because the capacity is so big but, of course, it would be another story if he'd done something that he needed to hide.

When I'm finished with his email, I check the hard drive of his computer. I see nothing interesting there. I then go back to the Internet browser and check his browsing history, wondering if it'll have been deleted. It hasn't.

I spot a listing for a jewellery website from a few weeks ago and before I even click on it, I know what it is. I click on it and sure enough, a page of engagement rings flashes before me. Then I realise that I shouldn't be clicking on these links because if Jake has reason to check his Internet history, he'll see that this page was accessed again today at this time.

I whip out my phone and open a web browser, then type in "How to delete an item in Internet browsing history". I find out how to do it and quickly delete the record of me having opened this page today. I skim through the rest of the history and see nothing suspicious. I quickly check the recycle bin to make sure the deleted record hasn't gone in there, then I shut the computer down and start on the house.

It isn't an easy job. As Jake isn't a tidy person, it's hard to spot anything out of place or hidden. Everything looks like it's just been thrown randomly everywhere. Again, I don't even know what I'm looking for as I scan the office. Just anything at all that strikes me as strange might help me to see where Jake's mind is at right now.

I see nothing untoward and as I leave the office, I decide to go outside to his shed. If he bought the rope that was used to tie me up, maybe I'll see some evidence of that in the shed. Although again, surely he'd have disposed of the rest of it and left no evidence, just like he'd have deleted any incriminating Internet browsing history. He might be untidy by nature, but he's well able to tidy things up if it's important enough for him to do so.

I find the key to the back door and try to open it, but as usual, it sticks. It's the dodgiest lock you could possibly get and I've often suggested to Jake that he should replace it. What if the house went on fire and he needed to get out in a hurry? But although he's said it's on his to-do list, he's never done it.

Eventually, after several attempts, I unlock the door and go outside to the shed. I rifle through the few shelves there are and check behind the lawnmower, but I see nothing of any significance. I wonder if there's any chance of finding a receipt for the rope Jake might have bought. He always holds on to credit card receipts to check them against his statement, but surely if he was going to buy something like rope he'd buy it with cash and throw away the receipt. It's worth a try, though. I go back inside, lock the door – again, with difficulty – and go to the drawer he keeps his receipts in.

I start rifling through it. The receipts are all for household items and daily things like supermarket food shops, clothes, fuel. I put them back in the drawer in the same haphazard manner they were in when I took them out then move around the kitchen opening and closing drawers, checking what's in each one. I've just banged a drawer shut, when I hear an unmistakable noise. I look up in horror.

A car has just pulled into the driveway.

Chapter 20

I close the kitchen door then race to the back door and try to unlock it. Again, it sticks. I try it several times, but it still won't open. I know that I only have seconds left before Jake comes in. I could try to run upstairs, but the likelihood is that Jake will come in while I'm halfway up the stairs.

The kitchen opens on to the dining room, which in turn opens on to the sitting room. All I can do is try to move from the kitchen to the dining room as he comes in, then into the sitting room, and try to get out unseen. But what if he goes to the sitting room first? Maybe I could say I've come round to collect some stuff. Then again, it still doesn't explain why I've seen fit to let myself into his house after ending things with him instead of arranging a time when I know he'll be there. Plus, he had his alarm set, so he'll instantly wonder why it's unset now.

I don't have time to think about it any further. Jake's key is in the front door. Wait a second – he's talking. He's either on the phone or he has company.

"Head into the kitchen, Dad, we'll get you a cup of tea," I hear Jake say as the door opens.

Oh God. What's happened? Why is he here with his dad in the middle of the day?

I have no choice now. I'll have to pretend I came here to collect stuff and brave it out. If Jake catches me trying to sneak out of the house while his dad is here, with Jake speculating on why the alarm isn't set . . . well, the shame doesn't bear thinking about.

I fix a smile on my face as Jake and his dad walk into the kitchen.

"Hello, Bob," I say to Jake's dad. "I just popped over to collect a few of my things, Jake. I thought I'd collect it while you were at work rather than bothering you in the evening. Let me put on the kettle for you two. You must be parched."

I turn my back and walk to the kettle, my cheeks blazing. I'm a disgrace, letting myself into someone else's house and trying to be brazen about it now, but I really don't want to upset Bob or embarrass Jake any further than I already have. I'll take whatever wrath Jake has for me another time, but I really hope it doesn't happen now while Bob is here.

"Why don't you go to into the sitting room, Dad," Jake says. "I'll bring you in your tea. It's much cosier in there."

I don't turn round until Bob has left the room. I know instantly by Jake's face that I'm busted.

He closes the door to the dining room and the door from the kitchen to the hall.

"What are you really doing here?" His face is like a sheet of ice.

"I left quite a lot of things here, Jake," I say. That's not a lie. That's just not the reason why I'm here.

"Where's your car?"

"I parked it a bit away and walked. I went back to my slimming club recently and they recommended that we do that. Remember, I told you about that before?"

And I had. My local slimming group had encouraged us to incorporate exercise into our lives by getting off a bus stop before our own one and walking the extra distance, parking the car a little further away from shopping centres and walking instead of circling around car parks, trying to get as close to the entrance as possible. They'd also suggested parking far away from houses and walking if it was safe to do so. I always used to park in the areas nobody else used whenever I went shopping with Jake, something that amused him but that he understood once I explained the rationale behind it.

He looks around the kitchen. "Where are your things, then?"

"I haven't gathered them yet. I'm not long here."

He walks closer to me. "What makes you think you have the right to let yourself into my house now?"

"I . . ."

He looks angry. It's a different type of anger to one he exhibited when I ended things. It's a quieter anger. It's a lot more menacing.

"I just want to get everything sorted, Jake. It's not good for you to have my things hanging around and as for me, I need them. I'm sorry I didn't ask you before calling over to get them. I didn't think you'd mind."

"Well, that's where you're wrong. I mind very much. And after what you accused me of earlier this week, I'd question whether or not you're telling the truth. I can't believe you had the gardai on to me."

"The gardai were on to everyone who was with me on the night I was drugged," I say.

"You should have told the gardai that the person who

did that wasn't me," Jake says. "Straight off the bat, you should have told them not to even question me. But you didn't."

"Penny was fine with it. She knows I just want to find the person responsible for drugging me. She's not taking it personally."

"You and Penny don't have the kind of relationship that you and I have . . . *had*. You're friends. You don't suspect her of anything. You suspect *me*."

"Is everything okay here?" I turn round to see Bob coming out of the sitting room, his face folded into a frown.

"Yes, thanks," I say, seizing the opportunity. "I was just leaving." I turn back to Jake. "I'll collect my things another time."

I walk towards the front door, oscillating between wondering if I'm a coward for leaving but fearing that this situation could escalate if I stay. I've never seen Jake look so angry.

"Good to see you again, Bob," I say as I pass Bob in the hall.

Bob continues to frown at me.

I leave as fast as I can, trying not to look as guilty as I feel for upsetting Bob. Once I get down the driveway and round the corner, I run to my car and drive away as fast as I can.

Chapter 21

When I pull into my driveway, I notice five missed calls on my phone from Jake while I've been driving. As I'm sitting there with the phone in my hand wondering what I'm going to say to him, he rings again.

I decide to answer, resolving to stick to my story. I only went round to collect a few things.

"Hi, Jake," I say as confidently as I can. "How are you? Sorry about earlier. I hope your dad didn't mind me being there—"

"Spare me the fake concern," Jake says.

"Jake, please. Can we talk about this?"

"I didn't ring for a chat," he says. "I want to make a few things very clear to you. First of all, never let yourself into my house again. You have absolutely no right to do that. I should really report this to the gardai, you know. I want you to give me back the key to my house. Post it or throw it in through the letterbox, but don't call in if you do. And if you're tempted to keep a copy, you should know that I've changed the code on the alarm."

"Jake, I'm sorry. It was a bad call to let myself in."

"You've made a lot of those recently."

"It's been a challenging time."

"I've tried to be there for you through it, but you wouldn't let me. Anyway, that's no excuse. The way you've treated me is beyond comprehension, accusing me of abducting you, getting the gardai to investigate my whereabouts and now letting yourself into my house . . . What was the point of that? To search for God only knows what?

"Is the word of the gardai not good enough for you, or is it only you as the investigative journalist who can ever find out anything properly? Well, you're wasting your time investigating this one. You have to accept that you had a hallucination and move on from it. And stop treating everyone around you with such huge disrespect."

"I never meant to be disrespectful to you," I say.

"It doesn't matter any more. You win. I'm finally done with you, Katie, and you're finally getting what you want from me. I've been far too sympathetic towards you. I don't need to be treated like a criminal by someone I've never been anything but kind to. Well, I think that's how I've been, anyway. You might see it differently. You must, to behave the way you have recently."

"Of course I don't see it differently! You're the kindest man I've ever met."

"But that wasn't enough."

"It's not that. Kind was good. Better than good. Perfect."

"And yet you wouldn't take the risk on starting a family with someone like that."

"Jake, that's not what this is about and you know it! You *know* my thoughts on having children. It's got nothing to do with you as a person. I don't want to have children with *anyone*. If I did, you'd be my number one choice a thousand times over."

"So you say."

"We've been through this over and over! Trust me when I say that the last thing in the world I wanted to do was to end it with you!"

"If that's true, you just wouldn't have ended it. If you really wanted to be with me, you'd have found a way to make it work. You wouldn't have been *able* to walk away like you did."

"You're wrong. It took everything I had in me to walk away and it broke me into a million pieces. I did it for *you*, so that you could find someone else to fulfil your dreams with. I hate life without you, Jake, but I didn't want to hold you back. I wanted to let you move on."

"It's going to be hard for me to move on when you're accusing me of all sorts of crazy stuff and messing with my head, isn't it? Not that I even wanted to move on before, but now . . . This is fucked up, Katie. And I'm not putting up with it any more. From now on, I don't want to see you, hear from you or have anything to do with you.

"I know that you and Penny are close, and I have no problem with that, but the three of us won't be in a room at the same time unless it's completely unavoidable. Yes, I've been contacting you a lot since we broke up, but it ends now. You were right. We need to get out of each other's lives. That's the only way this moving-on thing will work."

Goose bumps of fear rise on my skin. I don't know why. What Jake's saying is perfectly reasonable, after all. I pushed him away. I didn't want to, but I did. However, I did it for him. I did it for what I thought were the right reasons, although he doesn't see it that way. All he sees and feels is the rejection.

"Jake—"

"No. This is goodbye, Katie. Don't contact me again and don't drag me back into your life with more crazy accusations."

And with that, he hangs up. I'm seized by heartbreak, even though I know I have no right to feel that way.

Chapter 22

I take a deep breath, telling myself over and over to focus on why I'm doing what I'm doing. Feeling upset about what's just happened with Jake isn't an emotion I can indulge. I need to save myself. I need to think about my next move.

I get out of the car and put my key in the front door. Or rather, I try to. The key goes halfway in then sticks. I pull it out and insert it again, but it won't fit. I take it out and stare at it. It doesn't seem to have been damaged somehow. I try it again. It comprehensively will not fit.

My face goes red and I instantly start to sweat. This might only be a little thing in the grand scheme of things, but I don't need it right now. I need to get into my bloody house.

My neighbour, Helen, has a spare key for my house, but her car isn't in the driveway. I whip out my phone and ring her to ask when she'll be home for me to collect my spare key.

"Oh, I'm actually here," Helen says when she answers the call. "My husband has taken the car. I'll just dig it out and call round in a few minutes."

"That's brilliant, Helen. Thanks so much."

While I'm waiting for Helen to come, I try the key

again. I push it in harder this time – I mean, is it just me doing something wrong here? – and it goes in to some extent, but not correctly. I try to pull it out and it won't come. I try again. Nothing. Part of the key is now completely stuck in the door.

"For the love of God!" I scream then burst into tears. I need to get inside so badly.

"Katie?"

I turn round to see Helen staring at me.

"What's happened?"

I try to pull myself together. "It's just . . . " I point to the key. "It's stuck."

"But nothing else is wrong, no? Nothing serious has happened?"

Define serious, I think to myself, but I know Helen is wondering why on God's green earth I'm so upset about a key. And that actually makes me cry harder.

"I just need to get inside, Helen," I say.

"You can come to my house until we sort this key situation."

"Thanks, but I need my own house. Can you just try to get that key out, please?"

Helen steps forwards, looking very confused.

"What happened to your face, Katie?" Helen gestures towards the scrapes on my face.

"Oh! I had a fall while I was out, walking in the woods," I say.

If I'd said I got them from playing with a pride of lions that happened to be passing by earlier, I'd say Helen would have more readily believed that. She says nothing, but her face says it all.

She tries to get the key out, but her actions are as impotent as mine.

"I wouldn't say that's budging now – it's rammed in."

I start to cry harder.

"You can come round to my place, Katie, love. We can call a locksmith and get this sorted, but you can wait at my place."

Something hits me.

"The back door," I say through my tears. "I just remembered that I have a key for the back door under a flower pot."

I go round to the side gate and make my way round the back, hoping that the key is still there – I haven't checked it in ages. Thankfully, it is. I run to the back door. To my relief, it opens.

"Helen, I just need to turn off the house alarm," I say as the sound of insistent beeping hits us both. "Thank you so much."

I run to turn off the alarm. When I return to the back door, Helen's still standing there.

"Are you sure you're okay? You seem very upset about a key. Do you want to come over to my house for a cup of tea and a chat?"

"No, no, honestly," I say. "Thank you so much. You've been really helpful and I'm sorry if I alarmed you. I've just had a really bad day so far and this couldn't have happened at a worse time."

"Okay. Well, here's your spare key. You'll need it when you get the one that's stuck out. Look up YouTube. There's probably some sort of hack you can do to get it out and that'll save you the cost of a locksmith."

"Good point," I say. "Thanks again! Thanks so much! Bye now."

Helen walks away. I close the door behind me and stand

with my back to it for a few minutes before I pick up my phone and look up how to fix the lock.

Thanks to Helen's suggestion, and a spray of WD40 into the lock, I manage to free the key within ten minutes. Leaving the side door open, just in case, I close the front door and insert Helen's key into the lock. It goes in perfectly and unlocks the door instantly. I then try my own key again. Straight away, it struggles to go in again.

I decide not to force it after what happened last time, so I go inside and place the two keys side by side on the table. On first glance, they look exactly the same. As I inspect them more closely, I see that some of the grooves are slightly different. But that key worked perfectly yesterday, the day before and every other day for God knows how long! There's no sense to it. It's not as if someone could have replaced the key.

The more I muse on it, the more I feel the beginnings of a headache forming. I can't succumb to a headache now with so many other things to sort.

I resolve to put the key incident aside and try to think straight. What's next? Well, Jake catching me in his house leaves my plan to investigate everyone around me in tatters. I won't get away with checking up on Penny and Richard now, because Jake will tell them what I've been up to and they'll surely guess that I was going to check up on them, too. Penny will also tell Rose, Barbara and Gabrielle.

I check Facebook to see if Anna has replied to my mail. She hasn't. There is no "Read" stamp at the bottom of the mail, either.

My phone rings. It's Penny.

God, it didn't take long for him to tell her.

I think about letting the call ring out, but there's no point.

215

Penny will just turn up on my doorstep if I don't answer. It's probably better to face her wrath over the phone.

"Hi, Penny."

"Hey, Katie."

"Back from London?"

"I am indeed. How are you, pet?"

She sounds upbeat. Jake mustn't have told her yet – maybe he didn't have a chance to talk to her when she was in London. I try not to bristle at "pet", though. I can't help but find it patronising, as if I'm some poor fool to be pitied by the one who has it all sorted. I remind myself that Penny thinks she's more in control of her life than anyone else in the world and that it's not just me who gets the "pet" treatment.

"I'm okay, thanks."

"Hmm. You don't sound okay."

"Well, it's been a rough week, I guess."

"I know, and that's why I'm ringing. I have a rare night off, not to mention a few bottles of Moet that are begging to be drunk. Do you fancy coming over?"

"Oh, God, I'm not drinking. Drink helped to get me into the mess I'm in now, after all."

"Katie, nobody's going to spike your drink while you're in my house. Why don't you come over for dinner and we'll just chill out on the couch for the night with champagne afterwards? We're only talking a glass or two. And there are loads of movies on Netflix I'd like to see. I'm sure we can agree on one."

I should probably tell Penny what happened at Jake's house before he does. And it's probably better to do that face to face.

"I won't be drinking, Penny, but I'll come over for dinner and the movie. How about that?" I find myself saying.

"Okay, great. I understand your concerns about drinking. I think you should learn to drink in a responsible way though, rather than feeling like you have to give it up altogether, but that's just my opinion."

"Maybe," I say. "I'll look up the LUAS timetable and get the next one over, okay? See you soon."

I stand up and get ready to leave before I lose my nerve. Telling Penny about what happened at Jake's is hardly going to be the most pleasant conversation I've ever had. Tonight could really go any way.

I go to the radiator in the kitchen to get the jeans I'd washed the previous day and left on the radiator to dry, but when I take the radiator cover off, they're not there.

My heart jumps in my chest. I was sure I'd left them there.

I take a deep breath and run to the other radiators, thinking I must have left them on another one instead and just got mixed up. But there are no clothes behind any of the radiator covers. I run upstairs to my clean laundry basket. Perhaps I took the clothes off the radiators on autopilot and I just can't remember doing so. But the basket is empty.

I'm starting to panic now. I have a vivid memory of putting those clothes on the radiators. I took them out of the machine yesterday, went to the radiator in the kitchen first, worked my way into the hall and sitting room, then went upstairs with the remaining clothes. I can see myself doing it in my mind's eye. But the reality in front of me indicates something different.

I walk to the washing machine, deciding to retrace my steps from yesterday to see if I can make any sense of this. I pull back the wooden double doors that my washing machine lives behind. I notice straight away that there's a wash inside the machine. I open the door of the washing machine and claw at the clothes inside it to see what's there. My jeans, along with everything else I thought I'd put on the radiators yesterday, tumble out and plop at my feet.

I burst into tears all over again. I feel like I'm really, really starting to lose my grip on reality and it's quite terrifying.

About ten minutes of crying and rumination later, I manage to talk myself out of my fit. I remind myself that I'm under a lot of pressure right now and I'm probably going through my life in a trance when it comes to the daily chores that keep things ticking over. I'm not able to give them any of my headspace, because it's all needed for the bigger picture. That's all it is. I calm myself and try to get ready to face a night at Penny's.

It takes a while to pull myself together fully. I message Penny to say there's a delay on my part and that I'd be later than planned. I then catch the LUAS to Penny's house in Ranelagh, South Dublin. She answers the door done up to the nines.

"Should I turn round and go home? You clearly got a last-minute invite to a swish awards ceremony."

Penny flicks her hair over her shoulder. "I was just killing time while I was waiting for you by getting ready. Come on in."

I walk in, feeling like a tramp in my jeans, plain V-neck jumper and woollen coat. Although it's a cold November evening, the air in Penny's vast hallway is redolent of a summer garden. Fresh flowers have been placed on a beautiful mahogany dresser and the scent of a sweet pea candle wafts towards me. It feels inviting and yet, as always, I'm slightly uneasy in this house. It's so pristine that

I'm afraid to touch anything in case I mark it. And now, I have the associations of last Saturday night and Sunday to deal with here as well, not to mention the awkward discussion to come about Jake.

Penny takes my coat and puts it in the cloakroom, then ushers me into her vast kitchen and pours us two glasses of Moet.

"Look, take one and sip it – one or two won't do you any harm. It's drinking bottles at a time that's the problem."

She has a point. I do need to learn how to drink slowly and safely, the way everyone else does – and surely I'm safe here. I don't really want the alcohol, but maybe it'll take the edge off the way I'm feeling. I stare at the glass in my hand and despite myself, despite *everything*, I smile. Only Penny could drink Moet during the week! Well, Penny and now me, by proxy.

When I'm seated in the dining room, where our plates and cutlery have already been left out, Penny leaves the room for a moment and returns with a large quiche, a salad and a few other accompaniments. She carries it all to the table on a tray and lays it in the middle.

"Spinach, pine nut and brie quiche," she says. "Green herb couscous and bulgar wheat, and cranberry and rocket salad. Help yourself to as much as you want."

"I would say I'm impressed, but I'm thinking gourmet takeaway – am I right?"

"Avoca takeaway."

We both laugh. Penny doesn't do cooking. Sometimes, she doesn't even do *eating*. She's just too busy, she says.

The Moet goes down well. I'm starting to feel a little more relaxed after the first glass. Penny and I are dancing around the topic of Jake and I know it'll get to a point where I'll find that exhausting, but for now, I feel a lot better than I did when I was sitting in my room mulling over how messy my life has turned out to be recently.

But eventually, the time comes when I know I have to address it.

"I've had something of an altercation with Jake," I say. "He's mad at me. I called round to his house to collect some of my stuff while he wasn't there, but he came back with your dad while I was in the middle of it. He seems to think I was nosing around the house rather than collecting my things."

"And were you?"

"Of course not!"

"So why is he mad?"

"I hadn't arranged to call over. I let myself in with my key. Before you say it, I know it was a bad judgment call. I should have asked first. I just wanted to get it over and done with. I knew if I rang him to arrange it, the call would end badly with the way things are between us. We'd never get the job done. Not only is it not good for him to have my stuff hanging around the house, but I also needed all the stuff I left there. I thought I'd bite the bullet and just get it over and done with."

"You said my dad was there?"

"Yes."

"I didn't know Jake was meeting him today. He should have said. I'd have taken time off to meet them."

"Oh, right. He must have forgotten to mention it," I say, thinking that Jake probably presumed there was no way that Penny would be able to take time off.

I doubt very much that he was trying to exclude her, but she sounds miffed.

"Katie, I didn't want to say anything after you'd just

walked in the door, but Jake rang me while you were on your way over."

"Oh. It's to be expected, I suppose."

"Like you said, he's not happy."

"We need closure. I didn't want to make a big production of arranging a time to call round. In hindsight, like I said, it was a bad idea. I'm not thinking straight since last weekend."

"He said you didn't have any of your stuff gathered together when he came in."

"I wasn't there long when he came home."

"Why wasn't your car parked outside?"

"I have a habit of parking away from areas to make myself walk to them and get some exercise, remember?"

"Yes, but you usually keep that trick for shopping centres, not when you're visiting people's houses."

"You're wrong. I've started doing that all the time."

Penny sighs. "Katie, please tell me this has nothing to do with the hallucination. You weren't checking out Jake's house, were you?"

"Of course not!" I will my cheeks not to go red. I'm a hopeless liar.

"Good. You've taken enough of out of him already with the break-up. Try not to make things any worse for him, all right?"

I feel like a scolded bold child.

"Is he okay?"

"Oh yes, he'll be fine. You were only together six months, after all – it's hardly a lifetime. Don't feel bad about it. He just needs a bit of time."

"I presume the gardai contacted you?" I say while we're airing the elephants in the room. Might as well get this conversation over and done with, too.

"Yes."

"How do you feel about that?" I say tentatively.

I suddenly feel horribly embarrassed. Part of me feels like I really have some neck coming round here to Penny's house after I've had the gardai investigating her. Another part tells me to stop thinking like that and just continue getting to the bottom of this. But if I were Penny, I'm not sure I'd have me in her house right now.

"I know the gardai are just asking me about it as a matter of course because you've asked them to investigate it further. No hard feelings.

"I do think, though, that if they can't find the man who drugged you, you're going to have to let this go for your own sanity. This could really drag you down if you let it. Don't fixate on it or overanalyse it if you don't get answers from the investigation. Don't obsess. That's my advice, anyway – which you didn't ask for, I know." Penny shrugs. "Force of habit."

I don't know what to say, so I say nothing and hope the discussion ends soon.

We move into the sitting room. Once we're seated, we drift to other topics of conversation, but our exchanges are uneasy after what we've just discussed.

"While I'm here, Penny, I must collect my jeans from you," I say when silence falls.

"Oh, yes. I'll get them for you before you leave."

"Would you mind if I get them now? I can pop upstairs and get them myself if you like. I just don't want to forget them later."

"Oh, okay. I'll get them now, so."

"Thanks a lot. Was the blouse thrown out, or . . . ?"

"Do you know, I honestly don't know. My housekeeper

ironed all the clean laundry earlier this week, but she could well have chucked the blouse. I always tell her to throw away anything that's damaged or that's starting to look tatty. Let me have a look while I'm getting the jeans."

"That's great. Thanks."

I'm hoping to see both the jeans and the blouse, if possible. Despite the fact that the blouse has shrunk, surely signs of damage from the shrubs outside will be evident. If my face is anything to go by, the light material of the blouse should be destroyed. I can remember it catching on thorns. In fact, I can remember hearing the fabric ripping as I moved through the greenery. It's amazing how I didn't even register that at the time, but now I can remember it as clear as day. As for the jeans, I'm sure they got nicked on the greenery, too. Then again, the fabric would be a lot stronger in them and the damage might not be as evident.

I'm literally on the edge of my seat by the time Penny comes downstairs, dying to see the clothes. I know I won't be able to examine them too thoroughly in front of Penny, though. That will go under the "Katie is fixating, overanalysing and obsessing" category. She seems okay with me getting the gardai to investigate things further in terms of me wanting to find the person who drugged me. She also seems to be accepting that she and everyone else in this investigation being questioned is just standard procedure because I've asked for it to be looked into again. But if she realises that I still believe what happened in the cottage was real, she won't be able to stop herself from getting involved. The last thing I need is for her to contact my family – especially Mam.

Penny swishes back into the room, a plastic bag dangling from her hand.

"There you go." She hands the bag to me.

I peer inside, trying to feign disinterest.

"Oh, thanks, Penny. These jeans cost a lot of money, so it's good to have them back." I take the jeans out. "I might wear them again this weekend."

"I personally think they're quite overpriced for the quality of them. I had a pair of them a few years ago and they didn't last long before they started to fray. Do you want me to get you some jeans when I'm in the States?"

Penny starts to talk about a shopping mall she goes to whenever she's in the US office that sells designer jeans at a discount price. She's rattling off all the brands and I'm nodding, but I'm not fully listening. My eyes are travelling over the jeans, which I've unfolded as nonchalantly as possible. There are nicks on it. There are small frayed lines running down the thigh and calf areas. I can feel my heart pounding in my chest.

I flip the jeans over and look at the back of the legs. Yes, there are small frays on the back, too. They're entirely consistent with the type of fraying that brambles would cause.

"Why are you examining your jeans, Katie?" Penny says, dropping her conversation about jeans mid sentence.

"Just . . . wondering if I ruined the knees when I fell in the pub," I say.

"But you're looking at the back of the jeans now."

"As I said, they were really expensive. Just wanted to make sure I didn't destroy them in all that carry-on in the pub."

I refold the jeans and put them back in the bag.

"The blouse must have been thrown out, then," I say. "From what you said, it sounded like it was in quite a state."

"I didn't see it upstairs, anyway. I'll ask the housekeeper when I see her. Did you get your new blouse yet?"

"Oh, yes. It arrived. I meant to mention it. Thanks so much."

"You're welcome. There's no need for the old blouse anyway really, is there? Even if my housekeeper threw it out, does it make any difference? It was ruined anyway."

From the shrinkage, or from something else?

"Yeah, you're right. No need for it at all. Thanks."

I put the jeans back in the bag and leave it on the floor, hoping to close off this discussion.

Penny gives me a strange look but drops the subject. I try not to give her a strange look back, because I can't help thinking that if she and Richard had anything to do with what happened to me, it's very convenient that there's no sign of my torn blouse now, although I know I'm not being fair. Penny's housekeeper might know where it is, after all. I try not to sigh. All this second-guessing of every word everyone says to me is exhausting.

There's silence for a few minutes.

"Are we okay, Penny?" I find myself saying.

"Why wouldn't we be?"

"You sounded a bit peeved when I told you about Jake and me having words over me letting myself into his house."

"Oh, that. No, that's between you and Jake."

"Oh. Good."

"Look, Jake's bringing a lot of hurt feelings into how he's dealing with you. That's going to colour every interaction you two have from now on. Personally, I just want to stay out of it. Jake's always going to be in my life, obviously, but that doesn't mean you and I can't remain friends. I just think it'll be easier, though if I stay out of anything to do with the two of you."

"That's true, I guess."

"Realistically, now that you've broken up and won't be seeing each other any more, this problem is going to take care of itself anyway in time. Right?" Penny smiles widely. "Things always sort themselves out in the end."

"If only it were that simple . . . "

"It's as simple or as difficult as you choose to make it, Katie. You made your choice and you need to live with that now. You can mope about it or you can choose to look at the situation more positively.

"I don't mean to tell you what to do, but all I'm saying is don't indulge in the what could have beens. Find yourself a new direction and put your focus into that. I'll be telling Jake the same thing, too, as soon as I get a chance. That's my advice anyway, for what it's worth. You obviously don't have to listen to me, but that's my take on it as your friend." She shakes her empty glass. "I think it's time for a refill, don't you?"

Penny picks up my glass and takes it out to the kitchen, along with her own. She thinks problems are so easily solved – and for her, they are. I envy her that.

We've just started our second glass, when the doorbell rings. Penny raises her eyebrows at me before rising to answer it.

She returns with Richard.

I manage to stop myself from saying "Oh, no," out loud. I manage a grin that really must look twisted and a polite "Hello," said in a voice that doesn't even sound like mine.

"Katie, I didn't know you were here. I didn't see your car outside."

"I caught the LUAS."

Richard says no more. He looks less than happy to see

me here. I glance at Penny – perfectly made-up Penny. She was obviously expecting him.

"You didn't mention Richard was joining us," I say. "Maybe I should go and let you two have a night together."

"Not at all," Penny says. "Richard just popped by unexpectedly, didn't you, darling? Sit down and I'll pour you a glass."

She puts a hand on Richard's shoulder and almost pushes him into a seat beside me. As soon as she leaves the room, there's absolute silence.

One of us should really say something, but just as I'm about to open my mouth and come out with the first thing that comes into my head, I stop myself. Why should I be the one to make things more comfortable? Richard clearly can't be bothered speaking to me. I know he thinks I'm unworthy of his time. Only people at his elevated level are admirable enough to be spoken to. People like me in a mid-level career would just taint him with our lack of ambition, I think bitterly. As for Penny, I'm furious with her. Why did she invite me over here if she knew he was coming, too? What *is* she playing at?

I pick up my glass and sip it slowly.

"How's work, Katie?"

I almost splutter my drink back into the glass. If it wasn't for the fact that I'm quite sure I'm the only Katie in the room, I would have been convinced that Richard must have been speaking to someone else.

"Work is . . . busy, Richard." Typical though that when he does choose to speak to me, it's about work. What else? "I'm off this week, but in general, it's busy. Very busy, actually. You know yourself."

"I sure do," he says.

Silence again.

Dear God, Penny, how long does it take to fill a glass of champagne?

"So, what are your thoughts on the current political situation in the country?"

This time, I'm shocked. Richard never does small talk. You can tell – he's not very good at it. This break from our usual dynamic unsettles me, I have to admit. I usually know what to expect from Richard.

I silently berate myself for never being satisfied. I wasn't happy when he wasn't talking to me and now I'm not happy that he is. It just feels strange, that's all. I don't find him intimidating, but something about our conversation isn't sitting right with me, either.

I give my opinion on what's currently going on in Irish politics. The conversation feels forced and surreal.

I think of Penny's words about things sorting themselves out in the end and find myself saying, "As with everything, time will tell the story." I wish I felt the words were true. I pick up my glass again and throw back the last few drops. "Speaking of time, I should really go home soon," I say as Penny finally, mercifully, walks back into the room with Richard's glass of champagne.

"You must be joking! It's only ten o'clock!" Penny reaches out to refill my glass after putting Richard's down, but I cover it with my hand.

"Please stay, Katie. I'd really like you and Richard to get to know each other a little better. You're both very important people in my life. My partner and my best friend."

My eyebrows must raise involuntarily – I didn't think Penny and I were that close! – because Penny frowns.

"I mean it, Katie. Most women are threatened by me because of my career. I'm self-aware enough to realise that. You've always been confident enough to hold your own around me. And just because you and Jake aren't together any more, it doesn't mean our friendship can't continue far into the future, does it?"

"No, I guess not."

"For my part, I'm mature enough to know that all that business with the gardai this week is nothing personal. It's just something you needed to do to feel safe again. Richard's fine about it too, aren't you, darling?"

Richard nods. He doesn't look too convincing.

"Please, Katie, have another drink with us. Just one. I've waited ages to drink this Moet and I've had nobody to drink it with. It's good to have a friend around. It's good to have a friend, full stop."

I slowly remove my hand from the top of my glass. Sometimes, I truly feel sorry for Penny. I'm probably the only person in the world who does, but I've gained enough of an insight into her world to realise how solitary her life is. Other than Jake, she doesn't really seem to get on well with her family. She doesn't socialise with her work colleagues because she likes to maintain a professional distance from them. When she's at work events, she says she's always wearing her game face and that people only try to talk to her for networking purposes. Everyone has an agenda, she says. Other than Richard, she seems to have nobody close to her.

She's right – women are intimidated by what she's achieved in her career. I know this because the girls have said as much to me. Penny's attractiveness doesn't do much to endear her to most females, either. She and I have never had that dynamic. She's Jake's sister, so I obviously don't need to feel threatened about Jake in that respect. And I meet a lot of high-flyers in my own job – or at least, people who think they are. Although I'm not sure if it's just the drink talking now, I suppose I am the closest thing she has to a best friend, really. And I might never have seen her as being mine, but my allies are thin on the ground at the moment and Penny's one person who hasn't run for the hills since all this craziness started.

I still can't work out why she didn't tell me Richard would be calling round, though.

A few more glasses of champagne later, I'm more perplexed than ever as to why Penny and Richard are together. The tension between them is almost unbearable and I know I need to get up and leave, but I'm almost hypnotised by their interactions. Every topic that comes up for discussion ends as an argument, with my contributions slowly trailing off as Penny and Richard get into the flow of their respective viewpoints.

Now, they're bickering over local planning issues, a subject that isn't relevant to either of them but suddenly sounds like the most important thing in both of their worlds. It's all a game, I say to myself as their voices raise. It's a debate between the two most prestigious colleges in the country. It's all about winning.

I really shouldn't watch this blood sport any more. Time to leave.

"I'm going to leave you two to it and call a taxi," I say, taking my handbag, getting up and practically running from the room.

I expect Penny to object, but she's in the middle of an important match-winning point and barely looks up to acknowledge the fact that I've spoken.

After I've called the taxi, I go to the bathroom just to pass the time until the taxi gets here. After that, I wander as quietly as I can around Penny's vast hall, grateful that I've worn quiet flats. I'd love to take the opportunity to look around Penny's house and see if I can find anything that would help me to work out if Richard had anything to do with what happened to me, but I'd need time to do that properly.

I crouch down in front of a radiator cover and huddle against it, suddenly exhausted. The champagne has gone straight to my head and despite my problems, I know I'll be asleep within seconds as soon as I my head hits my pillow at home – if not seconds after getting into the taxi.

Richard's suddenly raised voice makes me feel wide awake again.

"You know what? I'm sorry I ever met you!"

I hear Penny saying something in reply, but her voice is a lot more muted and controlled. From her tone, she doesn't seem particularly upset.

"I've met a lot of selfish, self-absorbed people in my profession," Richard continues, "but you . . . you *invented* the concept of egocentricity. You're going to spend your life lonely and alone, Penny."

I can feel myself frowning. Although they'd been arguing, I hadn't anticipated the conversation going this way. This is starting to veer down a much darker path than the one I'd thought Penny and Richard were on. Less than an hour ago, Penny was talking about Richard being one of the most important people in her life. Right now, it sounds like they're on their last legs as a couple.

I hear footsteps. Quickly, I scramble up from my hunched position and run to the downstairs bathroom again. I've just closed and locked the bathroom door, when

I hear the sitting room door open, followed not long afterwards by the front door. Neither door opens again, nor had I expected them to. Penny doesn't follow people.

I leave it a few minutes and then come out of the bathroom, wondering how much I should say to Penny that I heard. Suddenly, I hear my mobile ringing in my handbag.

"Taxi. I'm outside," the driver says.

I enter the sitting room, not knowing what exactly I'll find. Penny looks up as I enter and smiles. Her glass of champagne is full to the brim.

"Ah, Katie," she says as if she's forgotten I was even here. "Sit down. Let me top you up."

"No, thanks – my taxi is outside."

"Oh. Another time. Thanks for coming over."

She smiles beatifically. It's as if the argument with Richard never happened. Again, I feel a rush of pity for her. Penny can never quite let anyone in – even her supposed "best friend".

"Oh, and I hope Richard wasn't rude to you earlier. He was in quite the mood this evening."

"No, no, he wasn't rude."

"Thanks, but you don't have to lie to make me feel better. He's always off with you, I've noticed that. But he's just wary of you because . . . oh, never mind."

"Because of what?"

She shrugs. "He reads *The Bulletin*. He's noticed you're writing articles about banking recently. And bankers."

"So? He's not in the fray."

"*Yet*." Penny shrugs. "I'm only quoting what he's been saying to me. He seems to think that because you meet him frequently through me, he'll be in your mind as someone to write about. I keep telling him it's nonsense."

"Yes, it is! I'll only be writing about him if there's

something to say, Penny, just like I would about any other public figure. It's my job."

Which instantly makes me wonder, *is* there something to say about him? Why is he worried?

"I know, Katie. I get it. For such an intelligent man, Richard lacks common sense sometimes. I suppose he has his demons and they come out in different ways."

"What do you mean?"

Penny rubs her eyes. "Sorry. Forget I said that. I'm tired after London. I shouldn't be talking about Richard. I should go back to work, actually."

"Are you serious?" It's half ten.

"Absolutely. I can bring this upstairs for company." Penny takes her glass and stands up. "Why are you looking at me like that?"

"Well . . . I'm exhausted just thinking about you going back to work right now." *Especially after a row with your boyfriend*, I say to myself, but I know better than to voice that thought.

Penny's face lights up. "I love it, Katie. It doesn't even feel like work to me. When you're passionate about what you do, you enjoy every minute. You understand that feeling, don't you?"

"That's true, I guess," I say. "Up until last week I had similar feelings about work. Since the . . . incident, it just doesn't seem important any more."

"Oh, come on, Katie! You'll pull yourself out of this. You just need to find a story to get passionate about. When you go back, maybe it's time to start digging up the dirt on someone. Just not Richard," Penny laughs. "Not that he has anything to hide, of course. Just a mistress." The bitterness in her tone is unmistakable.

"You don't have to put up with that," I find myself saying.

"With what?"

"That status. You should be more than that to someone."

"Katie, I'm not anything I don't want to be," Penny says. "This is my choice. I control this. Don't feel sorry for me. I'm no victim."

"I don't feel sorry for you! I just think you deserve better, that's all."

"I decide what I deserve," Penny says.

It's not said coldly – merely in a factual tone of voice – but it's enough to make me decide to leave the conversation there.

The taxi beeps insistently outside.

"I'm being rude. I'd better go. Thanks for dinner and the drinks," I say, not quite able to add "and for a lovely evening".

Penny escorts me to the door, glass in hand, waving me off with her free hand, a huge smile on her face. She reminds me of the Duchess of Cambridge, Kate Middleton, greeting her audience whenever Kate has a public engagement, minus the alcohol. I wonder what expression is going to be on Penny's face when she closes the door.

Jake often said to me that he never really felt like he fully knew Penny. Although she was his biological sister, she'd been adopted as a baby and had only come back into Jake's life a few years ago. Jake had told me the full story about a month into our relationship, after I'd met Penny several times. Sadly, their mother had died giving birth to Penny and their father, Bob, had felt unable to cope with a new baby. He already had three sons: Jake and his two elder brothers, one of whom relocated to Australia as an adult and the other to Germany.

The prospect of managing a new baby on his own while trying to rear three boys ranging in age from two to six was something he felt he couldn't cope with while he was in the depths of grief – not initially, anyway. The family offered to rally round. Bob's two sisters said they'd take Penny as much as they could, as did Jake and Penny's mother's sisters, but Bob was adamant that the baby was not to be passed from pillar to post like an unwanted nuisance. He asked the staff in the hospital to arrange for Penny to be fostered until he got his head together.

As the months passed, the thought of bringing her back into the home became unfathomable. He was barely able to cope with the boys, needing all the help his sisters and sisters-in-law could give him just to keep the house and the farm ticking over. How could he possibly put a baby into the mix as well? He thought she'd have no quality of life at all. Besides, he felt a baby needed a mother as well as a father.

He thought it over and decided it would be best for her to be adopted by someone who could give her the life she deserved. Jake said it broke his father's heart to make the decision, but he knew his wife would have wanted only the best for her daughter. The rest of the family were vocal in their opposition of his idea. However, he refused to bow to the pressure to keep her – anyone who was saying it was a bad idea had plenty of kids of their own to mind and he felt it wasn't feasible for any of them to adopt her.

"Why did it take Penny so long to track you down? Didn't she want to meet her biological family?"

"She didn't know we existed until both of her adopted parents died," Jake said. "They didn't want her to know. Her father passed first, then her mother three years later. She left Penny a letter telling her the truth, saying she and her husband wouldn't have been able to bear it if Penny had gone looking for her biological family when they were still alive, believing Penny would turn her back on them for not telling her sooner. They meant to tell her when she was eighteen, but she'd been going through a rough patch at the time and they weren't sure how she'd react."

"I wonder, did she ever suspect?" I said. "Penny seems on the ball about pretty much everything."

"If she did, she's never said. She probably had no reason to. She looked reasonably like her adoptive mother in terms of hair colour and skin tone. Her adoptive dad was tall, like she is. Her parents relocated after they adopted her. Nobody except their immediate family and closest friends knew she wasn't their biological daughter."

"So did the adoption agency set up a meeting between you, your dad and Penny, then, when she found out about her biological family?"

"No. Penny doesn't have much regard for following procedures unless they benefit her. She was too impatient to wait for the adoption agency's involvement. As soon as she got the information about my parents, she managed to track me down. She walked up to me as I was leaving work one day and told me she was my sister."

"Wow." That sounded like Penny's style all right. "How did you react?"

"I was shocked, naturally, but of course I knew I had a younger sister who'd been adopted. That much was never a secret in our family, so I assumed straight away that there was probably some truth to the matter. We went for a coffee and talked things over. Well, Penny talked, mostly. She was in deep shock herself at what had been kept from her. I felt sorry for her."

"Was she angry?"

"Yes and no. She said she could imagine how hard it would have been for Dad to raise her with no wife to help, but there was a part of her that wished he'd tried. She said it was hard not to feel rejected, or as if he blamed her somehow for Mam dying. She understood to some extent why her adoptive parents hadn't told her the truth when she was eighteen but felt they should have told her when she was in a calmer place – perhaps when she'd finished college.

"Overall, though, she felt like she couldn't complain with her lot. Her adoptive parents had given her an extremely privileged life. They were reasonably wealthy and lived in a beautiful house in Foxrock in South Dublin. They gave her every opportunity a young girl could have wanted growing up.

"They sent her to private school and gave her every means at their disposal so she could get good marks. She achieved the highest points possible in her Leaving Cert and was one of the top students in the country the year she took her exams. She plumped for Law and Business in Trinity College Dublin, although her adoptive parents wanted her to do medicine. But Penny wasn't one to do what she was told. She still isn't, as you know."

"And did she ask to meet your dad and brothers then?"

"Yes, although it took a while for Dad to agree to meet her. He was conflicted. He felt bad for giving her up, even though he did it for what he felt at the time were the right reasons. When he heard about what a privileged life she'd led, he started to feel a bit better about his decision. It justified what he'd done. His worst nightmare was that she'd ended up having a horrible life – one that was even worse than what he could have offered her.

"He came round, though. My brother in Germany came home to meet her, then my brother in Australia came home the following Christmas and he met her, too. It all went well. There was no hostility. My dad's a bit intimidated by her and all her success, though."

"How did she end up becoming the CEO of a multinational company at her age, anyway?"

"She's smart. She's a networker. She told us that her first job after she graduated from college was a very junior position in a multinational company as a business analyst. She worked her way up in that company to become a senior business analyst within a few years, then relocated to the company's office in the States. She worked there for a year before jumping ship to another multinational in the same city, to a more senior position with a lot more perks. Then she was transferred to Germany to help set up an office over there and she lived there for a year or two before getting poached by another multinational. That's been the trajectory of her career – moving around and getting headhunted."

"I can imagine that all right. So, how long is she back in Dublin?"

"She only moved back here a year ago from the UK office of the company she's with now, when she was offered the CEO position in the Irish office. Looks like she's here to stay now that she's bought a house, but you never quite know with Penny."

And what a house it is! It's a 2,500 square foot red brick detached house within walking distance of a LUAS station and close to the seafront, with a huge landscaped garden. It has five bedrooms, one of which is in the converted attic and contains a walk-in wardrobe the size of my master bedroom, a massive kitchen, a huge sitting room, a dining room, a conservatory and a study. Penny spends most of her time at work or travelling and the house is far too big for one person, but that's not the point. It's a statement home. It's the home of a CEO.

Everything about Penny just screams success. She looks the part, right down to her amazing bone structure. "She has the type of face that will age well," Mam once commented about Penny, and she's right. Mam doesn't usually see fit to comment on anyone's looks, but that's the Penny effect. People notice her. Coupled with her stunning looks, she has presence and a gravitas that's rare and impossible to miss.

One thing I noticed about her right from the start, though is that she didn't seem to have any friends, something she's clearly aware of when she made that statement in front of Richard about me being her best friend. It's hardly surprising, given the fact that she's spent the best part of the last two decades relocating from one place to the next through work. But as Penny said herself, you'd have to be a pretty confident woman to be her friend. Her looks and the self-assurance that oozes out of her would scare a lot of people off from being friends with her.

As for men, she's told me that most of them want more from her than just friendship. It doesn't seem to bother her hugely, though. She's so consumed with work that it doesn't leave much room for friendships. That said, she always takes me up on the offer of coming out with me and my friends whenever we arrange to meet up, and she's always gone out of her way to make time for me. I used to think that was down to wanting to make an effort with Jake's girlfriend for his sake. Yet, since Jake and I broke up, Penny has demonstrated that she still intends to keep our friendship up regardless. Maybe it wasn't the drink talking when she said I was her best friend. Who knows? Maybe even someone like Penny needs one of those, too.

Chapter 23

Although Mam is intermittently staying at my house as much as she can, she's currently at home in her own house, both for her benefit and mine. I think she needs the break from the worry of being around me and I need the space, too. Nevertheless, she said she'll call round again later in the day.

I'm putting the tea and coffee back in the cupboard where I like to keep it, rather than where Mam leaves it, when the phone rings. My manager's name, Henry, flashes on the screen. I hesitate before answering. At a guess, he's probably ringing to see how long it will be before I'm back in work, even though I told him I was signed off for the rest of the week. I know if I don't answer, though, he'll only ring again and again. Henry is relentless, which is one of the reasons why he's so good at his job. He reminds me of Penny in that respect.

Figuring I might as well get the conversation over and done with, I hit the green button on my phone to answer the call.

"Hi, Henry," I say as cheerfully as I can. "How are you?"

"It's you I'm worried about," Henry replies with his usual directness. "We received something in the office for you today. A large envelope."

"Oh. And that's bad because?"

"Because what was inside wasn't good."

"You opened it?"

"It wasn't addressed to you. It was a large padded envelope, just addressed to the office. Inside, it contained a warning addressed to you. For safety reasons, I thought you should know even though you're on sick leave. Do you want me to read it out to you?"

This is the last thing I want to hear right now, but what if it's related to my abduction? The abduction that nobody believes in. Maybe the gardai will sit up and take notice after this.

"Yes, please do, Henry," I say.

"Okay." Henry is calm. He's used to drama.

Katie Turner had better pick the subjects she scribbles about for your rag of a paper carefully from now on, or she'll end up with a bullet in her head. And one in each knee. And maybe one through each tit, too. Remember that. I'm watching everything you write, Katie Turner. You fuck up again and you're dead.

"Jesus. That's a threat, Henry, not a warning! But why? I mean, I haven't written anything contentious."

"What's harmless to you can be a huge insult to others," Henry said. "This could be some frustrated idiot who got offended because you wrote an article about short men being crap in bed or something. There are a lot of weirdos out there, remember. I'm always telling you that."

"I'm starting to find that out," I say. "And I didn't write an article about short men being crap in bed, by the way."

"And don't, either," Henry says. "I hear it's not true."

Henry is about five foot six yet swears he's five foot nine. Despite the situation, I giggle, but I can hear the fear in my voice as well as the amusement. Again, it's laugh or cry.

"Did the envelope contain anything else?"

"No. I presume the size of the envelope was to make sure the letter didn't get overlooked in the rest of the post. Someone badly wanted you to get this message."

"I'll need to take it to the gardai, Henry. Sick or not, I'd better come into the office and collect it."

Thankfully, the scrapes on my face are starting to heal and the bump on my forehead has gone down a lot. If I put on a few layers of heavy make-up, surely he won't notice anything.

"Are you well enough? I can swing by your house after work and drop it off if you're too sick to leave the house."

I think about this. If Henry calls, Mam will more than likely be here by then. If she meets him, who knows what she'll say to him about me if she gets a chance. It'll be coming from a good place, of course – the "don't make my daughter work too hard, she's been through a lot recently" angle – but I don't want Henry knowing too much in case it affects our professional relationship. I'm sure he'll think I'm losing the plot. Everyone else does. I could even end up losing my job if he thinks I'm a loose cannon and I really can't have that.

"I'm not feeling great, but I need to take action on this before someone makes me feel a lot worse. Do you want to send it to me through a courier and I'll pay for it? It'll save you the bother of going out of your way after work."

"No, it's fine. I'll be driving past the exit for where you live as I'm going home anyway, so it's only a detour."

Shit. I'll have to go in – it's too risky for him to come here.

"I wouldn't mind leaving the house, actually, Henry. What do you think? I'm getting cabin fever. I won't stay long, though – I'm still a bit weak. Will you be in the office for the rest of the day?"

"Right, whatever suits you. Yep. I'll be here, slaving away. And listen, don't be too freaked out by this."

"You think?"

"Course. We've heard it all before in here. If I had a tenner for every time someone said they were going to kill me, I'd be lying on a lilo in the Bahamas right now instead of gawking out of the window at the rain pounding against the window.

"This is the life we lead, Katie. It comes with the territory. We'll bring it to the gardai and I'm sure that will be the end of it. There are plenty of brave people sitting at home hating the world, but if they came face to face with you, they'd shrivel up inside. You're a bit scary when you're mad, you know. And I don't scare easily, so you must be terrifying to others."

"I doubt that somehow, but thanks for trying to make me feel better."

For a split second, my guard goes down and I'm tempted to tell Henry about the cottage, after all, and get his opinion on it, but it's probably not a good idea. He's my employer. Our workplace friendship could quickly take a turn if he thinks I might be nuts.

"I'll be in to you within an hour," I say before ringing off.

I catch the bus into town and get off at the nearest stop to the newspaper's office. It's only a two-minute walk from the bus stop to the door of the office and as I walk on the opposite side of the road towards the building, I look at the exterior of the office and notice that it's starting to look a

244

bit run-down. It's a grey brick building surrounded by shops, on a street just off the city's main thoroughfare, and the paper has had its office here for almost twenty years now.

The signage could definitely do with a revamp, but the profits of newspapers have been decreasing rapidly in recent years since online news became a more prominent and immediate source of information, so I know there's no point even suggesting a revamp to Henry. He's more concerned about what's going on inside that building. We all are. We're clinging on to our jobs by the tips of our fingernails, which is one of the reasons why I haven't challenged Henry more on why he didn't want to investigate the gardai after our initial quarrel. He's only looking for an excuse to get rid of people and much as I find his reticence morally objectionable, I want to hold on to my job. I love journalism. Sadly, the openings within the industry are few and far between right now.

A conversation I had with Jake on our first date drifts into my mind.

"What made you want to be a journalist?"

I shrugged. "I read a lot of books about the fictional supersleuth Nancy Drew growing up."

"No, really. What was it about journalism that made you say 'This is it. This is the job for me!' out of all the options out there?"

I took a long drink. "The pursuit of the truth. We need it in life. Without truth, life is all just one big perception and no reality. And that's dangerous. People who want to abuse power can take that mindset and exploit it unless there are people out there who are willing to ask the hard questions."

"And you're one of those people?"

"I hope I am. I want to be one of them."

"So, the truth is important to you?"

"Yes."

"Why?"

"The truth means the bad guys don't win. Where there's a lack of truth, there are people getting away with very bad things. Someone needs to stop them. It might as well be me as the next person."

I wonder if I'm going to be able to stop the bad person this time.

I find myself feeling nervous about seeing the letter as I walk into the building and towards Henry's office. Images of my time in the cottage flash into my mind, but I try to push them down. I'm glad when I reach the door of Henry's office, preferring the thought of what's ahead of me than spending another minute alone with my thoughts and fears.

I knock and hear Henry telling me to enter. The minute I see his face, I realise that my make-up isn't as efficient as I thought it was.

"Jesus! Your face. It's in shreds." Henry stands up and comes out from behind his desk. He walks over to me and stares at the cuts. "What happened?"

"It happened while I was out cold after the Rohypnol . . . I don't remember."

I'm taken aback. I thought I'd hidden the scrapes on my face well. Maybe they just look better to me now compared to how they were a few days ago, but to anyone who hasn't seen me since before the cottage, they must be immediately obvious.

"Did someone do this to you while you were drugged? And who drugged you?"

I sit down and tell Henry as little as possible. That someone put Rohypnol in my drink while I was out with my friends, that I collapsed and hit my head on the ground, that my friend told me I scraped my face myself with my fingernails while I was under the influence of the drug, and that I don't remember any of it. Although I'm again tempted to tell Henry about the cottage, I'm not going there.

Henry leans forwards over his desk and stares at my face again, frowning.

"You were very methodical in your scraping," he says, examining me in the usual forensic fashion he adopts whenever he's considering information in front of him. "The scrapes on both sides of your face are all the same length, even though there's more than five on each side. *Very* methodical for someone who must have been off their head on that date-rape drug. Why do you think that is?"

Thank you, Henry, I say to myself, thinking of the brambles, but to him I say, "I have no idea."

"And what's the story with the person who gave you the Rohypnol?"

"I don't know who it is. We were out, I'd had one too many and someone was chatting me up. I don't remember him, but my friends saw him. We presume it was him, but the CCTV from the pub wasn't of a very good quality, so the gardai say there's not much we can do about it."

"Well, that's shit. Nobody should get away with doing that, especially when you got a head injury out of it. How's your head now?"

"It's okay, but I'm still being a bit cautious," I say. "It's not a serious injury, but I was told by the hospital to take it easy." That bit is true. The reason why I was told to take it easy is slightly more expansive than that, though. "Can I see the letter? I'd prefer to get it over and done with."

Henry opens a drawer and takes out an envelope. As he

hands it to me, he doesn't tell me not to worry about the letter this time. Instead, he looks at the scrapes on my face again.

"It wasn't registered," I say, looking at the envelope.

There's nothing but Irish stamps on it, a succession of regular stamps lined up one under the other on the right-hand side of the envelope.

"No. It just came by regular post."

"No great surprise there. It could have been sent from anywhere in Ireland, so."

"Whoever sent it obviously didn't want to get it weighed in a post office, instead just chucking regular stamps on it and putting it in a post box. They didn't want to be seen on a post office's CCTV, I'd imagine, even though it'd be very hard to track them when they didn't send it as registered."

"Thanks," I sigh.

"You didn't need me to tell you that a non-registered letter is going to be pretty hard to trace, unless the gardai see something in that letter that I don't."

I shrug and open the envelope, taking out the folded piece of paper inside. I read the letter, butterflies rising in my chest as I do so.

"Do you think this is related to the Rohypnol incident, Katie?" Henry asks as soon as I put the letter down.

"I have no idea. All I can do now is bring this directly to the gardai."

I fold the letter and put it in my handbag. Henry crosses his arms and frowns.

"Is there something you're not telling me about all this?"

I shrug. "I'd tell you a lot more if I could remember it myself, Henry."

Again, I don't feel like I'm fully lying when I say this.

Henry's not buying it. I can tell by the expression on his face.

"Oh, I have a cert from the doctor for you," I say, grateful for the opportunity to change the subject. "I'll be staying off for the rest of the week, but I hope to be back next week. I hope me being out isn't putting too much pressure on the rest of you."

"We're managing," Henry says.

I try not to balk at his words. "I'm really sorry about this. I hate putting stress on anyone else."

Henry holds a hand up. "Stop. That sounded bad, but I didn't mean it to. It's just a week off. Nobody's died."

Tears instantly spring to my eyes. I don't know if it's because somebody could have died – I could have died – or because Henry is being vaguely . . . well, *nice*. This is as understanding as I've ever seen him be about any subject. My face must look *really* bad. It's clear that he smells a rat, though. And while in one way I think he could be a very valuable confidante, if things went wrong, it could cost me my job if I opened my mouth.

Henry sees the tears. "Are you okay, Katie?"

"Yes, I'm fine. It's just been a rough few days. Sorry about that." I stand up. "Thanks for this, Henry."

"Let me know what the gardai say," Henry says, standing as well.

Henry *never* stands when I'm leaving his office. He's definitely concerned. I think it might even be genuine.

I rush out as fast as I can, praying I won't meet any of my colleagues as I leave.

Chapter 24

I go straight to the garda station and ask for Brian. Thankfully, he's in the office. I fill him in as succinctly as I can.

"Surely this is proof that someone is out to get me." I say as soon as he's read the letter. "Can you reopen my case as quickly as possible?"

"We'll certainly investigate who might have sent this letter, Katie. We'll check it for fingerprints and we'll see what else we can do in the course of our investigation."

"Like what?"

"I'll keep you informed. Right now, all I can say is that we'll see what results we get from our investigations."

"Are you telling me that you'll need the results of these investigations before you can reopen the case?"

"We'll need to see if this brings any new information to light before we can take any further action," Brian says.

"And what about my safety in the meantime? Someone out there is making it very clear that they're out to get me!"

"Our focus now will be on finding who sent this letter, Katie."

"So what you're saying is, there's nothing else you can

do – or *will* do? There's a clear and present threat to my welfare out there, and you're doing nothing about it. That's the bottom line, is it?"

"Anything we can do, we will do."

"Rubbish, Brian! You're saying something while saying absolutely nothing. It's like my sister said. If I end up dead and buried in the Dublin mountains, you'll be to blame for this. *You*, personally. I've just come from seeing my manager at the paper, Henry, and he's also taking this very seriously. I'll leave you with that thought."

I turn round and march out, furious with Brian. I can't quite believe I've just had the cheek to threaten a guard and I'm sure it'll do no good for my cause, but it feels like no good is being done anyway.

I think about walking home instead of getting the bus – it would take a long time, but a long walk is exactly what I need now to clear my head – however, I'm too afraid. What if the person who's out to get me is watching me right now? In the current circumstances, I can't make a sitting duck of myself by walking the streets of suburbia on my own.

I wait at the bus stop, furious with the situation that's making me too afraid even to go for a walk by myself. This is a perfect justification of why I can't stop until I sort out this situation. I hate that my freedom is being eroded by fear.

On the bus, I relive the discussion with Brian. I have to concede that making a veiled threat to a guard wasn't my smartest move, but my anger and the frustration at being told over and over that there's nothing anyone can do to protect me just boiled over. Anyway, what was I even threatening to do? While my intention was to let Brian know that Henry could expose the gardai's failure to protect me should anything serious happen to me, I obviously know from past experience that Henry is averse to exposing the gardai to negative press. But I was hoping Brian didn't know that.

My previous worry related to the force knowing about my aborted investigation into garda bullying and harassment surely isn't founded . . . Surely it's not public knowledge. Still, I've probably made an enemy of Brian now with my big mouth. The mounting feeling of helplessness that I'm living with every day is making my behaviour more erratic than I'm comfortable with, but I can't seem to stop. My entire life is thundering out of control.

I spend the rest of the journey home wondering who could have sent the letter. The possibility that I might have pissed off some hardened criminal leaves me feeling like I'm going to be sick. And yet I honestly can't remember writing anything other than factual articles about court cases. But maybe that's enough. Maybe someone out there doesn't even want me writing that much. But to risk kidnapping me and then putting me back where they took me from . . . Why would anyone be bothered enough by me to do that? Unless my abduction and this letter are unrelated and the timing is just a remarkable coincidence, but that possibility seems unlikely.

I need to turn my thoughts back to closer to home and continue my investigations. If I don't do something concrete to help save myself, panic is going to take over again – and this time, it'll win. I can feel it coming down the tracks, hurtling itself at me at full speed.

Richard. He has to be next on my list. Richard . . . and Penny. I hate myself for doing this and yet I have no choice. If Penny's covering up for Richard, I need to know.

Later that evening, when I think she must surely be home from work, I call Penny.

"Penny, something's happened. I got a threatening letter. I know it's late, but do you mind if I call over?"

Penny looks exhausted when she answers the door to me half an hour later. I feel guilty for having disturbed her, not to mention the fact that I'm really here to snoop around her house if I can. Penny ushers me into the sitting room.

"Tell me about this letter."

I fill Penny in on the letter, warming my hands by holding them in front of the electric fire as I speak. The room is lovely and toasty.

"Have you passed it on to the gardai?"

"Yes. They're fingerprinting it, supposedly."

"Supposedly?"

I silently berate myself for letting my cynicism shine through. If Penny knew the full extent of why I'm angry with the gardai, she'd only give me another homily about how the cottage didn't happen: "Oh, I wouldn't hold my breath waiting for them to crack the case. They seem to have more urgent considerations, if I'm reading the vibe correctly."

"Well, that's just not acceptable. You make sure to keep pressure on them to take accountability for investigating it thoroughly."

"I'll do my best."

"What did your mother say when she heard about the letter?"

"I didn't tell her. She's worried enough – this will tip her over the edge." Although it might get her to take me seriously, the effect this would have on her stress levels would be unmerciful. "She's not staying with me tonight and I think that's for the best. The events of the last week have worn her out."

Penny nods then yawns. "You did the right thing, I'd

say."

"I think so." I suddenly notice the black rings under Penny's eyes. "Are you okay, Penny? You look tired, which is very unlike you."

Penny smiles. "Yes, actually. Work is somewhat . . . *challenging* right now."

"Oh?"

I've never heard Penny describe work as challenging. Busy, yes, but not challenging.

"It's okay. I can handle it. As for Richard, though – that man needs a good kick, although he'd probably enjoy it a little too much."

"What's going on with Richard?"

"Oh . . . " Penny sighs. "His tastes are a little . . . adventurous, shall we say. It's getting very annoying."

"His tastes in . . . ?"

"Yes. Let's just say that Richard has sexual proclivities that aren't in alignment with mine."

"What are we talking here?" the journalist in me asks.

"It's all fairly pathetic soft porn nonsense. Masks, role play, domination . . . He wanted to tie me up a few nights ago and had a bit of a hissy fit when I said no. Ah, I think he's just going through a bit of a midlife crisis, but it's fairly irritating."

I feel myself stiffen when Penny mentions being tied up. Is that what Richard is into? Penny doesn't seem to make any connection between my experience and hers, though. Probably because she doesn't believe me to begin with for that even to register. And I'd imagine she thinks Richard wouldn't look crooked at me sexually, anyway.

"So, you two are still together?" I say without thinking.

"Why wouldn't we be?"

Shit. "I just, erm, couldn't help overhearing you guys arguing when I went to the bathroom the last night I was here. It sounded pretty serious."

"What? Oh, that's just how we carry on," Penny said. "If I had a euro for every time we argue, I could give up working in the morning. Nothing I can't handle, and the same applies to this little deviancy of his. I'm sure a good night's sleep will sort me out and bring a fresh perspective on certain issues."

"Oh. Okay." I try to change the subject. "I could do with one of those myself. I haven't been sleeping too well since . . . you know. Mind you, the heat in this room is making me sleepy."

"Why don't you stay here tonight? The spare rooms are made up. You don't have to stay in the one you were in the last time if you don't want to – all three of them are ready to be used."

I can't believe my luck. This will give me a perfect opportunity to have a look around. But Penny being so hospitable makes me feel even worse about what I'm doing. Then again, if she had anything to hide, she wouldn't be inviting me to stay.

Although I do need to investigate Penny, Richard is my primary focus, especially now that I know it seems he likes to tie up women. I remind myself of that as I accept her offer, feeling like a complete Judas as I smile at her. Me, the person who's concerned about the truth . . . well, I feel like a total hypocrite and yet I can't stop. I'm on this path now and I need to stay on it until I find out what happened.

"I do have a selfish motive, I have to admit," Penny says. "I really need a decent sleep tonight rather than one of those where you pass out and then wake up again a few hours later, so I'm going to take a sleeping tablet. But I sometimes sleep in after taking one of those and all the alarms in the world wouldn't wake me. If you don't hear me moving around by seven, could you call in on me, please, and shake me awake if necessary?"

"Sure," I say.

I feel even worse for thinking that Penny surely won't hear me rummaging around after she's taken a sleeping tablet.

"Do you want a coffee?"

"Sure. Thanks, Penny."

Penny goes to make coffee. After another half an hour in front of the fire, we're both zonked. Penny excuses herself, saying she's fit to drop and will see me in the morning, but to feel free to stay downstairs and watch TV in front of the fire if I want to. I thank her again and tell her I'll take her up on that offer.

The fire has made me so drowsy that the prospect of nodding off here is so inviting, but as soon as it sounds like Penny has settled upstairs, it's time for me to get down to it.

About forty minutes later, when I've allowed plenty of time for Penny to fall asleep, I take off my shoes. Penny has a wooden floor in her sitting room – which wouldn't be to my taste, but she said it's easier to clean than carpet – and I don't want to risk being heard. I get up and examine the contents of the glass cabinets in Penny's sitting room. Penny's bedroom is at the opposite side of the house, so thankfully, she's unlikely to hear if I do make any noise and she happens to wake, which is surely an unlikely possibility after a sleeping tablet.

As in Jake's house, I don't even know what I'm looking for. Although the cabinets are full, there isn't a whole lot to work through, either. Penny has lots of expensive ornaments from all around the world and they take up about half the cabinet space. She also has several work awards on display. I lift each ornament and award up and look under them, feeling like an absolute fool but at a loss as to what else I should do.

Henry's theory on investigations at work is that you *comb*. You don't ignore the obvious while you're combing. You must lift up the ornaments and get that donkey work out of the way. So I lift them up one by one but, amazingly – or not – there's nothing sinister under any of them. Penny also has lots of expensive but probably never used glassware in her cabinets. I repeat the lifting procedure for the glassware and check that there's nothing in any of the glasses.

I keep expecting Penny to walk in any second, despite the fact that logically, I know I'll hear her if she walks down the stairs. I'm acutely aware that my entire friendship with her is on the line, though if I'm caught, especially after her graciousness in accepting that I wasn't actually going through Jake's things.

An enormous bookcase dominates the other side of the fireplace. I take the books out as quickly as I can, checking behind the spaces where they were and flicking through each one to see if there's any loose documentation in them. I feel absolutely ridiculous now. If Penny had anything to do with my disappearance and return, which is hugely unlikely to begin with, she's hardly going to keep a plan of how she was going to do it in a book as a bookmark or something.

And yet I continue with my task, not knowing what else to do. At least I feel a bit calmer now, though. It feels like I'm just looking through her bookcase for something to take to bed with me to read, although the tomes on this bookshelf would make for heavy reading before going to sleep: *Gaining Traction on Your Business*; *Turbocharge by Topgrading: How to Hire*; *How to Get Exactly What You Want*. I allow myself to smile at that one. I doubt very much that Penny ever needed to read that book in order to get what she wanted. You can tell from the minute you meet her that it's just in her to be like that. I admire her for it.

By the time I've gone through the bookcase, I'm exhausted. I pull out the couch and look behind it then put it back before removing all the cushions and checking to see if there's anything under them. I do the same for the armchairs. By now, I've moved from feeling foolish and embarrassed to wondering if I really do need help. This feels wrong. But I can't back down – I have no other plan. At least I'm taking some sort of action. I'm not sitting back like the victim I feel I've become.

I check every conceivable area in the sitting room then creep to the office at the back of the house. I open a filing cabinet, feeling like an absolute fraud of a friend. This is even worse than going through Jake's stuff. I felt some sort of justification with Jake, because crimes of passion are the most common crimes there are – sexual motivation is a strong one. But moving into the friends territory is a whole different ball game.

Richard. I need to focus on Richard to get me through this. I'm not going through *Penny's* stuff – I'm just looking for information on *him*. Penny told me before that Richard often works at her house if he's staying over. It doesn't happen often because of the obvious limitations in their relationship, but sometimes if he has business travel, he'll stay with Penny the night he comes back and he'll tell his wife he's flying home the following day. Invariably though, when he's caught up with Penny, the time will come when he'll need to go back to work before he can go to sleep.

My eye is immediately drawn to a folder on the right. It has text on its cover. Clearly visible text, because the folder is leaning against other folders and there's nothing at all to obscure my view.

It says: "Keep Calm and Rob a Bank".

I pull the folder out and notice immediately that the text is on a sticker that's been placed on a regular large black folder. It's clear from the banking reference who this folder belongs to, but who gave Richard the sticker? One of his children, most likely. Something about that realisation upsets me. The thought of one of Richard's children giving him something and thinking it'd be used in an office, when it actually ended up in the house of the woman he's cheating on his wife with, isn't a pleasant one. I'm not judging them – I'm in no position to judge anyone while I'm rifling through the possessions of someone who's been a good friend to me – but something about it saddens me nonetheless.

It's always the children who get hurt eventually. But as I know only too well, marriage is complicated. *Relationships* are complicated. There are no answers sometimes, no matter how much we think there should be. In the perfect world that we all aspire to live in someday, we feel we should have all the answers. Right now, I'd settle for finding out who's out to get me and resuming some sort of normality.

The important thing now is to see if there's anything of consequence in this folder. I hugely doubt that there is. If Richard has something to hide, he's not going to leave it in Penny's house, surely.

I rifle through it as quickly as I can and find nothing of

consequence. Again, I'm not even sure what I'm looking for, but this folder just contains work-related files that mean little or nothing to me.

I sift through everything else in the office, but nothing jumps out at me as being of any importance. I move to the kitchen and go through drawers. Penny's so organised that there are no receipts or documentation or anything untoward lying around where they shouldn't be. By the time 3 a.m. comes round, I realise I have to call it a night. I'm disappointed but not hugely surprised. It was never going to be that easy.

Chapter 25

I'm dressed and downstairs first the following morning. Although it's early, I'm kind of surprised by that. I half expected Penny to be up after her usual 6 a.m. workout. Sleeping tablet or no sleeping tablet, it really wouldn't have surprised me. As it happens, we meet in the kitchen shortly after seven, with no wake-up call from me required.

"Morning, Katie. Did you sleep well?"

"Yes, thanks. And you?"

"Far too well. I need to get out of here now. Actually, pretty much five minutes ago."

Penny fills a glass with water, knocks it back and slams the glass on the counter.

"Are you leaving now, or shall I give you the code to set the alarm?"

I can't think of a reason to justify why I'd want to stay after Penny leaves, given that I'm fully dressed and wearing my coat.

"I'm ready to go," I say.

"Great."

We go out into the hall, where Penny retrieves her handbag and coat from an ornate coat stand. As she does so, I curse myself for not pretending I slept in. I could have rushed into Penny's room at seven to wake her, Penny would have left in a hurry and she'd surely have said to me to stay on here. I could have had free access to look around upstairs for any clues. It would have been interesting to see if I could have found my old blouse anywhere. But surely if Penny isn't telling the truth about it, she'd definitely have thrown it out, just in case.

"Ready?" Penny has one hand on the alarm panel, standing by to set the code.

"Sure."

I open the front door and walk out.

"Do you want a lift to the bus stop?" Penny asks when we get outside.

I instantly feel bad for what I've just been thinking. I don't know who this whole scenario is turning me into.

"No, I'd rather walk. Thanks for having me to stay."

"Welcome. Talk soon."

Penny disappears into her car in a haze of heavy perfume, leaving a vacuum in her wake. She has such presence that I always feel a bit deflated when she leaves.

I trudge down the driveway and head for the bus stop. I've outstayed my welcome with what I've been up to.

Later that day, back home, I'm surprised when the doorbell rings. I'm not expecting anyone. I paddle out, hoping whatever is coming isn't going to bring me more trouble.

Rose is standing there when I open the front door.

"Oh, Rose, hi," I say, my surprise evident in my voice. "Is everything okay?"

"There's something I need to talk to you about. Can I come in?"

"Sure." I pull the door back further and stand aside. "Come on into the sitting room."

"I was talking to Anna earlier. I'm really sorry . . . I gave you false information about Jake. I didn't mean to, of course. I've only just found out that Anna was lying about Jake stalking her."

"*What*? Why?"

"She's in a bad place, Katie. It doesn't excuse her behaviour in any way, of course, but nothing is going right for her and she's taking it out on you. She's not over Jake at all. She thought there was some hope of them getting back together in the future, but obviously he met you and then that didn't happen. When were we talking, she said she just couldn't help saying what she did, in the hope that I'd relay it and you'd never go near him again."

No wonder she never mailed me back! She obviously just wanted to plant the bomb but not to have to explain her actions further.

"So why is she admitting it now?"

"I bumped into her again earlier in the TV station and she asked me what was going on between you and Jake now. I told her . . . "

"Told her what?"

Rose grimaces. "I'm sorry, Katie. I know you won't like me having said this, but I mentioned that you'd been drugged last weekend and things weren't going well for you in general, either. When she heard about that, everything changed. She felt sorry for you then and I assume she started to feel bad about the lies she'd told me when she heard the story."

"What did you tell her, specifically?"

Rose's cheeks flame. "I . . . I mentioned the hallucinations."

"Oh, Jesus. Everyone in the media knows each other, Rose. It's a small industry and I really don't want my private business being put out there by someone else!"

"Katie, I know it was a mistake. I really shouldn't have said anything. I'm sorry. I know it was very indiscreet of me. But it seems that me telling her about the hallucinations prompted her to tell me that she'd lied, so it's probably a good thing that I did."

I shake my head. "This is the situation that just keeps on giving and giving. As if being abducted wasn't bad enough."

"Oh, Katie." Rose shook her head.

"What?"

Rose bit her lip. "The abduction story . . . "

"Story? It's *not* a story. *Harry Potter* is a story. This *happened*!"

"I'm sorry, Katie, but I don't believe it did. It's not in any way feasible."

"I don't believe this."

But even as I said that, I did. I knew she wasn't alone, either, in her disbelief. Then again, *I* knew what was real and what wasn't.

"You probably need to be getting on," I say. "Thanks for calling over to tell me this in person. I'd appreciate it if you didn't tell anyone else my business from now on, though."

"Katie, I'm sorry!"

"So am I."

I walk to the front door, open it and stand there until Rose comes out of the sitting room.

Rose leaves with a hangdog look on her face. I'm not really all that mad with her, just disappointed that she saw fit to spread my business more so than anything else. Part of me is seething at Anna, though, while another part is relieved to hear that not only is Jake not a stalker, but also, he didn't want to marry Anna after a few months of being with her. That pleases me. But then I'm instantly filled with shame. I've got the gardai to investigate Jake. I've let myself into his house and searched it. Any feelings he had for me are surely dead and buried after that.

Dead and buried. As I could have been if I hadn't escaped from that house. Who knew what would have happened next?

I need to get to the bottom of everything, once and for all. I owe it to myself. I know now that I'm going to lose a lot of people along the way, but I could have lost my own life. I need to know who did this to me. Even if they don't come back for me, they could well go for someone else. And at this stage, it seems that nobody can stop this person, only me.

My phone rings. I look at the screen and see that it's Penny.

"Hi, Penny."

"Hi. Are you free? I need to talk to you."

"Yes, I'm at home on my own."

"Good. Katie, did you come across a folder belonging to Richard when you stayed at my house recently?"

I feel a sinking sensation in the pit of my stomach. How does she know? How can she possibly know?

"Em, no. At least I don't think I did."

I say the only thing I can think of. I can hardly say yes.

"Are you sure?"

"Yes, as far as I'm aware. Why, is a folder missing?"

"No."

"You've lost me, I'm afraid."

265

"When you called over and I asked you if you wanted to stay the night, you might remember that I was really tired and I went to bed quite early. We watched some TV and we didn't talk as much as we usually do because of that. As a result, I didn't get a chance to tell you that I got the external CCTV fixed. While I was getting that done, I also got *internal* CCTV."

Blood rushes to my face so fast that I feel like my cheeks will explode.

"You might remember that I left for work very quickly the following morning. I barely saw anything of the house before I left. But when I got home, I noticed that things weren't quite the same as how I usually keep them. The couch was at a slightly different angle, some of the books were sticking out further than they usually are . . . Just little things, but noticeable all the same when you live on your own and you're used to everything being exactly the same way all the time.

"I couldn't understand why that would be when there'd been no report from the alarm company of my house alarm having gone off over the last few days, but I just knew something wasn't quite right. It was niggling at me, so I took a look at the CCTV, just to make sure someone hadn't been in the house, even though nothing had been taken. And . . . well, you can fill in the rest."

I say nothing. I can't think of a single thing to say to explain myself. Sorry isn't enough. Sorry would be an insult.

"I should have listened to my brother," Penny says after an excruciatingly long silence.

"Penny, you've been nothing but good to me, but—"

"So, which of us do you suspect? Richard or me?" Her voice is hard now. "Or both of us? Are we working together

266

to ruin your life for some inexplicable reason?"

"Penny, it's honestly nothing personal. It's just that gardai's investigation has gone nowhere and I need to eliminate all possibilities."

"Katie, I really thought you were going to be okay," she says. And then she hangs up.

I'm shaking. I know I've lost Penny. Even though she didn't believe me, she was supportive in her own way and now that she's gone, through *my* actions, I feel utterly bereft.

As always, I have to remind myself that I had no other option. And yet I'm getting tired of telling myself that. All I'm doing is trying to uncover the truth, so why does it all feel so wrong?

Mam calls over and says she'll be staying the night. She tries to get me to talk at first. I make an enthusiastic effort for about two minutes, then run out of steam and fall silent. Mam then hovers around the sitting room, tidying and moving things that don't need to be tidied or moved. She's like a hen with an egg, and that usually means trouble.

She places an ornament back down on the mantelpiece and sighs heavily. When she turns round, her face looks tormented. She walks towards me and sits gingerly beside me on the couch, simultaneously reaching for the remote and muting the TV.

"Katie, what *is* it? What's wrong?"

I frown. "What do you mean?"

"You're not yourself at all today. You're jumpy. You seem almost hyper sometimes and other times you're a million miles away."

"I'm fine, Mam."

"Katie, you are *not* fine. I know you're not."

"You're wrong! Honestly, there's nothing wrong."

"Katie, I'm your *mother*. I *know* there's something up. I'm going out of my mind fretting about you. And I met your neighbour, Helen, outside there on my way in. She was asking how you were. She said you were in an awful state about your key the other day and she was very worried about you. Will you for heaven's sake tell me what it is so that I can help you? I'm worried morning, noon and night about you!"

I look at Mam, sitting beside me on the couch wringing her hands. A pang of guilt at what she's going through gnaws at me. But surely telling her what I'm really thinking – and doing – is worse.

"Katie, please. If you need help, I'm here for you. Whatever's bothering you is eating away at you, too. I can see it is."

I hesitate. Maybe Mam can help.

And she's clearly not going to give up asking until she finds out what I'm thinking.

I take a deep breath. "Mam, I know what happened in the cottage was real. I also know that nobody believes me when I say it was. But I *know* it was. And right now, I need to find out who did that to me. I won't have another minute of peace until I do. Someone is out to get me."

Mam's reaction is far, far worse than I expected. I thought she'd argue the toss with me again, telling me there's no logic at all in what I'm saying. Instead, she starts to cry. As she stares at me silently, tears spill from her eyes and drop down her cheeks. There are many of them. They come thick and fast. She remains motionless.

"Ah, Mam . . . " I touch her arm.

She draws back.

I give her the space she clearly needs, staring at the TV and wishing she'd say something. Anything. The silence, occasionally punctuated by sniffles and the rustle of tissue, is unbearable.

"You need to see someone," she says eventually. "A professional."

"I don't, Mam! I *need* someone to believe me!"

Mam shakes her head. She looks sadder than I've ever seen her, except when Dad died. The juxtaposition of the sadness I'm seeing now with the memories of how it was for all of us back then almost makes me shriek aloud.

"You heard what the doctor said to you in the hospital, Katie," Mam says, three times as slowly as she usually speaks. "It was a hallucination. Nothing more. Do you remember when you were young and you were convinced that the boogieman existed? After a long time – a long, fearful time – you realised and accepted that there was no boogieman. There isn't one now, either, Katie. Nobody's out to get you. A bad man wanted to take advantage of you, but it's over now. How can you not see that?"

"You're wrong, Mam," I say.

I notice that the pleading tone has left my voice now. I'm angry – angry that my own mother doesn't believe me – but I'm trying not to show it. Mam's too old. She's been through too much. It's not fair. I fervently wish I'd never said anything. I should have continued to lie to Mam about how I was feeling. Sometimes, honesty is not the best policy.

"Let me make you a cup of tea," I say, jumping up. Trying to break the tension. "You should have some tea and biscuits before bingo."

"I can't possibly go to bingo now," Mam says. "This is really serious, Katie. Can you not see that?"

"You should go. You never miss bingo. Let me make you that tea."

"No. No tea. I'm staying here and we're going to work out what we're going to do about all this."

Something rises in me. I'm not sure if it's anger, fear, nausea or an alternative that I can't quite identify. It's not pleasant, that much I do know. In fact, it's becoming more overpowering by the second.

"Mam, I'm going for a walk. I need some air."

I grab my keys from my handbag and run out as fast as I can before Mam tries to stop me. I need to get out of here. Now.

I run down the driveway and keep running until I'm well down the street, around the corner where Mam won't see me if she looks out. My heart is racing. I sit on a wall and wait for it to stop, but it doesn't.

My mind floods with thoughts, not just about the big picture, but also all the little things that have been going wrong. Texts being sent from my phone in the middle of the night, me breaking my key in the door and Helen seeing me so upset, my clothes being in the washing machine when I thought I'd put them on the radiator . . . all the little things that have been going wrong. Maybe I *am* losing my mind. Maybe everyone else is right and I'm wrong.

My heart starts to pound even heavier until I feel like it's about to burst out of my chest. A whooshing sound is flooding my ears. I try to take a deep breath, but I can't. The air won't seem to go in. I'm gasping now. I can feel beads of sweat forming on my forehead, even though it's a cold evening.

I start to pant in an attempt to breathe. I've no idea what's happening to me, but I'm scared. *Terrified*. For a few seconds, I think I'm going to die here and now. My heart is thumping against my ribcage so hard that it feels like it'll rip through my skin and land in my hands.

I do the only thing I can think of. I drop to the ground and put my head between my knees, forcing myself to attempt to take deep breaths. I close my eyes and try to empty my head of all thoughts.

Eventually, my breathing regulates. I can feel my heartbeat start to slow. I try not to think about what's happening in case focusing on it sets it all off again. Eventually, I get up and walk away as if nothing has happened. I tell myself everything is normal. Everything is fine. I don't even look around to see if anyone was there to see me sitting on the pavement with my head between my knees, gasping like a person at the side of a lake who just got saved from drowning. I pretend as if my life depends on it that I'm fine. Just fine.

I let myself in and go straight to the kitchen to put the kettle on. I unload the dishwasher. I force myself not to think about what just happened. I keep things normal.

This works reasonably well until Mam comes into the kitchen.

"Cup of tea?" I say when it becomes apparent that Mam isn't going to say anything.

"Katie, you surely don't expect me to drink tea and act like everything's okay?" she says.

This is bad. When Mam refuses tea – for the *second* time – things are truly serious.

"What do you want me to do, Mam?" My voice sounds calm. Disconnected. Disaffected, almost.

"You need to see a doctor," she says. "I'll take you to Dr McGuire in the morning. We need to take action on this as soon as possible."

I pretend she's talking about someone else's life. I need to stay calm.

"No action is required," I say. "Honestly."

"Katie, for the love of God—"

"I'm going to bed, Mam. I know it's early, but I'm tired. Thank you for wanting to help, but I have no more to say about this."

I walk out. Mam yells – *yells* – at me to come back. I pretend I don't hear. She follows me halfway up the stairs and I pretend she hasn't done that, either. When she follows me into my bedroom and tells me how much I'm in denial about how sick I am, I turn on my side in bed, fully clothed, and try to block her out.

When she eventually leaves, after a Trojan effort to talk me round, guilt creeps in. I mentally swallow it down. There's no room for guilt now. Guilt and all it entails will lead me back to the place I was in earlier.

Hours later, as I lie awake on the bed long after Mam has gone to bed in the spare room, I try to think about what happened earlier without delving into it too deeply in case it happens again. It's a delicate balance and one I'm struggling with.

I'm reluctant to put a label on what I just experienced, but everything is pointing to it being a panic attack. This thought makes no sense to me. I survived through the most horrific experience of my life in that cottage without experiencing what I did today. Why now? Is this some sort of post-traumatic stress coming out? My lack of understanding of what just happened is making me feel more anxious than ever. Given how I felt earlier today, that state would previously have been unthinkable to me.

It's a long time before I inevitably fall into a troubled sleep.

* * *

I meet Mam in the kitchen early the following morning. I couldn't stay in bed any longer than 8 a.m., my thoughts and worries invading my head too early for me to cope with. In the kitchen, I'm focusing on chopping fruit for breakfast, when Mam walks in.

"I'm sorry, Mam," I say instantly. "I didn't mean to be rude to you last night. I just needed some space."

"I see. And are you ready to talk about what needs to be done now?"

I hold back the sigh that's threatening to come out. "I'm only just up, Mam. I slept very badly. Can you give me some time to wake before we start the talking?"

"I'm only concerned about you, Katie! I'm trying to help you!"

"You don't need to be concerned and I don't need help. Mam, I know you're only trying to do your best for me, but please don't suffocate me. I'm a grown woman. *I* decide if I should see a doctor, or a shrink, or whoever it is you want me to see. I won't be railroaded into it, even if the railroading is coming with the best of intentions.

"I know you're only doing this because you care, but you need to stop treating me like a troubled teenager. That was all eighteen years ago. It's not now."

I hadn't intended for any of those words to come out.

At the mention of eighteen years ago, Mam looks at me as if I've slapped her cheek. I'm instantly annoyed. Yes, I did something wrong then and I caused my mother a lot of stress. But it was *eighteen years ago*. I've atoned for my sins by not giving her another minute of worry between then and now. How much longer am I going to be seen in the light of a shadow cast by a ghost from the past?

"I think I should go," Mam says.

"Ah no, don't. I didn't mean to sound cross."

Mam just shakes her head and walks out into the hall. As I follow her, she takes her coat and handbag from the coat stand and leaves without saying goodbye. I can tell she's furious. For once, she's not upset or worried. She's just plain furious at me.

I sit on the bottom stair for a long time after she leaves.

That evening, Mam's landline number appears on my screen. I swipe the phone to answer the call.

"Hi, Mam," I say tentatively. "How are you?"

"Fine, fine."

She doesn't sound fine. She sounds jumpy.

"About earlier . . . " I try.

"I don't want to talk about that. I was just ringing to ask you to come over tomorrow, actually. Tomorrow morning, please."

"Oh?"

"Yes, I need you to take me somewhere." She coughs.

"Sure. Are you sick?"

"Sick? No, no, I'm not sick."

"Okay. I just asked when I heard you coughing. I thought maybe you wanted to go to the doctor or something."

"No, no. But please be on time, Katie – ten o'clock on the dot, okay?"

"No problem."

"Grand. Well, I'll see you then." She coughs again.

"Where am I taking you?"

Yet again, she coughs. "I'll fill you in when you get here.

I must go now. Get to bed early, Katie, like a good girl. See you tomorrow – please, God."

She hangs up just as I'm saying goodbye. Mam *never* hangs up without a long round of goodbyes.

I put the phone down, staring at it as if I've just been smacked in the face by it. What was *that* all about?

Chapter 26

As I drive to Mam's the following morning, worry starts to kick in. She definitely wasn't herself last night on the phone. Something is wrong. I drive faster, worrying myself into a tizzy about the possibilities of what's up. I'm relieved when I pull up behind Mam's car in the driveway. Whatever she wants to talk to me about probably isn't good, but at least I'm here now.

As I walk towards the front door, I send a silent prayer up that she isn't sick and has been keeping it from me because of my troubles. Although Mam is of a somewhat nervous disposition in general, she never usually sounds quite so nervy as she did last night. Maybe it's just because of the words we had, but it feels like something more than that. Why would she decide to tell me right now that she's sick, though, when this is probably the worst time of all to do so? It can't be that. Still, my mind is going down the worst possible avenues and the sooner I hear what's going on, the better.

When I get to the house, I take my phone out of the glove compartment. I'm about to pop it into my handbag, when I see that I have a text. I almost drop the phone when I see who it's from:

Katie, this is Richard. I need to speak to you ASAP. Been ringing you for ages and no answer. Please ring me on this number as soon as you can.

At least that's the mystery of the withheld number solved, but why on earth would he want to speak to me? And why was the number withheld? Maybe he was ringing from a landline – numbers aren't always displayed on calls from them. If he wants to speak to me, he mustn't have been actively or purposely hiding his number.

I'm intrigued, perplexed and worried about this message and its implications, but now isn't the time to ring him. If I don't go into the house, Mam isn't above coming out to the car to get me. Catching me in the middle of a conversation with Richard wouldn't be a good thing. I mentally park the job until later.

I ring the doorbell. Mam opens the door faster than I'd expected, as if she was waiting for me.

"Hi, Mam. Is everything okay?" I say instantly.

I can already tell from her expression that something isn't right.

"Follow me," she says then walks towards the dining room.

As I walk behind her, I hear the sound of voices in the dining room. When I go inside, I see an expanse of familiar faces: Claire. Sandra. Penny. Gabrielle. Rose. Barbara. Jake.

I'm flummoxed. Their cars weren't parked outside. Where did they all come from?

"What's going on?" I say to Mam, who's walked into the middle of the dining room.

Mam lowers her head but beckons at me to enter.

"Mam?" I say, still standing at the door.

Shirley Benton

"We've all been so worried about you, love. I thought if all of the people in your life who care about you the most got together and we all talked things over, it would help."

Mam is shrugging now and looking very nervous. The penny drops.

"Is this an . . . *intervention*?"

"I didn't know what else to do."

"Dear God, I'm hardly in Kurt Cobain territory!" I look from one face to another, furious at them all.

"Who?" Mam asks.

"That grubby-looking singer in Nirvana who she was mad about twenty-something years ago. Claire got her into his music," Sandra says to Mam when I don't answer. "His wife got all of his people together to convince him to go to rehab because he had a serious heroin problem."

"Oh," is all Mam can say.

"And did it work, Sandra?" I say, remembering how Kurt sadly killed himself days after leaving the rehab unit some felt he was forced into going to.

"We're not here to talk about Kurt Cobain," Sandra says. "Mam was right to get us all together. We need to work out what to do about all this. You've been going around sussing people out behind their backs, Katie. That's not normal behaviour. That's paranoid at best. And at worst . . . "

"We're all just worried sick about you, Katie," Mam says. The tears are shining in her eyes. "Can't you just sit down with us for a few minutes?"

I shake my head at first, but I eventually sit. I can't let Mam down in front of everyone, even though part of me is livid with her.

I look them all in the eye. They all look uncomfortable,

278

except for Penny, who looks as if she means business. There's a hint of regret on her face, but not much of one. I suspect she's here to do what she needs to do and she won't be feeling too bad about it afterwards. That's how Penny operates.

I feel a flash of resentment towards her and find myself glaring at her. Penny, being Penny, doesn't flinch. I have a feeling the others are delighted to have her here. To say the hard stuff. The stuff that *needs to be said*.

"I've been talking to your sisters and your friends, love, and they're all worried about how you've been checking them out to see if they're a danger to you. Don't worry. This isn't an angry mob gathering. They're not offended, are you?"

Mam turns to everyone else in the room. There's a collective muttering of "No," and a few add-ons that that's not what this is about and they're just concerned for me.

"We're here purely to work out how we can help you. You need to see that none of us are a danger or a threat to you," Penny says.

"The jeans were frayed, Penny," I say. "When I got my jeans back from your house, they were covered in fray marks. That's from the brambles. How do you explain that?"

Penny looks at Mam and shakes her head as if this is a conversation that they expected to have. As if it's all been discussed.

"I didn't want to ruin your excitement about your expensive new jeans, Katie, but I have exactly the same jeans. I bought them way before you did. They're frayed also. They fray very easily."

"I saw Penny's jeans," Mam says. "They're frayed all right. It's just the material in them."

I honestly can't believe what I'm hearing. Penny has

279

been showing Mam her jeans behind my back. It's almost funny. For all I know, Penny could be deceiving me. She could be covering up for Richard. That's why the blouse "shrank" in the wash. The blouse would have been proof of the existence of the brambles. It would have been too much for both the blouse and the jeans to disappear, though.

Or is she covering up for Jake? Was I right from the start?

Jake's looking at the floor. He looks more uncomfortable than anyone else in the room.

I don't know who exactly it is, but I know someone in this room knows more than they're letting on. I can't let them know I'm on to them, though. I'll have to pretend to go along with this. I'll never find out the truth if I don't.

"So, what exactly are you all suggesting I do?" I say, staring at each one of them in turn.

Claire's eyes drop to the ground. She looks mortified. I'm not surprised, seeing as she was apparently on my side not so long ago.

"The first step is to go to your doctor and assess if you need medication," Penny says, taking the lead. "The doctor can also consider if you need further assistance from other health departments."

"What do you mean? What other health departments could I possibly need?"

Penny glances at Mam. Mam nods.

"Psychiatric help, Katie," Penny says softly. "I'm sure everything's fine, but I think it'd be best to leave no avenue unexplored, don't you? There's a way out of this. You're not alone. We'll all make sure you get the help you need."

Everyone in the room nods or mutters assent.

I feel like I'm drowning. I've never felt so hopeless in my whole life. I want to scream at them that I don't need help, but I won't be able to bear their pitying faces if I do. I also don't want to give them any more reasons to treat me like someone who needs psychiatric help.

This isn't me. This person they're talking about, it's someone else. It's *not* me. I realise I need to be seen to acquiesce to some level if I'm to get anyone back on my side. I can spend the rest of the day arguing with them all if I want, but there's no point.

I turn to Mam. "Okay. Tell me what you want me to do and I'll do it."

Mam's face almost collapses with relief.

"Katie, love, I want you to do it for yourself, not for me or for anyone else here," she says, grabbing my hands.

"I am," I lie. "I am."

Mam grabs me and pulls me into a hug. As I look over her shoulder, I see the reaction of everyone else in the room to my easy acquiescence. Some look relieved. Some look confused. Some just look plain dubious. Both Sandra and Penny are looking at me as if they don't believe a word. Jake's still looking at the ground. As I stare at him, he lifts his head. His expression is one of heartbreak.

I look away from him. Instead, I alternate my stare between Sandra and Penny. At that moment, I fully realise that neither of them believes a word I've been saying. Right then, I hate them both. If something happened to either of them, I'd like to think that I'd believe them. That I'd give them a chance. That I wouldn't assume that they were crazy and needed help. That's what this boils down to, as far as I'm concerned. They think I'm crazy. In fact, everyone in this room thinks I'm crazy.

The only person who can prove I'm not is me. And I won't give up until I do.

I smile at them both, more to discomfit them than anything else. Let them think what they want. I know what happened.

Mam comes with me to the doctor's surgery. I feel like a teenager again, for all the wrong reasons. We're at Dr McGuire's surgery, the local family doctor, not the one I've been seeing for the last few years. Dr McGuire's in his sixties and is someone Mam is much more comfortable speaking to than a stranger.

She needed to talk to a doctor about all this too, she said, and she was much happier confiding in our family doctor than in some young pup who's not long graduated. Me pointing out that my local doctor is in her forties if she's a day did nothing to allay her fears. Our local family doctor had known me since I was a baby, Mam said, even though he hasn't seen me in about a decade and a half and wouldn't know me from Adam if I passed him on the street.

He knew the young me – the daughter of Mr and Mrs Turner me. He doesn't know the current me, just that ghost of my past who's long gone. The fact that he's the person who Mam brought me to after my experience with drugs after Dad died isn't something I'm happy about. I'm sure he's predisposed not to look kindly on my experience as a result of that, but I say nothing. Because none of this matters and I'm just playing along anyway, I agreed to see him.

Dr McGuire smiles benevolently at us when we walk into the room. If he sees anything strange about a woman in her seventies accompanying her grown-up daughter to his surgery, it doesn't show on his face.

"What can I do for you?" he eventually says after we sit down and neither of us say anything.

"Katie needs a bit of help," Mam says, looking from the doctor to me and then back at the doctor. "Katie, why don't you tell Dr McGuire what's been going on recently?"

I glance at Dr McGuire, mortified. I feel more like a child now than even a teenager.

"Go on," Mam says, laying a hand on my arm. "There's nothing to worry about. Dr McGuire just wants to help."

I can't quite believe I'm in this situation, but I start to talk. Slowly at first until eventually, the whole story comes out. I tell him about what happened in the cottage, to which Mam adds a footnote that the gardai checked out my story and found no evidence that anything had taken place. I tell him that I've been finding it hard to trust anyone ever since.

Mam tells Dr McGuire that it's transpired that I checked out the activities of all of my friends on that night, as I knew she would. Dr McGuire doesn't look at me as if I'm mad. He just nods continually through it all. I can't help feeling that he's humouring me as we work through the story, though. Mam adds a few other details when I've told the bones of the story. That I've been under a lot of stress at work, that I recently broke up with Jake, and that in her opinion and that of those closest to me, I've been drinking far too much.

"I'm worried that she's suffering from some sort of anxiety," Mam adds when it seems like she has nothing else to say. "We're also concerned that it might be . . . something more serious." She glances at me.

"What she's saying is that she's worried I might need psychiatric help."

Mam cuts me with a look.

"There's no point in skirting around the issue, is there?

283

That's why you brought me here, after all. Penny said as much when she was in the house."

"What do you think of what we've told you, Dr McGuire?" Mam says, looking nervously at him.

"It sounds like you've had a very rough time of it recently, Katie," Dr McGuire says. "I'd like to do what I can to help you as much as possible."

He says the words without judgment and I find myself relaxing a little.

"As regards your anxiety in general, we often find ourselves experiencing a period of time during which there is more stress and demands than usual. It sounds to me like this has been the case for you in recent months. This can often lead to bouts of anxiety, which in your case has probably been exacerbated by the incident with the Rohypnol.

"I'm going to recommend an anti-anxiety medication for you, Katie. However, it's also possible at this point for me to refer to you to a specialist. Although what you're experiencing right now is a recent development, and sometimes in patients I'd recommend monitoring the situation further before taking any action, I think it'd be wise here to get a specialist involved."

"What kind of specialist?" Mam says.

I already know the answer. I think she does too, but the question still needs to be asked.

"I think it'd be beneficial for Katie to see a psychiatrist," Dr McGuire says. "Someone who's a specialist in mental health is the right person for you to see just now."

I'm not sure if it's the expression on my face or the sight of Mam raising a hand to her mouth and shaking her head that makes Dr McGuire add that seeing a psychiatrist isn't something to be alarmed about.

"This recommendation doesn't mean that the severity of what Katie's going through is high," Dr McGuire says. "I just want you to leave here today feeling you've been given the best possible chance to get better, Katie. Combined therapy is, in my opinion, the best way to achieve that."

"So, how severe would you consider Katie's behaviour of late to be, in terms of . . . well, mental health, as you call it?"

"I don't think either of you should be unduly concerned. From what you've told me, the cottage experience seems to be a hallucination – a known side effect of Rohypnol. This hallucination has led to paranoia, which is tied in with Katie's already existing anxiety issues."

A line from a Nirvana song comes into my head, paraphrased from a quote from Joseph Heller's book *Catch-22*, about how just because you're paranoid doesn't mean they're not after you. But I think it best to keep that to myself.

"Dr McGuire, you said in some people you'd recommend monitoring this type of situation further before taking any action in terms of specialists. Why aren't you doing that with me? Why the hurry to jump straight into a psychiatric assessment?"

Dr McGuire shifts in his seat. A flash of pink rises on his face.

"Having treated you in the aftermath of your father's passing, I just think it'd be prudent to jump in early here and make sure you have the best level of care possible at an early stage."

I can't help myself. "I was eighteen! You can't judge me now on the person I was then!"

"I'm not judging you at all, Katie. It's my duty as a

doctor to provide you with the means to move forwards with your health. This is the course of action I recommend we take."

Mam nods vigorously. "I couldn't agree more, Dr McGuire. We came here looking for help and now we have it, thank God."

"The main thing now is to focus on the future," Dr McGuire says, looking more comfortable now. "With treatment, I'm confident that you'll soon see an improvement in how you're feeling, Katie. However, I'm concerned about how the situation with the Rohypnol occurred in the first place. You said you were quite drunk and didn't notice the Rohypnol being placed in your drink. Was this level of intoxication a one-off?"

Mam looks at me pointedly.

"I do drink frequently," I say. "And sometimes in large volumes."

"In terms of nights of an average week, how many nights would you drink?"

"I have a glass of wine every night," I say. "Sometimes two. If I have a night out planned with a meal, I'd definitely drink a full bottle of wine with the meal, followed by either more wine afterwards or spirits. I might have one or two nights out a week."

"So, is it fair to say that you'd have one to two nights per week of heavy alcohol consumption?"

"I suppose it is. But to be honest, Doctor, I've barely touched a drop since . . . the cottage experience." I refuse to call it a hallucination just because everyone else is. "I've certainly had no desire to drink at all since then. I just shared a few drinks with a friend because she didn't want to drink alone. I personally feel my social drinking has just

286

become a habit – one I could give up easily. I don't feel it's a problem."

Dr McGuire asks me more questions about my drinking patterns. After what seems like an eternity, he concludes that while it doesn't sound like I'm an alcoholic, my drinking is something I need to keep a close eye on.

"Excessive alcohol consumption is something that could easily become a problem," Dr McGuire says, "so I'd recommend that you remain aware of that. I'd also recommend that you refrain from drinking excessively while on the medication I'm prescribing you. And if at all possible, avoid it completely."

Dr McGuire adds that he'll need to monitor my condition and gives me a date to come back. We leave with a prescription for an anti-anxiety drug and a referral to a specialist under way. Mam looks slightly less stressed as we walk towards the reception desk. As I pay for my consultation with the doctor, I throw the prescription in my bag and hope that it'll buy me some trust with my family and friends. I have no intention of using it, but they don't have to know that.

Chapter 27

When we leave the surgery, Mam instantly points out that there's a chemist round the corner.

"Let's go and get your prescription now," Mam says, taking my arm and physically leading me in the direction of the chemist.

I don't argue. It's easier that way. If it means I have to fork out for a prescription I have no intention of taking, so be it.

At the chemist, Mam takes the prescription out of my handbag and gives it to the lady behind the counter. After a short wait, my name is called. I'm given instructions on how to take the medicine correctly and I nod as I listen to them, feigning interest. Mam takes my prescription and looks at it with what seems to be great interest as we return to the car. She doesn't give it back until we're safely inside with our seat belts on, as if she's afraid I'll dump it in a bin when she's not looking if she doesn't take care of it.

We drive home in relative silence, punctuated occasionally by Mam repeating variants of the sentiment that things will hopefully improve with the medication and the visits to the psychiatrist. I nod or murmur assent every time she says it, hoping that I'm coming across as compliant in this whole exercise. I'm hoping my resentment at how my entire set of friends and family view me isn't coming across.

"Will you have a cup of tea, Mam?" I say as we walk into the kitchen of my house after we arrive back. "And I could make you a sandwich as well before you head off, if you like?"

"No, thanks. Sure, I'll stay with you tonight, pet," Mam says.

"Oh no, honestly, don't worry about me," I say slightly too quickly.

The thought of Mam watching my every move for the rest of the night isn't appealing. I quickly berate myself in my head for my ungratefulness. I know she's just concerned about me and I should be damn grateful that somebody is when someone else in the world is clearly out to get me. But I'm worried that I can't keep up the pretence for much longer. Mam may be innocent, but she's no fool, either.

"I insist," Mam says firmly. "Sure, what else would I be doing at home, anyway?"

I have no comeback to that. Mam has often mentioned how bored she is at home now that all of her children have flown the coop. I say thanks and set about making the tea.

"You can take your tablet with your tea now," Mam says as soon as we sit down at the kitchen table with our full-to-the-brim mugs.

"I'll leave it until after dinner," I say. "I shouldn't take them on an empty stomach."

"Does it say that on the prescription?"

"Well, em, I don't know. It's just never good to take medication without a meal first in case it makes you nauseous. So they say, anyway. I remember I took some ibuprofen and codeine before on an empty stomach and it made me vomit, so I don't want to take any chances."

"Right. Well, don't forget to take the first tablet straight after dinner, so," Mam says.

"I won't."

I sip my tea, wondering how I'll manage to get out of taking the tablet when the time comes. There's no way I'm taking medication I don't need. If anything, I need to feel anxious. It'll drive me on to get to the bottom of the situation.

My thoughts flit to the panic attack, but I immediately try to put that out of my mind. Anything that relaxes me could make me feel complacent and hopefully, the panic attack was a one-off.

I set about making the dinner, asking Mam to sit down in the sitting room and relax. She won't listen to a bar of it, though, and insists on helping to make the shepherd's pie. She's in the middle of chopping onions when her phone rings. She wipes her hands on kitchen roll before grabbing her phone and answering it hastily.

"Hello there," she says. "Give me a moment, please."

She scurries out of the kitchen without a backwards glance. I wonder who she's talking to – and why she's started to say "hello there" when she answers the phone, instead of her usual "how are ya."

I hear the front door open. She's gone outside. Clearly, whoever she's talking to, it's about me.

Jake. He came to the intervention, after all. Maybe he's still concerned about me, even though the last time we met he said he didn't want anything else to do with me.

She comes back in five minutes later, shivering.

"There's no need to go outside," I say. "You can go upstairs if you want to talk in private. I don't mind."

Mam looks at the ground. "I needed a bit of air," she says. "Right, I'd better get back to these onions."

We make the rest of the shepherd's pie in uncomfortable silence, something that's virtually unheard of for Mam. I wonder if she's afraid she'll let slip who she was on the phone to if she opens her mouth.

I'm loading the dishwasher after dinner when the doorbell rings.

"I'll get it," I say to Mam, who's washing a saucepan in the sink.

I walk to the front door, bracing myself to see Jake. When I open the front door, Penny's standing there.

A mix of emotions hits me. Shame at me rifling through the contents of Penny's house gets there first. It was different at the intervention when everyone else was there, when I was too shocked even to think about what I did in Penny's house. But now, I instantly feel like I should apologise, even though I'm not sorry for taking the initiative, either. Then I think about how the blouse conveniently disappeared and I start to feel angry at the thought that I might be right about Penny lying to me. But before I can say anything either way, Penny starts to speak.

"I know you probably don't want to see me after the meeting at your mother's house, but I'm only here because I care. I wanted to see how you're doing. I'm as concerned about you as everyone else."

I feel anger rise in my chest. While it's nice that people care about me, and while I appreciate it, I can't help but be sick of everyone saying how concerned they are about me. It feels so . . . *patronising*. As for Penny, it's hard sometimes not to view her as someone who thinks she's head and shoulders above everyone else. Plus, she's just so damn confident that it's hard not to shrink in her presence. And now here she is again, worrying about poor little me and all of my problems, while she has everything all sorted. And that's the best-case scenario. What if there's something more sinister going on here between her and me?

Regardless, I stand back and gesture at Penny to come in. What else can I do?

"Did you go to the doctor today?" Penny asks as we walk into the sitting room.

"Yes. I didn't have much choice, to be honest."

"What did he or she have to say?"

"He gave me a prescription for medication and a referral for a psychiatrist."

Saying the words aloud makes me feel even worse. This time last week, I was getting on with my life just nicely. Now, my friends, family and doctor think I need to see a psychiatrist.

"What type of medication were you prescribed?"

"An anti-anxiety pill."

"No, I meant what's the name of it?"

"Oh." I tell her the name of the brand.

She nods.

"Why do you ask, Penny?"

"Because I used to take anti-anxiety pills myself. I've taken that one. It's very good."

"Really?"

"Yes, it was definitely one of the best ones I was ever prescribed."

"No, really as in, you were really on anti-anxiety pills?"

"Why shouldn't I have been?"

"Well, it's just . . . you never struck me as being anxious, I guess."

"That's because I took anti-anxiety pills," she says, a wry smile on her face. "You didn't know me before I took them. Although I think I hid it well, but that wasn't the point. I needed to stop feeling like that, so I found a way to do that."

I'm shocked, but I try not to show it. I also feel slightly better. If someone who comes across as being as together as Penny can suffer from anxiety, anyone can. I'm not on my own in this.

"And when you say, 'one of the best ones I was ever prescribed', I take it you were on them for a longish period of time?"

"A year. I found some of them had no effect at all, so I kept going back to the doctor trying to find something that would work for me. The one you've been prescribed was definitely the best. I stopped taking it after six months."

"So it worked, then?"

"Yes, it worked in conjunction with me taking better care of myself at the same time. I had to make a lot of other changes as well, ones that I'd started to make when I was trialling the other tablets. But these ones definitely eased my anxiety."

"What were you anxious about?" I ask.

"Everything, really. My job, mostly. I was working from seven in the morning to after midnight every night during the week and then travelling or doing overtime at the weekends. I was neglecting myself – and also everyone else around me. That bothered me, as well.

"I still do long days, as you know, but I've pulled back a lot. I've learned a lot about delegation, too. That's helped. You can't do everything yourself, Katie. Similarly, you can't carry and solve a problem by yourself sometimes.

Occasionally, we all need help. If the tablets are going to help you in this instance, I'd strongly recommend that you take them."

I almost can't believe I'm hearing this. Penny never says anything about herself that might be perceived as a possible weakness. Instantly, I berate myself for even thinking that. I shouldn't be thinking of anxiety as a weakness. Everyone gets overwhelmed sometimes. Looking on it as a weakness is part of the reason why people aren't willing to talk about it. And yet, anxiety just isn't something I'd have associated with Penny.

Whether it's right or wrong of me to think that, it's something that I can't help thinking. It just goes to show how wrong you can be about others, though. Lots of people wear a mask every day – it's very hard to know what's going on in someone else's head.

And here I am thinking she's somehow involved in me being abducted. I look at her earnest expression and say to myself that surely she wouldn't do that – any more than Jake would do that.

I can't think straight. I feel like I'm on the cusp of going mad.

"I don't know if they *are* going to help me, though," I say, trying to return to the moment.

"Well, maybe not, but they can't harm you either, surely."

I think about this. Maybe I should take them. After all, I can't feel much worse than I do right now. My main concern is that I'll lose my focus on finding the person who did this, but I have to admit that right now, I'm all out of ideas as to how to do that. And besides, there's no reason for me to think that losing my edge will actually happen, other than my own surmising and supposition. And it would keep Mam happy. It would give her some hope that I'm going to be all right.

I shrug. "I suppose not."

Mam walks in. "Ah, Penny, how are you?"

Mam and Penny engage in small talk for a few minutes. For that short period of time, Mam looks like herself again. The worry that's been etched not just on her face, but also on her entire being, has faded. But I know it won't be long before it's back again.

"I'll go and make some tea for us all," I say, leaving Mam and Penny to chat.

I return with three cups of tea on a tray.

"Here you go, ladies," I say, putting the tray down and offering the tea. "I'd better take my tablet now with my tea before I forget," I say, glancing at Mam as I pick up the packet of prescription pills from the tray.

She says nothing. She doesn't need to. As I open the foil over today's tablet and then pop it in my mouth, I can see the relief on her face.

Penny stays for another few hours. Mam makes more tea and then later, Penny makes a third round. I'm sick of the sight of tea, but it feels good at least to pretend things are normal for a little while as we sit there sipping and dipping biscuits, commenting on various shows on TV.

I want to ask Penny for her opinion on why Richard wants to talk to me, but there's no opportunity to do that without Mam hearing the conversation. No good will come of Mam hearing about this, that much I know. She'll just think I'm accusing Richard of something, regardless of the fact that he's now the one trying to contact me. I need to be very careful about the transmission of this information – or any information – from now on. I decide I'll ring

Richard tomorrow when they all leave me in peace and quiet, and I'll see what he has to say.

Penny leaves shortly after ten. Mam declares herself to be exhausted and announces that she's going to bed early. I'm sure it's the relief of me deciding to take the tablets that's enabled her to allow herself an early night. She probably hasn't slept for God knows how many days, worrying about me.

Yet again, I feel guilty and although I'm ambivalent about my decision to take the tablets, if it means that it gives Mam a bit of peace of mind, it's probably the right thing to do. She looks like she's aged a decade since this whole thing began. Maybe I just haven't noticed old age creeping up on her and I'm seeing it now because I'm feeling responsible for some of the stress in her life, but every time I look at her now, I see her frailty. I don't want to add to it any more than I have to. I can't live with it.

And if I'm completely honest with myself, anything that may alleviate the possibility of me having another panic attack may not be a bad thing. I'm still doing my utmost not to think about that, as if recalling it will induce another, but that's the second time tonight that it's crept back into my head.

I decide that an early night might not be a bad thing for me, either. Maybe more sleep will help me to think of what I'm going to do next. Other than pretending to everyone that I'm going along with getting help, I'm all out of ideas. The person who's out to get me could strike again soon. I need to think of something that I can do to protect myself. But right now, that feels like another day's work. There's been enough drama today.

Chapter 28

When I wake, I'm there again.

I'm in the cottage. I'm back. I'm *back*.

It's dark. It's pitch-black, but I know where I am. I know by the smell.

I'm tied up again.

This time, I'm gagged. It's as if the person who did this knew I'd been wondering why I hadn't been gagged last time. The ropes are tighter now. There are more of them. They're thicker. I can't see them, but I can feel them. They start at my neck and wind all around my body, right down to my ankles, like a whole army of pythons have melded into each other to form one deadly beast that will remain on me for ever. Well, until I die. Which will be soon.

And yet, it'll be an agonisingly long wait until I finally reach oblivion. There's no escape this time, I know that. Instinctively, I know I'm here for good this time. That whatever mistakes the person who put me here made last time round won't be made again.

I'm not sure if I've moved yet. It's only been a few seconds since I woke, but it feels like much longer. Did my head jerk awake? If someone's in the room with me, could they possibly detect my movement in this pitch-darkness? Did I make any noise? But then, how could I when everything's tied so tightly?

The only noise I can make is from my throat. I must keep the noise in. I force the scream that's fighting its way out to stay inside. If the person who did this is here, in this room, I don't want them to know how scared I am. I won't give them the satisfaction – I just won't. *Fuck* them. They won't get a reaction from me. Not now, at least. Who knows what horrors await me in the near future, though, that will leave me powerless to fight my screams?

I try to remember how I got here. How he got me back. Do I remember being taken? What do I remember?

Nothing. That's all. Absolutely nothing. I try to work out what the last thing I remember is, but I draw a complete blank. It's as if my memory has been erased.

All I know is that I was here before. I remember what happened then. I remember how I escaped. I remember going home and checking out everyone around me to see if they were a threat to me. But then, where did the memories end?

Scenes pass through my mind of being with Mam, with Claire, with Penny, even with Jake, but I can't order them. I don't know which of them was the last one before I got here. And I don't remember anyone taking me. Did he come into my house and knock me out somehow? Was I alone in the house?

And then I remember. Mam. Mam was in the house with me. She was staying with me. I remember. Oh, God, what if he's done something to Mam?

Terror – sheer, raw terror, much deeper than anything I've felt up to this point – envelops me. What if she's *here*? What if he's done this to her, too?

What's he going to do to her?

Then I feel it. A touch on my arm.

He's here. He's in the room with me. Right beside me. I can't see him, not even an outline or a shadow of him. I can't smell him, but I can feel him. His hand is still on my arm.

He's back to do what he didn't get to do the last time. To finish the job, whatever that entails. That's why I'm here. That's why I'm back. How did he even get me back here? Why can't I remember?

It's too much. It's all too much. I scream and scream against the gag, horrific, mangled sounds that don't go where they should and threaten to choke me. To my own ears, I sound like someone being tortured. All that's come so far, though, is a touch on my arm. There's so much worse that can come. There are so many screams left.

And then I hear a voice.

"Katie, I've waited a long time for this . . . "

I open my eyes.

I stare at the wallpaper. I remember how long it took me to choose that wallpaper. I wanted something uplifting. I eventually chose a beige background with hundreds of little yellow sunflowers on each strip. It wouldn't be to everyone's taste, but I've always found it put a smile on my face when I woke. But not today. Today, I barely even register it because instantly, I find that something's niggling at the back of my mind. It's something that's happened. But although I'm grasping at the memory of what it is, I can't quite catch it.

After a few seconds, it comes back to me. The cottage. I was back there. Or . . . was I?

No. No, I *dreamed* I was back there. I was tied up, much tighter this time. I was gagged. The person who was in the room with me touched my arm and I screamed for what felt like an eternity. I was also terrified that he'd done something to Mam. God, it was a vivid dream. Now that it's coming back to me, the details are flooding my mind with acute precision. After the lengthy bout of screaming, though, there's nothing. That's where it ends. Did I wake and I just don't remember it? Did the new tablets make me sleep more deeply?

I look at the clock. It's 8.10 in the morning. I must have had the dream hours ago, which is why I couldn't instantly remember it when I woke. There's a distance between when it happened and now. I know that much. It's not like when you wake from a bad dream, and you've instantly left where you were in your head and found yourself back in reality. There's no bridge from those kinds of dreams that make you wake screaming. One minute you're there, in that horrible place, and then you're back in your own bed, beyond grateful to be back in your normal life.

Unable to shake the dream off, I decide to go in and check on Mam. As I walk towards her bedroom, though, I hear the noise of cutlery being put away downstairs. Of course – 8:10 a.m. is practically lunchtime to Mam. I change direction and paddle to the bathroom, still feeling half asleep. This morning, for some reason, I feel lazier than I usually do in the mornings, even though I went to bed much earlier than usual. Moving is a big effort. My arms feel sore, too. I look at them and see that bruises have started to form. I have no idea why.

Maybe I hit my arms against the bedside table in the middle of the night, but the position of the bruises, on the back of my forearm and not the inside, aren't consistent with how I'd surely have hit the bedside table. And if I'd hit myself hard enough to bruise, surely the pain would have woken me. Did the anti-anxiety medication put me out cold or something?

While I'm in the bathroom, I hear footsteps on the stairs. They sound heavier than usual.

When I return to my room, Mam and Penny are sitting on my bed.

I look from one to the other, waiting for an explanation. Nobody says anything.

"What are you doing here?" I direct my words to Penny.

Penny looks at Mam. "Your mother rang me last night and asked me to come over."

Last night? "Why? Is something wrong?"

Mam starts to cry.

"What? What is it?"

Penny just shakes her head.

"One of you, will you please just tell me what's going on! Is it Jake?"

"Jake? No, no," Penny says as if the thought that something might have happened to Jake never occurred to her.

What else am I supposed to think, though, when she and Mam are sitting on my bed shortly after eight in the morning, with Mam crying?

If it's not Jake, that only leaves . . . me.

I can't even bring myself to ask again. I wait.

"You were hallucinating again," Penny said. "I take it you don't remember anything?"

I feel like a cannonball has just been fired into my chest.

"I . . . I had a dream about being back in the cottage.

But no, I didn't have a hallucination. That's not what it was."

"You're wrong, Katie. Let me prove it. You were afraid that he had me, weren't you?" Mam says in a shaky voice. "The man who took you. You thought he'd taken me as well. And he touched your arm, and . . . " Mam's face crumples again. "I'll never forget those screams."

"What . . . what happened last night? Did I wake you screaming? I can't remember. Was I talking in my sleep?"

"I found you downstairs," Mam says. "You were running around the hall, screaming and thrashing against the walls."

The bruises on my arms. They're long. They're consistent with thumps against a flat, even surface.

"You didn't even know I was there. You couldn't even see me. You just kept talking. You were living out what you were seeing."

"No . . . "

I can't remember a single thing. The realisation that I'd be none the wiser if they'd chosen not to tell me terrifies me. Have other things happened that I can't remember? Things that people haven't told me about.

"You talked me through it all. Everything that was going on in your head, you recounted, but it wasn't to me. You were just talking out loud."

"I . . . I don't understand this."

I sink to my knees and sit on the floor. I've never been a sleepwalker. I've had bad dreams and occasional nightmares, but nothing at this level.

"It must have been the anti-anxiety pill, Katie," Mam says. "You've had a reaction to it. I rang Dr McGuire and told him what happened. He's on holiday abroad at the moment and can't come to see you, but in his opinion, that's what's happened. You've had the same hallucination again because you're allergic to something in the medication."

"It's the same thing happening again, but for a slightly different reason," Penny adds. "You obviously must be susceptible to adverse reactions to particular medications."

"No," I say firmly. Too firmly. It came out as a shout. "This wasn't the same as the last time. I knew when I woke that this was something my brain had fabricated. I thought it was just a bad dream, because that's all I remember it as. But what happened before was real!

"This was just some sort of memory of it. Or I hallucinated about it because it's on my mind morning, noon and night since it happened. It was very clear to me when I woke that it hadn't happened again. The first time, I woke and knew it was more than a memory. The two situations couldn't be more different."

Mam and Penny look at each other. It's a knowing look. They expected me to say this.

"We need to take you to the hospital, Katie," Penny says.

And end up in the psychiatric ward? Not a hope.

"No. Absolutely no way," I say. "I'll go to the doctor tomorrow. Whoever's covering for Dr McGuire, I'll go to see them first thing."

"You need to go to the hospital, Katie. This isn't right."

Mam's voice is firmer now. She's determined not to take no for an answer.

"I just won't take any more of those tablets and then all will be fine. Clearly, as you said yourself, this is a reaction to the medication. I was fine before I took that tablet last night. The medication is the problem and that can wait until tomorrow to be addressed."

"Katie, we're not taking no for an answer," Penny says.

"And since when is this your call?" I say, my tone sharper than I've heard it in a long time.

This is insane. I am thirty-six years of age. I can't allow Penny to come in here and railroad me into making decisions that aren't right for me. I've had enough of everyone telling me what to do. I'm in the right here. *They're* the ones who won't believe me. Maybe *I* should be bitterly disappointed in *them* for not supporting me the way I need to be supported. For not believing me. My family and best friends don't want to hear what I have to say. They're only concerned with implementing the endgame of what they believe to be my reality. Well, they're all wrong.

"Stop interfering and coming into my home telling me what to do," I add to Penny, unable to stop myself now. "You seem to think you can control everything and everyone. Well, I'm not having it. As I said, I appreciate you wanting to be a good friend, but you're crossing a line here."

"We only want to help you," Penny says. "That's all we're trying to do here, to do our best for you."

She actually sounds hurt. I've never heard Penny sound hurt before. And I don't like how she's turning this into "we". I wasn't referring to Mam, just her. Penny and Mam seem to be as thick as thieves right now.

"I appreciate that and it's good of you, it really is. But you're getting too involved, Penny. You're overstepping the boundaries. I don't mean to sound ungrateful, but it's not up to you to make these decisions."

"She's only here because I called her," Mam says. "I

thought you might have enough sense to listen to Penny. God knows, you don't listen to me or your sisters."

"You're both making this situation worse," I say, folding my arms across my chest. "I obviously need to revisit my medication tomorrow with the doctor. In the meantime, please stop infusing my life with more drama than it needs. I know you're trying to help – believe me, I do know that – but you're not helping. You're not *listening* to me. You're not doing what I actually want you to do. You're doing what you think you should be doing.

"If you want to help me, stop stressing me out even more. I'm taking anti-anxiety pills to try to stave off anxiety, something that you say you want to help me with, and yet you're both making me more anxious right now. I'm sorry, but that's the truth. Please, just give me a bit of space to breathe, okay? I'll go to the doctor tomorrow. I'll get all this sorted."

"Katie, you don't seem to be in a position to be able to sort yourself any longer," Penny said. "You need us. You need help – a lot of help. You're not yourself any more."

I stare at Penny, feeling something rising inside me. And before I know it, my mouth is off, working independently of my mind.

"You're always around when bad things happen to me," I say. "Always."

"Katie—" Mam starts.

"And bad things never happened to me before you came into my life."

"Katie, that's enough!" Mam says. "Penny's only trying to help."

"No, Mam. Think about it. Penny's been there for every bad thing that's happened to me."

"Exactly, Katie," Penny says, her voice sympathetic. "I've been here for you for everything. You haven't been the easiest friend, but I've never turned my back on you. And now you're saying I'm responsible for your problems? I find that really hurtful."

"You have total access to my life, Penny. The more I think about it – for every situation that's happened to me that doesn't make sense – you are the one with open access to walk into my life and do whatever you want."

"Katie!" Mam says as agitated as I've ever heard her. "Mind your tongue! This is ridiculous!"

"I think I should go, Jackie," Penny says to Mam.

"Oh no, Penny—"

"No, honestly. I'm in the way here. This is a family issue." Penny pats Mam's hand and gives her a sympathetic look. "You have my phone number if you need to talk," she says in a lower voice.

Obviously not so low that I can't hear her, though. I'm standing right beside her, for God's sake. Anger rises in me again. I can't stand this feeling of being a huge concern to everyone. *I'm* okay. It's whoever's out to get me who's the problem.

"Goodbye, Katie. We'll talk again soon."

Penny puts a hand on my shoulder and pats it before leaving. It's a very non-Penny thing to do and I don't quite know how to react. Eventually, I nod and say, "Mind yourself." One of my standard goodbyes for everyone. She looks at me as if I'm being sarcastic. Of course! I'm the one who needs minding, aren't I?

Mam walks Penny downstairs. I brace myself for what's to come when she returns.

But she doesn't return. The minutes pass and ten minutes

later, she still hasn't come back. I can hear her pottering around downstairs, making tea and unloading the dishwasher.

I go down.

"There's no need to do any work, Mam. I'll take care of the dishwasher. You sit down and drink your tea."

My words get no reaction. She doesn't even turn round.

We continue like that for a few moments, with me making small talk and Mam completely ignoring me or occasionally rewarding me with a grunt. The silent treatment is bad. Very bad.

I go back upstairs, closing the kitchen door as I leave. In my bedroom, I reach for a pen and my writing pad. Between the speed at which I'm writing and my shaking hand – I've been trembling quietly ever since I heard about how I was running around the house last night hitting myself off walls – my writing is erratic. But it's legible all the same. I make my bed and leave the note on the pillow. Then I pick up my phone.

"Claire, would you be able to come round here as soon as you can?"

It's relatively easy to sneak out without Mam seeing me. She's retired to the sitting room and she's put the TV on, so I unlock the side door, close it quietly and leave the house by the side entrance. The blinds are still down in the sitting room from earlier in the day and unless she happens to put them up at that very moment, I know she won't see me as I walk down the driveway.

I walk down the street, glancing back at my house as I do so. The blinds are still down and there's no sign of Mam running down the street after me. I've escaped.

I make my way to the bus stop, having decided to leave

the car at home. I'll catch the bus to the city centre and find a hotel to stay for the night. Soon, Claire will arrive and they'll find my note. I know Mam will be upset when she finds out that I've left, so at least having Claire there will help her to deal with it. But I can't stay around Mam a second longer.

I'm thirty-six years of age and I'm sneaking out of my own house. I shake my head. How did things come to this?

PART THREE

Chapter 29

Three weeks later . . .

I take a deep breath as I leave the office and step out onto the street. Logically, I know it's highly unlikely that anyone's about to jump out from somewhere and attack me, but I still can't help feeling nervous. I hold my head up high and walk out, hoping I look more confident than I feel. *I'm fine*, I say to myself. *Everything is fine.* This is the game I play with myself now – telling myself my troubles are over and hoping I'll start to believe it.

As for what happened a few weeks ago, I can't explain it and I have no idea how to move on from it, either. I know my family and friends are watching me like hawks after my "running away" episode, and I can't have that. So I pretend. I'm trying to present myself as the person I was before all this happened. It's all I can do. At least one good thing came of me running away, though. Mam realised that pushing me to get psychiatric help was only going to result in her losing me. Now though, I have to make sure I appear to be okay at all times to everyone around me. It's exhausting.

I'm relieved to get home and turn the key in the door of my house. Although I'm frightened of living alone now, I'm more threatened at the thought of being around people who are watching my every move. As the weeks have gone on and I've become more adept at pretending I'm back to my old self, my family have given me a little more breathing space. Mam knows I have two days off tomorrow and the following day, though, so I'm sure she'll be over tomorrow checking up on me.

After the intervention, she and Sandra insisted that I return to work on a phased basis only. Claire stayed out of it. She said only I knew what I was currently able for when it came to work. I wanted to go back to work full-time, but Mam and Sandra wouldn't listen. There was a huge argument over it, in which I told them they had no right to try to organise my life at my age. In the course of it, Mam collapsed with chest pains and we had to call an ambulance. She was fine afterwards, thank God, but it was game over for me when it came to arguing my case to go back to work full-time. What else could I do after that but what she wanted?

I never found out what Richard wanted. I returned his call and he said he wanted to meet me in person to tell me things he couldn't tell me on the phone. We made an arrangement to meet, but he stood me up. I rang him many times after that and got no answer. I didn't bother telling the gardai, because really and truly, what was the point?

As for Penny, we haven't spoken a word since I accused her of being out to get me. And as convinced as I was at the time that she was behind what happened to me, I now feel like I have no clue if I was right about that, either. I have no clue about anything any longer. I just have to try to put one foot in front of the other and get on with things until I somehow find some more clarity in life – if it ever comes.

I pour myself a glass of sparkling water and sit down at

the kitchen table. I should cook dinner, but the motivation to do so is just not there. I decide to allow myself five minutes to sit down and wallow, then I'll get up and cook dinner.

This is how I live now. This is who I am. Trudging from one task to the next, never really feeling enthused about anything, doing things because I have to. It scares me. I was never like this, except for that period after Dad died. It's so hard to find my way back and with everything unresolved, I don't know if I ever will.

If nothing happened in that cottage, that means I have no choice but to question my sanity on a daily basis. Mam and Sandra keep telling me I need to go to see professionals. They're probably right and yet I just can't bring myself to do it. I can't help feeling wronged. I'm not taking any medication since what happened with the anti-anxiety pills. I'm avoiding seeing the doctor. I'm going round in circles, but I can't see any other direction at the moment.

When my five minutes are up, I realise that I should probably check my phone in case Mam has contacted me to see how I am – she gets worried if I don't reply fast. Slowly, I get up and retrieve it from my handbag.

When I do so, I see a missed call from the garda station, a notification of a voicemail and three missed calls from Jake. Something flutters in my chest. Fear, I assume, but mixed with the sense that something's going on and I don't know if it's good or bad.

I'm about to click the voicemail icon on my phone, when I hear the doorbell.

I walk to the front door with trepidation, wondering what's ahead. I open the door and see Brian standing there. His expression is unreadable.

"Hello, Brian. Come in. What's going on?"

313

Brian steps inside.

"Hello, Katie. How are you today?"

"Brian, what's happening?" I shake my head. "I'm sorry – I don't mean to be rude, but I assume you're not here for tea. I don't even make very good tea."

"I'm not here for tea, Katie. I have news relating to your case."

"Oh?"

"Yes."

"And? Good God, Brian, spit it out!" I instantly inwardly berate myself at my lack of respect towards a garda, but I can't take the tension for another second.

"Katie, Richard Stapleton has confessed to your abduction."

Chapter 30

After Brian leaves, I ring Jake. I don't know why. Or maybe I do.

Jake picks up almost instantly.

"It was Richard, Katie. Penny found out."

"I just had a visit from Brian saying as much," I say, but I find myself unable to continue.

"Are you okay, Katie?"

"I don't know." I take a deep breath. I'm suddenly finding it hard to breathe, so I try to buy some time by getting Jake to talk instead. "What did Penny tell you? I don't know how much to relay to you from what Brian told me . . . "

"Penny said she sussed it last night. Richard came over to her house pretty late. She said he was deranged. He'd taken cocaine at the end of a staff night out and he was acting pretty crazy. He started talking about you and it all came out.

"As I'm sure Brian told you, Penny started recording the conversation on her phone without him noticing and she took what he said to the gardai. They caught up with him and he confessed. But the recording was pretty damning and there would have been no point in him lying any further. Penny played it for me. He wouldn't have had a leg to stand on by lying after that."

"I can't even remember what Brian said about the contents of the recording. I was so stunned at hearing the news that I just heard white noise when he was talking about that."

"It was about Penny more so than you, but what he said was enough to prove that he did this to you. He said that he wished he'd taken Penny to the house and left her there instead of you. He called her every name under the sun in the course of it. He's absolutely nuts, Katie. If you'd heard the anger in his voice . . . Penny's lucky he didn't murder her last night. The whole thing is absolutely sickening."

"And Brian said the house Richard left me in was one he inherited – did Penny tell you that?"

"Yes – she said it was his great-grandparents' house in County Westmeath, located in the Midlands. It was left to him, along with 30 acres of land around it, when his father died last year."

"He sent me a message recently saying he wanted to talk to me. What was he trying to do there? Play with my mind?"

"Probably trying to cover his tracks in some way, I'd imagine."

A sense of being overwhelmed floods me. It's all so much to take in. I don't think I can even hear any more for now.

"Jake, I accused you of this. I'm so sorry. Why are you even speaking to me?"

Jake says nothing.

"I can't even begin to apologise enough. There's nothing I can say to make this better. I am truly, truly sorry, Jake."

I hang up before I start to cry. I know I should be feeling

something else – some level of vindication for the fact that I was right all along and nobody believed me – but it's a pyrrhic victory to be right about something like this. Especially when you've suspected all around you of doing it, including someone who clearly had my back all along.

Richard. Good God. And he sat there in Penny's house talking to me about Irish politics. It's almost funny.

I turn my phone off and take ten minutes out to breathe and think. I have no answers from my thinking ten minutes later, but I feel a little calmer. I decide to ring Claire and ask her to let Mam and Sandra know. After that, I don't know what I'll do.

I sit down and think about my conversation with Brian again. He was clinical in his delivery and gave me the high-level facts first: that Richard had confessed, that he'd been arrested and that he'd be charged with abduction. We'd teased out the details that Jake had mentioned as the conversation went on, but as I'd said to Jake, some of it had been white noise to me with the shock of it all.

"But . . . why?" was all I could say.

"He said it was a sexual game that he ultimately couldn't go through with. He panicked – left you there but then came back for you."

"Jesus Christ. Brian, he tried to contact me a few days ago. He left a message saying he needed to speak to me. Maybe he was going to confess and chickened out. Or maybe he was going to do something else to me."

"We have him now, Katie. His confession is on record."

I was almost sure I could hear sympathy in Brian's voice, but I suppose he can't be seen to be too apologetic in case it's deemed to be an indication of guilt or an inference of negligence.

I stare into space. I feel like I should be angrier with all those who didn't believe me, or who didn't try harder to help me prove this, but I'm not – not now, anyway. Although I can logically reason that it's a huge relief to know that I was right all along and that the person responsible has been arrested for it, I just feel like a deflated balloon overall.

I know I'm lucky and that this situation could have been a lot worse, but I feel almost numb now. It's such a horrible thing to have happened and a part of me still can't take it in that it has happened. I feel like I'm swimming through mud now as much as I felt it back in that house. It must be shock.

Penny. I should contact Penny, too.

I ring Claire first. She turns the air blue with expletives about Richard, which makes me smile for the first time today, before turning her rant into a heartfelt apology that she didn't do more to help me. I swat her apologies away and tell her I need to go and ring Penny. My energy is ebbing by the second and I need to get all this talking over with.

"Katie, I'm glad you rang," Penny says without preamble when she answers. "I've been in two minds about ringing you. I can't believe I didn't realise all this sooner. I've been blind to it all. Also, I brought that man into your life. Your paths would never have crossed only for me. It's to my detriment that I didn't get to the bottom of all this a long time ago – when it happened, actually. Perhaps I didn't want to see what was right in front of my nose—"

"Penny, please stop." I hear the sound of my own voice doing something that resembles a laugh. "It sounds like you've been rehearsing that speech or something."

"I've certainly been planning what to say to you all right that adequately covers how regretful I am about this entire sorry situation."

"It's nobody's fault, only Richard's," I say. "You were in love, Penny. As you said, it blinds a person."

"You sound a lot calmer about this than I expected," Penny says. "You'd have every right to be furious with me."

"Penny, I accused you of doing this! You'd have every right to be mad at me, too!"

"But I didn't help you. I didn't believe you. Nobody did. We were all wrong."

"None of that can be changed now, though. I guess I'm just glad it's over. I don't know what I feel, to be honest. Actually, Penny, I think I'll have to go. I've had a few conversations in a row here and I'm just mentally drained."

"Okay, Katie. I'll ring you tomorrow. Again, I'm dreadfully sorry that I brought that – *creature* – into your life."

"You also solved the mystery and took a recording to the gardai that proved his guilt, from what I heard, so I should really be thanking you for that."

"No need to thank me, Katie. Just forgive me. As I said, I'll call you tomorrow. Thank you for ringing."

Penny hangs up. I'm grateful that I don't even have to say goodbye and that the talking is over for now. I feel more tired than I've ever felt in my life. I thought I'd feel on top of the world if I got to the point where I proved this happened, but I don't. All the adrenaline that I've been carrying around since all this started seems to have just left my body in one gigantic swoop.

I crawl upstairs and throw myself on the bed. I try not to let my guilt about Jake consume me, or to think about how comprehensively I've messed up our relationship – among many others that have been tainted by this whole thing.

Chapter 31

True to her word, Penny rings at ten the following morning.

"Hi, Penny."

"Hey, Katie. You're off work for the next two days, right?"

"Yes."

"Great. Do you fancy a trip down to County Clare tomorrow?"

"*Clare?* What about work?"

"I've booked a few days off to deal with what's happened with Richard. I can't focus on work right now. I'd make a fool of myself – and I'm not prepared to let that happen. This is the most prudent way of dealing with things."

"I see. I can understand that, I suppose."

"So, what do you say to Clare? Free accommodation . . . good company . . . The weather might even be good, who knows?"

"It does sound lovely, but I can't."

"Why ever not?"

"Not after the last few weeks."

"Oh, come on, Katie! You can't sit in for the rest of your life. It'll do you good to get away for a few days."

"What if something happens?"

"What could possibly happen to you in Clare?"

"Penny, I'm . . . well, I don't know what I am. I think I'm in some sort of shock over everything. I keep expecting the worst still. And I'm useless company right now."

"That's fine, Katie. Look, I just need to assuage my guilt at bringing Richard into your life by trying to do something nice for you. I don't know how else to cope with this and I'm no good at repeatedly apologising. So, what do you say? I could really use the company. Maybe you could, too."

I don't want to say yes. I want to crawl under the duvet and not come out until I have to go to work again. But Penny needs help to deal with this. As Jake said to me before, love is a great leveller. This is as much of a cry for help as she's going to make. And it's not like I'm up to anything else, is it?

"Okay. Let's do it."

Penny calls for me at 2 p.m. on the dot the following afternoon. I have to admit to myself that I'm not any more in the mood for going anywhere today than I was yesterday, but I told Penny I'd go and I won't let her down.

Penny isn't as upbeat on the way down as she had been on the phone yesterday. I can only assume that what happened with Richard is really hitting her and is bringing her down, but I say nothing and instead wait for her to bring it up. By the time we're halfway to Clare, though, the subject of Richard and what he did hasn't raised its head and it's starting to become an elephant in the car. Quite aside from what he did to me, I don't want Penny to think I don't care about her relationship with Richard falling

321

asunder, either, so I tentatively ask her how she's feeling about the whole thing.

"Oh, fine. I'm better off without him. How are you feeling about Jake?"

I wasn't expecting her to throw the topic back at me and I'm somewhat lost for words.

"Okay, I suppose," I eventually say. "Sad about how things have turned out, really."

"You don't have to worry about Jake bothering you any more, though," Penny continues. "He seems to be starting to move on."

"Oh?"

"He . . . Oh, it doesn't matter. I shouldn't have said anything."

"He what, Penny?"

Penny hesitates. "Do you really want to know?"

"I'm asking, aren't I?"

"Well, he said he was . . . with someone at the weekend."

"Oh."

"Someone he met in a pub," Penny says. "I'm sure it was no big deal – possibly a one-night thing that won't go anywhere – but it's probably best for both of you if he starts to do that kind of thing."

"Maybe," I say, but I feel completely flattened.

For the rest of the journey, I can't take my thoughts away from how messed up everything is – and to dwell on the role I played in it all.

By the time we get to Clare, I'm an emotional wreck but I'm trying not to show it. Since I brought Richard up, Penny's keeping the conversation going by talking about pretty much everything other than Richard. And I'm happy to let her do so if it helps to mask what's going on inside my head.

The holiday home is part of a reasonably large development of self-catering units. We stop at a house near the entrance of the development to collect the keys. Penny goes inside with a printout of her Internet booking confirmation while I stay in the car and continue to wonder if me coming on this trip was a good idea at all. I thought the change of scene might lift my mood and divert my thoughts, but so far nothing has changed for me except my location. I promise myself that I'll try to put everything out of my mind for the next few days, though. I'll work out what I'll do with the rest of my life when we get back from Clare.

Penny returns with a set of keys in her hand. I force a smile onto my face as she sits back in her seat.

"There's a path at the back of the development that leads directly to the beach," Penny says as she pulls into the driveway of a detached bungalow a minute later.

"Sounds great."

"You know, if we can just stop thinking about what's happened, I think this has the potential to be a really fun break," Penny says as we retrieve our bags from the boot of the car.

I'm not sure I agree, but I say, "I could do with some of that," and force a smile.

We go inside. The house is spacious and immaculately clean, if somewhat minimalistic, with three bedrooms, a sitting room, a kitchen-cum-diner and a large garden. We assign ourselves bedrooms and then cook dinner from the food we've brought down with us. Penny opens a bottle of wine, which I abstain from. There's plenty there – Penny's brought three bottles – but I have absolutely no desire.

Whatever else people might think about me, I know I'm not an alcoholic. I'm a woman who drank too much, yes, but my problem isn't with alcohol. That, at least, is something to be happy about. And yet, over the course of the night my mood doesn't lift at all.

Dinner is tense. Something has definitely changed with Penny. I think she's taking the Richard scenario much harder than she's letting on. You could argue that I'm the one who has the right to be in this form, but Penny seems much angrier than I am. She drinks two large glasses of wine with dinner and pours a third when she puts her knife and fork down and pushes the plate aside, half of her food uneaten. I decide to broach the subject again, hoping that talking about it'll ease the tension.

"How are you feeling about Richard now?" I say as nonchalantly as I can.

I want to make sure that there's no trace of pity in my voice – Penny *despises* pity – or judgment, either.

Penny takes a long drink and shrugs. "I should have seen what was happening. I'm far more tolerant in my personal relationships than I should be. People wouldn't think that of me because of how they perceive me as a businesswoman, but I'm completely different when it comes to close relationships. I blame my parents – my adoptive ones, the Thorntons. They were such cold, distant people that it's no wonder I put up with more than I should have from the likes of Richard and the men who came before him."

I'm stunned. I've never heard Penny say anything negative about her adoptive parents before.

"I'm sorry, Penny. I didn't know that."

Penny takes another long drink. "How could you have?

I'm sure Jake told you that my parents were great people and I had a great life. The *perfect* life."

"He said it sounded like things had gone well for you," I say carefully. "You seemed happy."

"Nobody ever knows how someone else is really feeling."

"You should tell Jake and the rest of your family how it really was. Why haven't you? You and Jake are close."

"We *were* close. Not any more." She throws the rest of her wine back and refills the glass with the little that's left in the bottle.

"Why?"

"Things change. It was different at the start. He was so excited about having me in his life. And then . . . well, he got excited about other things. The novelty of me wore off."

"Excited about other things like what?"

She shrugs but looks straight at me.

"Oh, Penny, he didn't stop being excited about finding his sister when he met me! He talked about you non-stop from the minute we first met. If you weren't his sister, I'd have been jealous – that's how much he spoke about you. Believe me, he was thrilled about you being in his life and that didn't stop when I came on the scene. You should never feel you're not as close just because of me. You should have told him this, Penny."

"It's not just Jake. Bob is an old man now – old, frail, weak. Jake said Bob never fully came to terms with my birth mother dying and I've always been an iffy subject to bring up. Too many memories for him to cope with, Jake says. If he finds out that my life wasn't so great, after all, who knows what it'll do to him?"

"You could just tell Jake not to tell Bob—"

Penny cuts me off mid sentence. "Why do you think I'm so driven to succeed? I'll tell you why. Success is all I have. It's all I *know*. My adoptive parents were very successful people in their chosen field. In our house, though, that success meant that they had no room left within them to look after a child emotionally when they got home. They were always totally and utterly sapped from work and preoccupied. Either that or maybe they never had it in them in the first place.

"Maybe they weren't the right people to adopt a child at all, but they looked good on paper, so they got me regardless. I was another tick in the box on the list of things to be achieved or gained."

"Penny, I'm sure you were much more to them than that."

"You weren't there. You can't say. Is it any wonder I end up with unsuitable men who aren't worthy of me? People who use me as a place to moor their boat for a while before going home to their wives. But no more. I'm done with that. I won't be a victim of the people who mess me around any more."

The last word in the world I'd have used to describe Penny is victim, but I don't say that. It won't help. And what does she mean by *wives*?

She finishes the rest of her wine. "Are you shocked? You *look* shocked."

"I . . . I just wasn't aware that you felt like this, Penny."

"Of course you weren't. I make people believe what I want them to believe, Katie."

"And when you say wives, do you mean you've been with other married men?"

"All the men I've been with over the last five years or so

have been married," she says flatly. "They seek me out. They want to screw a powerful boardroom woman during the week and also to go home to their perfectly clean homes with their perfect little wives and perfect-sized families. And I've let them.

"It's wrong. It stops now. As for Richard, he's been the worst one of them. I've known for a long time that Richard was something I should have got rid of."

And then just like that, Penny's face changes. "Enough of all that."

"No, Penny. It's good for you to talk—"

"No. No more talking about that. About the Cliffs of Moher, do you mind if we do that tomorrow afternoon? I might have a lie-in tomorrow morning and get some decent rest. Maybe you should sleep on, too."

"Well, my version of a lie-in and yours are probably quite different," I say. "Your idea of sleeping on is until about nine!"

"No, I think I'll do things properly tomorrow."

Penny gets up and goes to the kitchen. She returns with another glass of wine, in a bigger glass this time.

"I hope you don't mind, but I'm going to bed with this drink. I'm shattered."

"Penny, are you sure you don't want to go back to what we were talking about?"

Penny closes her eyes. Her expression is almost a grimace, but she manages to turn it into some form of a smile.

"Katie, that's as much as I can say for now. I've said enough. In fact, I'm *spent*. I'm not a talker when it comes to these things. Do you understand?"

"Okay, Penny. I don't want to force you. I just thought that talking it out a bit more might help."

"Tomorrow will help. The fresh air will do me good. You too, I'd imagine. You were the one who was abducted, after all."

"It certainly can't do any harm."

"See you tomorrow, Katie."

Penny smiles again, looking a lot more like herself this time, and leaves the room with her wine. I have a strong feeling the lie-in plan has less to do with getting rest and more to do with the anticipation of a huge hangover.

Chapter 32

I get up at ten the following morning, expecting to see Penny when I go downstairs, but there's no sign of her. Wine or no wine, it's still unlike her. At eleven, I tentatively knock on her door.

"Are you okay in there, Penny?" I say when I get no response.

"No," she shouts back. "Very hung-over. Can't get up yet."

"Okay," I say. "Can I get you anything?"

"No, thanks," she shouts. "I just need my bed for a while. We'll go to the cliffs later, for sure."

I go to the kitchen and make myself a cup of coffee, just for something to do. As I'm boiling the kettle, I notice that the sky looks like we're going to have rain later. I take out my phone and check what the weather conditions are going to be like for the rest of the day. The forecast predicts rain and drizzle – not exactly perfect conditions for visiting the cliffs.

This trip is going to be *miserable*. I'm surprised Penny didn't check out the weather yesterday before she got it into her head to visit the cliffs today – she's usually always so thorough. The break-up with Richard's definitely affecting her more than she's letting on.

As for me, I feel awful because of what Penny said last night about her and Jake not being as close after he started seeing me. I certainly don't think it's true, but I can see why she might perceive it to be that way. I realise that I'd never even considered that Penny could have been jealous of Jake being with me. I'd have thought that it was something Penny would have been above feeling, which is probably unfair of me. I suddenly remember how she reacted to the picture of Richard's wife and it reinforces the thought that she's not above jealousy.

It's half twelve before Penny comes downstairs.

"Are you all right?" I immediately ask. She looks a lot less polished than usual.

"I'll live," she says. "I hope."

"It's probably a shock to the system. You don't usually get bad hangovers." I stand up to get Penny a drink of water.

"I don't usually drink that fast."

I return from the kitchen with a large glass of water and hand it to Penny. She thanks me and sips it slowly.

"Do you mind if we try getting something to eat before we go to the cliffs?" Penny asks. "Something like a carvery in a local pub, maybe."

"We don't have to go to the cliffs at all today if you're not feeling great, Penny. We could leave it until tomorrow if you like."

"About tomorrow . . . " Penny shakes her head. "I'm so sorry, Katie, but I got a call from work earlier. They need me back. Someone's pulled out of an important presentation to my counterpart in the States and I need to step in. I sincerely apologise for cutting the trip short after I dragged you all the way down here, but I'll have to leave first thing in the morning."

330

I shrug, privately relieved that this strained trip will come to an early end.

"Even a day or two away is better than none at all. Don't worry about it."

"Are you sure?"

"Absolutely."

"Thanks, Katie. I'll go upstairs and have a quick shower, then let's get that bite to eat. I'm suddenly starving."

It's half one by the time we sit down to order in a local pub. In her hung-over state, Penny's shower wasn't so quick, after all. I'm ravenous myself now. I quickly decide on lasagne, chips and salad, but Penny takes so long to order that I'm afraid the pub will stop serving lunch soon. She eventually decides on an open chicken sandwich, a surprising choice given how long it's taken her to make up her mind. I was expecting a request for a spectacular customised option to be given to the waitress.

"And two Irish coffees while we're waiting for the food, please," Penny says as the waitress is about to walk away.

She nods and scribbles the order on her pad.

"I hope they're both for you. I don't want one," I say. "And someone will have to stay sober to drive."

"One is for you – you can surely manage to drive after only one drink – but I'll drink it if you don't want it."

"Hair of the dog?"

"Yep."

When the waitress returns with the Irish coffees and puts them down on the table, Penny pushes one in my direction.

"Up to you. I'll have it if you don't."

I pick it up and smell it. It smells delicious. For the first time since the incident, I actually *want* to drink something with alcohol in it. It suddenly vexes me to feel like I can't or I shouldn't, and not because of driving. I had *no* desire to drink that wine last night. I don't have a problem with alcohol. I shouldn't have to behave like I do.

"You know what, I'll have it," I say. "You're right – the small amount of alcohol in that will be out of my system by the time I drive again. Lunch will balance it out. I obviously wouldn't have more than one and then drive, though."

Penny clinks her glass against mine.

The food arrives five minutes later. I eat fast, but Penny picks at her lunch.

I glance at my watch: it's well after 2 p.m. now. We need to hurry if we're to make the most of the trip to the cliffs, but I know if I say that to Penny, she'll just say she's had enough. She's such a poor eater at the best of times and right now she needs nourishment.

I wait another ten minutes before saying anything. It's clear by now that Penny has eaten as much as she will eat.

"We should make a move," I say.

"I need to pop to the bathroom first."

"Sure."

I take out my phone while Penny's away. I have no new messages or emails, so I flick through photos to pass the time. It's a bad idea. There's still some of Jake in my bank of photos. Seeing his face makes me experience countless conflicting emotions. I'm so busy thinking about it all that I don't notice Penny walking towards me with two drinks in her hand until she's right at the table.

"What's all this?" I say as she places two glasses on the table.

"A gin and tonic for me, and a glass of alcohol-free beer for you. It'll give you time to work that Irish coffee out of your system before driving."

"Penny, we need to get moving!"

"I know, I know. Can we just knock this back and then get going? I need to go on the sauce for a bit."

"Why?"

"Richard."

"Penny, don't let him do this to you!"

"This one's for the road and that's all."

"That better be all. If we don't get going soon, we might as well forget about it."

"Sure. We didn't come all this way just to sit in a pub." Penny drinks at least half of her gin and tonic in one go.

"Give me the car keys," I say.

I have an awful feeling that she'll say she's fine to drive when we get out, which she clearly won't be, and I want to cut that argument off at the pass before it happens. Penny throws me a dirty look but hands over the keys. By the time she's finished her drink, I'm less than a third of the way through mine.

"Drink up, Katie! I know you're well able to do that. And it's alcohol-free, for crying out loud!"

As a waitress passes, Penny calls her over and orders another drink for herself.

"This one's your fault," she says. "I can't sit here watching you drinking."

"Cancel that order and I'll just leave this drink," I say. "I didn't even want it."

"No. I'm not leaving until you've had that drink."

I look at Penny in disbelief. I've never seen her like this.

"Not leaving," she repeats. "I mean it. Drink that up."

"Are you sure you're okay? You seem totally out of it or something."

"I'm fine! I'm absolutely fine. I had to take prescription

333

medication earlier, but I'm perfectly okay."

"Prescription medication for what?"

"Anxiety. The friend you and I share."

"Anxiety? I thought that was in the past for you?"

"It's back."

The waitress returns with Penny's drink. Penny pays the waitress and immediately knocks back half of the drink.

"And should you be drinking while taking medication?"

"Who cares?"

I pick up my glass and throw back my drink. I need to get her out of here. I'm putting my glass back down, when Penny's phone rings.

"It's that bastard," she says.

"Richard? Surely the gardai haven't released him?"

"I'm sure he can still make phone calls, Katie. I doubt that the local cop shop is like Alcatraz in terms of security measures."

"Don't answer it, Penny."

"Why not? I'm not afraid of him."

She presses a button, says a curt hello and walks away towards the toilets. I call her and tell her to come back, but she keeps walking. I know following her and trying to persuade her to hang up would be useless.

"Shit." I shake my head, suddenly wishing there was alcohol in front of me, after all.

I don't even see the point of driving to these cliffs now with things the way they are. I have no idea what to do with Penny. What I do know is that she needs help or support from somewhere through this Richard situation. I don't seem to be helping much. There's only one person I can think of who probably can.

I take out my phone. I think it's safe to assume that

Penny will be on her call to Richard for quite a while, or as long as he can get away with, anyway. I'm surprised when Jake answers. I was hoping he would but was realistically expecting to have to leave a voicemail.

"Jake, hi. I'm sure I'm the last person you were expecting to hear from, but I need to talk to you in confidence about Penny. I'm very worried about her."

I fill Jake in on the Richard situation, and how Penny feels she and Jake have drifted apart somewhat since he started dating me.

"Please don't tell her I said any of this," I say, "but I really feel like she's lost and she needs support from her family. She'll never admit that, of course. When we come back from Clare tomorrow, maybe give her a call in the evening and arrange to meet."

"You're in Clare?"

"Yes. We went on a short break to Liscannor, near the Cliffs of Moher. We're going to climb them later." Hopefully, I add to myself as I glance at my watch. "Penny needed to get away after the situation with Richard."

"I see."

After a long silence, I say, "Well, that's all I wanted to say. Again, please don't mention that I contacted you. I just felt it was for the best to say something."

"Okay, fine. Thanks."

"And, Jake . . . I'm sorry it all had to end this way between us." The words are out before I realise they're coming.

Jake says nothing for a long time. Eventually, he finds his voice.

"I'm really sorry I didn't believe you. I should have. And I should have helped you to find out who did it. But, Katie,

I'll never understand how you felt that I could have harmed you."

"You don't understand what it feels like to fight for your life then, Jake," I say. "But I'm deeply sorry if I hurt you."

"You did," he says.

I don't know what to say that I haven't said before.

As I'm trying to formulate a response, Jake says, "I have to go now. Thanks for the information."

And with that, he hangs up.

I stare at the phone in my hand for a long time after the call, wondering how it all came to this. I eventually put it down and sip my beer absently, just to keep myself occupied with something.

Penny finally returns. She looks incensed. Her face is flaming and her mouth is set in a firm line, her eyes as wide as saucers.

"What happened?"

"Let's get out of here," Penny says.

"What did he say?"

"I'll tell you on the way to the cliffs." Penny opens her handbag and throws some money on the counter. "That'll cover both of us. Let's go."

And with that she's up and off, leaving me no choice but to follow.

It takes less than ten minutes to drive from Liscannor to the cliffs, but it feels like a lifetime. Penny's mood is so foul that it's like a fog in the car. I can barely breathe for the tension coming from her. I ask her repeatedly to tell me what Richard said, but she says we need to keep that conversation for the cliffs. I can't reach her.

She either seems to have retreated inside herself or else

she's blocking me completely. When we went outside the pub, I suggested to Penny that we forget about going to the cliffs – it was late in the day and it'd be getting dark in the next few hours – but she wouldn't hear of it. She needed to do a quick visit to keep her mind off things, she said, otherwise she'd go mad.

I'd never heard Penny speak like that before. I acquiesced just to keep her from losing the plot, but this was definitely going to be a quick visit and I doubted that she'd take in a single second of it. I'm not feeling too good myself, either. I shouldn't have had that Irish coffee. My head is quite woozy and I'm almost nervous driving, even though the small amount of alcohol in it should have worn off by now and shouldn't even have had much of an impact after eating a big lunch.

Despite the fact that I want this journey to the cliffs to be over as quickly as possible, I drive slightly slower than usual, just in case.

I almost faint with relief when we get to the car park for the cliffs. I'm feeling completely smothered by Penny's mood now. She stares into space as I buy the admission tickets, looking completely disinterested in being here. As we make our way down the path from the car park to the cliffs, I try to make small talk.

"It's quiet here, isn't it?" Unsurprisingly, given how late it is in the day, I add to myself.

"It's off-peak season. Of course it's quiet. Isn't that the best way?"

"I guess."

We walk for a few feet in silence.

"How about we go to O'Brien's Tower first? It's the highest point on the cliffs." I suggest.

337

"Can we keep that for the walk back? The few people who are here will all go there first. If we leave it a little while, we'll have it all to ourselves."

"Okay, but we wouldn't want to leave it too long, either. It's going to get dark soon."

"I know. I just don't really want to be around anyone right now. Can we just leave it a while?"

I stare at Penny like I've never seen her before. The woman who has no issue with getting up and speaking in front of huge audiences at work doesn't want to be around the handful of people who seem to be here today. People who won't engage directly with her, or give her more than a passing glance. She really is in a bad way.

Penny walks on without waiting for my reply.

I look wistfully in the direction of O'Brien's Tower, where there's a group of senior citizens walking towards the tower, with some of the group talking to the cliff safety rangers – the only group that's here, by the looks of it. Given how late it is, I have a feeling that I won't be seeing the tower properly today at all.

I follow Penny. We soon reach a fork on the path. Penny walks left, in the opposite direction from the tower. She's walking fast. In fact, she's practically running. The ascent is reasonably steep to begin with and I struggle to keep up with her. I lose track of how long we walk, alone for the most part on this miserable day when anyone in their right mind is anywhere but here.

"Penny, wait up! Where are you going?"

"I saw on a map that there's a lovely quiet area further down this path," she yells back. "It's just a brisk walk away."

"Can you slow down a bit?"

My words seem to make her walk faster.

The view from this part of the path is amazing, even given the bad weather conditions, but I can't appreciate them right now. Penny's erratic behaviour is really starting to unnerve me. I don't believe she's going to do anything stupid – of course I don't. And yet something's not quite right. Something that has to go beyond her being upset about breaking up with Richard. And we're on the top of a cliff, yet she's running along blindly. Although the path is clearly delineated, I still can't help but feel nervous. There's a reckless air about her and this isn't the time or the place to unleash that behaviour.

"Penny, wait for me!" I run after her. "Please stop! I don't feel well," I say. It's the first thing I think of. "Walk beside me, will you?"

She turns round and gives me a look of pure disdain. It shocks me.

"What's wrong with you?"

"I'm . . . feeling a bit dizzy."

"That's probably from the beer."

"It was alcohol-free beer."

"No, it wasn't." Penny walks faster.

"What do you mean? Why would you buy me beer with alcohol with it when you knew I had to drive?"

"A few drinks won't kill you." She laughs. "Unless you get kidnapped again. Who knows what might happen then?"

I'm as shocked as I would be if Penny had randomly produced a gun out of nowhere and aimed it at me.

"Penny, what the hell is wrong? Where have *you* gone to? I don't know this person."

"That's right, Katie. You don't know me at all."

Penny starts to run again. She runs towards a sign that

I can see all too clearly from where I'm standing: Please do not go beyond this point.

No. No, no, no. I race after her as she passes the sign and stops dead at the cliff edge. She's only inches away from a steep, endless drop into the Atlantic Ocean.

"Penny—"

"Join me," she says, beckoning at me.

"It's not safe."

"Join me or I jump."

Chapter 33

I thought I knew what being terrified felt like. I didn't think I'd ever experience anything worse than the fear that engulfed me in that cottage. I was wrong.

I edge closer to Penny. I'm petrified at what she's potentially going to do – not only to herself, but also to me. I've no idea if she's playing me here, trying to frighten me, and why she'd even want to do that. I've no idea if she actually wants to jump and again, why in the world would she want to do that – Richard or no Richard?

I've no idea if she wants us *both* to go down.

I look up as surreptitiously as I can to see if there's anyone around, especially a safety ranger. My visibility from this area is limited, but I know there's nobody in the immediate vicinity. I can't hear anyone and the limited number of people who were here when we arrived were all in the area of O'Brien's Tower. Where we are now is out of their range of vision.

My only hope is that someone behind us saw Penny running towards the area you're not supposed to go past. There wasn't anyone in front of us – I know that for sure. It looked to me like a lot of the rangers were being asked questions by the group at O'Brien's Tower, though. They might be occupied for the next while and away from their usual posts. And even if they come back, we're probably outside their line of vision in the place where Penny has brought us to.

I can of course walk away, back towards the path, and cry for help or run back to the visitor centre. But that might be all it takes to make Penny jump. I can't risk it. I can't do that to her. If she jumps, I'll never, ever forgive myself.

But what if she wants to take me with her?

Penny reaches into her handbag and takes out a bottle of water.

"Drink this with me," she says. "It's vodka. Straight."

My heart thumps furiously. If she starts drinking straight vodka at the side of a sheer cliff drop, there's no hope at all of keeping her alive.

"Okay. Give me some," I say.

I'll have to get closer to her to get the bottle, but it's my only chance of making sure she doesn't drink it. I take an infinitesimal step towards her, trying with my body to make it look like it's more of a movement than what it actually is, and reach out for the bottle.

Penny smiles, opens the bottle and takes a long drink.

"Your turn," she says, handing the bottle to me.

I take it, my hand shaking. I'm ashamed to realise that I'm afraid she's going to grab me and throw me over the side of the cliff. But she doesn't. I take the bottle and edge back, closer to safety. The proximity to the edge makes me want to vomit. I can't understand how Penny can stand there looking as cool as a breeze. It makes me think she really isn't afraid of dying at all and that maybe this is what she actually wants.

My stomach convulses at the thought. I lean over and vomit, dropping the bottle. It was always my plan to spill the drink as soon as I got the bottle, but this wasn't how I'd planned to do it.

Eventually, my stomach stops heaving. I stand up straight again and look at Penny. She's just staring at me, expressionless.

"Come over and stand beside me," she says.

"I . . . don't want to go so close to the cliff edge, Penny."

"Why ever not?" she asks in a tone that suggests that this is a reasonable question.

"I've just been sick. I'm dizzy. It's dangerous," I say, managing to avoid mentioning the most obvious reason. "Let's move elsewhere. Let's go and talk somewhere."

"I can't think straight anywhere else. It's either here, or there."

She leans over and looks down. Her sudden movement makes my heart jump. All it would take is for her to lose her balance to fall right into the sea. And she's been drinking, so that could happen easily. Then she throws herself down and sits at the edge of the cliff, her legs dangling over the sea.

Before I can rationalise it, instinct takes over and I walk over to her.

"Penny, sit back," I say. "Sit back, *now*."

She turns round slowly. Her face is hard, but when she speaks, her tone is softer.

"Will you hold my hand if I do?"

"Of course," I say.

I'll say anything now to keep her alive and get her out of here.

She arches her back and slowly moves her body backwards. Once she's sitting back, still on the cliff edge but no longer hanging over it, she makes a sudden move upwards and grabs my hand. Her grip is firm. It takes every

343

ounce of willpower I have not to yank it away. I'm far too close to the cliff's edge to feel comfortable. My instinct now is to get away from here and to run as fast as I can to safety, but I know if I do that, it could all be over for Penny.

"Sit with me," she says.

"Let's move somewhere safer."

"I need you to sit with me. These could be my last moments. There are things I need to talk about."

"Oh, Penny, please don't say that. We can turn all this round in a heartbeat just by getting up from here and walking away. There's nothing so serious that it merits this."

"Then sit with me. Talk things through with me. Help me to change my mind."

She's vacillating – she wants to live. I need to pounce on that and help her before it's too late. Slowly, I reach out my hand. She takes it.

I sit down beside her. My entire body is shaking from my proximity to the cliff's edge.

"How are you feeling now?" Penny says.

"Sick," I say honestly. "I don't think there's anything left in my stomach to throw up, though."

"It's like the night of the cottage incident all over again," Penny says slowly. "Vomiting must be your thing. At least by the time I'd bundled you into the car, though, there was nothing left in you to come out. I probably would have killed you if you'd been sick in my car."

My heart almost stops. I stare straight ahead for a few seconds, taking deep breaths. Eventually, when I've composed myself to some degree, I turn my head to face her.

"It wasn't Richard. It was *you*," I say.

"Of course it was me, darling. Why do you think we're here?"

Chapter 34

I'm screaming for help. My screams come immediately and instinctively. I scramble to my feet and start to move towards the path we came down, but Penny's right behind me. She jumps at my back and pushes me to the ground.

"Try not to fight this, Katie. Your balance is going to be bad after that Irish coffee and the beer. Plus, the drugs I mixed with your beer. You haven't a hope of winning against me."

I'm stunned at hearing I've been drugged again. So stunned that I stop fighting against Penny for a split second. It's long enough for her to throw herself to my right. Now, I'm right between her and the edge of the cliff. I'm still several feet away from the very edge, but it wouldn't take long to breach that gap if I was pushed hard enough. Whatever she drugged me with, it's not like last time. I didn't even finish that beer and I've been sick, so hopefully some of it has gone out of my system now. I can feel the drug, but it hasn't floored me.

I refuse to look down. Instead, I look at Penny. I can't take my eyes off her now. She's coming for me. It's a matter of when. Right now, though, she's fiddling with something in her handbag.

"Don't worry about spilling the drink, Katie. I have something far better here. My prescription medication."

She takes out a small, flat tin. She scuttles backwards for several feet, clearly protecting herself against me, in case I make any sudden movements towards her, then sits on the ground and puts the tin on her lap. As she opens it, she huddles in on herself, simultaneously throwing glances at me. The tin also contains what looks to be a credit card and a rolled-up note. She cuts up the white powder contents into lines, glances at me again, takes the note and furiously sniffs two lines.

"Why do you look so shocked, Katie? I've been taking this stuff every day for a very long time. You never noticed?"

I don't answer.

"No, of course you didn't. Too wrapped up in yourself." She closes the tin carefully. "I'd offer you a line, but it'd be a waste, considering where you're going." She makes a fist and points her thumb towards the edge of the cliff. "I gave you enough of my drugs, anyway, when I put LSD in your tea. I didn't think you'd go quite as mental as you did, though. Your poor mother. I felt sorry for her, having to look at you that night."

It was *her*. It wasn't the anxiety pill that made me hallucinate. Dear God . . . !

A part of me wants to speak up, but I say nothing. Anything I say will antagonise her. Pleading with her for my life would increase her desire to do this quickly. All I can do is try to buy time through silence.

When the drugs kick in, as they will soon, surely her balance and reaction time will be affected? Although maybe her system is so used to it that that won't happen. As she's just confirmed, she's no stranger to what she's just done. But I'm fighting for every second of life now and all I know for sure is that saying anything rash will hasten my demise.

Maybe someone will come. Maybe a ranger was meant to be at this point and got called away to the group of senior citizens. If someone returns to their post here, they'll see us. But what if their presence makes Penny decide to push me before they can help me?

Penny hugs her knees to her chest and rests her chin on them, staring at me all the time. I stare back.

"How did you manage to convince Richard to take the rap for this?"

"Because I know way worse shit about him that I was ready to divulge if he didn't. After the intervention, Jake was starting to make noise about potentially believing you and that maybe we'd all judged you too harshly. He was starting to pry too much. Someone had to get the blame in case he threw a spotlight my way.

"Richard's punishment for abducting you would be a lot less than the punishment he'd get if the rest of the truth came out. He'd just get a great lawyer and plead some insanity mixed with sexual issues bullshit for that."

I try to process this. Jake was starting to believe me. This isn't a time to care about that factor and yet I do.

"Fucking Richard. Fuck him."

I say nothing. Agreeing or disagreeing could be fatal.

"If he wasn't such a yellow-bellied wimp, this would all have been taken care of ages ago," she continues.

Although it's getting darker, I can clearly see her staring at me again after she says this. Her eyes penetrate me, full of disgust and hatred. It's then that I truly realise that Penny's absolutely insane. And capable of *anything*.

347

There will be no getting out of this unless I get to her first. One of us will not make it down alive.

"You're very quiet. Don't you want to know what I mean by that? Or are you too yellow-bellied too to ask? You're all the same."

I shrug. "Go on, then. Hit me with it."

"You're only here right now because of Richard," she says.

As I suspected, Penny's desire to hear her own voice has overtaken her desire to kill me immediately.

"Not that this was his idea. You jumping off the Cliffs of Moher is all my idea. You've been through a lot, after all. After your recent difficulties, people will assume you wanted to end your suffering. No, you're still here, as in alive, because Mr Big Shot is a coward. When it came down to it, I was the one with the balls to take action and solve my problems. Not him. But he ruined everything."

I try to process what Penny's saying. After mulling it over for a few minutes and realising that Penny isn't going to say anything else, I know I can't stay quiet any longer.

"Was Richard the one who brought me back from the cottage?"

"Of course. It was hardly me, darling. I don't change my mind about things once I've made a decision."

"And Richard did?"

"Oh, please. As if Richard would have had the guts to do what I did. He had nothing to do with it."

"But I was told there was a recording of Richard saying he did it . . . "

"What Richard said makes it sound like he did it, but that's not the case. He was talking about his involvement in it all – it doesn't mean he actually did it. It was all me."

348

"What exactly *did* you do, Penny?"

I'm banking on the fact that she might want to boast about it. I take a deep breath and hold it, praying she'll start to speak. It's almost dusk now, but even through the muted light, I can see that Penny's smiling. She looks almost euphoric.

"Wouldn't you love to know," Penny says, tapping her nose.

"You had help," I say instantly. "You couldn't possibly have done this by yourself."

Penny smiles wickedly. "Nice try, Katie. Do you really think you're going to get the story out of me that way? Do you think my desire to show how clever I am is going to outweigh my ability to keep the details to myself?"

I say nothing. Disappointment floods me. I should have known that Penny wouldn't fall for my goading, but I had hoped her ego would win out.

"But then, does it really matter?" She looks around. "There's nobody here but you and me. Soon, you're going to die. If you want the full story before you leave the world, I'm the only person who can grant you that. Even a man on death row gets his favourite meal, after all."

I'm torn between relief and fear at what she's going to do after she finishes speaking.

"Well, first of all, I drugged you. That was fun."

Penny looks off into the distance, a huge smile on her face. Then she stops talking. I don't know if it's the effect of the cocaine, or if she just wants to make me wait. While she seems distracted, I take a few steps sideways, away from the cliff and towards safety. Eventually, I can't wait any longer and I can't stop myself from speaking.

"Why did you bother with the drug at all? You said I

was drinking faster than the rest of you. Why didn't you just let me drink myself into oblivion? You took a risk putting the drug into my drink in a place where there was CCTV."

"I drugged you because you're a horse, not a woman, and I was afraid closing time would come and we'd still be there. There's only so much patience any woman can have. The amount you drank would have knocked someone else out, but not you. Look at the size of you." She throws a hand dismissively in my direction and makes a face. "You're so . . . wide. You're built like a man. I honestly don't know how Jake found you attractive at all.

"As for drugging your drink, well, that was easy. I'm sure it's a given that you don't remember us going to the bathroom after we bought our drinks – just you and me. It was just after we'd moved to the back of the pub to find a quieter place to stand. You left your drink on the sink when you went into the bathroom. I was going into a toilet cubicle at the same time, so I picked up your drink and brought it into the cubicle with me, along with my own drink.

"If anyone saw it happening, they wouldn't have thought it was strange. You were clearly drunk and I was sober. I was just minding your drink. Who leaves their drink on a sink where people are washing their hands and putting on make-up? You just don't leave drinks lying around publicly, Katie. Who knows, they could be spiked?"

"Or they could be spiked by the person who's supposed to be looking after you, but who would suspect that?" I take a few more steps sideways.

"Exactly, Katie. *Exactly.* You're not quite as stupid as you look. I don't make a habit of carrying Rohypnol in my bag when I'm going out, but I did worry that I might need it. I've been out drinking with you before, after all. As for the guy chatting you up, well, that was just a stroke of very good luck. I really didn't think anyone would bother chatting you up at all.

"I think he just saw that you were very drunk and might not notice just how ugly he was. God, Katie, I don't know how you managed to get Jake at all in the first place. I think my brother suffers a confidence deficit if he thinks you're the best he can do. No wonder I went out that night with the intention of getting rid of you for good."

I can't help shaking my head, although I know I shouldn't give her the satisfaction.

"You went out with me that Saturday with the express intention of getting rid of me at the end of the night . . . Penny, that's fucked-up."

Penny laughs. I can hear the pride in her laugh.

"Isn't it?" she said almost gleefully.

I say nothing this time. I won't rise to her again. Let her talk. That's what she wants – to hear the sound of her own voice and reflect on the glory of how great she thinks she is. This time, I wait. I step sideways again.

"The scene in the pub couldn't have gone any better," she eventually says. "It was a great idea to knock you out publicly with the Rohypnol. Everyone saw just how 'drunk' you were and even if you'd eventually drunk yourself into a coma in the pub, it probably wouldn't have been as dramatic as you collapsing on the floor was.

"I was planning on saying that you must have wandered out of my house in the middle of the night, at which point I'd report you as a missing person. People would assume that you'd walked down to the beach. You've often mentioned to people how much you love watching the sea.

You certainly told Jake, because he told me you loved it. Maybe you fell asleep on the beach and got swept away when the tide came in. There are so many possibilities when you're dealing with someone as drunk as you were.

"I brought you home to my house in a taxi. When we got inside, you vomited all over my floor. While I cleaned that up, you used my bathroom and you made an awful mess in there, too. I won't even repeat the details, because they're too disgusting, but suffice to say that you're a vile creature who needs to be potty-trained all over again.

"You stumbled out of the bathroom and staggered to the kitchen. You fell asleep on the kitchen table while I cleaned up the bathroom. When I finished and came out to find you snoring on the kitchen table, I knew it was time.

"You've always been such a nuisance. Ever since you came on the scene, Jake's never been available. He's always at your place doing something with you and when he's not with you, he's talking about you. When you ended things with him, I figured it'd be a matter of time before you got back together again. I hoped you wouldn't, but I know even *you* aren't stupid enough to let a man like Jake go.

"He was convinced that you'd made a mistake and that there was a way back for you two. Bad and all as it was listening to him going on about you when you ended things, I knew it'd be worse when you got back together. Then it'd be back to me hearing about you non-stop every single time I spoke to him.

"I was *bored* of it. The drama of the break-up made me realise that I needed to sort this problem long-term. I wanted my brother back. And when something stands in the way of me getting what I want, Katie, I eliminate the bottleneck."

352

The air turns cooler. I feel chilled to the bone, for many reasons.

"My car was parked out the back. I put some chloroform on a dishcloth and made sure you were well and truly out of it. Although the state you were in, I probably didn't really need it."

The shock I'm feeling must be visible on my face, because Penny stops and laughs.

"What? You didn't think I was capable of doing something like that?"

Right now, I think Penny is capable of doing just about anything, but I'm not going to say that.

"Just . . . wondering where you got it, that's all."

"Honey, when you're at my level of success and fortune, you can get anything you want, no questions asked. If you were going to stay alive, you might have known someday, if you kept on beavering away in that little job of yours. Or you might not. Don't beat yourself up about it. There aren't many people like me in the world."

Thank God for that.

"I dragged you out to the car in your precious new blouse and jeans that you'd vomited on. Jeans that I had to buy a pair of and manually fray myself, thanks to you. Not to mention the cost of the replacement blouse because the original one was so torn. Then I put you in the passenger seat and drove you to the cottage.

"The CCTV was turned off, of course. Not broken. I didn't think anyone would question it and sure enough, they didn't. And you know why, Katie? Because nobody believed you. Nobody thought your story was worthy of a more thorough check, because it sounded like such complete and utter nonsense."

"Where did you take me?"

"Charming, wasn't it? A real little bijou property. If by some miracle you survive going over the side of that cliff, I can find out if Richard will sell it to you, if you like. On your salary, you probably can't afford much else."

"So, it *is* actually Richard's house? That much was true."

"Embarrassing for him, isn't it? What a pile of rubble his father left him. He's still trying to decide what to do with it. He took me out to see it one day. I'm not sure why. He definitely wasn't trying to impress me with it, that's for sure. Maybe he thought I'd be impressed at seeing how far from his roots he'd come, though."

It hits me again how completely crazy Penny is. She tried to kill me because of a bit of sibling jealousy. My "best friend" is truly, madly insane – and highly dangerous.

"So, Richard wasn't involved in taking me there?"

"No, of course not. I told you, he'd never have the guts to risk it."

"So, how did he know where I was? Did you tell him?"

"I didn't mean to. I had a line when I came home and it loosened my tongue. Taking it on top of the alcohol I'd had that day made me say too much."

I hadn't even thought about how Penny must still have been drunk when she drove us to the cottage until she says that. It's an absolute miracle that I'm still alive at all – for however long that lasts.

"Of course, he had to charge off then like a mad bull and bring you back. If I'd known that was where he was going when he left, I'd have drugged him first and left him there to rot, too.

"In the recording, he said he should have taken me to

the house and left me there instead of you ever having been there. It sounded incriminating. If I'd written a script for him, it couldn't have gone any better for me."

I try to quell the anger that's finally rising inside me. The gardai knew that Penny was the last person to see me before this happened, but they never probed it properly because she had Richard as an alibi. And surely the CEO of a multinational company and a banker at Richard's level would never lie, right? Did their high-powered positions in life protect them, while I was left stranded in no-man's-land, completely helpless?

But anger won't help me now. I need to keep a cool head, to prepare for the attack and fight for my life. Penny didn't kill me last time. I won't let her kill me now.

"I thought the cottage would be the perfect place for you to curl up and die. It's miles from civilisation. Nobody would be visiting. I was surprised you managed to free yourself, though. I didn't think you'd be capable of it. I didn't even bother blindfolding you. I thought it'd be a nice touch for you to see the place you were going to die in in all its glory.

"You were never meant to get out of that house, but if Richard hadn't come back for you, you'd have died out in that lane where he said he found you. And the best bit is that even if you were found, you'd be on Richard's land. Who would the finger of suspicion have been pointed at then?"

"Do you really hate Richard that much?" I say. "He loved you!"

"Not enough to leave his wife and family, though. I was just a younger, prettier bit on the side for him. He didn't take me seriously. That was a big mistake.

"The next time he went to his cottage he'd find your dead body and he'd either have to dispose of it, or go to the gardai and say that a dead woman had been found on his property. A dead woman he knew, who'd have been reported missing. He'd be the chief suspect in your murder."

The way Penny talks about disposing of my body really makes it hit home that she's ready and willing to try to kill me again. Right here, right now. But I'm bigger than her. I'm stronger. If she attacks me, I'll give her the fight of my life to survive. Even if she has the chloroform with her, she'll have to get near me first. I won't let that happen.

"God, you were so clueless that it was actually pathetic. You searched Jake's house, and I knew you'd come to mine and try to do the same thing. I went to bed early and let you search the house to your heart's content. Did you not find that odd – how convenient I made it for you? Did you not see that I was completely mocking you with that *Keep Calm and Rob a Bank* sticker on the folder? You deserve to die for your stupidity alone.

"It was funny when you actually finally copped it, though, and accused me of it all in front of your mother. I was sorry it meant I had to stop doing fun things like sending emails from your work account and putting your washed clothes back in the machine. Or getting new house keys cut that looked almost exactly the same as your old ones . . .

"Oh! and coming into your house at night and getting you to unlock your own phone with your thumbprint so I could message your sister was a personal highlight, as memories go. Who has the code for your house alarm, Katie? Me. I knew you wouldn't wake when I came in, or even when I took your hand to place your thumb on the phone – you sleep like the dead. And you'll soon sleep like the dead again."

Through the haze of impending darkness as dusk falls, I see Penny moving towards me. Through my panic, I register that she's running – *charging* now that she's built up momentum – towards me. I run at her, prepared to meet her head-on.

Terror envelops me and yet I know I must fight.

Our bodies meet and hers has travelled at the faster speed. I stagger backwards in the direction of the cliff. I know that every step I lose will bring me closer to its edge. I throw myself at Penny, clawing at her face, trying to dig my long fingernails into her eye sockets. I'm horrified at my viciousness, but I'll do whatever it takes to keep myself alive.

As I push again, the force of my body against her slight frame causing *her* to lurch backwards this time, I know in that moment that I'm capable of killing another person to keep myself alive. That thought also horrifies me and it's something I know I'll struggle to live with if I do it.

But I don't want to die. I won't stand back and let it happen to me.

I charge forwards again. I know Penny won't have any hidden surprises, such as a knife, to attack me with. She purely wants my injuries to be those consistent with leaping off a cliff, so that it looks like I've jumped voluntarily. But Penny ducks sideways a millisecond before I land on her and I fall face first on the ground. As soon as I'm down, she lifts up my legs and starts to drag them.

No.

I scream. I can't help it.

Penny starts to laugh. She thinks she's won. She continues

to drag me to the edge of the cliff. I kick and wiggle furiously until I escape her grasp. Her birdlike wrists are no match for my heavy legs. I'm on my feet again within seconds, but she's already coming for me.

We jostle furiously, but Penny's getting tired. I can feel it. Her light body is no match for my heavier frame now and within seconds, I've pushed her to only inches away from the edge of the cliff. If it was even ten minutes later, it would be completely dark and I wouldn't be able to see it. But for now, it's clearly visible and one, or both, of us are only seconds away from going over the side.

Penny reads my thoughts and grabs the lapel of my coat.

"If I'm going down, bitch, I'm taking you with me."

The ferocity of her tone chills me. How did she grow to hate me so much that things came to this? But I can't let her see that she's rattled me. Penny's crazy. If it wasn't me she'd chosen to do this to, it would be someone else eventually.

I raise a foot and kick her leg as hard as I can. She flinches but doesn't release her grip.

I hear something, not fully registering. A whirring sound, I think it is. I wonder if it's in my head. It gets louder. It gets closer.

I can't see it. I don't dare take my focus off what I'm doing for a millisecond, or Penny will finish me off. But I'd swear on my life that it's a helicopter. Penny's grasp on me loosens for a split second and I know her attention has been diverted by the sound, too.

Somebody knows we're here.

"*Bastard*!" Penny squeals and pulls me towards her with a new ferocity.

She's going backwards. And she's bringing me with her.

"*No*, Penny. Don't do this. He's not worth it," I say,

knowing there's no point appealing for my own life. "Don't let Richard diminish you like this. This is exactly what he wants."

Penny says nothing. She stands still for a moment as if she's considering my words but tightens her grip on me. I try to pull her back, struggling to gain a foothold and keep my balance as I pull her weight onto me. Then she tugs at me with everything she has left in her and somehow manages to drag us another few steps backwards. We're inches away from death.

I hear the helicopter coming closer. It's hovering over us now.

"Is this how you want to be remembered?" I scream. "Everyone will think you couldn't hack it any more. Richard will think it. So will his wife. She'll have won."

I know I'm playing dirty now, but I have no choice. I have to play Penny's game if I have any hope left.

"Think of your legacy, Penny. Think of how you've represented women in business. You can go on to do plenty more great things. You can show Richard what he missed out on. But you can't do anything if you take so much as one more step behind you. Move forwards, Penny."

She doesn't budge. I know she's worked out my game. And yet, she's not dragging me backwards any more, either. I can see her face now, illuminated in the glow from the aircraft above us. Her eyes are flickering towards the helicopter and I know – I can *see* – that she wants it to rescue us. She doesn't want everything that's Penny to end right here, right now.

I see my moment and I seize it. I throw myself backwards, pulling her down with me, then roll on top of her. I pin her chest down with my knees and push my hands onto her arms. We're still dangerously close to the edge, but the helicopter is landing now. Penny tries to push me off, without the same ferocity as before. She wants to live now. I know it.

And then the helicopter lands and the rescue team are jumping out and running towards us.

Chapter 35

Claire arrives at the garda station just after I've given a statement to Brian. She's shown into the room I'm being interviewed in, as per my request to Brian and his colleague prior to the start of my interview.

"Hello, Claire. Sit down." Brian indicates the seat beside me.

"Katie, I'm so sorry," Claire says, hugging me so tightly that it becomes a squeeze. "I should have done more for you. If I had, this might never have happened."

The anger I felt earlier that nobody believed me has totally dissipated and all that remains is relief that I'm still alive. I tell Claire that it's okay.

"It's not. You could have been killed!"

"But I wasn't. And don't take offence when I say this, but can you let me go now, please? I didn't escape Penny just to die of suffocation."

We all laugh a little, even Brian.

"I don't understand, Katie," Claire says as she sits down. "You said you were rescued by a helicopter. How did the gardai know you were in trouble? Did you ring them, or . . . "

"No. I don't know all the details myself at this point."

"Let me fill you in," Brian says. "I've been on the phone all the way down here, trying to piece it all together. My colleague was driving, before you ask." He smiles.

Despite everything that's happened, I return Brian's smile. He didn't have to travel down to Clare when I rang his station in Dublin to report everything. He could have left me to make my report to the gardai in Clare and then spoken to me when I got back to Dublin, but instead, he travelled down as soon as I rang him.

Maybe it's guilt, or maybe it's just how he works. Either way, I'm glad he's here instead of me having to make my report to a different garda. They weren't going to let me leave without me giving a statement to someone and I wasn't ready to talk to anyone for quite a while after I came to the station. I was still too shocked.

After Penny and I were taken into the helicopter, she didn't utter a word either to me or the rescue team. She stared straight ahead, utterly impenetrable. A part of me wanted to rant at her, but I couldn't even vocalise the horror of how I was feeling. It was too surreal, too hurtful.

The reality of knowing that I was right all along gave me no comfort, although at least I knew now that I wasn't going mad. But the truth had brought a horrible emptiness with it, a void that I didn't know how to fill. Knowing that someone close to you wanted to kill you is more devastating than I could ever have imagined.

Penny continued to remain wholly detached until we came to land, whereupon we were met by ambulances and gardai and separated. She didn't even look at me as she walked away. I refused to go to the hospital. I couldn't bear the thought of a busy hospital just then. I was brought to the station and checked out by a doctor, but not before I rang Brian, Claire . . . and Jake.

"Richard got in contact with the station earlier. He told us Penny was sending him strange texts about you, so he phoned her. She told him she was going to finish a job that should have been done a long time ago. He tried to get the details out of her, but he said she just spoke in riddles for a long time before hanging up. Although, she did allude to how it would be terrible for someone to be present while you committed suicide and to witness such an awful event.

"He felt she was under the influence of an illegal substance at the time and capable of anything, including killing you. He then rang Jake to see if he knew where you were. Jake told him you'd gone to Clare with Penny and you were planning on going to the Cliffs of Moher. Fearing that Penny could make an attempt on your life there, Richard rang the station and we liaised with our colleagues in Clare to send a helicopter to the cliffs, just in case.

"Richard said his confession was false and was made under duress. He was quite insistent that you could be at serious risk. It turned out that his suspicions were well founded. My understanding is that a safety ranger also spotted you and Penny from a distance in an unauthorised area and reported it to the office, and the helicopter's pilot was informed of your location."

"Penny said Richard knew that she'd left me for dead in that cottage. Why didn't he report her, then? Why did he let things escalate as far as they did? Penny said she knew stuff about him – was it because of that?"

"Penny had damaging information on Richard, yes," Brian says. "Information that she decided to divulge to the gardai in a station near her home a few days ago.

363

Presumably before she went to Clare and after Richard's 'confession'. He said nothing about Penny taking you to the cottage because he was afraid he might be charged in relation to conspiring to defraud investors and depositors."

Brian went on to explain that Richard had confided in Penny that he'd become caught up in bad practices at work relating to financial transfers involving various banks in an eight-month period the previous year. Erroneously, they gave investors the notion the bank had sums of money that were billions larger than they really were. He'd been stressed that the truth would come out and had told Penny the reason for his stress.

"Penny also threatened to kill his children," Brian said. "It wasn't something that Richard felt he could take lightly."

Jesus. She wasn't content with just killing me, she was going to bring innocent children into this. I'm guessing that's why Richard suddenly went quiet. And in case she was seen as a suspect in my "suicide", she'd set things up for Richard to take the blame for the abduction. And all because Richard wouldn't leave his wife for her. Good God.

"What will happen to Richard now?" I ask.

"He'll be charged with conspiracy to defraud investors and depositors," Brian says. "It's in the hands of the law now."

I probably shouldn't care what happens to Richard – he could have gone straight to the gardai after Penny abducted me and corroborated my story about the cottage – but he chose to try to save himself. However, I know I wouldn't be here right now if it hadn't been for him. Even though the truth was out about his dodgy dealings before we left for Clare, he could still have let Penny kill me. It surely looks even worse for him now that he has to admit he didn't take any action after what happened at the cottage. He could have made that particular issue go away. But he didn't.

"I can't believe Penny did all this," I say aloud, but mostly to myself.

"Richard mentioned that Penny had been fired from her job. Drug-taking had become an issue with her."

"And what else do you do when you lose the prestige of your high-profile position except decide to shove your best friend off the Cliffs of Moher?" I find myself saying.

And as for the drug-taking, a lot of things are making sense in hindsight. The fit over Richard's wife and the way she behaved the night she asked me over for champagne immediately come to mind.

"Richard also said that after reporting his fraud to the gardai, Penny rang a national newspaper, who then contacted Richard. He didn't make any comment, but he knew his goose was cooked. He's admitted everything to us and wants to comply with the investigations as much as possible. He's probably hoping he'll get a more lenient sentence when this goes to court if he's compliant."

"Where's Penny now?"

"With the superintendent."

"What's going to happen to her?" And me, I silently add. Am I safe now?

"She'll be charged with attempted murder," Brian says. "Don't worry, Katie. She won't be in a position to hurt you again. We'll make sure of that."

"You'd better," Claire says. "If we'd all listened to Katie when she first reported the abduction and you'd done something about it, she wouldn't have been almost thrown over the side of the Cliffs of Moher. You wouldn't want the media to get wind of your negligence, I'm sure!"

"Claire, leave it," I say. Anger isn't going to help anyone at this point. "It's over now."

Brian looks genuinely rueful, but he's probably not going to say that in case it gets him into trouble – trouble that I certainly don't intend to start. It won't do anyone any good.

Claire sighs. "I'm sorry, Brian. I'm mad at myself more than anything."

I put my hand on Claire's arm. "At least you listened when everyone around me was dismissing me. You *tried* to believe me. And Brian, thank you for your help. I know you did the best you could."

Brian and Claire both look surprised. I guess they expected me to be angrier, but I don't know how else to deal with this. Staying calm and not playing the blame game seems as good an approach as any right now. I've probably hurt a lot of people myself with my accusations in the course of finding out the truth – one in particular more than anyone. The truth may be out, but there are no winners.

When I leave the interview room a few minutes later with Claire, I see Jake sitting in reception. He stands up as he sees me walking in.

"Can you give us a minute?" I say to Claire.

"I'll wait outside in the car," she says. She nods at Jake, who nods back.

I walk over to him. "I presume you're here for Penny?"

Jake shrugs. "For both of you, I suppose. Don't get me wrong, I fully condemn what Penny's done, but she has nobody else. When the gardai called me and told me what happened, I didn't feel I had a choice but to come."

I sit down, suddenly exhausted. Jake does, too.

"I need to apologise again for suspecting you, Jake. I didn't truly think you were capable of doing such a thing, but *somebody* was. Everyone was a possibility until I found out the truth. The instinct to survive took over. But I know you probably can't ever forgive me. I'm so sorry."

"I'm sorry, too. That bloody intervention . . . I was part of that. I started to feel after that that something wasn't right, though – that we were all ganging up on you. I should have believed you."

"It's not your fault," I reply. "Nobody did. I didn't even believe myself sometimes."

"I feel responsible. I brought Penny into your life. But I obviously would never, ever have thought she'd be capable of doing something like this."

"Neither would I. She fooled us all, Jake. She clearly needs psychiatric help and you'll have to help her to get it. She won't accept she has a problem. She'll need to be convinced."

"I got a call from Richard a while ago," Jake says quietly. "He's of the opinion that Penny suffers from a narcissistic personality disorder, but she hides it well. And covers her tracks by moving from place to place and job to job when the cracks start to show. At her job level, she can do that. He also thinks she now suffers from psychosis, exacerbated by her drug use."

"What do *you* think?"

"I think I don't know who my sister is."

I put my arm around Jake's shoulder, my pity for his plight increasing. I immediately wonder if I'm overstepping the mark after what I've put him through, but he doesn't flinch or shrug me away.

We sit like that for a long time. It feels like there's so

much to say and yet it can't be said yet. I need to let the horror of it all settle for a while. I expect Jake does, too.

"Claire's waiting for me," I eventually say.

"Are you done here?"

"Yes."

"I suppose you're going back to Dublin?"

"I haven't thought that far ahead. I presume Claire needs to get back tonight, though. What about you?"

"I booked accommodation in Liscannor for tonight while I was sitting here waiting. I've no idea what's about to happen, but I'd better stay around to find out. Someone has to."

Jake puts his head in his hands. I feel sorry for him. The burden of managing Penny is going to rest entirely on his shoulders.

I stand up to leave, but Jake puts a hand out and stops me.

"Do you have to go?"

I should be shocked and yet I'm not. A lot has happened and I've made mistakes that probably should be unforgivable, but ultimately the only people who understand the awfulness of what's just happened are Jake and me. Whether that will be enough to get past my wrongdoings long-term, I don't know. All I know is that right now, we need to be together. Jake just acknowledged it before I did.

"I can tell Claire I have somewhere to stay here tonight."

Jake smiles. For the first time since I got on the helicopter, I allow myself to believe that it's all over.

It happened – it truly, unequivocally *happened* – and now it's finally over.

The End.

www.ingramcontent.com/pod-product-compliance
Lightning Source LLC
Chambersburg PA
CBHW070632180626
46817CB00006B/2099